Praise for *Salty, Bitter, Sweet*

"A story that will fill your heart and warm your belly."

Ismee Williams, critically acclaimed author of
Water in May and *This Train Is Being Held*

"Poignant and heartfelt, *Salty, Bitter, Sweet* has it all. Full of culture, love, and loss, every page is a feast for the senses in a story that never shies away from exploring complicated family dynamics. Cuevas's writing is pure magic."

Nina Moreno, author of *Don't Date Rosa Santos*

"*Salty, Bitter, Sweet* sparkles with wit, humor, and heart. Cuevas's debut is as delectable a morsel as the gourmet creations aspiring chef Isa creates along her journey to find her place in her family, the culinary world, and her first romantic relationship. I devoured this charming novel in one sitting and can't wait for more from this talented author."

Gilly Segal, author of *I'm Not Dying with You Tonight*

"Sweet, delicious, and beautifully layered—not unlike the perfect mille crêpe cake. You'll want to devour this book immediately."

Rachael Allen, author of *A Taxonomy of Love*
and *The Summer of Impossibilities*

"Both deeply poignant and laugh-out-loud funny, Mayra Cuevas's *Salty, Bitter, Sweet* expertly blends heartbreak, romance, and the joy that comes from letting go of expectations and learning to love yourself—the perfect ingredients for this deliciously satisfying debut!"

Marie Marquardt, author of *Dream Things True*,
The Radius of Us, and *Flight Season*

"In addition to being an incredible YA romance that will absolutely sweep you off your feet, *Salty, Bitter, Sweet* is also an honest meditation on slowing down and appreciating the simpler things in life. Isa's tunnel-vision on winning the kitchen apprenticeship is relatable for so many teens who feel pressure to achieve at a certain level, all the time, and her journey illustrates that taking care of yourself is more important than any award or grade or job. I loved this book!"

Norah, Little Shop of Stories

"What a magnificent treat. This novel is delicious and nutritious, with a captivating romance garnished in family drama. Cuevas has crafted a page-turning tale that explores our most private motivations."

Kimberly L. Jones, writer/director and coauthor
of *I'm Not Dying with You Tonight*

SALTY, BITTER, *Sweet*

MAYRA CUEVAS

BLINK®

BLINK

Salty, Bitter, Sweet
Copyright © 2020 by Mayra Cuevas

Requests for information should be addressed to:
Blink, 3900 *Sparks Dr. SE, Grand Rapids, Michigan* 49546

Hardcover ISBN: 978-0-310-76977-4

Audio ISBN: 978-0-310-76980-4

Ebook ISBN: 978-0-310-76983-5

Cover design: Brand Navigation
Interior design: Denise Froehlich

Printed in the United States of America

20 21 22 23 24 / LSC / 10 9 8 7 6 5 4 3 2 1

For my abuelas Cuqui and Josefa,
who taught me that love arrives through the kitchen

Para mis abuelas Cuqui y Josefa,
quienes me enseñaron que el amor entra por la cocina

Chapter 1

The Perfect Souffle

Happiness, like love, arrives through the kitchen. At least that's what my abuela Lala used to say.

I ponder her words, feeling every bit happy in the kitchen as I wipe a cheesy smudge off my recipe book then lick my thumb.

I sigh in pleasure.

I may not know much about love, but judging by the perfect balance of Gruyère and parmesan, I definitely got the kitchen part down.

Though I can't take the credit for this French marvel. My copy of *Larousse Gastronomique* is so worn I could probably taste each dish simply by licking the border of the page.

Larousse—also known as the French culinary bible—says an ideal soufflé should have a melting texture, a creamy center, and stand for two to three minutes without deflating. Currently, my deflation time is one and a half minutes—at least thirty seconds short of passable and a full minute and a half away from perfection.

"Morning, kiddo." Papi saunters in and heads straight for the coffee maker. "Did you sleep in the kitchen?" He fills his favorite mug, one that reads *I'm as corny as Kansas in August*—God, he really is.

How a Cuban American born and raised in the Midwest ended up living on a cherry farm in France is beyond my comprehension. Life is so weird sometimes.

7

"Ah, the nectar of the gods," he sings. The cup of black coffee he pours looks and smells like jet fuel.

"I made café con leche—it's in that thermos if you want some." I nod toward the tartan-print thermos, a staple in Lala's kitchen.

Oddly enough, Lala's thermos was part of my inheritance. My name, Isabella Fields, is written in Lala's old-fashioned cursive on the cardboard box it came in. Under it she wrote, "For my *morenita*"—the sweet term of endearment she often used to celebrate my darker skin tone. Yet it's not the color of my skin that makes me almost the mirror image of both Papi and Lala; it's the wild, curly mane of cocoa-brown hair, my full lips and high cheekbones. This is my Latina side, the morenita me. The only feature I inherited from my fair-skinned French mother is my nose. A small, straight-edged thing that, to me, looks out of place in the mishmash that is my face—not because I prefer one nose over another, but because it's a constant reminder I come from divergent worlds while not wholly belonging to any of them. Never Cuban enough, or French enough, or American enough— that's me, a dissonant three-course meal.

Along with the thermos, Lala left me her cookware, baking pans, and her handwritten cookbook, which I've yet to unpack. Just thinking about it—with its red, tattered binding and yellowed pages full of her notes—makes my heart tighten in a way I can't focus on now. Too many memories to untangle at once.

"I'll have some of your cafecito later," Papi says. "Today, I need my first cup black and straight." He takes a long sip, idling by the kitchen counter like a puppy waiting for a treat. Papi loves to eat my food. And I love that he loves it.

He watches me as I slip my hands into heat-resistant gloves and open the oven door. The heavenly smell of melted cheese and butter envelops the kitchen. Inside, delicate clouds of pure, cheesy bliss burst from the ramekins. I instantly smile.

"Still on the soufflés, huh?" he asks, peering over my shoulder.

"They have to be perfect," I say, removing the baking tray

from the oven. "Nothing else will do." The scalding water filling the bottom of the tray sloshes precariously as I ease it onto the kitchen counter.

This time, I tried a new method recommended in *Larousse*—placing the ramekins in a bain-marie before sliding them in the oven. It's a way to steadily bring them up to temperature and keep the heat consistent. I pray it worked.

"The eggs have to be infused with the right amount of air bubbles. And the oven temperature needs to be exact." I balance a wispy slice of honeycomb on top of each ramekin. "They're all about precision."

I add white chamomile flowers and a fig compote drizzled with honey to the plate. Seen from a distance they look flawless, but the real test is in the taste.

"What are these?" Papi asks, peeking into a tin of freshly baked pastries.

"Those are for Jakub." I swat away his hand. But he still manages to steal a pastry from the tin.

"That's nice of you." He bites into the fruit-filled roll.

"He actually gave me a list of things I need to bake for him." I chuckle to myself, thinking of the kid's beaming face every time I bring him sweets. I've never met a five-year-old with so much spunk. "He wrote it in Polish. It took me hours to figure out what he wanted. I had to research and translate all these recipes."

"His mom said you promised him some American cookies?" Papi asks, finishing the pastry in two bites.

"Chocolate chip." I smile, staring at the powdered sugar on his face. "You got some on your nose," I say, passing him a cloth napkin so he can wipe it off. "No one told me how impossible it would be to find chocolate chips in France. I have a few leads in Lyon, but I've been too busy preparing for the big day tomorrow."

"Luck favors the prepared," he says, raising his *Corny as Kansas* mug in a mock toast. "So proud of you, honey."

"Thanks, but I was lucky just to get in."

"You beat a thousand kids for a spot in this program. That's not luck, Isa. That's talent."

"You're my dad. You're supposed to say that."

"Just let me know when we have to start calling you Chef Isabella. I'm buying you one of those tall hats so you can wear it around the house." He kisses my cheek and reaches for a leftover piece of honeycomb. He slides the sweet wafer into his mouth and hums in delight. I grin in spite of myself.

Luck or talent? I guess I'm about to find out.

A little over one hundred restaurants in the entire world are decorated each year with a three Michelin star award—a title that says you are the best of the best. Or as the guide puts it, "worth a special trip."

And only one of those restaurants, La Table de Lyon, owned by world-famous Chef Pascal Grattard, has an international apprenticeship program. They accept fifteen students each summer for a special three-week course. At the end of the course, the top student gets to stay for a year-long apprenticeship. This year, I am the only American.

When the acceptance email arrived, I couldn't believe my crazy good luck. This is not just any job—it's a life-changing opportunity.

Lyon is the gastronomic capital of the world. If I can make it here, I can make it anywhere. Past apprentices have gone on to open their own successful restaurants and win their own Michelin stars. At the very least, saying you trained under Chef Pascal Grattard and graduated from his intensive course is guaranteed to open doors at the most sought-after restaurants.

"Are you still visiting your mom next weekend?" Papi asks. The mood suddenly shifts between us.

I clear my throat. It's been six months and we have yet to have the why-did-you-cheat-on-Mom conversation. I can't bring myself to ask and he can't bring himself to tell me. I love my dad, but I hate the awkwardness growing between us. Mostly, I hate what he did to Mom.

The only reason I agreed to stay with him and Margo—his new wife—is because they live thirty minutes away from Grattard's restaurant. As much as I tried, I couldn't come up with a good excuse to stay in the city.

If I land the apprenticeship, I'm moving out. No more feeling like an unwelcome guest around Papi's new family. A job like that means a brand-new life—a reset button to erase everything that's happened in the last year. To make everything I've sacrificed worthwhile. A redemption of sorts.

"Do we get to eat these?" Papi asks, eyeing the soufflés while pulling a stool and sitting by the kitchen island, across from me.

"I made one for Margo—is she coming down?" I ask.

"No idea." He reaches for his plate. "Where's my spoon?"

I open the silverware drawer and grab two spoons, then close the drawer harder than I intended.

"Do you realize she hasn't tried any of the food I've made? She didn't even taste the cassoulet last night. Or the chicken with butter and wine sauce from the night before. I thought you said it was her favorite." The cassoulet alone took me three hours to make. I had to prepare the duck confit, the beans, and a pork ragù before assembling everything in a casserole dish.

"The smell of cooked meat makes her nauseous. I think it's a pregnancy thing," Papi says apologetically. "But I liked it."

I shake my head and let out a long exhale. I've run out of ideas on how to connect with this woman. Why do I even bother?

"These are perfect, Isa," Papi says of the soufflés. He takes the spoon to his mouth, closes his eyes, and hums. I wish I knew he was humming because this is the best soufflé he's ever had, but Papi always reacts the same way no matter what I put in front of him. He's an unreliable taster—he only likes to eat.

"Can you taste the delicate notes of thyme?" I split apart my soufflé and inspect it for air pockets and moisture.

"Oh, is that what I taste?" He's already scarfed down his and now is moving to the one intended for Margo. "These are the best ones you've made so far."

"It's still not right." I turn my plate toward him. "You see right here—" I point my spoon to a lumpy section, the product of too much moisture. "This should be fluffy and airy. It's no good." I push my plate aside and then try to do the same with the rush of disappointment that follows. I remind myself it took Julia Child at least twenty-eight tries before she perfected her strawberry soufflé. I have eight more to go.

Papi makes a second trip to the coffee maker to refill his mug. When he sits back down, I notice his deep brown eyes look tired around the edges and an overgrown beard has taken over half his face. He reminds me of the Cuban rebels photographed in a book about "La Revolución" Lala used to keep on her coffee table. The only thing missing is a beret.

"You okay?" I ask. "You look a bit . . . tired."

He makes a face. "Are you trying to tell me I look old?"

I laugh, leaning over the kitchen island to kiss his cheek. "Never."

"Margo didn't get any sleep, which means I didn't get any sleep," he says.

"Is she feeling any better?"

Papi shrugs. "I ordered her a special pillow so she can sleep on her side. Let's see if that helps."

"I was thinking about making ratatouille for dinner," I say. "It's all vegetables."

He stops eating. I catch an almost imperceptible wince before he looks up to meet my gaze.

"Don't get your hopes up, honey."

"It's worth a try." I shrug, adding *aubergine* to the market list I've been working on all morning. I whisper the French pronunciation a few times—*ohburgene*—loving the sound of the word on my tongue. It makes eggplant sound even tastier.

Papi finishes the second soufflé and pushes his plate to the side. "Loved these," he says, licking the last of the honey drizzle off his spoon. "When are you making Mami's apple pie? That's two birthdays in a row you've forgotten."

I swallow the knot that immediately forms in the back of my throat. I haven't forgotten, I want to say.

"Margo got you that chocolate cake. Remember?"

He raises an inquisitive eyebrow, completely oblivious to the soul-crushing effect his pie request has on me.

"No point in having two desserts," I say dismissively.

"Said no one ever," he teases. But I don't laugh. Instead, I turn around and pretend to busy myself in arranging and rear-ranging the pots and pans hanging from a rack next to the stove.

Lala's apple pie is not happening. I locked that recipe in a dark corner of my heart and threw away the key. How can a source of so much love and joy become a vessel for so much grief?

I baked him the apple pie for his birthday last year, as was our tradition. Then I went to his office in the Loop—which con-tains Chicago's financial district—to surprise him.

Turns out, the surprise was on me. I stood on the other side of the street holding a hot pie in my hands and watching him kiss Margo on the lips—repeatedly.

That's how I found out about their affair.

I didn't tell anyone, however—not Lala and definitely not Mom. I didn't even confront him, even though I felt pure rage coursing through my bloodstream. It was too much to process.

The pie went straight into the nearest trash bin along with the childish belief my parents' love was indestructible. I ran to the nearest L station and got on the first train heading to God knows where. I just sat inside the train car, watching the city landscape through blurry, tear-filled eyes.

After that, I enrolled in more baking classes and decided nothing existed outside the kitchen. I needed a reason to get out of our house while my parents fought their way through an excruciating divorce. It got to the point I couldn't look either one in the face. It hurt too much.

In the kitchen, no one could harm me—hot pans aside. In that sterile, stainless steel environment, I was in complete control.

In the end, all those extra classes worked out in my favor. That focus got me into Grattard's program. And I'm not about to let up now.

"I can make you an apple clafoutis instead. I have to practice that anyway."

"It's not the same," he argues.

As my saving grace, Margo enters the kitchen.

"Bonjour," she says, pinning her long blonde hair up in a loose bun over her head. She stops next to Papi and plants a kiss on his lips. I look away. It's still too soon to call this normal. It may always be too soon.

"I'm so hungry," she says, the hungry sounding like *ungry*.

Margo opens the fridge and peers in. It's full of my leftovers and all the meals she hasn't eaten. She glances over a few containers but doesn't take any out. Finally she closes the fridge, walks over to the bread box, and takes out a loaf. "Bread and butter est all I can eat."

Her overextended belly rubs against the counter as she spreads half a stick of butter over two slices of bread. I really hope *this* is a pregnancy thing.

Papi and I watch her take the bread layered with butter to her mouth, bite, and moan as if this is the best thing she's ever tasted. No matter how hard I try, I can't compete with French butter.

"Four more weeks," she says, sitting on a stool and rubbing her belly in a circular motion. It's impossible to imagine that in a month I'll be someone's half sister. We'll be seventeen years apart. It's weird.

"I'm going to the market. Can I borrow Margo's car?" I ask Papi.

"Margo and I are heading to Lyon to get some things for the baby's room," he says.

"James is painting the walls a soft yellow," Margo adds, resting her hand on Papi's arm. He reaches for her, covering her hand with his.

"Gender neutral yellow." Papi winks in my direction. They decided to keep the baby's gender a surprise until it's born, which has only added to my big-sister anxiety. It will be hard enough being the sister of a girl. But a baby boy is a whole different ball game. When I babysat for our neighbors back home in Chicago, the boys were always dirty, stinky, and messy. Boys are like ghost peppers—pain-inducing interlopers whose nature is to wreak havoc.

Papi doesn't care about the gender as long as the baby is born "happy and healthy," but I think Margo wants a girl. I've seen the starry-eyed way she beholds pink baby clothes. It's the same way I look at designer cake stands.

"I'll only be a minute," I say, shuffling my notes into my market bag. "I'll be back before you know it and you guys can leave."

I catch the sideways glance Margo shoots at Papi. One of her eyebrows raises so high it distorts the features on half of her face. She doesn't say anything, though; she simply walks out of the kitchen.

"I swear, I'll be back in half an hour, tops," I plead.

"Isa, honey, the market is like a black hole with you. It sucks you in and spits you out half a day later. Take the bike."

"When are you getting a *real* car?" I ask, exasperated.

"I already have a car."

"An old truck that is permanently hitched to a trailer doesn't count as a car. That thing is too big to park in town."

"It's a great day for a bike ride. And I'm pretty sure Jakub would love to get his pastries." He stands, kisses the side of my head as he always does, and leaves.

I watch him stroll down the hallway, his shoulders loose and his feet bare. He seems so at ease in his worn-out jeans and faded T-shirt. It's unnerving. He's so not the overstressed father I grew up with. I barely recognize this man. And I have no idea what to make of him.

I sling my bag over my shoulder and across my chest. Then I head outside to pull Margo's old cruiser bike out of the garden shed, placing the tin of kołaczki cookies inside the basket between the handlebars.

Papi was right about one thing—the weather is perfect for a bike ride. The midmorning sun warms my arms as I pedal down the driveway.

I veer from the main road and take the long way to the town market, riding through the cherry orchards.

Villa des Fleurs—as Margo's family estate is called—sits on a hill in the town of Bessenay, surrounded by acres of cherry trees.

I slow down as I pass a group of farmers dangling from high ladders. The way they almost defy gravity reminds me of circus acrobats. With the harvest at its peak, their days are consumed with collecting red fruit from the trees. The work looks grueling, but somehow they always manage to wave and smile when I pass by.

I look around, searching for Jakub or his parents. They're a sweet family of Polish seasonal workers. Papi said they come every year to help with the harvest.

I find Jakub playing with a toy truck under the shade of a tree. I smile and wave the tin in the air for him to see.

"Isabella!" he yells, waving me over.

I rest the bike on its kickstand and sit on the blanket next to him.

"What did you bring me today?" he asks in his basic French. I don't speak Polish and he doesn't speak English, so we practice French on each other.

"Kołaczki," I say, lifting the lid off the tin to reveal two dozen (minus one) perfectly assembled Polish pastries. "I made you three different flavors: blueberry, apricot, and cheese." I point at a piece of paper taped to the lid with the three flavors translated into Polish.

He takes the tin from my hands and sets it in front of him,

then stares at the pastries for a long time before finally choosing one with the blueberry filling. I wait expectantly for the verdict.

He scarfs it down, then reaches for a second. This time, he goes for the apricot.

"So?" I ask.

He shrugs, reaching into the tin for a third with his free hand. The boy is double fisting the pastries, has crumbs on the sides of his mouth, and his little fingers are covered in powdered sugar. Baking doesn't get any better than this.

"Do you like them?" I ask.

"My mama's are much, much better," he says, his mouth full. "Yours are okay too."

I laugh hard. A five-year-old just became my toughest critic.

"You promised the chocolate chips," he reminds me.

"I know, I know," I say apologetically. I dust off some of the powdered sugar that has covered the front of his overalls. "Next time, I promise."

I take the tin away from him and put the lid back on. "These are for later." His mom won't forgive me if I feed him so much sugar, he's bouncing off the walls—or trees in this case.

"I have to go. I'll see you later, okay?"

He plants a sugar-dusted kiss on my cheek, then takes the tin and runs to his parents' side. I watch him pop the lid open and offer them a treat. They each take one and grin. I wave a hello in their direction as I get back on my bike and pedal away.

As the sun hits my face, a wave of optimism swells in my chest. *Great things are about to happen*, I tell myself. Nothing can ruin this perfect day.

Chapter 2

Fruits, Vegetables, and a Motorcycle Guy

A dozen market vendors cram the town square in what feels like a small gastronomic festival. Baskets of fresh produce gleam on the tables alongside huge slabs of various meats, crusty loaves of bread, and bunches of lavender gathered from the fields of Provence.

It's heaven. But today St. Peter let in some idiot who is zipping down the street in an old motorcycle with a sidecar. The roaring and crackling of the engine has no place among the sounds of voices and footsteps around me.

The bike turns at the end of the street and heads back in my direction. It's not the rider who catches my eye but the white bulldog wearing aviator glasses who sits in the sidecar. His tongue flaps all over his face, making him look like he's smiling.

I snicker in spite myself. Then I turn to give my undivided attention to the vegetables at hand.

Earth and damp saturate my sense of smell as I hold a porcini mushroom near my nose. I press its rubbery surface with my thumb, gently pushing down—checking for the right amount of bounce.

"It's all the same!" Monsieur Barthélemy waves his arms in the air. "Pick one already. We're both getting old here." His French accent is so pronounced that when he spits, he sounds like he's singing. He turns around to help another customer, but I hear him mumble something about the *fille américaine*—that's what he calls me.

I've asked him to talk to me only in French so I can practice, but after a misunderstanding over a box of zucchini, he's been pushing his English on me. I never knew my French was so bad until I came here. Even though Mom and I always spoke French around the house and I took classes in school, I'm not a native speaker. It makes me wonder if Lala lied to me about my Spanish too . . .

Sadly, my first language is English, where a *champignon* is just a mushroom. I add three more champignons to my basket and move to the tomatoes. These will take a while.

I dig around for a deep-colored tomato, firm but with a little give. As with the mushrooms, I bring them to my nose and sniff, this time searching for a sweet, woody smell.

For an instant, I'm transported to Lala's kitchen and the herbal smell of her sofrito simmering as part of some guisado. A symphony of garlic, onions, and peppers play among the pots and pans, and I find myself longing for her arms tying an apron around my waist.

I was born to be a culinary artist. But the universe, with its messed-up sense of humor, thought it would be hilarious to give me a French grandma on my Mom's side who would rather starve than cook her own dinner. And a Cuban abuela who knew nothing of classic French technique but who habitually grew (and killed) her own food.

A loud pop brings me back to the market. The black motorcycle parks across the street from Monsieur Barthélemy's stand and the rider dismounts. I watch him check the exhaust pipe, which is making all kinds of crackling noises even though the motor has stopped running. That thing belongs in a museum. The rider then sets a bowl by the bike and pours a bottle of water into it. He unloads the dog and ties him next to the bike so he can drink.

At this exact moment, I should turn around to mind my own

business. But no, instead I stand there in a daze as the rider takes off his helmet, his riding glasses, and his jacket to unveil the definition of crazy hot.

I drop the tomato.

This guy could melt the icing off a cake with one look. If his lips were fruit, they would be juicy pink plums. The kind you want to sink your teeth into.

I quickly bend down to pick the produce up before Monsieur Barthélemy chastises me for disrespecting his fruit. Motorcycle Guy leaves his white dog tied to the bike and swaggers to Monsieur Barthélemy's booth. He grabs an orange and tosses it into the air like a ball.

That's when he starts to lose me. If Monsieur Barthélemy and I agree on one thing, it's that fruit shouldn't be disrespected in that way. I don't care how hot he is.

I go back to my search for the perfect tomato but find myself squeezing them a little too hard.

"A lot of people think tomatoes are vegetables, but they're actually fruit," someone says in broken French. My head turns to find Motorcycle Guy next to me, cleaning an apple against his shirt. I realize he is talking to me. "It's because of the seeds," he explains, biting into the skin.

I stare at his face for a moment—something about the way his eyebrows bunch up over his dark eyes makes it hard to look away. But then he opens his mouth again. "That one is no good," he says, eyeing the tomato in my hand.

It takes me all of two seconds to decide this guy's cockiness greatly outweighs his looks.

I ignore him and drop the tomato into my basket. I step aside and toss three different-colored peppers in as well. I don't even smell them first. I check off my list and get ready to pay.

"Monsieur Barthélemy, s'il vous plaît," I say, keeping my eyes on the old man.

"Oh, record time. Only one hour to pick. Only le best for ma fille américaine."

I ignore his sarcasm. If he didn't have the best vegetable and fruit stand in the whole market, I wouldn't bother with him at all. He looks over my basket and adds the amount in his head. "Ten euros," he declares from behind his stand. My hand digs through my purse, trying to find the right bill, though Monsieur Barthélemy has moved on to Motorcycle Guy, who is carrying a bag of fruit and an oversized bunch of flowers. "They're for my mom," he says—this time speaking English with an accent that reminds me of Lala's singsong-y intonation. If I had to guess, I'd say he's Spanish.

"I'm visiting for the summer," he offers.

I nod but don't say anything. I'm not sure what else I can do to make it clear I'm not interested. This guy reminds me of a flambé gone bad. A little too much alcohol in the pan, a flame that's too hot and too high, and you can kiss your eyebrows goodbye.

"Are you American?" He cocks his head to the side and smiles.

"Um-hum." I hold out the ten euro bill for Monsieur Barthélemy, but he gets called away by a woman confused about the weight of a melon.

"Are you here for the summer?" he asks.

Motorcycle Guy steps in closer and leans his shoulder against one of the wooden beams that hold up the stand. I roll my eyes, not that it likely makes a difference.

"I'll be around all summer and have absolutely nothing to do," he says, then licks his lower lip. The confidence in his voice leaves no doubt this guy is used to getting his way. I bet where he's from, girls swoon over his flawless olive skin, broad shoulders, and the toned chest he's probably hiding under that tight black T-shirt. But his arrogance makes me want to hit him over the head with a cast iron pan.

I'm not one of those swoony girls. And I'm definitely not a fan of the Rico Suave type.

"Right . . ." I say, searching for Monsieur Barthélemy over the boy's shoulder. He is still dealing with the melon drama.

"I know a great cherry field down the road." He plucks a cherry from one of the baskets, then casually places it in my hand. I'm too stunned by the exchange to pull away, so the ripe cherry sits on my open palm like a foreign object.

"I can take you there, if you wish. You can pick as many as you want."

"Wow," I scoff. "Sure. I would love to disappear into a backwoods field with a complete stranger . . ." *To do who knows what.* I look over his shoulder again, waving the bill at Monsieur Barthélemy to catch his attention. "That sounds amazing. Every girl's dream."

"Huh?" He frowns as if he could somehow read my lewd thoughts.

"Okay . . . I'm leaving now." I push past him and drop the cherry back inside the display basket.

Monsieur Barthélemy is waving both arms in the air, emphatically defending the weight of his melons. I leave the ten euro note on the counter and walk away.

Sugar, butter, and flour are still on my list. And I may have to stop at the little baking supply shop that had some pretty cake pans in their window display.

I drop my things inside the basket of my bike, then swing my leg over the seat and put my foot on the pedal. I don't intend to look back, but I do. Motorcycle Guy is standing on the street, leering in my direction and biting into his apple.

I make myself turn back around and push down hard on the pedals.

What a jerk. If I never see him again, it'll be too soon.

I hate taking the bike to the market. The flat road through town ends at the bottom of a hill, and from there it's a steep climb up to Villa des Fleurs. The way down is no big deal, fun even if you consider the sun in your face and the wind in your hair. But as of right now, I've given up trying to pedal my way up the hill with a basket full of groceries and a bag slung over my shoulder.

Plus, I went a little off list and picked up some extras—a couple of cake pans and a few oval-shaped ramekins that will be perfect for a crème brûlée. I'm quickly regretting my purchases as they are beginning to feel like one-ton weights. By the time I get to Margo's house at the top of the hill, I'm panting and sweating.

I stop to catch my breath when I notice the same black motorcycle and sidecar from the market, parked in front of our house.

My pulse instantly quickens.

Did that guy follow me here? How does he know where I live?

I grip the handlebar tighter, trying hard to think of what to do next.

No way this is a coincidence. Villa des Fleurs is as tucked away as it gets. It has its own private access road, and the closest house is a mile away. You'd have to know it's here to find it. And what's worse, if I scream, no one will hear me.

A cold chill runs down my spine as the first symptoms of panic set in. Under normal circumstances I'm not the panicky type. But I'm more than four thousand miles away from home, living in a villa in the middle of nowhere.

I search my bag for my cell phone and find it's not there. *Crap!* I left it in the kitchen. I can almost see it sitting on the counter next to the oven gloves.

Should I turn around and go back into town? But what if he chases after me? My face will end up plastered on some missing girl poster. And let's face it, the French probably don't care much about missing American girls. And what's more, the Americans don't care much about missing Latina girls.

My hands grip the bike handles and I rack my brain for everything I learned in that self-defense boot camp Mom and I attended back in Chicago. In one day, we learned to fight off a rapist and escape a kidnapping. They told us that when in doubt, always call the police.

I need to get to a phone.

I walk the bike to the front door, which is unlocked. This could have been Papi and Margo's doing; the doors of this house seem to be perpetually open. When I tried to protest, saying someone could break in, they both laughed at me. "We're not in Chicago anymore, honey," Papi said. *Who's laughing now?*

Besides the normal old-house creaking, the hallway is eerily quiet. I slowly make my way to the kitchen. Once I find my cell phone I dial 112, the European equivalent of 911. I nervously whisper my name and address into the receiver, closing the kitchen door and jamming the door handle with a chair.

I tell the operator there's an intruder in our house. She tells me to stay locked in the kitchen and wait for the police to arrive. I hang up and wipe my sweaty palms on my pants, then open the knife drawer and search for the most menacing blade we have. A vintage meat cleaver seems like a good choice. It's a little rusty around the edges but that only adds to its Jack the Ripper vibe.

I call Papi's cell—though, big shocker, it goes straight to voice mail. When he lived in Chicago, I used to complain about having to go through his secretary for everything. Little did I know, I should have been thankful I had a real person to take a message. I call Margo's cell, but it also goes to voice mail. Why do these people even bother carrying their phones around?

I grip the meat cleaver tighter. This is why I hate the countryside. In Chicago, I could've gone to our neighbor's house and waited for the cops.

I glance around the kitchen and realize the curtains are drawn back. This entire time, I've been a sitting duck. Motorcycle Stalker Guy could be out there watching me, waiting to strike. I move around the room, quickly closing the curtains. When I reach the sink, I gasp. He's by the pool.

Only he's lying down on one of the lounge chairs, wearing sunglasses and propping his feet up on the chair. The flowers he bought at the market lie on a side table beside him. Would a stalker do that?

I wait for him to move, but he doesn't. Is he asleep?
I search for the white dog and don't see him anywhere.
What the heck do I do?

a. The 112 lady told me to stay put until the cops arrive.
    But they aren't here yet. Are they even coming? How
    long is the response time in France?
b. What if he needs medical assistance? Or what if he's
    drunk? Or on drugs? Maybe he went to the wrong
    house.
c. Motorcycle Guy followed me here from the market.
    I mean, that whole invitation to a field was kind of
    creepy. Do I just wait and pray he doesn't see me?

Ten long minutes pass.

The police are never coming. I glance out the window and
watch him for a moment. He doesn't even flinch. If he's passed
out, maybe I can surprise him.

I move the chair blocking the door and make my way to
the pool.

Be like a mouse, I tell myself, unable to remember the French
word for mouse.

I softly push open the double doors that lead to the patio,
enough that I can squeeze myself out of the house.

Souris. The word for mouse comes to me as I step outside
and am blinded by the sun. My hand automatically shoots up to
my forehead to block the rays, though my vision remains blurry.
All I can see is a big, white thing running in my direction. I
want to scream, but my heart is pounding so hard I can't form
the sound. I turn around and try to open the double doors—the
handle won't turn. I've locked myself out of the house.

A scream comes out at the exact moment the white thing
jumps onto me. I freeze against the door, the meat cleaver
pressed up against my chest.

"Beluga! *¡Quítate!*" Motorcycle Stalker Guy yells in Spanish.

When he finally looks at me, he chuckles. "Ah, of course. It's the *friendly* American."

I hold the cleaver out in front of me and blurt out, "I called the police!"

He stands there, silent, with his dog sitting by his side.

"They are on their way. Right. Now." I press my back harder against the door, as if I could melt myself through it.

"You really should put that thing down. You may hurt yourself." He turns around and walks back to the lounge chair. The dog follows his every move.

"Did you not hear me?" I scream after him. "The police are coming. You should leave."

He lies back on the chair, intertwines his hands, and rests them over his chest.

"Wake me up when they get here."

We don't have to wait long. I shriek when someone taps on the door behind me. Two policemen are standing on the other side of the glass. One waves at me to step aside, then they both saunter onto the patio as if they were here for a pool party. Apparently the 112 lady forgot to relay my sense of emergency.

"I called you," I say in French.

"Where is the intruder?" one of them asks, glancing at the meat cleaver in my hand. He frowns but doesn't say anything.

I nod in the direction of Motorcycle Stalker Guy, who is walking toward us.

"*J'habite ici*," he tells the cops. I'm about to say, "No, you don't live here," but then he turns to me and says, "I'm Diego, Margo's stepson. Nice to meet you."

The policemen glare at me, as if I'm somehow responsible for wasting an hour of their precious time. They should be glaring at our unwelcomed guest instead.

"I'll be here all summer," Diego adds, sidestepping me and heading inside the house, dog trailing behind.

I grip the meat cleaver a little harder. I can't stand this guy.

Chapter 3

Chicken Legs and Lemon Tarts

I s there a sauce for this?" Diego asks, biting into a cold chicken leg straight out of the fridge.

"Can you please use a plate?" I take the leftover containers from his hand and set them on the kitchen island. "Here." I place a dish next to them when it's clear he ignored my plea. "There's a wine and butter sauce on the second shelf to go with that chicken. It's labeled."

"Aha," he exclaims, pulling out another tower of containers.

I try to ignore the chicken leg attached to his mouth and go back to slicing a Japanese eggplant through a mandoline. *At least he can multitask.*

My hand moves quickly over the metal contraption. Each slice must be exactly one-sixteenth of an inch for the perfect ratatouille presentation.

Diego piles three pieces of chicken onto his plate and gives a leg to his overexcited dog.

"Don't you have dog food?" I ask. I want to tell him that chicken was marinated overnight and braised for two hours, but instead I breathe out slowly.

"Chicken legs are his favorite," he says, heaping a mountain of rice, carrots, and potatoes onto his plate.

"Well, you can't keep him here. It's not hygienic to have animals where food is being prepared."

I reach past him to grab a bowl, and end up knocking my

27

shoulder against his. It's like hitting a wall. How can this enormous kitchen suddenly feel so small?

"Sorry," he says, handing me the bowl.

"Thanks." I look down, feeling like an alien species has invaded my safety bubble. Since I got here, the kitchen has been the only place in this house where I can be me—at-ease me. Now Mr. Alien Intruder has found a way to suck all the peace out of every square inch of space.

I push the last of the eggplant down the mandoline blade. The slices are too thick, but it's too late; I've cut up the whole thing. I struggle with the tiny screws of the mandoline while adjusting the slicing blade to the right thickness. I test it on a piece of squash before I begin slicing again. At this rate, the whole dish will be ruined.

"Oh, and by the way, he's not an animal. He's Beluga." The dog perks up at the mention of his name. The so-called Beluga has inhaled the chicken meat and is now chewing on the bone.

"What's wrong with his eyes?" I ask. "Is he sick? If he's sick, you need to take him outside." *And please go with him.*

"He's not sick. He's albino."

"Should he be chewing on that bone? I heard something crack."

"Are you a cat person or do you just hate dogs?"

"I've never had a pet, so I couldn't tell you."

"You are the first girl I've met who doesn't like Beluga. Everyone likes him."

I scoff. "Oh, I bet."

The dog is kinda cute in that scrunched-face bulldog way, but I'm not about to admit it. And I'm certainly not about to become one of those girls who drools over a cute guy's dog.

Diego hands Beluga another chicken leg, which he quickly devours. And before I can protest the continued dog feeding, the kitchen phone rings.

"I'll get it," he says, walking toward the receiver on the wall. The way he's making himself at home is nerve-racking.

"Bonjour," he says into the receiver. Then nods and says, "Yes, yes, she's right here.

"It's your mother," he says, handing me the phone.

I take it from his hand, avoiding any unnecessary contact. My eye is literally twitching with irritation. Great. Just what I need going into Grattard's kitchen—a nervous tic. I'll be the girl spasmodically winking at everyone in the room.

I clear my throat, shifting my tone. I utter a cheerful "Hi, Mom" into the receiver. "How's your visit with Mamie going?"

I press my shoulder against a cabinet and stare at the wall. Every time we speak, I feel guilty for choosing to spend the summer with Papi and Margo, instead of traveling with her to visit my grandmother on the coast. Not that it was much of a choice, but still. It's like I'm betraying her somehow.

"Lovely, but I miss you terribly, darling. I wanted to wish you good luck tomorrow," she says. "How are you feeling?"

"Fine," I say, looping the phone cord around one of my fingers. There's so much more I want to tell her, but not with Diego listening.

"Oh, and I finally settled things with the principal at your school. He assured me an apprenticeship would count toward your senior year. Isn't that wonderful?"

I bounce from foot to foot, unable to display the full extent of my excitement. Since we got the acceptance email to Chef Grattard's program, Mom has been working with my school so that if I get the apprenticeship, I can stay in France and not have to waste one more year learning about human anatomy and nonlinear equations. The only math I'll need in Grattard's kitchen is figuring out how to convert ounces into grams.

"That's great, Mom," I say, clutching the phone harder. Listening to the sweetness in her voice makes me realize how much I miss her. "I can't wait to see you next weekend."

Mom goes on about her visit with Mamie, and her plans for the weekend, but my focus involuntarily drifts back to Diego and his horrible culinary etiquette. I turn my head to find him drizzling the wine and butter sauce all over a big bowl of food he's preparing. I mean, he's using a serving bowl! It looks like a volcano exploded on the dish. *Gross.*

"Mom, I'm sorry, but can I call you back later? We have a visitor. Margo's stepson decided to pop in *unannounced.*"

I watch Diego, eyes on the plate, slowly shake his head.

"Is everything okay over there?" she asks, clearly picking up on the annoyance lacing my voice.

"It's fine. I can't wait to see you. I'll call later. Okay?"

"Yes, darling. See you soon. I love you."

"Love you too," I say before hanging up.

When I turn around, Diego has pulled two more containers from the fridge so that the entire kitchen counter is covered in open receptacles.

"Eat much?" I mutter to myself. He might as well be eating out of a trough. I grab a zucchini and quickly slice it against the mandoline's blade.

"I'm not a visitor," he says after a long pause.

"We'll see," I say. There is no way Papi is going to let us sleep under the same roof. That man is crazy overprotective.

"Yeah, we'll see." Diego puts his bowl into the microwave and presses *start.*

I concentrate on the peppers in front of me, charring them over an open flame until the skin turns black and the kitchen fills with a smoky, sweet aroma.

Behind me, looking over my shoulder—and way too close for comfort—Diego says in a low voice, "You know those are burning, right?"

My entire back absorbs the heat coming off his chest. I fold in my shoulders and step closer to the flame. My face feels like it's about to melt off.

I clear my throat and manage to say, "That's the point."

He moves aside and I step away from the flame, and from him. Then I set the peppers in a covered dish so they can steam.

When the microwave timer dings, I utter a *thank goodness* under my breath.

"Beautiful day to eat outside," I say emphatically. Then turn off the burner and pray he takes the hint.

"Not a cloud in the sky," he says, plopping himself on a stool by the kitchen island. The albino dog drops onto the floor beside him.

"Maybe you can find a cherry field or something." I fake smile.

"Oh, you've changed your mind, huh?" He lifts his head and raises his eyebrows.

"Yeah, right," I huff.

He puts his fork down and takes off his leather jacket. Immediately I wish he'd put the thing back on. This guy is seriously cut. I make a mad dash for an onion and sink my knife into it, hoping the eye-irritating gases will mask the redness rushing to my cheeks. For some reason that Michelangelo statue pops into my head. The *full* body image.

Get a grip, Isabella.

"Does Margo know you're here?" I grab another onion even though the recipe calls for only one. "She didn't say you were coming."

"It's a surprise," he says between bites. I've never seen anyone eat that fast.

"You said you're her stepson?"

"She was married to my dad—her first, his second. Didn't end well. He's a bit of a control freak . . ." He stares at me and shakes his head.

"What?"

"Nothing." He scrapes the last bite out of the bowl like he's going to lick it clean. "Did you make this? It's pretty good," he says offhandedly, moving to the sink to wash his dish.

I know I should be grateful for the compliment, but I bet he would probably say a meal that came out of a box is also "pretty good."

"Thanks," I mutter reluctantly, gripping a head of garlic. I place some cloves under the blade of my knife and strike with the heel of my palm. A loud thump echoes in the kitchen, making the albino dog whimper.

"Maybe you should take him outside," I say—for the second time.

"He's fine," he says. "He doesn't like loud noises."

Am I getting lost in translation or is this guy incapable of taking a hint?

I peel off the skin around the cloves and proceed to practice my mincing technique.

Diego stands and walks to the fridge. He opens the door and peers in, moving a few things around on the shelves.

"Can I help you find something?"

"Dessert?"

"Second shelf on the left. Blue container. It's labeled lemon tarts." I turn back to my recipe, rereading it for the hundredth time like I'm some amateur. "You know, those tarts taste even better when you eat them by the pool," I say.

"Did you make these too?"

"Uh-huh."

He bites into a tart, tucking the container under his arm.

"Not bad," he says between bites. *Not bad?* The two words sound like the long, pointy prongs of a fork scratching the surface of a chalkboard. Then he grabs an entire milk jug from the fridge and a glass from the cupboard.

"Come on, Beluga, let's go outside so Mademoiselle Chef can have her kitchen back."

The moment they leave I exhale, long and loud.

This guy needs to *go*—for good.

An hour later I'm staring at my almost-finished meal—thin, round slices of tomato, squash, zucchini, and eggplant arranged in neat rows inside a baking dish. I sprinkle salt and pepper and drizzle olive oil before placing the casserole in the oven. The dish would be perfect if it weren't for those too-thick pieces of eggplant.

Margo and Papi arrive in time for dinner. Margo screams *"Mi amor!"* the moment she sees Diego and lunges at him with her arms spread wide. I had no idea she could speak Spanish. She only uses English around me even though I've repeatedly told her I need to practice French.

Diego and Margo launch into a rapid Spanish exchange, way too fast for me to follow. Apparently, Lala did lie to me. My Spanish is worse than my French.

"James, this is Diego," Margo says, turning to Papi and throwing her arm around her stepson.

Papi is quick to shake his hand. "I've heard so many good things about you," he says, and I begin to wonder, where is the father who would erupt at the prospect of a hot guy sleeping under the same roof as his teenage daughter? Clearly, that dad stayed back in Chicago.

I pretend not to listen as I set the table for dinner, practicing the French table setting I've memorized—the silverware placed in the order it will be used, leaving one inch of space around the plate; the napkin folded in a triangle; the water and wine glasses in front; and a side plate for bread. Every setting is a model of uniformity.

"When did you get here?" Margo asks.

"Early afternoon," Diego says. I nervously wait for the meat cleaver and policemen story, but instead he says, "We left Barcelona at sunrise. Beluga loves to watch the sun come up over the ocean."

The dog barks as if he can add something to the conversation. The sound resonates through the dining room. I decide to draw the line at having a canine at the table for dinner.

Papi bends down to pet Beluga. He's making all kind of weird noises, like one of those women who go crazy every time they see a baby.

"I've been thinking about getting one," Papi says, and I almost drop the water goblet in my hand. Every time Mom and I talked about getting a puppy, he said they were too much work. "We're never home," he used to say. But that was *old dad*, I remind myself with a twinge of resentment. Farmer Jaime here has all the time in the world.

"Margo tells me you really enjoy running the farm," Diego tells Papi. I take a little longer filling the water glasses, lingering to hear Papi's response. Even though I've been around him every day for a few weeks now, I haven't got a clue as to how he *really* feels about his new life. On the outside, he seems happy, I guess. But how can he be truly happy when he had to forgo the life he had with me and Mom? My own question stings. Part of me—a big part—doesn't want to know the answer.

"I'm loving working outside again," Papi says. "My parents owned a farm in the Midwest, back in the States. That's where I grew up. I miss that life. I've been helping Margo's family with some plans to expand, maybe create a product line. Marmalades, preserves, that kind of thing."

"James est a brilliant businessman," Margo gushes, planting a kiss on his cheek. Papi drapes his arm over her bare shoulders.

"I got you something," Diego says to Margo, handing her the flowers he bought at the market and a brown carry-out bag. "We stopped in Montpellier for breakfast. I got you that cheese you like."

"Oh! From La Fine Mouche?" Margo opens the bag and sniffs the contents. I've never seen her look so delighted over food. "You are so thoughtful. I'm surprised you remembered." She turns to Papi and says, "I used to take Diego to the beach in Montpellier when Dario was too busy."

"When was he not?" Diego retorts.

"I'm surprised your father gave you permission to come visit. What about your training?" Margo asks, tilting her head to the side. Her right hand absently rubs her belly in circles.

Diego shrugs, and for half a second glances in my direction. Our eyes meet but he looks away first. "My coach said I could take a break. Can Beluga and I stay in the cottage?" He taps against his leg and the dog is instantly by his side, staring up at Margo with pleading puppy eyes.

"Of course," Margo tells him, bending down to rub Beluga behind the ears. He closes his eyes, lifts his head, and moans at the touch. "Some of your things are still there."

"The table is ready," I say loud enough so they can hear me. "Dinner will be out in a minute."

They gather around the table, pulling out chairs. The albino dog lingers as if he's expecting someone to pull out a seat for him.

"Can you please take your dog outside?" I ask Diego as politely as I can muster.

He looks at Margo. She sighs and nods in agreement. Diego grunts, but doesn't say anything. He opens the patio doors and Beluga rambles outside, his head hanging low. It's weird how sometimes you can tell dogs are disappointed.

Back in the kitchen, I pull out the ratatouille and mentally get ready to plate, considering the dish's color contrast and height.

I'm about to position the first element when I hear Margo say, "It's like living in a restaurant . . ." before lowering her voice.

I tightly press my lips and turn off the oven.

Who else am I supposed to practice on?

Whatever. Papi doesn't seem to mind.

My fingers firmly hold on to a ring form as I arrange a bed of couscous on the plate and spoon the ratatouille on top. I garnish with fresh basil and inspect the dish, painfully aware that during the next three weeks someone else will be scrutinizing every element on my plate.

"Michelin stars come only to those fully committed to excellence," Chef Grattard was once quoted as saying.

As I carry the plates to the dining room, my chin inches a little higher than usual. Tomorrow, Chef Grattard's kitchen will be mine.

Chapter 4

The Omelet from Hell

Of all the days for Papi to try to be Super Dad, why did he pick today? And why did I let him?

This morning Papi decided it was time for a father-daughter breakfast in some out-of-the-way pâtisserie. "It's the best in Lyon," he kept repeating. But when we got there, all I could do was stare at my pain au chocolat and take a few sips of my café crème. My stomach churned with anxiety and anticipation for the day ahead. By the time we left the pâtisserie, traffic had reached its peak.

My irritation was worsened due to the fact I didn't get enough sleep thanks to a recent string of kitchen nightmares. In the final one, I served Chef Grattard a plate of undercooked pasta. He walked the plate to the trash bin and tossed the whole thing in, fork and all. "*Chef Boyardee* makes better spaghetti than this!" he screamed. I woke up drenched in sweat.

Our car finally pulls in front of the restaurant, and I tumble out.

"Good luck, honey!" I hear Papi say as I shut the car door.

My chest tightens as I take in the bold, gold letters that read *La Table de Lyon*. I stare at my reflection in the lettering, still not believing my insane good luck.

Papi says luck favors the prepared. That's me, the girl who's spent the last three years training for this moment. After-school culinary courses, weekend jobs at any mom-and-pop restaurant

that hired teens, and a million test recipes from a million different cookbooks—all for this moment.

I force the door handle down and enter. I've seen countless
photos of this dining room, but none did it justice. The black-
and-white checkered floor glistens under my feet. A massive
gold chandelier hangs from the middle of the room, an unusual
contrast to the modern aqua-and-yellow armchairs surrounding
each table. Floor-to-ceiling windows adorn the sides of the room,
bathing everything in sunlight. It's the most beautiful restaurant
I've seen in my whole life.

And now I'm a part of it.

"You're late," a disembodied voice calls out in French. My
breath catches in my throat. I search the room and find a short,
stocky man waving from the back of the restaurant. "Hurry, now,"
he spits. I jog to meet him, trying to explain there was traffic, but
he holds up his hand and shushes me. "This is not my problem,"
he says while leading me through a narrow hallway and down a
flight of stairs. We pass several security cameras as we walk. I
get the impression I'm being watched at all times.

"Through there," he says, pointing to a set of stainless steel
double doors before returning upstairs.

I smooth down my hair and walk the twenty feet to the doors,
sweaty and disheveled. This is so not how I imagined beginning
my first day in Chef Grattard's kitchen.

I'm the last one to arrive. Fourteen overachieving teenage
cooks from all over the world—forming a rainbow of cultures
and colors—turn to look at me as I burst through the swinging
entrance.

I force down the urge to be sick.

As I step into the test kitchen, I immediately notice two
things: the room is freezing, and the other students have gathered around a stainless steel island in the middle of the room.
Everyone is already dressed in the same uniform—a white chef's
coat, white apron, white toque hats, and gray pants. I didn't
realize we would have to wear a toque—a staple in traditional

high-end kitchens. I've never worn one, but really, how hard can it be to keep that tall thing on your head?

My uniform sits alone in a pile at the center of the island. I edge my way between two tall, lanky guys and reach for the change of clothes, ignoring the multiple sniggers and stares.

"You must be Isabella," a girl says. She has a British accent and the looks of a Paris runway supermodel—even in her uniform. She towers over me, and her glowing ebony complexion is something generally found on magazine covers.

"I go by Isa," I tell her, rubbing my arms for warmth. I swear the temperature has dropped a whole ten degrees in the time I've been here.

"We were wondering if you were gonna be a no-show." She extends her hand and says, "I'm Pippa, nice to meet you."

I shake her hand and mean to say, "Nice to meet you too," but what comes out is a nervous, "Do you know where I can change?"

"Ah, you're the American. Right. All business, I see," Pippa says, a warm smile still on her face. Behind her someone snickers. She glances back. Her eyes roll when she sees the source of the noise—a tall blond with pale white skin and ice-cold blue slits for eyes.

"That's Bruno, but I say we call him Snake Eyes," Pippa whispers.

Snake Eyes's feet are firmly planted on the floor and his arms are crossed over his chest. I notice he's the only one carrying pens and a thermometer in his sleeve pocket.

I stand a little taller, trying to remember if I brought a thermometer.

"Changing room is through that door," Pippa says, pointing toward a hallway at the back of the kitchen. "There are lockers in there for your stuff." I thank her and walk-run in that direction.

My clothes come off as if they're on fire. Then I tumble into my uniform, almost tripping on my pant legs. Even though it's Arctic cold, my armpits are sweating buckets, making me second-guess if I remembered to put on deodorant this morning.

I try to calm myself by repeating one of Chef Grattard's pillars of excellence: "Technique is not enough. Only passion guarantees greatness." I tell myself I have tons of passion—passion out the freaking wazoo.

With one reassuring breath, I turn to glance at my reflection in the mirror. Big mistake.

Huge. Freaking. Mistake.

A child wearing an adult costume stares back at me. *Are you effing kidding me?*

The pants are saggy, the apron almost touches my feet, and the coat sleeves are way too long. The toque only adds to the cartoon character I've become. Did I order the wrong size?

I pull the back of my collar forward, trying to catch a glimpse of the tag—it reads 42. I attempt to do the US conversion math in my head. *Twelve!* Three sizes too big. I might as well be wrapped in a potato sack.

"It's fine," I tell myself between clenched teeth. "It's perfectly fine." I nod at my reflection and lift my head. I shove my things into the locker and join the others. I will deal with the uniform after class.

Do. Not. Freak. Out. Isa.

As I walk back into the kitchen, I ignore the incredulous stares and the hand that flies over some guy's mouth to conceal a snicker. And I especially ignore Bruno, aka Snake Eyes, who is outright laughing into his closed fist.

Never in my life have I ever wanted a do-over day so badly.

I stand next to Pippa, half hoping I can hide behind her. She gently elbows my side and says, "They got my size wrong too." I smile back, but I can see her uniform doesn't look like a potato sack. It hugs her in all the right places like she stepped off some culinary uniform fashion show.

"As I was saying," Snake Eyes says, giving me a sideways glance like I interrupted some great speech. "My father is a MOF."

"They're like culinary gods," another guy interjects.

"Father says the Michelin inspectors are all about consistency . . ." Snake Eyes drones on about the workings of the
inspection process like he's an expert. Most of the students hang
on to every word, except Pippa and me, and a third girl who's off
to one corner, absorbed in a set of knives. She has a tiny frame,
dark hair mostly hidden under her toque, and the same olive skin
tone as Diego.

"That's Lucia," Pippa says, following my eyes. "She's from
Catalonia. She won some teen cooking show on TV. Apparently,
she's a big deal in Spain."

"Really?"

Pippa shrugs. "I found a clip on YouTube, but it was in
Catalan. She seemed pretty badass, though. The quiet but
deadly type."

My pulse picks up. No one said I'd be competing against
the son of a MOF and a Catalonian teen star. Suddenly, all my
preparations seem downright inadequate.

After a quick scan of the room, I realize we're the only girls
in the program.

That's until the double doors open and a woman dressed in
full chef garb walks in.

Everyone goes silent.

"Welcome to La Table de Lyon," she says, standing at the
head of the island. She sets down a clipboard in front of her. "I'm
Chef Sabine Troissant, Grattard's executive pastry chef. I teach
the summer program."

Snake Eyes moans loud enough that everyone can hear him.

"Is there a problem?" Chef Troissant's lips are pressed into
a thin line, and it must be noted her uniform is definitely not a
potato sack. Her chef's coat is impeccably pressed, spotless, and
correctly fitted, with her name embroidered in royal blue letters
over the left front panel. And her light brown hair is neatly placed
under her hat, not one hair out of place.

"*Je suis désolé*, Chef Troissant," he says in the perfect French
of a native speaker, but anyone can hear his apology lacks

conviction. "I was told Chef Grattard himself would be teaching," he adds.

I want to say I was told that too, but there's no way I'm siding with Snake Eyes.

"*I'm* teaching," she says, pausing to give him the cold stare of death. Her piercing gray eyes make her gaze even more menacing. "We received one thousand applications from fifteen countries this year. This is the *only* international program of this caliber. Someone would be more than happy to take your place. The wait list is very long."

Snake Eyes nods and doesn't respond, though the smirk plastered on his face speaks for itself.

"*Alors*, let's get started. I will speak English, but some terms cannot be translated." Chef Troissant flips through the papers on her clipboard. "*Bon*," she exclaims, clapping her hands together. "First lesson: the French omelet. I will demonstrate. Then you will have three minutes to do it yourself. Your work stations are behind you."

An assistant rolls in a cart equipped with a countertop burner, utensils, and ingredients.

My shoulders relax and I unclench my hands. I've been making French omelets since I was a kid. This should be easy.

"Please—you shouldn't even be here if you can't make an omelet," Snake Eyes mutters to a guy next to him. "I guess *some* people need to learn the proper way—not that overcooked egg travesty they make in America."

I want to grab an egg from Chef Troissant's table and smash it on his head so he can get the full effect of the American version. Instead, I step closer to the demonstration table and listen.

"The herbs: chives, tarragon, parsley, and chervil," she says, cutting them with a precision that only comes with years of experience. "Three eggs. Break the egg flat, like this." She cracks the eggshells on the table and drops the contents into a bowl. "Don't break the yolk. You will introduce bacteria." Chef Troissant pauses, squinting in my direction.

"No notes!" she spits. "You must remember this!"

I instinctively search my hands but come up empty. My head turns from side to side—the same as everyone else—and I realize she's talking to the girl behind me, Lucia from Catalonia.

Lucia fumbles while trying to put away her notepad and drops her pen in the process. I bend down, pick it up, and give it back to her. She doesn't look at me, but I can see her face is beet red. She mumbles a nervous mix of *gràcies*, *gracias*, and *merci* and takes two steps back.

"I believe the instructions were very clear," Chef Troissant says. "No personal items are allowed in this kitchen. No notebooks. No cell phones. No anything. *Comprende?*"

Everyone nods. My hands fly to my pockets to make sure I left my phone in the locker.

Chef Troissant continues with the demonstration, beating the egg mixture with a fork. "Very important—add salt and pepper. Beat your eggs," she says. "You don't move like a wet mop. Move quick. Really beat your eggs." Her hand is moving so fast it's like some kind of superpower. My wrist hurts from watching hers.

She adds butter to the hot pan and swirls it around. "Bon, I mix with one hand and shake with the other hand. Make the smaller possible scrambled eggs. Very tender. Very scrambled. We will break the mixture on this side. Bring the two lips together without letting it brown. Wet in the center. Very important."

My head is spinning. She's rocking the pan back and forth at lightning speed with one hand while she scrambles the center of the omelet with the other. Her fork moves around the pan like it's all part of one unit.

I thought I knew how to make a French omelet but turns out I've been doing it wrong all along. My stomach drops to my feet. Is this what we're expected to do in lesson one? I try to remember the last time I made a French omelet, and for the love of me, I can't. I can't even remember how it turned out. I think of Mom teaching me how to move the pan around, but her movements were akin to a slug's compared to this. I struggle to remember anything I learned at the French cooking course I took back home—the one that got me accepted here—but my mind goes blank. It feels like the world's heaviest cast iron pot has fallen in my stomach: I've forgotten how to make a stupid French omelet.

"Bring the lip back. Make a nice half moon. Bring up and fold. Wet in the center," Chef Troissant explains, but she might as well be speaking Mandarin. My armpits start to sweat profusely, to the point that it doesn't matter if I put on deodorant or not.

"Let it set. Bring it to the edge. It has to be beige in color. Slightly wet in the center. *Et voilà!* The French omelet," she exclaims, presenting her dish.

My lungs collapse inside my chest. I must have blinked or something because I missed the part when the omelet went from the pan to the plate looking like it jumped out of a page of *Thuriès Gastronomie Magazine*.

"Now please take your stations. You have three minutes."

I step behind my work station. My legs feel as if they're made of gelatin. I move a few things around, waiting for Chef Troissant to give us an official start.

"They may have margarine in the back if you prefer," I hear Snake Eyes say. He's taken the station right next to mine. I bite the inside of my cheek and count to ten in my head.

"What do you call this margarine? I Can't Believe It's No Butter?" he asks, laughing at his own dumb attempt at a joke.

"For your information, margarine is a French invention," I spit back, ready to launch myself into a Napoleonic history lesson.

"Of course, but it was meant for the lower class," he says, staring me down over the bridge of his pointed nose. "Your people ran with it."

I'm left with my mouth open as Chef Troissant calls, "*Faites attention!* Everything you need is on your work stations, including an identifying number. No names. Only numbers."

Mine is thirteen. *Great. Does anyone have a black cat they wish to lend me? Or a ladder I can stand under?*

"Your three minutes start now," Chef Troissant announces.

My ingredients all blend into a blur. The other students—including Snake Eyes—move around me at freakish speed while I'm swimming in a sea of molasses.

I mangle my herbs with a knife that is too big for my hand. I crack the eggs over the bowl but realize I skipped the first step: turning on the stove. The pan is as cold as a body dumped into Lake Michigan. In a panic, I let my eggshells fall inside the bowl. I turn on the range and dump in a spoonful of butter that sits lifeless in the pan.

"One minute and thirty seconds left," Chef Troissant calls out.

What happens next can only be described as an out-of-body experience. I watch myself from somewhere in the ceiling as I plunge my fingers into the egg mixture to fish out the shells, then beat the eggs like I'm a human stand mixer. Meanwhile, something is burning. It takes me a moment to realize it's coming from my station. The butter has turned black inside the pan. In a panic, I turn so fast that my stupid toque flies off my head and lands on Snake Eye's station. I swallow a scream.

Snake Eyes doesn't even reach for it. He only stares at the white pleated thing in absolute disgust.

"Can I have my hat back?" I say, trying to regain control of my pan's temperature. I turn down the flame to a minimum but it's still smoking.

Snake Eyes lifts my hat with a pair of tongs and dumps it on my station. "They sell clamps in the hardware store," he grumbles. Then he coughs dramatically, waving the air in front of his face. "Do you need an extinguisher?"

I open my mouth to tell him exactly what I need, but he obnoxiously turns his back to me.

His omelet is almost finished and he's getting ready to plate. It looks as good as Chef Troissant's.

I wipe off my pan and put in more butter. This time it melts into a nice creamy foam. I pour in my egg and herb mixture and swivel the pan around … but nothing happens. There's no cooking. No "very tender. Very scrambled." The pan is now too cold. And there's no way I'm serving a plate of salmonella to this woman. I turn the flame all the way up.

"Fifteen seconds. Time to plate," she calls out.

I fold the omelet and drop it onto the plate, then sprinkle some herbs over it as garnish.

"Time's up," she says.

I stare down at my dish. It's an all-American omelet with fully cooked eggs and the telltale golden crust. And what is worse—if that's even possible—I forgot to add salt and pepper.

Chef Troissant stops at each station, individually inspecting every student's dish. She takes one bite of the omelet, then passes judgment.

"Bon," she says to Snake Eyes. His face sparkles like he won the lottery.

She then moves to my station. I scramble to balance the toque on my head. *I hate hats!*

I badly want to say something. How great it is to be here. How I'm looking forward to the next three weeks. How excited I am about the two-day pastry intensive course offered at the end of week three. It's world-class!

But I don't say any of this. Her no-nonsense approach to my dish stops me cold. She picks up the plate and cuts a piece of the omelet with the side of her fork but doesn't bring it to her mouth. Her left eyebrow shoots up as she returns the plate to the table and moves on to the next station. To my left, Lucia from Catalonia has also managed a textbook French omelet. It looks smooth as silk, even better than Snake Eyes'.

I want to fall through a big, black hole in the kitchen floor— and take my overcooked eggs with me.

Chapter 5

Cherries Jubilee

To top off my day from hell, I'm forced to take a taxi home. Papi texted that he and Margo were in town getting some baby stuff. He asked what time he should pick me up. Of course, since my phone was stored inside a locker the entire day, I didn't see his message until they'd already left the city.

I press my forehead against the cab's cold window as we drive past the rolling hills of Bessenay. It's raining hard and the fields have taken on an ominous shade of grayish-green. I watch a few cows skip toward the shade of a massive tree, where others have taken shelter. *At least I'm not a cow standing in the rain.* This becomes my consolation for such an abysmal first day.

The entire ride home, I can't shake the omelet disaster. I tell myself it's a matter of practice, like the soufflés. So for dinner, I decide to make everyone an omelet—four omelets, four chances to practice. The thought eases the tension welled up in my chest. These will be the best omelets anyone's ever had. Given the appropriate amount of time, I know I can do this.

After the test fiasco, Chef Troissant explained some of the techniques we would cover during the program—all French classics. She then gave us a copy of La Table de Lyon's menu and told us to familiarize ourselves with every dish.

"Learn to respect the ingredients," she told us. "Memorize them. Understand how they come together."

But I can't figure out how to even begin to re-create dishes described in only a handful of words. Take the salmon dish, for example: confit, Roosevalt fondant, saffron pistils—that's it. What am I supposed to do with that? The only dish on this menu I find remotely doable at home is the cherries jubilee listed in the dessert section. Mostly because the main ingredient is readily available in our backyard.

When I finally arrive at the house, I make a beeline for the kitchen. Today's omelet lesson plays in my mind like a video on a loop. I need to get it right soon or I'll be tossing and turning all night.

Before I can reach the kitchen, I'm sidetracked by laughter coming from the dining room and the distinct sweet, deep-fried smell of General Tso chicken.

I enter the dining room to find Papi, Margo, and Diego seated around the table, eating from paper plates with plastic utensils. The table is covered in take-out containers, and I was right about the General Tso chicken. But there's also Mongolian beef and Singapore noodles.

"What's this?" I ask, as if the scene before me needs an explanation.

"Chinese. You hungry?" Diego asks. It would take me two days to get through all the food piled on his plate. Has this guy ever heard of portion control?

I glance down at his feet. Even the albino dog is treating himself to a chicken wing.

"Diego picked up some takeout. We saved you some," Papi says. He pushes out a chair for me, but I've lost my appetite.

"Thanks, but I'll pass," I say. "Have homework to do."

"You have to open your fortune cookie first, even if you don't eat. It's tradition," Diego says, tossing me a fortune cookie across the table. I catch it midair.

"You know these messages are mass produced, right?" I say, but tear into the wrapper anyway, hoping for one of those uplifting fortunes like *All your hard work will soon pay off.* I crack the cookie open and pull out the strip of paper.

"What does it say?" Diego asks.

"It says . . ." I pause, my eyes stinging. "It says . . . *The fortune you seek is in another cookie.*"

Diego and Papi laugh. *Because this is so funny.*

"I have stuff to do." I walk away, holding my back straight until I leave the room.

"Wait, Isa," Papi calls out. "How was your first day?"

"Great," I respond before I disappear into the kitchen. "It was great."

I mean, really, what does a fortune cookie know?

If I can't make the stupid omelets—because *someone* decided to mess with my dinner plans—I'll focus solely on the flambé. Today, I'll take even the smallest victory. I can't go to bed feeling like the world's most incompetent cook.

I open *Larousse* and read all about the flambé technique—the act of pouring spirit over food and then igniting it, both to enhance flavor and "demonstrate culinary showmanship." Perfect. I badly need some showmanship. And what's even better, I get to use my blowtorch.

I go back to the dining room and tell everyone, "Save room for dessert."

"Yum. What are you making?" Papi asks.

"Cherries jubilee," I say.

"There's a fire extinguisher under the sink. Just in case . . ." Papi chuckles to himself, reaching for what's left of the Singapore noodles. It's a dig at a past "incident" in Lala's kitchen that has become family lore. Usually I laugh it off, but today the joke grinds against my very bones.

"Funny," I say, walking back to the kitchen.

Once I get my ingredients and utensils ready, I launch into action. First, I pit the cherries, then place them in a skillet with sugar, lemon juice, and vanilla bean seeds. The cherry mixture must cook on medium to low heat until the sugar dissolves. I'm standing by the stove, stirring the skillet, when Diego comes in.

"There's still some food left if you get hungry later," he says, shoving a few containers into the fridge and totally messing up my color-coded storage system.

"I'm good, thanks." I make a mental note to rearrange the fridge after he leaves.

He shuts the fridge door and then lingers next to me, forgoing any measure of personal space. "Need some help?" he asks.

I sidestep him, trying to add some distance between us, while breathing through the sudden flurry of heart palpitations that come when his arm (accidentally) rubs against mine.

"I'm good," I repeat, clearing my throat.

"Is this that dessert with the flames?" He grabs the brandy bottle from the counter and scans the label.

"Yup."

He twists the lid open and smells the contents.

"You use alcohol for the fire, right?"

"Um-hum." I watch him set down the brandy and reach for my blowtorch. I resist the urge to take it away from him. For the uninitiated, a blowtorch may be something of a plaything, but for me it's an instrument for culinary perfection.

"Is this a real blowtorch?" An amused grin takes over his face and I catch a mix of excitement and curiosity dance across his eyes.

Oh no. Heck no.

"It's not a toy." I grab the blowtorch from his hands and set it back on the counter, hoping he will leave it—and me—alone.

"Come on! Let me give it a whirl. I'm great with the flames." His eyebrows shimmy over his eyes. If I wasn't so tired, or annoyed, I might find it kinda charming.

"I bet you are."

The cherry mixture bubbles to life, which means it's ready for the alcohol to go on top. This whole back and forth is messing up my timing.

I turn from the pan to the counter, searching for the bottle of brandy, but again it's in Diego's hands.

"Are you sure you know how to do this?" he asks, waving the bottle in front of my face like this is some silly game. The childish smirk across his lips assures me he doesn't get the skill that goes into a flambé.

"You know, usually, I like doing this on my own," I say, nice and clear, then grab the bottle away from his hand. Mercifully, he lets go and steps back.

"Your dad said you almost burned down your grandmother's kitchen. Is that true?"

My jaw clenches. *Really, Papi? Traitor.*

"It was an accident," I say, gripping the bottle harder. "And if he had changed the batteries in the fire alarm over her stove— like she asked him to—I would have known the pie was burning."

"I'm pretty sure the batteries in this fire alarm haven't been changed in a while either." He points at a round plastic disc on the ceiling. "See? No red light," he says.

"Thanks for your concern," I say through gritted teeth. "I think I can take it from here."

He doesn't leave, though. He makes himself comfortable on one of the stools around the island countertop. What do I have to say to get rid of this guy?

"I'll be here in case you need an extra hand," he says, leafing through the pages of *Larousse*.

I turn around and ignore him.

I pour a few tablespoons of alcohol into the skillet and get ready to light it. I hit the blowtorch's ignition button and watch the blue butane flame come to life. The most thrilling thing about cooking torches is knowing I'm holding pure heat in my hand—2,700 degrees Fahrenheit, to be exact.

Every girl should have a blowtorch.

I'm about to light the pan on fire when it occurs to me that maybe I should add a pinch of cinnamon. I've never tried it myself, but I've read that the powder ignites. Bring on the showmanship!

I set the blowtorch next to the stove and dash to the pantry in search of cinnamon. When I first took over Villa des Fleur's kitchen, I organized all the spices in alphabetical order. The effort has now paid off. I quickly find the cinnamon jar and turn back to the stove. But to my absolute horror, Diego is already there, holding *my* blowtorch and getting ready to ignite *my* flambé.

"What are you doing?" I yelp.

"The alcohol was about to evaporate," he says plainly.

"Seriously, what do you know?" My patience for this guy—and this whole day—has run out. "Put it down!"

When I check the pan, as much as it pains me to admit it, he's right. It needs more brandy. I reach for the bottle and pour a healthy amount, completely unaware Diego is still holding the blowtorch in his hand.

"Now for the best part," he exclaims.

"I told you, I don't need your help!" I call out, incredulous I've let this guy highjack *my* flambé. Then, it all happens as if in slow motion—as I'm wrestling him for the blowtorch, the butane flame hits the skillet, and the bottle I'm holding goes sideways, splashing alcohol all over the pan. In the span of half a second, the skillet goes up in flames.

I swear in two different languages and jump back, landing on Diego's hard-rock chest.

The flames are so high, they lick the extractor hood over the stove.

"Where's the fire extinguisher?" His hands grip the sides of my torso as he moves me out of the way. I don't know if it's the way his hands fit perfectly around my waist or the giant flame taking over the kitchen, but the heat becomes intolerable.

"Isa! The fire extinguisher, where is it?"

"I got it." I open the kitchen cabinet and pull out the red canister. I've never used one of these before—last time, Lala put out the fire—so I get stuck reading the instructions.

Diego grabs the canister out of my hands, pulls on a red cord, and aims the hose at the skillet. Within seconds, my flambé—and the entire stove, hood, and back wall—are covered in white fire-suppressant foam.

Papi and Margo come rushing into the kitchen.

"What happened?" Papi asks, taking inventory of the damage. "Are you guys okay?"

I don't say anything. I'm so furious, you could probably put an ignition switch on me and I'd light to 2,700 degrees.

"We're fine. Not sure about the stove, though," Diego says.

Diego and Papi hover over the stove, inspecting the hood. Margo watches them from a distance, scowling at the scene.

"I'm going to bed," she finally says. Then mutters something unintelligible before the door closes behind her.

"This is exactly why I cook alone," I snap after she leaves.

Papi and Diego exchange a glance. "I'm sure Diego was just trying to help," Papi says.

"I don't need help," I say forcefully. "I made that crystal clear." I stare hard at Papi, waiting for him to stand up for me, to tell Diego to just back off.

"I'm sure you could use some help cleaning up," Papi says, squeezing my shoulder. "It doesn't look like there's any damage."

He takes one last look at the stove, and I'm thankful he doesn't bring up the burned pie incident.

"Do you want me to help you clean?" Papi asks, resting a hand on my shoulder.

I shake my head no. He looks way more tired than me.

He kisses the side of my head in passing as he leaves the kitchen. "Don't stay up too late," he says.

Diego fumbles with a sponge and a bucket he finds in the storage closet. My eyes shoot long, sharp knives in his direction. His back is turned to me. If looks could kill, he would've dropped dead right then and there.

"What are you doing?" I ask.

"Cleaning up this mess." He reaches inside a drawer for a dish towel.

"I said I'll take care of it. You can go now."

I toss the burnt skillet into the sink, where it lands with a loud clank. My shoulders drop and I hear myself release a loud groan.

"I want to help—" he starts to say, but I cut him off.

"Can't you see I don't need your help?" I snap. "How many times do I need to say it? The only thing I want is to be left alone. Is that too much to ask?"

He drops the bucket in his hand. "Fine. Have it your way."

I grab a sponge, squeeze some dishwashing liquid onto the pan, and start scrubbing hard against the charred bottom.

Behind me, I hear the kitchen door swing, followed by a harsh silence.

My eyelids blink open and shut a few times, forcing back the tears.

I don't know if it's the god-awful day, or the ruined kitchen, or this mess of a new family, or the vivid memory of the day I burned Lala's pie that unexpectedly rushes to the forefront of my mind. Suddenly, I'm standing in a puddle of my own tears, feeling like the biggest loser.

As I scrub and scrub, harder each time, the pangs of grief I've spent months stuffing down threaten to choke me. Lala's absence stabs my heart and burns the hollow of my chest, like I've swallowed a mountain of embers that refuse to be extinguished.

I squeeze my eyes tight, wishing I could rest my head on her shoulder. Wishing everything could go back to the way it was before, when she was still with us.

But all I see behind my closed eyelids is the stupid pie, like a big ball of fire inside her oven. An omen for the string of unfortunate events that, when summed up, could be directly linked to her death.

In middle school, when my friends asked about my plans for the summer, I'd tell them I was going to a sleepaway camp. It was kind of true, I guess. Back then, I was a little embarrassed to admit I was spending summer with my Cuban abuela on her farm in Kansas.

For one, I'd had to dive into our complicated family genealogy—Kansas farmer falls in love with a Cuban immigrant, they have a mixed-race baby who later marries a French girl and, *voilá*, here I am, so mixed I constantly get asked "where I'm from." It's not the question itself that bothers me, but the assumptions behind it. The underlying message that "you don't belong here" and "you are other." You'd think a second-generation American wouldn't have to deal with this crap, but people somehow seem confused by my Midwestern accent, mostly Latina features, darker skin tone, and French-speaking mother.

Complicated family dynamics aside, none of my friends liked their grandparents as much as I loved being around Lala. I quickly learned the joy I felt in her presence wasn't a universal teenage experience.

What they didn't know, however, was that Lala was no ordinary granny—she was my abuela and she was my friend. Her home was like a sanctuary or a refugio. It was where I learned how to cook, how to grow my own herbs, and how to take eggs away from the chickens. And eventually where I went to escape the war between my parents.

It was also where I learned about the consequences of our mistakes, when our family pie recipe got stolen.

I was fifteen, and Mom had gone back to France for the summer to visit Mamie. Papi usually went with her for a few weeks but this time he stayed in Chicago, using the lame excuse he was too busy at work and couldn't take time off. I should have known then that things were on a downward spiral.

I decided to head to Kansas to spend time with Lala. After Grampa Roger died, Papi and I insisted she move to Chicago, but she'd refused.

"Isabela," she would say, pronouncing my name in Spanish, "my life is here. Why would I leave, morenita?" She would caress my long brown hair, as if addressing the parts of me that were undeniably her.

Lala always used to say we were like two cafés con leche

poured from the same pot. Except she had more leche and I had more café. She taught me that it was a point of pride to be a "café con leche Cubano." It was that simple—two Cuban coffees with milk. And I agreed, even if my friends sometimes argued that using food to compare skin color was inappropriate.

Lala's closest friends, and a big part of the reason she didn't want to move, were a group of ladies from her gardening club. There was eighty-year-old Hazel, an Austrian lady who made the best carrot cake I've ever tasted; a former beauty queen and professional quilter named Therese, whose sugar cookies were out of this world. And Barbara. Good ol' Barbara—or so I thought at first—with her elaborately coiffed hair and her stories about coming from old family money. Barbara was the devil. I hated her as much as I hated her oatmeal raisin cookies that tasted like cardboard.

Their group would gather every week in Lala's kitchen and bake pies for a women's shelter in the city. In that kitchen, I watched them swap recipes like they swapped stories, with a zest for life many would envy.

It was during one of those baking sessions that Lala, for some godforsaken reason, felt the need to share the award-winning, secret apple pie recipe that had been in our family for four generations.

That recipe had made Lala the Pie Queen of the Wyandotte County Fair ten years in a row, to the dismay of many Kansas City natives, including Barbara.

"You are so brave for competing," I heard her tell Lala once. "Who knew Cuban pies would be so popular? Is that even a thing in Cuba?"

Her tone was so condescending that it made me want to punch her in the face.

But Lala didn't need me to defend her. That woman was fearless. Year after year, she put her "Cuban American" pies—that's what she called them—on the judges' table even though she was a transplant to that community and even though people sometimes treated her like she didn't belong.

"They gave us a number," she told me the first time she competed. "That's how I knew they would be fair. The judges didn't know which was my pie."

She was so proud of her blue ribbon that she framed it and put it over the mantel.

"They didn't see it coming. A Cuban lady making apple pies?" Lala laughed to herself. "But you tell me, nena, what does being from Cuba have to do with knowing how to work a stick of butter into the dough? Not one thing. You do what you love, mija. Jealous people are always going to try and get in your way."

She should have known one of those jealous people lurked in her kitchen.

The day Lala gave away our recipe, I was there. It was the same day I almost burned down her kitchen.

Barbara held on to that recipe like she was holding on to one of Lala's blue ribbons. Her eyeballs practically bulged out of her skull as her long red nails scanned the ingredients and method on the page.

As Lala explained to the group the exact technique she used to cut the apples and prepare the syrup, Barbara took copious notes. When Lala demonstrated how to trim the pie crust to form her well-known lattice pattern, Barbara made a step-by-step sketch on the back of the page. And when Lala told them her unique baking method—using a paper bag to create the crunchy top crust and the light, flaky bottom—Barbara pulled out her phone and started taking pictures.

After it was all said and done, Lala took her pie out of the oven and declared it her "best one yet." Barbara folded the piece of paper with the recipe and slipped it into her purse.

I had a feeling Barbara was up to no good. In fact, I was so absorbed in keeping my eye on her that I forgot to set the timer for my own pie. First, I saw the billow of smoke seeping through the oven door. When I opened the oven, my beautiful pie had turned into a fireball; the paper bag had caught on fire. I grabbed a towel to smother the flames—big mistake. The blaze spread to the towel and all the way up to my gloves. Lala had to push me out of the way so she could use the fire extinguisher.

My abuela wrapped me in her arms and assured me there was no reason to cry. "*No hay por que llorar, morenita.*" Later, I learned she was quoting some Celia Cruz salsa song.

"*Mija, el que nunca se equivoca, es porque nunca hace nada,*" she said. She was always pushing me, my Lala. Not to get stuck in my mistakes but to turn them into something worthwhile.

"You have to live, mija. You can't be afraid of making a big mess every once in a while. To make an omelet, you have to crack some eggs."

Mistakes, she said, made you stronger.

Lala, Hazel, and Therese helped me clean the mess—but not Barbara. Barbara got into her Mercedes and left.

Later, we found out that good ol' Barbara had taken Lala's famous apple pie recipe to her daughter, who was opening a pie shop in Kansas City. A few months later, Lala's pie was featured in the *New York Times*, under the name Granny Barb's Apple Pie. They called it "the best pie in America."

Papi wanted to sue. But Lala wouldn't have it. She blamed herself for being so trusting. I blamed her too. Some mistakes, you can't fix. Some mistakes make you wish you had never tried in the first place.

Chapter 6

Finger Soup

I was already awake when the alarm went off. The determination to rise above yesterday's double fiasco served as motivation to get out of bed before sunrise. By the time the others woke up, the kitchen island was covered in textbook-quality French omelets: beautiful egg creations with the perfect light-yellow color and the "slightly wet" center.

Now back in the test kitchen, I am armed with newfound confidence. Today, I can make an omelet blindfolded.

"Precision cuts," Chef Troissant announces to the class as she enters the kitchen. She stands firmly behind her station and displays a set of knives in front of her. "Show your skill and craftsmanship."

I'm slightly irked we won't be giving the omelets another go, but at the same time relieved we are moving on to something new. Plus, I get to use the Nenox knife Mom bought me when I received my acceptance letter. It's made of a Japanese steel so sharp, it can slice through a hardcover book. I've been waiting for the right moment to put the blade to the test.

Chef Troissant's assistant walks in, pushing a cart with a bowl of peeled potatoes floating in water.

"The omelets showed me your skill level." She scans the room, and it feels like her deathly stare lingers on me longer than anyone else. "Unsatisfactory," she says, shaking her head and clicking her tongue.

My hand wants to shoot up into the air. *Chef Troissant, my omelet did not show my skill level. I'm so not unsatisfactory.* I wish I could yell it at the top of my lungs.

But the omelets are quickly forgotten the moment I notice The Spoons.

On the back wall of the kitchen hangs a vertical spoon rack painted barn red that holds fifteen large metal spoons. They're made of a rough, almost hand-forged metal, something straight out of the Middle Ages. Each one sits in its own slot, stacked one above the next. Someone took the time to paint numbers in bold, black type on the back of each spoon. They don't seem to be in any particular order. It's like some kind of abstract artwork.

Then I remember what Chef Troissant said yesterday: "No names. Only numbers."

It hits me like a brick—the numbers aren't random at all. These are the kitchen rankings and number thirteen is dead last.

The bottom of the rack, as if I needed a fresh reminder of how much my first day sucked.

A gush of inadequacy pools in the pit of my stomach. "Tears mess up your makeup," Julia Child always said. Not that I'm wearing any makeup, but I get her point. The kitchen is no place for wusses. I need to step up my game.

"*Faites attention!*" Chef Troissant calls, placing a potato on the cutting board. "Come, come," she says, waving us to her station. "Today, you must master the stick cuts. I want to see long, uniformly shaped sticks with perfectly square ends."

There is complete silence as we watch her slice the potatoes into the traditional cuts. Pippa stands behind me, watching over my head. Lucia is next to me. She has a pen in her hand but no notepad.

"There are five stick sizes: pont-neuf, bâtonnet, allumette, julienne, et fine julienne. Why should you care about sticks? Master the sticks, master consistency. There are rulers in your stations. The measurements must be exact. Pont-neuf: two centimeter square by seven centimeter long," she says, demonstrating the cut on a potato. In the span of seconds, she creates four identical pieces.

Lucia pulls up her sleeve and scribbles something on her arm. *What is she doing?* My heart stops at the thought of Chef Troissant seeing her and unleashing *No notes!* wrath on both of us simply because I'm standing next to her. I want to move to the other side of the group, but Snake Eyes is there.

"What are you doing?" I whisper.

"I can't remember the measurements," she whispers back.

"She's gonna see you."

"Mademoiselle Fields, is there a problem?" Chef Troissant calls out.

"Je suis désolée," I apologize, wondering if I should bow down or something.

"You will cut yourself if you don't listen to my instruction. I don't want your finger floating in the soup. Do you understand? No finger soup!"

"Yes, I understand." I nod solemnly, blood rushing to my face.

"No one gets cut in my program. If you get cut, I will know you did not listen. Do you understand?"

"I understand." I can barely hear myself through the ringing in my ears.

"I can't hear you, Mademoiselle Fields."

"Yes, I understand," I say louder this time.

"Do you think this is funny, Monsieur Legrand?" I thank the heavens when she turns to Snake Eyes.

"Je suis désolé," he says. But like yesterday, he isn't désolé at all. But unlike yesterday, Chef Troissant looks like she's ready to pounce. She could hold a spoon between the tension lines in her eyebrows.

"Monsieur Legrand, do you care to refresh the class on what I just explained?"

"Do you want me to go up front?" he asks, almost giddy.

Chef Troissant points the butt of the knife in his direction, as if to say, *Knock yourself right out.* An eerie stillness takes over the room. It's like watching a hunter set a trap for an unsuspecting animal. I almost feel sorry for Snake Eyes. But whatever Chef Troissant has in store for him, he's had it coming.

Chef Troissant steps to the side to let Snake Eyes explain the various cuts. And I hate to say it, but he doesn't do a bad job. He stacks up his sticks against Chef Troissant. They are practically perfect. Without a ruler it would be hard to distinguish the two. Unfortunately for him, she has a ruler. Several.

Everyone seems to hold a collective breath when he's finished his presentation. A self-satisfied smile is plastered across his face. We all turn to look at Chef Troissant, waiting for the verdict. She doesn't speak; instead, she claps. Not an excited clap—this is the slow, methodical clap of a psychopath.

"Monsieur Legrand, why are you here?" she asks him.

His smile falters. The question seems to catch him off guard. He sets the knife on the table and his hands drop to his side.

"You know this already, oui?" she asks.

"Yes, I do," he responds by inching up his chin. It's a subtle movement, but I'm certain it didn't go unnoticed. This woman can smell fear.

"Well then, maybe you should spend a day in the restaurant kitchen. Would you like that, Monsieur Legrand?"

He nods.

"Our normal shift is eighteen hours. Is that too much for you?"

"No." His jaw hardens into a square.

"Perfect. The micro parsley station is all yours for the next eighteen hours."

No one dares move, or even breathe. The micro parsley station is like the torture chamber of high-class restaurants. Snake Eyes will spend his eighteen hours hunched over a bowl of micro parsley floating in iced water, picking out leaves with tiny tweezers, which will be served on the plates that go out. In a documentary on Michelin-starred chefs, I saw the chef lose it when a half-wilted leaf—one tiny leaf!—of micro parsley touched one of his plates. "Put that crap in the garbage, where it belongs!" he screamed at the poor guy who had dared pluck and place it. I almost feel bad for Snake Eyes. Almost.

The moment Snake Eyes leaves, the kitchen seems to double in size. The stainless steel shines brighter. The ingredients smell fresher. And even Chef Troissant seems more relaxed—or at least the scowl on her face has been replaced with a neutral expression.

We take turns picking our potatoes from burlap sacks clustered on the floor. Fifteen potatoes each—three for each of the five cuts.

"Take your stations," Chef Troissant commands. "*Allez!* You have one hour." Then she leaves the kitchen and locks herself in her office.

"Sorry about earlier," Lucia leans in to say. She's retaken the workstation next to mine. "I can't understand half of what she says."

"I'm just glad we weren't the ones sent to pick parsley leaves," I respond, taking my new knife out of its case. When the kitchen lights hit the steel, the blade gives off a reflective metallic shine. I smile to myself. This is the knife of a winner.

"Is that a Nenox?" Lucia asks, leaning over my station.

"Yeah," I say, totally showing off like a kid with a new toy.

"Can I?" she asks, holding her hand out. I carefully place my knife in her hands like a newborn baby.

"What's the handle made of?"

"Desert ironwood. They use one-hundred-year-old carbonized roots from the desert." I read all about it on their website. "It was a gift from my mom."

"That's so nice," she says, passing the knife back. My eyes linger on a knife callous on one of her fingers. "I'm Lucia, by the way. I don't think we've met properly."

"I'm Isa."

"Do you two have a death wish?" Pippa whisper-shouts from her station at the other side of the kitchen. "She said no talking."

She looks over her shoulder but Chef Troissant's door is still closed. "Do you guys want to go somewhere after class?"

Lucia shrugs and nods.

Part of me is hesitant to get friendly with my competition, but then I look around and see a roomful of guys. None of whom has even bothered to introduce themselves.

"Sure, I'll go," I say.

"There's a bakery down the street. The pastry chef's brilliant," Pippa says.

Somewhere across the room one of the guys shushes us, so we lower our voices.

"Do you know if they make churros?" Lucia asks Pippa. "I've been craving them so bad."

"They make bugnes, Lyon's answer to the fried pastry. With a side of chocolate sauce!" Pippa says. "They're delicious."

"I'm definitely in," Lucia says.

"After class." Pippa nods toward the clock on the wall. "Keep your eye on the time, ladies. We have to peel."

We've lost a whole five minutes on chitchat and I have yet to start peeling. I double down knowing I'll need enough time to cut and measure my sticks. It occurs to me that Chef Troissant knows her task is impossible to complete in one hour. I turn to Lucia to complain, but she is peeling potatoes like a maniac. I count the seconds in my head—ten. Ten seconds per potato. This girl is a kitchen marvel.

"Where did you learn how to do that?" I ask in awe.

"A chef in Barcelona taught me. It's easy," she says, grabbing an unpeeled potato. "Stand it upright, like this." She props the potato up on the chopping block. "Then take the peeler and move it up and down very fast. You turn it around as you go. The ends are the last part."

I try her trick on my next potato and cut my time in half.

"Peeling is easy. It's the cutting that's hard," Lucia says. She's peeled all her potatoes and is now working on her cuts. Meanwhile, I am so behind.

I use Lucia's hack to peel the remainder of my potatoes in record time, then start cutting, impressed with the feel of my new knife in my hand. It's heavy enough to make itself known, but not so heavy it will tire my wrist. The blade slices through the vegetables like they were made of air.

The pont-neufs, the frites, and the bâtonnets are not that hard to cut. They're thick pieces and easy to measure. It's the delicate allumettes and juliennes that take the most time. I'm going as fast as I can, but every time I glance at the clock it's like time has jumped forward.

Chef Troissant comes out of her office with five minutes left. I still have five potatoes left. *One potato per minute,* I tell myself. *Julienne as fast as you can.*

I'm ultra-focused on every cut, but my hat, once again, is sliding all over my head. *What is it with this thing?* I force myself to ignore it. Meanwhile, my beautiful knife is flying on the board. I can't even see my fingers between the blade and the potatoes. In fact, I'm going so fast that I don't even feel the blade slice away my knuckle until I notice my potato sticks are soaked in my own blood.

No, no, no!

I instinctively raise my arm to my chest to stop the blood flow. My arm is throbbing all the way up to my heart, like my chest is getting hit with a meat pounder.

Chef Troissant has her back turned to me as she inspects the cuts at the first station. Across the kitchen, a first aid kit hangs from the wall. I half walk, half run to it. I bandage my finger with one hand and swallow every ounce of pain coursing through my arm. When I turn around, Chef Troissant is standing by my station. Her arms are crossed over her chest and the spoon-holding scowl is back on her forehead.

"Mademoiselle Fields, did you carry blood across my kitchen?"

I don't answer. Mostly because the throbbing has moved to my head and is impairing my speech.

Chef Troissant moves to the back of my station and pulls out a first aid kit. She drops it with a loud thump onto my worktable—on top of the bloodied potatoes.

"What two very specific instructions did I give?" she asks into the air. "Anyone?"

"Not to cut ourselves. And if we cut ourselves to use the first aid kit in our station," one of the guys says. Because apparently mansplaining is a talent all guys share, regardless of what country they come from.

"Did you not hear that instruction, Mademoiselle Fields?" Her eyes slice into mine. I want to tell her that no, I didn't hear it, and ask her if she said anything about needing stitches.

"Mademoiselle Fields?"

"No, I didn't hear."

"Alors, maybe next time you'll pay more attention." She pauses and nods to my left. "The cleaning supplies are in that closet. You will clean up your mess. I expect you to properly sanitize my kitchen—the entire kitchen."

For a second, I envy Snake Eyes and his micro parsley station. While he gets to work in the kitchen, I'll get to clean it—again! As if last night wasn't enough.

"Blimey, it smells like a hospital ward in here." Pippa shoves a mop bucket into the closet. "I think our work here is done, ladies."

"I can't believe you guys stayed behind to help me," I say, taking off my apron. "That's, like, the nicest thing anyone's ever done for me."

Back home in Chicago, my friends didn't really get my dedication to this "chef thing," as they called it, which made it hard to sustain any meaningful connections. And they definitely didn't get why I spent all my free time engrossed in recipes instead of going to parties or getting drunk in someone's basement.

In retrospect, my friendships were mostly superficial, not the open-hearted, say-anything kind of bonds. If I'm honest, they often left me feeling a profound sense of loneliness. I was better off alone.

I guess you can't have it all when you're striving to be the best at something. Sacrifices must be made.

But as I take in Pippa and Lucia sauntering across the kitchen in their aprons and chef's coats, I can't help but wonder if it could be different this time. Maybe here, I don't need to choose between friendships and my passion. Maybe I've finally found my tribe.

"No thanks required," Lucia says. "If it were me, I would want someone to stay." She shrugs and her lips settle into an easy smile. I love how comfortable the three of us seem in the kitchen now that the guys are gone.

"Thanks. I totally owe you one," I say, aware that Lucia's punishment odds are highly unlikely. Her spoon is in first place. Mine, needless to say, remains last.

We head to the changing room and take off our uniforms.

Lucia removes her toque and I catch a glimpse of the elaborate bun hidden under it. She has bobby pins sticking out in every direction.

"Is that how you do it?" I ask.

"What?" She's plucking pins out of her head.

"Keep this silly thing balanced on your head," I say. "I've never had to wear one of these before."

"Ugh," Pippa huffs. "I hate these hats. Mine always gets stuck under the hood of the stove."

"Here, let me show you." Lucia and I stand in front of a mirror as she twists and turns my wavy mane into a bun halfway down my head, sticking a million pins to keep every lock in place. She sets the toque on top of my head and expertly holds it with extra pins hidden on the inside of the hat.

"Try moving now," she says, stepping back.

I move my head from side to side, then up and down. I even

try bending over. All the while, the hat remains planted firmly on my head.

"You're a freaking genius," I exclaim, jumping and bending my body, as if to test the limits of her hat trick. "Well done!" We high five each other. "Now, I'm afraid of taking it off."

Eventually—after more prancing about the changing room—I do take the hat off. Lucia and Pippa share their pins and hairbands and show me a few more techniques. They're both experts on kitchen hair, it seems.

We change into our regular clothes and walk outside, wondering if the pâtisserie is still open. Pippa exits the restaurant first and steps onto the sidewalk, whistling as she goes.

"Mmm-*mmm*. That is one fine morsel," she says. I follow her eyes to a black motorcycle with a sidecar and Diego leaning on the side.

I double my stride until I reach him.

"What are you doing here?" I ask.

"Nice to see you too," he says, taking off his sunglasses. "James and Margo were busy. I was in town, so he asked me to come get you."

"I could've taken a taxi."

"You know, in some countries, *thank you* is considered an acceptable response. I'm not sure how they do things in America, but you may want to try it sometime. *Merci* is very popular in France." He gives me the smuggest of smiles.

Pippa and Lucia quickly appear by my side, both wearing the wide-eyed, giggly expressions of boy-crazy girls the world over. I save a perfectly acceptable *merci* retort for a later time.

"This is Diego," I say. "Pippa. Lucia." Everyone nods. Everyone smiles (except me).

"Is this your boyfriend?" Pippa asks.

"God no!" The response comes out even before she's finished asking. I glance at Diego, but he's not smiling anymore. When I actually think about it, I don't know what I should call him. Family friend? Annoying houseguest?

"He's my dad's wife's stepson from her first marriage . . ." They both look at me like I'm making no sense. "It's complicated." I sigh.

"Are you Catalan?" Lucia asks. "I saw the Catalonian flag sticker on your windshield."

Diego turns his full attention to Lucia.

"Barcelona," he says.

"Me too!" Lucia's smile bursts even wider.

"Where did you go to school?" she asks.

"Lycée Français," he murmurs.

"Wow, fancy. I wish I'd gone there. Maybe if my French was better, I could understand what our teacher says." She giggles and flips her hair back.

Gimme a break. I can see now why Diego probably thinks every girl he meets will fall for him.

He shoves his hands into his pockets and shrugs. "It was my dad's idea."

Diego glances back in my direction, then turns to solely face Lucia and launches himself into a rapid half-Catalan, half-Spanish conversation that as far as I can tell is about the inner workings of his French international high school. They use too many words I don't understand, so it's impossible for me to follow.

I stand around trying not to be awkward.

"Where's that pâtisserie of yours?" I ask Pippa.

"It already closed. We'll have to go tomorrow," she says.

"Tapas!" Lucia exclaims, switching to English. "Diego said there's a great tapas place a few blocks from here." The girl is beaming. I mean, her face could rival the sun.

"That sounds great. Another time? We really should get going," I say, feeling a sudden urge to separate my two worlds, which are unexpectedly colliding.

"I have to make dinner," I continue, stepping closer to the motorcycle. The seat looks way too small for two people.

"James asked me to pick up some roasted chicken," Diego says.

"But I have plans," I argue. "I posted the menu on the fridge."

His hands go up into the air. "You can take it up with him," he says. "And after last night, maybe you need a night off." He smiles, though his lips are tight and hard. I can't tell if that was meant as a backhanded insult. Though I'm pretty sure everyone can see the fumes coming out of my ears. I spent hours working on the week's dinner menu, even researching some lighter dishes that might be good for Margo's upset stomach. Thinking that finally, I'd make something she could actually eat.

"I got a whole chicken for Beluga, if that's what you're worried about," he adds, almost begging me to get into the dogs-shouldn't-eat-chicken-bones argument.

"What's a Beluga?" Lucia asks.

"It's my dog." Diego pulls out his phone and slides through several pictures.

"Aww," they both half-say, half-sing.

"Okay, time to go. Where's my helmet?" I ask.

"She hates dogs," he says, nodding toward me.

Lucia and Pippa both look at me like I've murdered someone.

"I don't hate dogs," I say defensively.

"He's adorable. You should bring him next time," Pippa says. *Next time?*

"We really should get going," I say, trying to sound nonchalant but failing miserably. "Don't want that chicken to get cold." I force a smile and step closer to the motorcycle.

"See you later, ladies," he says, putting his helmet back on. "There's a seat belt in there." He glances at the sidecar.

I don't protest the sidecar seat. I don't say the sidecar is the dog's seat and I should be riding on the back of the motorcycle—like a normal person. I don't say anything.

I step in, wriggle to a sitting position, and extend my legs inside the black metal bullet, certain I look absolutely ridiculous partially hidden inside this thing.

I put on my helmet, strap on my seat belt, and seethe all the way home. The last thing I want is for my home life and my restaurant life to intersect. Is there anywhere I can exist without the shadow of our family drama? When and where do I get to be my own person?

Yeah, I'll admit, the guy isn't *technically* doing anything wrong. And it's not *technically* his fault I was already having problems fitting into the new family arrangement before he got here. But I can't help feeling like his mere presence is upsetting the delicate balance of my new world order. I just want him gone. For good.

When we arrive at the house, I drop the helmet on the seat and head for the front door. As I'm about to enter the house, I decide I've had it.

"Can you please not flirt with my friends?" I spit out.

"I wasn't flirting." He holds a box full of roasted chicken in one hand and a brown paper bag in the other.

"Oh really?" I switch to a mock Spanish accent. "Oh, tapas. Let's go to tapas. Everyone loves tapas!" I suck in a deep breath, my voice getting higher. "What's so good about tapas? It's an appetizer. Why don't they call it that? It's not even a full meal!"

"It's called being nice. You should try it sometime. Like right now." He shoves the paper bag into my hand and walks away grumbling, "I got that for you."

"I am nice!" I yell after him, but he's already crossed the hallway into the kitchen.

I open the paper bag and immediately feel like the world's biggest ass. Fortune cookies. A bag full of them.

Chapter 7

Of Love and Pies

"So, Isa, dish out the details. What's the deal with Diego?" Pippa asks.

I shrug and bite into the best fraisier cake I've ever had. I chew slowly, hoping they'll find something else to talk about—something that isn't "the hot Spaniard."

It's finally Friday. Week one in Chef Grattard's kitchen has come and gone and all I have to show for it is a bandaged finger and spoon thirteen sitting at the bottom of the rack. Not exactly what I had in mind.

To celebrate this grand accomplishment, Pippa invited us to Pâtisserie Lulu, her favorite spot in Lyon, where we've been sitting outside, watching people walk by on the street.

The only good thing to came out of this week is my new uncanny ability to memorize Chef Troissant's instructions. It turns out fear is a great motivator. Take yesterday, for example: she was teaching us about French cheeses and opened a wooden box containing a small wheel of Époisses de Bourgogne. It has a sticky orange rind and a smell reminiscent of sweaty gym socks and filthy barn animals that's led to it being called the stinker of all cheeses. While everyone else scattered in disgust to various parts of the kitchen, somehow I managed to focus through the nausea-inducing smell and hang on to Chef Troissant's every word. If I didn't know any better, I'd think she was a little impressed.

"This is so good." I take another bite of the fraisier and lick a dollop of cream off my fingers. "What does she put in this stuff? Is this champagne?" I pass my plate around so they can try it.

"I told you, Chef Lulu's brilliant." Pippa bites into a fruit-filled pastry. "Cherry and thyme. It's delicious. Here, try this one." She gives me a bite and I close my eyes in pure, sugary bliss.

"This French churro-thingy is amazing. It's filled with mascarpone and dulce de leche." Lucia dunks her fried pastry into a small porcelain cup full of hot chocolate. When she brings it to her mouth and chews, her body sags into the chair in evident pleasure. "I'm not sharing mine," she teases.

"Okay, Isa, I'm not letting you off the hook. Back to the hot Spaniard . . ." Pippa says, and I roll my eyes. "I need to know, does he run around the house in his underpants?"

I shush her, glancing around at the nearby tables. Lucia giggles into her cup.

"No, he doesn't run around the house in his underwear." The heat rises to my face just thinking about the image. "He's staying in a cottage in the back, and only comes inside to raid the fridge."

"He can raid my fridge any day of the week," Pippa snorts. She and Lucia, lean into each other. All the sugar must be making them giddy.

"Looks aren't everything," I say, trying to sound blasé. But the underwear image is stuck to my eyelids and doing weird things to my brain.

"But he must be smart too. His school is one of the best in Spain. A few kids from the royal family have gone there," Lucia says, with a little too much enthusiasm. I don't know why, but the fact that she knows that insignificant detail bothers me—more than I care to admit.

"You wouldn't believe the first thing he ever said to me." I tell them how we met in the market before we knew who the other was. "He told me he wanted to take me to a field! I mean, how creepy is that?"

"I think it's kinda nice," Lucia says hesitantly. "There are some beautiful fields around here."

"Call me crazy, but I'm not in the habit of meandering into desolate fields with total strangers. That's how girls go missing. Or worse!"

They burst out laughing, clearly not taking any of it seriously. In her laughing fit, Lucia stumbles forward and almost spills all her chocolate onto the table. We blot the mess with a pile of napkins.

"Oh come on, Isa. Give the guy a break. He doesn't strike me as the serial murder type," Pippa says. "Too hot."

"Maybe he just wanted to go to a field and pick cherries," Lucia adds. "I'd go with him."

"Yeah, I guess." Maybe I do need to work on this city-girl paranoia thing.

"All I'm saying is," Pippa adds, edging closer and looking only at me, "if you don't want him, someone else will." Then she points at herself and Lucia. "We have two takers at this table."

Lucia gives a loud *um-hum*.

I shift on my chair, suddenly uncomfortable. Why am I so bothered by the idea of Diego being with someone else? It makes no sense.

They can have at him, for all I care. Right?

"A date with the guy is not gonna kill you," Pippa suggests.

"I don't…" I begin to say, searching for the right words to express the nagging doubts I've felt connected to anything to do with guys, relationships, and love. Lala gave up her family in Miami to marry Gramps, then moved to middle-of-nowhere. Mom gave up her career to be a wife and a mother. Maybe I'm selfish for thinking in this way, but I don't want to sacrifice my life for love.

After a long breath, I say, "I just don't want to give up anything for a guy."

Pippa nods in understanding. "I broke up with my boyfriend before I came here." She sets both hands on the table as she says, "It had to be done."

"Really?" Lucia asks. "Why?"

"He was older and thinking about the future. I mean, I don't know where I'll be at the end of Grattard's course!" Pippa says.

"Was it hard to break up?" Lucia asks.

"A little," Pippa says, resting back on her chair. "He was pre-med at King's College. He knew a lot about the human anatomy." She lifts both eyebrows, and her cheeks crimson. Lucia and I cram closer over the table, leaving no space between our shoulders. Pippa's British accent makes her story all the more compelling.

"Once, we sneaked into a lab after hours and fooled around a bit," Pippa snickers. "Nothing too wild. Making out, that sort of thing."

"When was this?" I ask.

"Last semester," she says.

What was I doing last semester? Not making out in a lab, that's for sure.

"Were you in love with him?" Lucia asks.

"Not really." Pippa shugs. "He was nice and all, but I just wanted a good time, you know?"

I nod. Like I know. But I really don't.

"At our age, who wants anything serious? Who has time? We're in school for a million hours every day. And an apprenticeship is going to be even more work. I don't want to be pining after some bloke who's sucking all my energy. There's no room for distractions, ladies. I mean, less than ten women hold three Michelin stars in the entire world! It's total bollocks."

We all go silent for a moment. I consider the odds stacked against us. It *is* total bollocks.

"Totally," is all I can say, even though I've never had what you'd call a "proper boyfriend." Tack it onto the list of things I've sacrificed for extra time in the kitchen. The most I've advanced in the "fooling around" territory was that time my next-door neighbor and I made out one afternoon after school. He was a year older than me and we'd grown up together, so inevitably, after the awkward puberty phase passed, we had an "I'll show you mine, you show me yours" moment.

We finally made out, but it was wet and sloppy. He fumbled with the clasp of my bra and after a long five minutes of trying and failing, I told him to stop. I mean, how hard can it be to undo a hook? Then Mom showed up, so that put an end to the misery—thank goodness.

It was weird and uncomfortable. It wasn't love and it definitely wasn't a good time.

After he left, I lay on top of my bed, frustrated, wondering if all guys were this awkward and inexperienced.

I bet guys like Diego are perfectly comfortable with all of it—bra clasp and all. An image of Diego pushes itself into my mind. Suddenly I feel warm, flushed, and uneasy.

What am I thinking?

I take the last bites of the fraisier, hoping to distract myself with the taste of strawberry and champagne. But no matter how hard I push against the image of Diego, it refuses to leave. It roots itself to the back of my mind like a weed that won't die. And what's worse, part of me wants it there.

"Sometimes I hate being a girl," Lucia says with an air of resignation. She leans back on her chair and takes the last bite of her pastry.

"Why?" I ask.

"We have to deal with all this extra stuff guys don't even think about," she says.

"What extra stuff?" I ask.

"Womanhood stuff," she says in a solemn tone. "If Legrand got a girl pregnant, do you think it would matter? He'd still have his own restaurant in ten years—or less! And all the Michelin stars. It's not fair."

"Absolute rubbish," Pippa says. "I'm picking career. I don't see what's so much fun about changing nappies. Trust me, I've done it all. I'm the youngest in my big Jamaican family, so my mammy's house is usually a menagerie of nieces and nephews. I love them all, but they are rowdy, dirty, and loud. I can't imagine having to take care of a kid all the time."

"Not me. I want to fall in love. And I want to get married and have babies," Lucia says, her voice full of conviction and idealism. "When I'm older, I mean—not now. My mom got married and she works as an English teacher. She didn't have to choose."

"All I'm saying is, from what I've seen so far, when you fall in love your brain shuts down," Pippa says. "I'll be damned if that's gonna be me. I'm reaching for those stars and nothing is going to get in my way."

"What about you, Isa?" Lucia asks.

I don't hesitate when I say, "I want all the stars."

"Frente al amor y la muerte, no sirve de nada ser fuerte" was one of Lala's favorite Spanish sayings. It means it's useless to fight against love or death.

"Roger and I have been married for fifty years," she once told me. We were in her farmhouse kitchen, where she expertly rolled pie dough between her fingers as a Spanish ballad played in the background. Her soft curls were up in a loose bun over her head. Even in her seventies, Lala's hair was dark brown, not even a hint of gray. She kept a standing appointment at the hair salon every four weeks to make sure of it.

"Pour me a cafecito, mija," she said. This is how I knew she was about to tell me one of her stories about leaving Cuba after Fidel Castro's revolution in the fifties. When it came to Papi and me, Lala tried hard to instill an appreciation for our immigrant roots. She even kept a record of our family's history in her red notebook, along with special recipes and comments on ingredients and methods. The same notebook she passed on to me.

I reached for the tartan-print thermos, the one I brought with me to Bessenay, and poured us each a mug of her signature café con leche. The secret, she said, was to add a stick of Mexican cinnamon to the pot of milk as it simmered to a rise.

We sipped on our warm mugs of coffee and I retook my spot at the table, peeling apples across from her.

"I was twenty-five when I came to this country on one of the freedom flights—that's what they called them," she recalled. "President Johnson sent his planes to Cuba twice a day. Three hours later we had a new life in Miami."

She sprinkled flour on the countertop, wiped one of her hands on her apron, and took another sip of coffee. I followed the movement of her hands, entranced by the deep ridges in her skin. To me, they were the most beautiful hands I'd ever seen. I wondered if I'd have hands like hers someday.

"My tía Gilda was waiting at the airport when I arrived. And I still remember what I was wearing—a blue, billowing dress with buttons along the back that I had bought with my own money." Lala paused, a faint smile on her red-tinged lips. I don't remember ever seeing her without lipstick. "I was a nurse in Cuba. Graduated top of my class at the University of Havana." She beamed with pride. Her nursing degree became a thing of the past as soon as she landed in Miami. If she wanted to work as a nurse again, she would have to start all over—improve her English and go back to nursing school.

"On the second day I was in this country, Tía Gilda took me to a cousin's wedding at the Fontainebleau Hotel. I had to borrow a dress from my cousin Rosita—soft pink with a tulle skirt that flowed down to my midcalf. Let me tell you, mija, I was something back then."

I chuckled at the way she shimmied her hips. I knew she was right. I've seen the pictures of that wedding—she looked like a vintage movie star.

The music changed to a tropical beat and I could almost imagine Lala entering the Fontainebleau's grand lobby. In previous versions of this story, she'd described in great detail the dazzling stairways, majestic chandeliers, and dramatically colored murals.

"I told my tía I didn't want to go, that I didn't know anyone. But she wouldn't hear it. She said I didn't leave Cuba to sit at home—*y vestir santos*. She said, 'You're too pretty to be single.' And it wasn't like I hadn't had my share of suitors in Havana." Lala pushed a strand of loose hair behind her ear, then reached for the rolling pin and began flattening the dough.

"I had plenty of suitors, let me tell you. But I wasn't interested in any. They wanted me to leave the hospital and stay home. Bah." She waved a hand in the air like she was swatting away an invisible force. "Latin men. They're all the same. Don't fall in love with a Latino, morenita. They expect you to be their wife and their mother."

I was twelve at the time, so I rolled my eyes and just said, "Okay, Lala."

A pile of tart Granny Smith apples lay sliced on the table in front of me. I tossed the green peels into the compost can and began preparing the caramel syrup while Lala worked her magic on the dough.

The syrup was our own family recipe—butter, flour, water, white and brown sugar, vanilla, cinnamon, and nutmeg.

"Roger was the first person I saw when I walked into the ballroom," she told me. My hands stopped stirring the syrup. This was my favorite part of their story. Every time she told it, Lala's face would light up with the unmistakable glow of a woman in love. What was even more amazing was knowing someone could carry those feelings for fifty years.

"Roger was a handsome man. Tall with thick, dark hair." She divided the dough in two equal parts, wrapped it in plastic wrap, and set it in the fridge.

"He was wearing a dark suit and black tie. When our eyes met, it was like I was landing in a new country all over again. He came to our table and asked me to dance. The band was playing 'Dos Gardenias' . . ." She hummed the song to herself, then moved to the radio. "I think I have it here," she said, fishing for a CD inside a basket. "This is the original, by Antonio Machín," she explained as the sound of a 1940s orchestra filled the kitchen. A man's silky voice sang a bolero, a serenade set to a rumba beat.

"By the end of that song, I knew it was useless to fight. It was love and resisting would be futile. That gringuito stole my heart on that dance floor."

As if on cue, Grampa Roger sauntered into the kitchen, carrying a bunch of wildflowers he picked from Lala's garden. They didn't say one word to each other as he poured water into a vase, arranged the flowers, and placed them by the windowsill above the sink. Before leaving, he kissed Lala on the cheek and whispered something into her ear. Lala's cheeks went pink and a smile spread across her face. Grampa glanced in my direction and winked. My faced turned pink too. They were too much sometimes.

After he left, Lala and I finished our coffee, and when the dough had rested enough we covered the pie dish and then filled it with apple slices dripping with syrup.

After dinner all three of us sat on the porch to devour a big slice of pie. Grampa Roger always said this was his favorite meal to eat in the whole world.

"It's dessert. Not a meal, Roger," Lala countered, elbowing him softly.

I sided with Grampa Roger every time. It was my favorite meal too.

Frente al amor y la muerte, no sirve de nada ser fuerte. Lala taught me about giving in to love, but she never explained how to give in to death.

A server appears by our table outside Pâtisserie Lulu and clears our dishes. "We'll be closing soon," he says in French. "Last call for pastries."

"Last call, ladies," Pippa says, tossing her head back in the direction of the pastry counter.

"This place is so much better than a bar," Lucia remarks.

"I'm going inside. Getting a box to take home," I say, rushing in. Since the fortune cookie bag incident three days ago, I've been contemplating what kind of dessert says "I'm sorry I was such a raging lunatic." But mostly, I've been stuck on what kind of dessert would make a hot (and thoughtful) Spaniard forgive a neurotic American. I've come up short, every time.

Inside the pâtisserie, the pastry cabinet runs the length of the shop. Row after row of the most decadent creations fill the glass shelves with a full spectrum of colors and a symphony of flavors.

I'm pleasantly surprised when I find large bags full of gourmet chocolate discs in the chocolatier section. They're the size of a dime, perfect for the chocolate chip cookies I promised Jakub. I reach for a top shelf and grab two bags.

Next, I move to the pastry cabinet and its overwhelming selection. What would Diego like? Is he a fruit tart kind of guy? Or does he prefer a more traditional éclair? I get one of each, just in case. I add a sampling of macarons: *pistache, fleur d'oranger, coquelicot,* and one called the Marie Antoinette, stuffed with raspberries and rose crème. My box is almost full, but there is still room for a couple of flaky palmiers and a crème caramel cup.

"*C'est un cadeau,*" I tell the counter attendant, and in response he wraps the box with a pretty bow and places it inside a gift bag.

I'm rehearsing what I will tell Diego—some version of "I think we got off on the wrong foot"—when his motorcycle pulls up in front of the store.

My initial surprise turns into unease as he gets off the bike and kisses Lucia on both cheeks. He nods toward Pippa and smiles. I watch him and Lucia from inside, talking and pointing, gesturing with their hands, surely speaking Spanish or Catalan. I shouldn't feel jealous. I shouldn't feel anything, really. But I do. I feel everything.

"Mademoiselle?" The counter attendant gives me my box. The big bow now seems like a silly gesture.

When I step outside, the only thing that comes out of my mouth is a "hey."

Diego says hey back. This is our first exchange since Tuesday. Somehow, we've managed to stay out of each other's way all week.

Pippa is the only one who seems to notice the gift bag in my hands. "That's some big bow you've got there. Who's the lucky guy?"

Thankfully, Lucia interjects, cutting off my response. "Diego and I are grabbing tapas," she says eagerly. "You guys want to come?" She's already strapping on a helmet.

"I have to get home and pack," I say, reaching for my backpack so I can half hide the gift bag. "I'm flying out to see my mom tomorrow."

"Sorry, I have other plans," Pippa says, but I can see the *I'm not playing third wheel* on her face.

"Ready?" Diego asks.

Lucia gets in the sidecar like she belongs there. She doesn't even complain about the dog hair.

"Must be the Spanish thing," Pippa jokes as we watch them disappear around the corner.

"Do you want to share a cab?" is all I say.

Chapter 8

Doggie Tarts

Someone is playing a ukulele inside my room in the middle of the night. *That can't be right.*

I reach for the cell phone on my nightstand and glance at the time. It's three in the morning.

What is he doing?

Papi has as much musical talent as a cardboard box and Margo doesn't strike me as the ukulele type, so it must be Diego.

I groan, falling back on the pillow. Why did I pick the room closest to the pool? Oh yeah, because I wasn't expecting a ukulele-playing Spaniard to drop in for a visit.

All I can do is listen to the melody of strings floating in through my window. It's the kind of music that transports you to a sandy beach on a remote island, waves crashing on the shore and palm trees swaying to a tropical breeze. The thing about ukuleles is that they make even the saddest songs sound happy. The kind of happy that swells in your chest and, against your better judgment, slaps a smile onto your face.

I get out of bed and walk to the window to watch him play. He's lying on a pool lounger, cradling the ukulele in his arms, Beluga curled up on the floor by his side. Did he just get home?

I close my window shutters and sit on my bed, trying to talk myself out of walking down to investigate.

What would I even say? *So, do you normally stay up all night*

*playing island music? Or are you celebrating a late-night escapade?
With my new friend!*

My fist hits a pillow as I drop back onto the bed and stare at the white ceiling.

Why am I even considering walking down there? I mean, this is the same guy who, without even knowing my name, had the gall to try luring me to a cherry field. Who sauntered into this house, and—unlike me—instantly fit perfectly into this messy family. Who almost burned down the kitchen and ruined my flambé. And who just this afternoon took off with Lucia. Couldn't he find someone else to date in all of Lyon?

I sigh—a deep, long sigh.

Given the solid argument against him, any practical girl would go back to sleep. But what is it about this guy that makes me wish I was more impulsive?

I can be impulsive, I tell myself. *I don't need a guy to be reckless.*

So I get to my feet, slip my arms into a bathrobe, and tie the waistband tight.

On the way out, I grab the box of pastries and peel off the gift bow and delicate wrapping. The box, now a plain cardboard cube, is intentionally unassuming.

Hey, here's an impersonal peace offering, like a plant or a basket of fruit.

I debate whether to get two glasses of milk as I round the kitchen but decide against it—he may interpret it as thoughtfulness on my part. And I'm not ready to go there.

"Can you keep it down? Some of us are trying to sleep," I grumble, sitting on the lounger next to him.

He jolts up, surprised to see me. Beluga whimpers and raises his head.

"Did I wake you?" he asks, moving the ukulele aside. "I'm sorry—I couldn't sleep. I didn't think anyone could hear."

"Don't stop playing. I'm already up." I set the pastry box on a small table between our chairs. "I got these today, help yourself," I say, opening the lid.

Diego's eyebrows shoot up, impressed with my selection. I bite my lip as I watch his fingers dance inside the box, choosing carefully.

"Is this flan?" he asks, lifting the crème caramel cup and the little spoon that came with it.

"The French equivalent."

"Thanks," he says, holding the cup and spoon and pushing the box in my direction. I reach for a green macaron.

"Consider it an olive branch," I say. "A really yummy olive branch."

We exchange a smile and a new feeling flutters deep inside me. His dark brown eyes hold mine with an intensity I didn't expect. I look away, uncertain of what this feeling is.

My attention darts from the water lapping on the sides of the pool to the patio umbrella someone forgot to close and finally to the now-snoring dog splayed on the ground.

"Did you get a new fortune?" he asks, bringing the ukulele back against his chest. One of his hands rest on the shiny wood surface as his fingers jump back and forth between strings.

"I did. Want to guess what it was?"

"Long life and riches await you," he teases in a low-pitched TV-presenter voice.

"Not even close. It said: I cannot help you, for I am only a cookie."

His fingers abruptly stop moving. He stares at me, one eyebrow cocked. "You have the worst fortune cookie luck of anyone I have ever met."

"I intend to file a complaint with the cookie factory, first thing in the morning."

"Put me down as a witness."

I interpret the playful sarcasm in his voice as a sign that all is forgiven. I hold his gaze, conflicted by the divergent emotions rippling through my chest. Why do I feel so attracted to a guy whose mere presence aggravates me to no end? Someone who by all appearances is my polar opposite? It makes no sense.

This time, Diego looks away first. He shifts in his lounger, playing with the knobs at the head of the ukulele.

I let my head fall back against the lounger's headrest, staring past the pool to the horizon. The hillside is dark with the exception of Bessenay's streetlights flickering in the distance. During the day, you can see the rows and rows of cherry trees from where we sit, but now everything is dark. The only sign of cherries is the faint smell of ripe fruit in the air.

We sit in silence for a while, listening to the dainty sound of the ukulele as Diego plucks at the strings.

I want to enjoy the music and everything else about this unexpected night, but there's a question I can't seem to ignore.

What happened with Lucia? And why did he get home so late? I mean, how long does it take to eat tapas?

The thought of them doing God knows what vexes me more than I care to admit. Did she finally decide to have a good time instead of waiting for love?

I turn to face Diego, but my mouth can't seem to form the right question. Instead, I'm transfixed by everything all those other girls see in him: the rich brown of his eyes, the long eyelashes that rim them, the tousled black hair, and the deep ridges of his collarbone. What would it be like to lay my head there?

"Are you okay?" he asks. "You look like you have something on your mind." He leans in slightly, a knowing look on his face. For the briefest of seconds, I consider what would happen if I just closed the gap between us and kissed him.

A warmth blooms in my chest and spreads in every direction. It reaches my neck and face in what I know are red blotches of heat.

But then I realize, as much as I want to be the "cool girl," I'm not the type who jumps into something I don't understand. That's just not me.

"How was your date?" I finally ask. He inches backward, away from me, taken aback by the question.

He clears his throat before answering. "It wasn't a date," he says, riffing through the strings a few times.

"It looked like a date."

"It wasn't," he answers curtly.

The mood shifts between us. Even the strings sound strained and awkward.

"Are you sure she knows that?" I say, remembering Lucia's beaming face as she stepped into the sidecar. I didn't recognize it at the time, but her eyes had the same determined expression I'd seen her wear in the kitchen.

"Why? Jealous?" His eyes cut to me, a sly grin on his lips.

"Ha! Jealous of what?" I reach into the pastry box and pull out a cream-filled Napoleon, biting hard into the flaky surface. "I'm not a fan of finger food dinners."

Beluga stirs awake, lifts his head in my direction, and whimpers.

"What?" I ask the dog.

"He's probably wondering why you haven't offered him any food."

"You really have spoiled this dog."

Beluga walks toward the pastry box and nudges his pushed-in nose against the cardboard.

"He likes the blueberries," Diego says.

"I thought dogs weren't supposed to eat sweets," I say, lifting a tart out of the box. Beluga follows the movement of my hand, then rests his head next to my feet on the lounger. His wide-set eyes are barely visible in the thick folds of his skin, but they're begging for even the tiniest scrap.

"It's only a few bites. Not like we're feeding him an entire chocolate cake, although I'm sure he'd like that." Diego reaches to pat Beluga on his side. But the dog's undivided attention is on the tart in my hand.

Beluga tilts his head to the side, mouth drooping, and whines.

"Fine, you win." I bring the tart to his mouth. He gorges it in one bite, then licks my fingers, searching for crumbs. When he can't find any, he lifts his paws to the lounger and nuzzles my thigh.

"You only get one tart," I say, softly patting his head.

"He wants you to scratch him," Diego says. "He likes it behind the ears."

"I have to feed him and scratch him too?" I say in mock irritation, my fingers already digging into the folds of Beluga's thick neck.

"Think of it as penance for threatening him with a meat cleaver."

Beluga leans against my hands, eyes closed, wagging the folded nub that forms his tail. I scratch him harder and he emits a low rumble, something like a cat's purr.

"You found his happy place," Diego says.

"You like that?" I ask Beluga. He barks in answer to my question.

"How long have you had him?" I ask.

"Since he was a puppy."

"And just to set the record straight, I like dogs. I wanted one but my dad always said they were too much work," I say, watching Beluga go back to Diego.

Diego taps an empty space on the lounger. The dog climbs on top and settles down, face planted on a cushion.

"He was a consolation prize," he says, moving his legs so Beluga has more room to spread out.

"What? Your parents missed a birthday or something?" I chuckle awkwardly.

"Nope."

"Then what?"

He keeps his eyes on the dog when he says, "I got him after my mother left us."

"Oh . . ." I have no idea how old this dog is, but he looks fully grown to me. He must weigh at least fifty pounds. Diego must've been a kid when his mother left. "I'm sorry to hear that."

"Ancient history," he says dismissively, thumbing the strings hard. "What would you like to hear?"

I stare at him, confused. What just happened? You don't bring up an absent parent and then burst into song.

"Don't tell me," he says while strumming a few chords, "you don't know any ukulele songs."

I want to press this mom thing, but a wall has gone up inside him. New creases appear on his forehead and his jaw is tight with tension.

"Something from Elvis?" I say to lighten the mood.

"Elvis?"

"You know, the King?" I ask with my best southern drawl.

"I know who Elvis is. I'm just surprised you're a fan." He cuts me an impish sideways glance.

"I'm not!" I laugh, hitting his arm. "He's the only musician I've seen playing a ukulele."

"There's no shame in being an Elvis fan," he says, rubbing his arm in pretend pain. The lines on his face soften and the wall seems to come down just long enough for me to get a glimpse of the real guy behind it. The recognition stirs a new wave of mixed feelings inside me. I wonder what it would feel like to bring his lips to mine.

"How did you get into Elvis?" he asks.

"I'm not *into* Elvis. My grandfather made me watch *Blue Hawaii* once. The Elvis character was always trying to pick up girls with his ukulele. He was kind of a womanizer."

"I don't know any Elvis songs, but what about something French?"

When he starts to play, I'm mesmerized by the fluid movement of his fingers on the strings. The unmistakable melody of "La Vie en Rose" springs from the instrument and floats around us. I find myself wishing I knew the lyrics so I could sing along.

When the song ends, I clap. "That was amazing," I say. "Where did you learn?"

"YouTube. This lady in Hawaii has a tutorial channel."

"I could never do that," I say.

"It's like learning how to cook. Just takes practice."

He sets down the ukulele and reaches for a palmier from the pastry box. "These are better with milk. I'll be right back. Save my seat." He stands, careful not to disturb Beluga, then saunters off into to the kitchen.

I watch him disappear. After he's gone, I realize how much the temperature has dropped. I fold my legs against my chest and wrap my robe tighter around me.

Diego returns carrying a glass of milk in each hand.

"Here you go," he says, passing me one.

We both grab a palmier, dipping them into the milk at the same time. When I put it into my mouth, the buttery flakes mix with the crunch of caramelized sugar.

"Thanks for the pastries." He polishes off the last of his palmier and drinks what's left of the milk.

"I should get back to bed," I say when I'm done with mine.

"Probably a good idea," he says. He feeds Beluga another tart and this time I don't protest.

"Some of us have a flight to catch in the morning." I set both feet on the patio pavers and make to leave, but don't stand.

"What big plans do you have this weekend?" I probe. Is there another non-date with Lucia in his future?

"Nothing big." He shrugs and doesn't offer any details.

"Tomorrow should be a perfect pool day," I offer.

"Can't stand the smell of chlorine . . ." His voice trails off.

"Huh?"

"This is my favorite ukulele song," he says, abruptly changing the subject with music. "You may want to stay for this one." Instantly, I recognize the tune of "Somewhere Over the Rainbow."

Raising my feet back onto the lounger, I rest my shoulder on the backrest and listen, completely lost in the melody.

Half a dozen songs later, the first rays of sunlight peer through a horizon of dark clouds.

"I have to get ready for my flight," I say, standing to leave.

"Papi will wake up soon and start pacing outside my door if I'm not packed. He's such a stickler about being on time to the airport."

"Have a good time with your mom." He yawns, eyes sleepy. "Beluga and I are going to bed."

He stands in front of me and I tilt my head up to meet his eyes. As tired as we both are, the space between us fills with a palpable electricity. Something like a living, pulsating force pushing us toward each other.

Behind us, I hear a door open.

"Have you guys been up all night?" Papi says, holding the patio door with one hand.

Diego moves aside nervously and nods at Papi with sleepy eyes. "Good morning," he says, then snaps his fingers at Beluga to move. "*Venga*," he tells the dog.

I hide my hands inside the pockets of my robe and walk to meet Papi.

He kisses me on the cheek. "Are you all packed?"

"I'll be quick," I say.

"I've heard that before," he says, walking toward the kitchen, to get his coffee, I'm sure.

I step inside the house and close the patio door behind me, watching Diego and Beluga disappear into the cottage.

I don't need this, I tell myself. He will just be a distraction. An unwanted complication.

I chastise myself for every reckless thought that entered my head tonight. For wanting to kiss him. For thinking there could be something more between us.

Chapter 9

The Blessed Pie

In her quest to help the unlucky and downtrodden, Lala inadvertently taught me the culinary pleasures of the hole-in-the-wall. Some people may see these greasy dives as the dumps of the culinary world, but for Lala, the mishmash of furnishings and décor, the motley crew of characters waiting for their meals, and the cheap, life-changing food was like finding a diamond in a trash heap.

My favorite in her long list of holes-in-the-wall was Bubba's Sticky Fingers BBQ. Hands down the best BBQ in Kansas City—in both states. Or as Lala used to call it, Bubba's *lechonera*, the Cuban name for a roasted pork house.

Bubba was a big guy who used to be part of a biker gang—or so Lala said. I have no idea how he and Lala became friends.

At his BBQ joint, Bubba greeted us carrying two plates on each arm. He served us the works: a full slab of ribs, brisket, sausage, slaw, and a few slices of Wonder Bread to soak up the sauce. After we stuffed ourselves into a coma, Bubba refused to take Lala's money. "You've given me enough for a lifetime, Miss Lala," he would say. But Lala—being Lala—always left a twenty on the table.

When I asked her what Bubba meant, she brushed off the question. "A little compassion goes a long way, morenita. People forget to have compassion with themselves."

She never told me this, but later I realized she probably met Bubba on one of her Blessed Pie runs.

I don't know when exactly my Lala became the Blessed

Pie lady, though I suspect it was shortly after Barbara became famous for Lala's recipe and not long after Grampa Roger died.

We were still trying to get her to move to Chicago, near us, but she didn't want to leave her farm. "Who's going to take care of my chickens?" she'd ask.

Hazel and Therese kept her company. And the volunteer work at her church gave her a sense of purpose, but I imagine it wasn't enough.

Lala had lost the love of her life and her companion of fifty years. And news had spread that Barbara and her daughter were turning her pies into a franchise. Lala's apple pie was about to go national.

Anyone else would've taken Barbara to court. But Lala just started making her pies and giving them away for free.

She bought an old van off Craigslist—a 1970s classic VW painted bright yellow.

At first, I didn't get what Papi was so upset about. "This is dangerous," I heard him say once during a heated argument. I stood in the hall listening, my back pressed against the wall.

"If you want to sell your pies, why don't we open a store? I can write the business plan," Papi offered.

"I don't want to sell them," she spat back. "If people want to buy my pies, they can go to Barbara's store!"

"Let's get an attorney then," Papi countered.

"Attorneys and lawsuits are a waste of time and money. I have my own plan," she told him.

Papi grunted in frustration and left the kitchen, slamming the back door that led to the garden. I jolted at the sound.

After that, Lala agreed to let me tag along on a Blessed Pie run under the condition I didn't tell Papi.

"Jaime doesn't get it," she said, pronouncing Papi's name in Spanish. "But you'll understand. You have your abuela's spirit, mija. I see it in your eyes."

I smiled, wondering what else she saw.

Lala put the key in the ignition. It took a few tries to start the run-down hunk of metal, but when it did the Buena Vista Social Club's "Candela" came through the speakers.

We set off in the Blessed Pie van with a chorus of "*candela, me quemo aé*" playing in the background. I had no idea where we were going, though the last place I expected was an awful trailer park in the middle of nowhere.

The arrangement of mobile homes was more like a postapocalyptic maze than an actual neighborhood. The street signs had been ripped off their posts. Rusted abandoned cars sat on cinder blocks. Beach towels and broken shades were the standard window coverings. A net-less basketball hoop was bent beyond repair. And small plastic kiddie pools were strewn across the tiny patches of gravel and weeds that passed for front yards.

But the most striking thing about this park was how dirty everything was. As if a film of dirt covered every nook and cranny. Lala's soundtrack of tropical beats and vocals sounded way, way out of place.

We finally stopped by what looked like the most broken-down trailer in the whole lot. A couple of scruffy kids in diapers played in the front yard. A woman came out the main door to meet Lala. Her clothes fit like bedsheets over her skinny body. This woman was barely there at all.

We stepped out of the van and walked toward the home. I had no idea why we had come to this place and why we were delivering a pie to someone who hadn't eaten in the last decade.

"Thank you, Miss Elena," the woman said, calling Lala by her given name. It was me who came up with the moniker Lala when I couldn't pronounce *abuela* as a baby. My two-year-old brain kept getting stuck on the last syllable, *la-la*. My parents gave up on the whole abuela thing and the name Lala stuck.

Lala handed the woman the pie and a small paper bag. The woman gave Lala a one-handed hug and then they exchanged a second brown bag.

"You take care of yourself, now." Lala waved at her as we left. "May the Virgencita bless you."

Lala opened the back of her van, where she kept a bright yellow container that read: Infectious Waste Material, DANGER, Destroy by Incineration. She stuffed the bag the woman gave her inside.

"What's going on?" I asked when we were back in the van.

"That's Mary. She's a heroin addict," Lala explained. "She gave me her used needles and I gave her new ones."

"Okay . . . Are you supposed to do that?" This was a little too much, even for Lala. "I mean, is that even legal?"

My sweet pie-baking, salsa-dancing Lala was giving needles to drug addicts and I was only now finding out. How long had this been going on?

She turned to me and said, "You sound like Jaime." I still remember the sting of her words.

"No, I mean, it's great you're helping people. I just . . . I don't understand." And I wanted to understand. I wanted to be one hundred percent by her side, helping her do whatever it was she was doing. Even if I didn't fully get it.

We left the trailer park and turned onto a main road.

"These people are sick, Isabella," she said forcefully.

The sound of my own name jolted me. Suddenly, I was Isabella and not her "morenita."

"They aren't ready to get help. So if I give them the needles, maybe they won't get HIV or hepatitis. And when they're ready for help, at least they'll be healthy. Like Bubba."

It took me a moment to realize she was talking about BBQ Bubba. The old black man who handed me a hot fudge sundae every time we visited. Bubba was one of the sweetest souls I'd ever met.

"Is it safe, though?" I asked tentatively. "It's nothing contagious, right?"

"I've been volunteering at a needle exchange program for months. I'm a trained nurse," she said, her voice defiant. "I know what I'm doing."

I backed off and didn't ask anymore questions.

We pulled into a beat-up truck stop by the highway and Lala

got out. This time, I stayed in the van. The place gave me the heebie-jeebies. Some women milled around the trucks. Their skimpy outfits left little to the imagination. A chill ran down my spine when I saw one of them disappear inside a truck with a man who had that greasy, pervert quality.

Lala exchanged a bag and a pie with one of the women. She had long brown hair that cascaded down her shoulders and heels so high I thought she might topple over. Lala nodded in my direction and the woman waved. Hesitantly, I waved back.

"Is she a prostitute?" I asked Lala when she returned to the van.

"She has a name. Milly."

"Why do you give them pies?"

"They're blessed," she told me. "The mind is very powerful, mija. As I make the pies, I pray to the Virgencita, 'Guide them back to the light.' Everyone loses their way at some point. But not everyone has someone to say, 'It's gonna be all right, your life is a gift worth living'—that's love, mija."

Lala paused. She took a deep breath and her face softened. "Look around you, morenita. Who else is gonna bake a pie for people like Bubba, Milly, and Mary?"

We both knew the answer.

"It makes them happy. And happiness around here is in short supply. I may not be able to heal their addictions, but at least I can take away some of the loneliness."

Safety concerns aside, I felt proud of Lala. She had turned her gift with food into something meaningful. Her pies meant something to these people.

"I want to help you," I said. "We can make the pies together."

"Good," she said, a smile spreading across her face. "But this stays between us. Okay?"

"Okay."

When we got back to Lala's, though, Papi somehow knew what we were up to. I'd never seem him that angry.

"Are you going to take her to a crack house next?" he yelled at Lala. "How irresponsible can you possibly be?"

I listened from the hallway.

"She is old enough to understand things, Jaime," Lala shot back. "There is more to life than business plans and making money." There was a pause in their conversation. I wanted to come in and tell Papi that Lala was right. Stand by her side and show him we were a united front.

I took a step forward but paused when I heard Lala ask, "What happened to you? I know something's going on with you and Adeline."

And suddenly my body couldn't move. Once again, I was standing on the sidewalk, holding a pie while watching Papi kiss Margo.

"Don't turn this on me," Papi spat. "You got sick and now you're putting my only daughter at risk."

Sick?

A cold shiver ran from the top of my head to the soles of my feet. It felt like glacier water slowly flowing down my body, freezing me in place.

I willed myself to step closer to the kitchen. I had no idea Lala was sick. She'd never said anything.

"You know I would never do that." Lala's voice was suddenly small. "That was an accident."

"An accident? You got hepatitis from one of those needles. People die from that. Don't you tell me it was just an accident. You don't get to say that."

"It's hepatitis—not a death sentence. It's not the end of the world, Jaime."

"That's not what the doctor said, and you know it," Papi said. "I'm done. Do whatever you want. But you're not bringing Isa into this."

He burst into the hallway, almost crashing into me. Before he stormed up the stairs, I noticed his eyes brimmed with tears.

We left early the next day. No one said another word about the pies, or the needles, about Lala's sickness or Papi's affair. No one said anything.

That was the last time I saw her.

Chapter 10

Dessert Cart Trainwreck

The moment I step off the plane in the South of France, my lungs fill with the salty coastal air. A soft breeze weaves through the loose strands of my hair and the sun kisses my face. It's a familiar place tied to many memories of happy family vacations as a child. The soothing effect is almost instant.

I take a taxi to Villefranche-sur-Mer, the seaside village where my French grandmother, Mamie, lives. As the car zips through the Basse Corniche from Nice to the Ville, I take in the familiar sight of the French Riviera. People associate this place with glamour and glitz, but for me it's the home of the salade Niçoise, the fleur de courgette, and the socca. My mouth waters just thinking about the deep-fried stuffed zucchini flower or the addictive chickpea crêpe, the type you can only find in the market square.

But knowing Mamie, she will probably want to go to some chichi restaurant where the portions are small and the waiters never smile.

In the realm of grandmothers, Mamie and Lala are like sugar and salt. The white crystals may be indistinguishable at first glance, but they deliver two very different experiences.

Mamie's house sits on a hill overlooking the ocean. No farms here. Pretty much every house in Villefranche-sur-Mer overlooks the ocean.

It's a picture-perfect hillside of soft-orange buildings and a harbor colored in pastels. A steady traffic of sailboats and luxury yachts glisten in the bay. This is the land of Chagall, Matisse, and Picasso, with the splendor of the Belle Époque era.

I take in the beach below us, dotted with big blue umbrellas and topless sunbathers, and am flooded with memories of playing on the sand as a child with both my parents; a long time ago, before everything changed.

"My pretty girl!" Mamie greets me in French when my cab pulls up. She kisses both my cheeks and then holds me by the shoulders with both hands. I can tell she's inspecting me. "Darling, we need to do something about your skin," she says, taking my face in her hands. "Have you been wearing the sunscreen I sent you?"

"I've been busy," I mutter, pulling away, painfully aware that here I'm no one's morenita.

With her red lips, shoulder-dusting crop, and highlighted cheeks, Mamie is the epitome of the French woman: perfectly imperfect, without ever trying too hard. I didn't inherit this gene. I have to try. Hard.

Mom interrupts with a hug and two kisses. "I've missed you so much," she says. I linger in her arms, drinking in the fragrance of Chanel No. 5.

"Darling, go get changed." Mamie drapes her arms over my shoulders and ushers me inside.

"We have lunch reservations," Mom injects with a quick nod. Translation: chichi restaurant.

"I got you a lovely dress you can wear." Mamie gives me an up and down look. "We're going shopping this afternoon. And to the salon. You need a haircut."

There's no use arguing with Mamie, so I sigh and nod. I can tell her I don't need new clothes, that I gave away the last set she got me; or that I don't need a haircut because I'm always in the kitchen with my hair under a hat. But to her, it won't matter. She's hell-bent on turning me into a proper French girl. If only her efforts came with proper French culinary skills. Now *that* would be worth the pain.

I slip on the outfit she bought me, a short white summer dress that shows off my shoulders. I don't own anything like this. My wardrobe is what you'd call practical. No lace, no bows, and definitely no dry-clean only fabrics.

Mamie also got me a hat with a wide, floppy brim. *Subtle.*

I know she loves me, but her obsession with keeping my skin from getting "too dark" is downright colorism. Why can't she just let me be?

I catch my reflection in the mirror and wonder how long this dress would last in the kitchen—a whole three seconds before it would be covered in sauce spatter. I loosen my bun and my soft dark curls fall around my face, but it doesn't look quite right. My hair has no volume and no sexy, mussed-up quality to it. It's just . . . there. I pull it back into a bun, the way I'm used to seeing it.

I don't even bother with the emergency kit of creams, quick-fixes, and makeup Mamie left on the vanity for me. Not that I even know where to start. For one, no matter how many creams I apply, I won't get Mamie's desired effect: to make me more French.

Whether she likes it or not, my face is a hodgepodge of Latina, Midwestern, and French genes. In middle school, I used to think I got the reject genes—like the leftover soup at the end of the week. I didn't get Papi's towering height. Or Mom's slightly pouty lips. But later I realized that you can make a heavenly sancocho from the leftovers. In fact, the best chefs can create something spectacular out of scraps.

That's what I told myself, anyway.

Once I entered high school, the pretty girls were so predictable, daubing on lip gloss in the bathroom mirror or styling their hair with a curling iron until it had the "messy-after-sex" look. I never knew what they meant.

And what's so special about using lip gloss and curling irons?

Ask any of them to make the perfect lemon zest whipped cream and they would probably go to the store and get a tub of

Cool Whip, an artificial imitation. There's nothing more ordinary than Cool Whip.

I take one last look in the mirror and see myself dressed in pure white. *You are fresh whipped cream with lemon zest, and most definitely not Cool Whip.*

Mamie orders for the three of us. She doesn't let me try the pork belly with lavender appetizer.

"It's not good for your complexion," she says in her thick French accent. "I ordered consommé."

"But that's just broth," I respond in plain English. Every time I try speaking French around her, she interrupts me midsentence with a correction.

Mamie doesn't budge on the lunch order. She closes the menu and waves off the waiter. Meanwhile, Mom is on her second glass of wine. She practically chugged the first one.

"Well, this is nice," Mamie says with a pleased smile. "Just us girls."

I nod, uneasy at the "friendly" tone in her voice. I don't like it one bit.

Mamie turns to me and asks, "So, how are James and his new"—she clears her throat—"wife? Did they marry?"

I glance at Mom, who's taking a long sip of wine.

"They're fine." I adjust the silverware in front of me. For such a fine establishment, they should do a better job at getting the soup spoon placement right.

"Those *Américains* and their antiquated conventions around marriage," Mamie adds. "Would be lovely if they had such conventions around being faithful." And it becomes clear to the entire universe she's not gonna drop it.

I search for our waiter. I should've ordered something to go with the broth. And where is the bread basket?

"Will you have a new sister or a brother?" Mamie asks.

"They want it to be a surprise," I say.

"It was, indeed, a surprise," Mamie adds.

"Where's our waiter? I want a salad. The one with the pear slices. That sounds nice, doesn't it?" I ask her. "Mom, do you want a salad?"

"I already spoke to the *serveur* about the appetizer," Mamie responds curtly. "Have they selected names?"

I'm waiting for Mom to interject, but she doesn't. She sits there stoically as if this conversation doesn't bother her at all. As if we were talking about someone else's family. Someone else's husband.

"I don't know," I say.

"I still find it absurd that James moved to France." Mamie brings her wine glass to her lips and sips.

Other than walking out and taking Mom with me, I'm out of ideas on how to stop the train wreck I know is coming. I feel the tracks rumble under our table.

"All those times he assured us he'd never be able to leave the cosmopolitan pleasures of Chicago . . ." Mamie scoffs.

The train approaches at full speed. Horn blasting. Wheels screeching.

"I suppose that, in the end, such cosmopolitan pleasures simply don't compare to the pleasure of an extramarital affair."

CRASH. There are no survivors.

The waiter finally comes. Talk about timing. He places a few small plates on the table and leaves. I want to grab his sleeve and beg him not to go. *Please sit down, let's talk about your family instead.*

We sip on our tasteless broth in silence.

"I didn't want to leave either," Mom finally says. She glances at me and half smiles. I search for her hand under the table and squeeze. She squeezes it back.

"Don't be silly, darling. Who would prefer Chicago over this?" Mamie says. "You were confused, that's all. But it's over now. No need to rehash the unpleasantness of the past."

I almost drop my spoon. I press my lips hard to prevent any kind of snarky response.

"Let's move on to something else," Mamie says, suddenly cheerful. As if she didn't create the train wreckage surrounding our table. "Isabelle, how's culinary school?" She turns to me, pronouncing my name in French.

"Excellent," I lie, eyes on my plate.

"I told Adeline I was delighted to know you'll have the proper French classical training. Heaven forbid you end up flipping burgers at some—what do you call those? Diners?" She chuckles to herself.

I decide to order the biggest dessert they have—make that two desserts.

"Or worse yet, end up like James's mother, feeding prostitutes and drug addicts."

My eyes cut to Mom. They're about to bulge out of my skull. She glances back at me and gives a slight shake of the head, the one that says *Let it go*. But I don't want to let it go.

"Bubba, Milly, and Mary," I say quietly, as if reciting some mantra I memorized long ago.

Mom and Mamie stare at me like I'm speaking some foreign language.

"Bubba, Milly, and Mary," I repeat a little louder. "Those are their names. The drug addicts and prostitutes have names."

A long, uncomfortable silence takes over the table.

"Adeline, darling," Mamie says, shifting in her seat. "I saw the loveliest blue dress in the window display of that boutique by the house."

Unable to sit in this catastrophe of a lunch for another second, I excuse myself. I place my napkin on the table and stand. "I have to go to the ladies' room."

But I walk toward the kitchen instead. I grab our waiter and ask for the dessert menu. "One of each," I tell him in French. His eyebrows tick upward. That's the most expression I've seen on his face since we got here.

To hell with my complexion. And to hell with Mamie's no sugar rule. Bring on the dessert cart.

Chapter 11

Chicken Cake

Les poulets," Chef Troissant proclaims, as a cart full of dead chickens rolls into the kitchen. They've been plucked clean but their heads and feet are still attached.

Their lifeless, accusatory stares take me back to Lala's farm. "This is as fresh as they come," she'd say, meticulously selecting a chicken from her coop. Then she'd take it to the back of the barn, away from all the others, grab it by the head, and break its neck with one swift jolt. I almost passed out the first time I saw her do it. At dinner, I guiltily ate the poor bird, lying roasted on a bed of vegetables.

"Today you will prepare for me coq au vin," Chef Troissant tells the class. She's inspecting the chickens as she speaks. "You must follow proper butchering technique. I will observe very carefully. As for the dish, I am giving you a certain . . ." She pauses for a breath, then surprisingly utters, "liberté."

A shared gasp echoes in the kitchen at the sound of the word *freedom.* The slight upward tick on Chef Troissant's lips makes me suspect she's enjoying this. "Think originalité. Think depth of flavor. Impress me," she tells us, waving both hands in the air. For a second, I wonder if she's been drinking too much of the vin.

"No time for a long marinade. You will use chicken instead of old rooster. Very young. Very tender. Allez," she says, waving away the cart.

I glance at the spoon rack on the wall. My number remains

last in spite of all the extra hours I logged in the kitchen last week. In a moment of desperation, I even went on YouTube and watched all of Julia Child's *The Way to Cook* lessons—as if I hadn't watched them a thousand times already.

But this is chicken, and coq au vin at that. Mom has been feeding me coq au vin since I was old enough to chew. If I fail at this task, I should voluntarily turn in my apron.

"If my father's coq au vin is good enough for the president of the République, it should be good enough for Troissant . . ." Snake Eyes mutters to himself from the station next to mine. Apparently, his dad is the official chicken-in-wine expert for the entire country. Whatever. The president has never been to my mom's kitchen.

A dead chicken lands with a thud on my work station, courtesy of one of Troissant's minions. The rest of the ingredients are ours to grab from the pantry.

"Did she say if we have to use blood to thicken the sauce?" Lucia asks, flipping through a hidden notebook behind her workstation. "That's the traditional method, you know." She looks up at me. "I swear her accent is getting thicker by the day."

"I think you can use whatever you want. She wants *originalité*." I mockingly wave my hand in the air. Lucia giggles into her fist.

"How was the weekend with your mom?" she asks.

"It was nice to see her. I wish we had more time, though. How about yours?" I smile, trying to sort out how to ask what I really want to ask without actually asking.

"Pippa and I tried this new Moroccan place by the river. You must come with us next time." An unexpected sense of relief washes over me when she doesn't mention Diego.

"Allez, mind your stations. No chitchat," Chef Troissant calls out from her perch by the instructor's table.

"Je suis désolée," Lucia and I call out in unison. Then we both get back to work in silence.

Usually Chef Troissant hides in her office after giving

instructions, but today she's watching us like a hawk. This must mean serious points in the apprenticeship deliberations.

I call out to Lala, who is surely circling somewhere above my head. I need her chicken butchering skills and I need them fast. My hand reaches for the butcher knife and it's like I become possessed. The chicken's head falls off first. *Whack!* One swift drop of the blade is all it takes. Then I remove the feet, one by one. Everything comes back to me in full detail as if I were watching it in a movie.

"Remove the oil gland, then make a slice above the cloaca to put your hand inside," I hear Lala's voice in my ear. "Don't be afraid, morenita."

I jam my entire fist inside the chicken. In addition to the other organs, out comes the heart, the liver, and the giblets—the makings of the perfect chicken stock.

Then I open up the legs and pierce the skin, pulling the drumsticks back and popping out the bone from the joint. The knife slices down the carcass, cutting off the drums and thighs, then the wings. And just because I feel like showing off, I take a drum and, halfway down, slice through onto the bone. I scrape the tendons and cut off the knuckle, giving it that finished haute restaurant look. I saw this once in a Gordon Ramsey cookery class video.

To finish, I slice my knife through the center of the chicken and cut through the wishbone. Most people cut across, which Lala would say is a mistake. When I'm done, two amazing, plump chicken breasts are on my cutting board. As Ramsey would call them, the Rolls-Royce of chicken parts.

I'm so consumed by my chicken that I don't notice Chef Troissant standing in front of my station. When I look up to meet her eyes, she doesn't say anything. Her eyebrows ascend lightly and I think I detect a shadow of a nod. After she walks away, I'm left wondering if that was—maybe?—an expression of approval. I try hard not to get my hopes up, but dang. I need to get this right.

For the coq au vin, I turn to Mom. I think of her in Mamie's house and feel a pang of guilt for leaving her there. I decide to make this coq au vin for her. After Lala, Mom is the best cook I know, even if she didn't go to culinary school. Mamie convinced her it wasn't a *real* career for a woman. She tried to pull the same nonsense on me, but I'm more headstrong than Mom was at my age. And Mom didn't have a Lala to encourage her.

Mom marinates the chicken overnight in wine, but I don't have twenty-four hours for my pieces to sit in the fridge, so I grab a bottle of the nicest Burgundy from the wine rack and walk over to the food vacuum sealer. I stuff my chicken pieces into a plastic bag, douse them with wine, and place them inside the machine. A few seconds later, the air has been completely sucked out of the bag, pressuring the wine into the chicken. *Voilà!* A twenty-minute marinade.

I'm walking back to my station when I pass Snake Eyes on his way to the vacuum sealer. *Of course.* I bet he thought of that just now.

We're the only two students who have finished the butchering. Everyone else is still struggling with their birds. Even Lucia is having a hard time cutting through the carcass. A band of sweat has collected on her forehead as she plunges her knife into the chicken in all the wrong ways. Chef Troissant is standing on the other end of the kitchen, so I lean in and whisper, "Through the wishbone."

She looks at me like I'm speaking some alien language. I scramble my brain thinking of how to say *wishbone* in Spanish— *hueso deseo?* That can't be right.

"Here, let me show you," I say, trying to repay her kindness in helping me clean the kitchen on our second day. I grab her knife and cut through the chicken myself.

Next to me, a metal bowl hits the floor, and I watch in slow-motion horror as Chef Troissant turns around and catches me, knife in hand, leaning over Lucia's station.

The deep scowl on her face needs no translation. The kitchen cleaning assignment is going to be child's play compared to whatever she has in mind.

My heart rate doubles. A surge of blood pumps hard against one of the veins on my neck.

Snake Eyes leans to pick up the metal bowl that landed next to my feet. I glance down at him, shooting death darts out of my eyes.

"Oops," he says, grinning.

"Mademoiselle Fields, would you like to butcher everyone's chickens?"

I slowly set the knife on the table—no sudden movements here. I even try to hold my breath for as long as I can. I don't answer her question either. This is a trick question. I know it. She knows it. Everyone knows it.

I set my eyes on the chopping board. My breath gets caught somewhere between my throat and my heart.

Chef Troissant waits a few beats for an answer that never comes.

"Let me make myself clear," she finally says. "This is not a team sport. Only one of you will get the apprenticeship. One." She proclaims this to the entire room, as if the numbered spoons on the wall are not enough of a daily reminder.

Then she turns to me and says, "Tomorrow, mille crêpe cake on my station. I want to see it as I walk in. *Comprenez-vous?*"

"Oui, Chef Troissant," I say, staring at my apron. But the only thing left to understand is that Chef Troissant is a drill sergeant, the kitchen is her battleground, and food is her weapon of choice. And more so, the mille crêpe cake, with its twenty impossible paper-thin crêpes, amounts to nothing short of a suicide mission.

"You smell delicious," Papi jokes as I slide into the passenger seat of his car.

"Coq au vin," I say. "Mom's recipe."

"Ah." He nods and goes silent. We both know that was his favorite meal. He used to ask Mom to make it at least once a month, and when she did, he would linger in the kitchen for the entire preparation—one of those rare occasions when he was home early from work. They would drink wine and listen to a playlist of French songs Papi jokingly titled "Pepé Le Pew." They would talk and laugh and look at each other with eyes of love. God, how long has it been?

After a long pause he asks, "How is she?"

They haven't seen each other since the divorce six months ago—when Papi signed away our life in Chicago so he could move to France with his pregnant girlfriend. And the only times they speak are to discuss something me-related.

"She's fine," I say, wondering if this is the right time to have the divorce-mistress conversation.

"Did she seem okay?" He pauses before hesitantly adding, "Is she happy?"

I can't discern if it's concern or guilt I hear in his voice. Maybe both.

"Happy enough," I say. Then, without thinking, I let a question of my own slip. "Are *you* happy?"

"Happy enough." He glances at me, feigns a smile, and shrugs. And for some unexplainable reason this feels like the most honest moment we've had in a long time.

I'm about to ask him if he misses Mom, but he steers the conversation with his own question.

"How's your grandmother?"

"Fine. Same as always."

The moment passes, and we go back to driving in silence.

I stare out the window as we make our way through Lyon towards Bessenay. We drive by majestic buildings erected over six hundred years ago. The beautiful architecture and monumental town squares are lit from all sides, like works of art inside a living museum. On the streets, people mill around cafés and bars. The scene makes me long for home. Couples saunter down the sidewalk arm in arm, seemingly without a care in the world. I find myself wishing I was one of them. And not here, trapped in this car, wondering when the right time is to ask Papi why he did it. Why Mom and I weren't enough?

Now is not the right time, I tell myself. Not when I smell like chicken and wine, my hair is matted with sweat, and my feet ache from standing for twelve hours. And I still have to make a mille crêpe cake when I get home—twenty translucent crêpes layered with pastry cream.

Lucia offered to help. "This is all my fault," she said more than once.

But it wasn't. She didn't ask me to cut the chicken for her; I did that all on my own. It was a stupid mistake that will cost me greatly. And for what? I know better than to think I should help her because we are on some sort of girls' team. Chef Troissant is right: there're no teams in that kitchen.

"How did the coq au vin turn out?" Papi asks after a while. "Did you bring home any leftovers?"

I glance at him, and the sadness in his face makes my heart ache a little. There's something like longing in his eyes.

By all outward appearances he seems to enjoy his new life with Margo. But how can he forget about Mom, when at one point in his life he promised to love her forever? He must feel something. Right? I *know* he must.

"We had to turn in our dishes," I say. "Chef Troissant will taste them and we'll know tomorrow how we did." *Those cursed spoons.*

"Did you sauté the onions, mushrooms, and carrots in the lardon drippings?" he asks, as if he was talking to an amateur.

"Yes."

"What about the sauce reduction? You used her stock recipe?"

"Papi, seriously? You have to ask?"

"I'm sure it was amazing." His voice trails off and I'm left wondering if he is still talking about the coq au vin.

Back at the house, Papi and I are greeted by Margo's voice booming from the living room.

"You have to talk to him!" she demands, her voice rising.

Papi and I pause, standing side by side in the empty foyer.

"He doesn't listen," Diego fires back. "What am I supposed to do?"

Papi and I glance at each other, trying to make sense of their argument. And judging by the blank expression on his face, he's as clueless as I am.

"I'll be upstairs," Papi whispers, setting his keys on the entry table. He takes the stairs to the second floor and leaves me standing alone. I'm sure Margo will fill him in later.

I stand in the foyer for a few minutes, unable to tear away from the unfolding drama.

"Fifteen years, wasted," Margo snaps. "All that work for nothing."

Diego doesn't respond.

"And Cambridge?" she asks. "Alfonso says you got in."

"I'm not going," he says emphatically.

"Diego, you can't do this." Margo's voice softens as she pleads.

"The whole thing was his idea. He never asked me. He doesn't care what I want," Diego spits.

A long silence follows, and I begin to walk away, anxious that one of them will catch me listening. I know this is voyeuristic, but in a sordid way it eases my own pain a little to know I'm not alone in this messed-up family.

"Maybe things would have been different if you hadn't left," Diego tells her.

"That's not fair. You know why I had to leave." Margo sounds on the verge of tears.

"Well, now it's my turn. I thought you would understand." His voice cracks and I take it as my cue to leave, but then the living room doors abruptly swing open, and in an instant I'm face-to-face with Diego. We both open our mouths to say something. For a moment, his eyes are vulnerable and heavy with anguish. But then he shifts and raises every barrier within him. He brushes past me and strides down the corridor leading to the patio. Beluga struggles to catch up, running behind him toward the guest cottage.

Inside the living room, Margo is slumped on a chair, holding her belly, her head leaning against the backrest. She's never looked more miserable.

Before she can notice me standing there, I retreat into the kitchen, thankful for the silence and the solitude. And weirdly thankful to Chef Troissant for the mille crêpe cake I'm about to throw myself into.

By two a.m., the pastry cream is cooling in the fridge and I've almost finished making the twenty crêpes I need to create the cake. Next to the plate of selected crêpes sits a second plate, about four times higher, piled with all the discards. The thing about a perfect mille crêpe cake is that all the crêpes need to be the same thickness—that of a sheet of paper. The internet teems with bloated crêpe cakes thrown together with bulky, pancake-like crêpes, and thick creams straight out of a pudding box. Grotesque.

The authentic mille crêpe is refined, sophisticated, and elegant. Layered flavors merge overnight, creating the epitome of a French dessert.

At long last I exhale as I transfer the last crêpe from the pan onto the plate.

I pull out my favorite cake dish from the cupboard, made with handblown glass and delicate colored inlays. I got it at the town market a few weeks ago, when I still had time to wander around town.

I rest the first crêpe on the dish and bring the pastry cream out of the fridge. I dip a spoon into the cream and taste, closing my eyes as the flavors hit my tongue. This is my best batch yet.

Tiny flecks of vanilla bean are embedded throughout the cream, and a hint of Grand Marnier liqueur adds a hidden note of citrus.

Spatula in hand, I get to work. The layering is the easy part. One crêpe covered in cream, then another on top and so on, until twenty flawless crêpes are stacked into a textbook cake. But I'm not done yet. Knowing Chef Troissant, the actual cake will only take me so far.

The presentation will require a blowtorch. Thank goodness I have the kitchen all to myself.

I set the new fire extinguisher next to me just in case. Then I sprinkle granulated sugar on the top crêpe and cover the sides. I slowly burn a translucent crust of caramel around the cake so that it resembles a sugar shell.

I step back and take in the result. The picture-perfect cake surprises even me. This is a dish I can truly be proud of. I snap a photo and upload it to my social feed. Instantly, I get a few likes and comments of approval. Everyone loves a gorgeous food shot.

I store the cake in the fridge and head to my room floating up the stairs. I don't bother to undress as I crawl under the sheets. All I care about is the culinary masterpiece sitting in the fridge. In the morning, I will walk into Chef Troissant's kitchen like I'm carrying a trophy. The thing radiates its own light! I smile into my pillow and fall asleep. They'll have to call me Queen of the Crêpes.

Chapter 12

Everything Tastes Better Fried

A ray of sunlight hits my face, and I'm instantly wide awake. My only thought is to run downstairs to check on my crêpe cake. Enough time has passed for the pastry cream's moisture to redistribute into the crêpes. This cake can only go from perfect to legendary.

I take off my apron as I walk down the stairs, trying to detangle the strings around my neck from the rat's nest that is my hair. *Note to self: take off apron before going to bed.*

Not only did I manage to leave part of my hair attached to the apron, I also stink—like day-old coagulated chicken fat and sour wine.

Second note to self: take a shower.

When I reach the bottom of the stairs, I'm startled by the laughter coming from the kitchen. *Oh no! No! No! No!* My mind goes blank as I leap across the hallway. For the love of me, I can't remember if I put a *do not eat* sign on the cake.

I swing the kitchen door open so hard that it slams against the wall.

The laughter goes silent as someone screams—a blood-curdling scream that sends goose bumps down my back and arms. It takes me a moment to realize the deranged sound is coming out of my own mouth.

I practically vault from the door to the kitchen island, where Papi and Diego are eagerly tearing into my cake.

"Put it down," I scream, reaching for Papi's fork. I rip it from his hand and take away his plate. "What are you doing?" I also take Diego's plate and pull the fork right out of his mouth.

"Hey, I'm not done," he complains, trying to get his plate back.

"You touch this plate and I swear to God, the meat cleaver is coming out."

Diego retreats. "Okay . . . Good morning to you too," he says, standing to refill his coffee cup.

"Isa, honey, what's wrong?" Papi's looking at me like I'm the crazy one. Doesn't he realize what they've done?

"It's ruined," I wail into my beautiful cake, now missing two big slices. "It was perfect and now it's ruined." I take in deep, slow breaths. Tears sting my eyes. I'm not going to cry. Not in front of these two.

"For such a fancy cake, I thought it tasted pretty good," Diego says from across the kitchen.

"This was my special assignment," I say through gritted teeth, clenching and unclenching my hands to prevent them from swiping the smudge of pastry cream at the corner of his mouth. "You ate my homework."

"You should have put a sign on it or something," he says offhandedly.

I may rip his head off.

My fingers grip the sides of the island until my knuckles physically hurt. One of the veins on my neck is throbbing so hard and fast, it may actually burst.

"Sign? *Sign?* You see this pile of crêpes?" I point at the plate sitting in the middle of the island and a white paper with the words *EAT ME* written in big, bold letters. "Eat me!" I call out, waving the paper in the air. "There's a sign. Why couldn't you eat *these*?" I want to cry so badly. I really do. But I don't have time for tears. I need to fix this. Fast.

"Those don't have the cream," Diego says, stirring sugar into his cup. "The cream was the best part."

"Honey, why don't you make another one? You still have an hour. Diego can borrow the car and take you to the restaurant."

I stare at Papi for a hot second, wondering how a person can be so clueless.

"It took me seven hours to make this cake." That's all I say, because I'm afraid if I try to explain anything beyond that, my head will literally explode.

"Sweetheart, did you get any sleep?" he asks, pouring a cup of black coffee that he sets in front of me. I don't dignify it with an answer. I take a big gulp from the mug and then go into full-on cake-fixing mode.

I trim what is left of their slices and squeeze them back inside the cake. Slowly, I remove the damaged top layer. With it, goes the perfect crust I created a few hours ago. I drop it onto a plate in front of Diego, where it lands with a splat.

"You can eat this. There's no fixing it."

Diego pushes the plate forward and gets up. "I'm good," he says, walking out of the kitchen with his mug of coffee. "I'll be out front when you're ready to leave."

"Do you need help?" Papi asks, but he's so close to the door he practically has one foot in the hallway.

Yeah, fine, leave, I scream inside my head. *Like you left Lala's house the day of the Blessed Pies. Like you left us in Chicago after your affair. Every time things get too difficult, you just leave.* "No, thanks," is what I actually say, turning away from him to deal with my cake. Alone.

If I replace the top crêpe layer and re-caramelize the cut-up side, I may be back in business. I dig through the pile of discarded crêpes and pull out a decent replacement for the top. Thank goodness I left some pastry cream in the fridge, mostly because I was too tired to clean out the container.

I daub some cream on top of the cake and gently rest the replacement crêpe on top, all along ignoring the sinking feeling that it looks as bad as the gallery of deformed mille crêpe cakes online. I also ignore the fact there is not enough pastry cream to fill the gaping hole created by the bites Diego and Papi took. I ignore all of these things, because I don't have time to think.

The clock has once again jumped forward, and if I don't hurry, I will be late for class. Meaning, the cake won't be sitting on her station as Chef Troissant walks in. Meaning, I might as well pack up and go home.

My fingers dig out handfuls of sugar and I sprinkle it on top and on the sides of the cake, making a mess everywhere.

I pull out my blowtorch and pray there's enough butane gas left to finish the job. The flame goes out with a sputter the moment I'm done caramelizing the cut-up side. I toss the empty gas can into the garbage, along with what is left of the former crêpe topper. My heart breaks as I watch the caramel splinter inside the garbage can.

The almost-repaired cake sits on the island, laughing at me. This version most definitely does not radiate its own light. Instead it is sucking all the light—like a black hole, or canned vegetables.

I step back and draw all the oxygen out of the room in one long inhale. My head turns from left to right, searching for an angle from which the cake looks as good as it did last night. But such an angle does not exist.

I write *DO NOT EAT* in all caps on a piece of paper. Then I run up the stairs back to my room, peel off my dirty uniform, apply some deodorant, change my underwear, and wriggle myself into a clean chef's coat and pants. My hair gets pulled into a bun. It's so greasy you could fry an egg in it. I don't give myself a second look in the mirror as I walk out. It's not worth the extra pain. I know how I look—like someone who is about to get her butt handed to her.

"Can you please go faster?" I'm in the passenger seat, cradling the cake on my lap. "And watch out for the potholes."

"It's rush hour," Diego says, changing the radio to a Spanish music station playing a Latin reggaeton song. He hums the lyrics and taps his fingers on the steering wheel to the beat of the music.

The dash display announces the singer's name is Maluma and the song is "El Perdedor"—translation: *the loser*. How very appropriate.

"Can we listen to something else?" I ask, propping the cake against a pillow on my lap. It's the best shock absorption system I could conjure in a hurry.

"What do you want to listen to?" he asks.

I shrug, staring out the window. Outside, it's one of those idyllic French summer days with its bright blue, cloudless sky and seventy degree temperature. I sort of wish it were raining.

"Something *not* about being a loser," I say.

Diego smirks while shaking his head and turns off the radio.

"What?" I ask.

"Nothing," he says.

The car inches forward, but we get stuck at a red light. I wonder if I should get out and walk.

"Why are you doing all this?" he asks, glancing at the cake on my lap.

"What do you mean, why?" My voice comes out edgier than I intend.

"What do you mean, *what do I mean*? Why are you doing it?"

"Because I enjoy it," I say simply.

"You enjoy being *on* all the time?" he asks in a cynical tone.

"I'm not *on* all the time," I snap.

He glances at me, eyebrows raised.

"For your information, this has been my dream for as long as I can remember. Three Michelin stars. One is the beginning. Two is not enough."

"So, let me get this straight. You don't sleep. You don't shower. You scream like a crazy person because someone had the wrong slice of cake. And this is supposed to get you stars. Did I get that right?"

My face goes hot at the shower part. Do I really smell that bad?

"Whatever," I say. "Sometimes you have to make sacrifices to get what you want."

We finally get a break in traffic and the road opens. We cruise through four green lights. La Table de Lyon is ahead, within walking distance.

"All I'm saying is, if you really enjoyed this, you would be happy. You don't look happy to me," he says, pulling up to the curb.

I open the door and step out of the car, balancing the cake in my hands.

"Thanks for the ride," I say, slamming the door shut.

I am happy, I tell myself—over and over again.

When I finally arrive at the test kitchen, everyone is huddled over the center island. I set down the cake on Chef Troissant's station and walk over to see what's going on. There's murmuring and a collection of somber faces.

"What happened?" I ask Pippa.

"It's terrible," she says, shaking her head. "Chef Bernard Martin, the owner of Le Illusionaire, committed suicide."

I gasp. "*What?* How? His restaurant is one of the best in the world." I'm shocked by the news. Mom and I used to watch his TV series, where he traveled to remote places around the world and talked to people about food and culture. The best part of the show was Martin himself. He was honest, humble, and unguarded, and the people he spoke to responded in kind. "Great food," he used to say, "is but a conduit for deeper human connections."

"Is the news online?" I ask.

"It's just starting to cross some news feeds. That guy knows someone who works in Martin's kitchen," Pippa says, pointing at a tall, blond student—a quiet Belgian guy, who seems uncomfortable with all the attention he's now getting. "It's a senseless tragedy, if you ask me."

Lucia joins us. "Did you hear?" she asks.

We nod solemnly, and suddenly my stupid crêpe cake doesn't seem that important.

"Is that your mille crêpe?" Lucia asks with astonishment. I move out of the way so she can get a better view of my little disaster. "*What happened?*"

"A Spaniard happened." I sigh, then turn to Lucia and add, "No offense."

"None taken," she replies, amused.

"It's not *that* terrible," Pippa says. "I'm sure it tastes *amazing.*" Her *amazing* sounds like she's trying too hard to say something nice.

"Why did he just eat the middle?" Lucia asks, holding back laughter.

I elbow her gently. "You guys, it's not funny!" But still we laugh, trying to release a little of the tension and sadness. We get some disapproving looks from the rest of the class. Pippa tries to shush us, but then she glances back at my cake and starts laughing again.

"I'm so sorry," she says, trying to control herself. I'm laughing along in a demented fit of hysterics, fueled by stress and lack of sleep.

When we all catch our breath, we debate ways to fix the sinking middle—where the soul-sucking hole is located.

"What if you plate a slice?" Pippa proposes. "Maybe drizzle caramel sauce on the plate?"

"And some berries?" Lucia suggests.

"Is it that bad?" I ask, painfully aware of the answer. I can't believe Diego did this. God, sometimes he makes me want to wring his neck!

"I'll get a plate," Pippa says, already moving across the kitchen.

"Caramel sauce and berries—I'm on it," Lucia tells me. "Don't worry, Isa, we'll fix it." She gives me the saddest lost puppy look before disappearing into the walk-in cooler. I hate that look. It's the look I saved for kids back in high school who signed up for a culinary elective because they thought it would make a nice hobby. Because they thought it would be an easy A.

"Incroyable!" Snake Eyes stands next to me, chest puffed out and arms akimbo. This guy loves taking up space. "It's like you're trying to lose on purpose."

I stare at him, incredulous, like my face has hit the floor and he's kicking me in the teeth.

"Did I do something to you?" I spit out the question. It seems to catch him off guard. He blinks a few times, then grins and says, "You don't do anything to me." His eyebrows tick upward slightly, as in *Did you get that double meaning, sweetheart?* Today, though, I ain't having it. It's already been an awful day, and class hasn't even started.

"Why are you such a jerk all the time? Do you hear yourself? What is your problem?" I move away from him and try to refocus on the crêpe cake. Where the heck have Pippa and Lucia gone?

"My problem is that you don't belong here," he says very matter-of-fact. "Grattard is the standard for excellence. This," he says, tapping his creepy long fingers on the table next to my cake, "is not excellence."

I open my mouth to tell him where he can put his excellence (and his finger), but then I glance at the cake and all the fight leaves me. He's right. *This* is not excellence.

"Hey, Legrand, I think the butcher delivered a pig's head with your name on it. It's sitting in the cooler, in case you were wondering," Pippa says, pushing him out of the way.

Snake Eyes's lips curl into a snooty sneer. "Tell me now, did you Brits invade India just to steal their cuisine, or was that a side benefit? I guess mushy peas and fish and chips weren't enough, huh?" He doesn't wait for Pippa to respond before walking away.

"Wanker," Pippa mutters after he's gone. "I'll make him a *special* Jamaican jerk. Extra hot peppers."

"I've never had Jamaican jerk, but I do love fish and chips," Lucia tells Pippa.

"Everything taste better when it's fried," I say. "Maybe we should dunk the cake in the fryer."

"That would be so American," Pippa teases. We all snicker.

I drizzle caramel sauce on a plate in a loop pattern around the edges.

"Is it true they fry whole sticks of butter at carnivals?" Pippa asks.

I snort and nod, remembering the time Lala took me to the Kansas State Fair, an otherworldly medley of carnival games, farm animals, and every kind of fried food known to mankind. It was a miracle people didn't drop dead on the sidewalk from a heart attack.

"Have you ever tried the fried Oreos? I've always wondered about those," Lucia says.

We transfer a slice of cake to the plate and strategically position a few berries.

"You guys should come over sometime—we can have a Friday Fry-a-Thon or something," I say. I can't remember the last time I had friends over. During most of high school, there wasn't really anyone I wanted to hang out with that much. I'm actually excited when Lucia says, "That would be awesome!"

"I've been dying to make my auntie's fried chicken," Pippa says. "She uses pork lard—like the real deal. It's out-of-this-world good. You know, if you don't mind the whole clogged artery thing. Sometimes I want a sensible home-cooked meal. You know?"

"Yeah, those are the best." Lucia passes me a handful of berries to finish decorating the plate. "I miss my mom's cooking. She makes a killer arròs negre. It's like a paella, but we use squid ink to turn the rice black."

We take a step back and admire our work.

"Much better," Pippa declares.

"Ah, the moment of truth," I say, watching Chef Troissant enter the kitchen, trailed by a tall, hulking man in a chef's coat.

We all scatter back to our stations.

Chef Troissant and the other chef stop short of the apprenticeship area. He is talking down to her, literally. Chef Troissant's head barely comes up to his shoulders. Her face is even more rigid than normal, and her shoulders are pulled back so tight her back might snap.

When she enters the room, she doesn't even notice the mille crêpe cake.

You have got to be kidding me.

"Faites attention!" Her voice is even more tense than usual. How is that even possible? "Please welcome Chef Augustus Legrand, Meilleur Ouvrier de France."

Oooohs and ahhhhs instantly fill the kitchen. Even I squeak in amazement. A real-life, flesh-and-bone MOF stands in front of us, someone even rarer than Michelin-starred chefs.

My eyes narrow on the colors of his chef's collar—blue, white, and red. It's all I can see. Wearing that striped collar is considered the ultimate recognition of excellence.

The MOF award is given only in France and only to French citizens. (Thank you, Mom!) It is a competition held every four years, with the French president himself handing out the medals along with the lifetime title. The grueling preparation process takes years. Some chefs spend their whole lives chasing after the award, only to end up in tears when they fail. Grown men crying is a thing in the MOF world. Earlier this year, when I was bingeing documentaries on Michelin stars, I heard a chef say that the MOF competition is not about doing the best that you can, but about doing the absolute best that can be done—the ultimate quest for perfection.

"Alors, Chef Legrand will be teaching today's class, at the request of Chef Grattard," Chef Troissant says in a flat tone.

At the second mention of his name I glance at Snake Eyes. He's standing tall with his arms tightly crossed over his chest and his chin inched upward. It is obvious to me—and everyone with a pair of eyes—that Chef Legrand is his father. This should be interesting.

Chef Troissant turns to leave but pauses midstep when she sees my cake. She doesn't idle by the table; instead, she grabs both the plated slice and the cake and takes them into her office. She shuts the door and pulls down the shades.

"Bon! Who is ready for fun?" Chef Legrand scans the room.

His face is one big smile, and his arms are open wide as if he's trying to take us all in. "Today, beautiful day. Why stay inside, I say. Let's find l'inspiration! Come along. We must waste no time." And with that, he leaves.

We look at each other, wondering if it's okay to follow him out the door, outside the restaurant. But when Snakes Eyes goes after him, we quickly follow. I mean, if a MOF tells you he's gonna show you where to find *l'inspiration*, you follow him to the ends of the earth.

Chapter 13

Trumpets of Death

"Le Marché Saint-Antoine," Chef Legrand declares as we arrive at Lyon's famous Saint-Antoine Market. He had a minibus waiting for us outside the restaurant.

The ride from La Table de Lyon was a total whirlwind. My brain went frantic, scrambling to think of every question I've always wanted to ask a MOF. When will I get this opportunity again?

And why didn't Chef Troissant tell us he was visiting today? I could've prepared. Done some proper research, instead of googling his name on my phone and speed-reading his life story during the raucous bus ride.

Everyone exits the minibus and gathers on the sidewalk, waiting for instructions from our leader. We are all practically bouncing on our heels with excitement. It's nice to be out of the kitchen for a change.

"If you need l'inspiration, you will find it here. Bon, gather around," Chef Legrand says, doing that thing where he stretches out his arms and joyfully grins from ear to ear. "I will give you each forty euro." He pulls out a wad of bills from one of his chef's coat pockets. "You must each buy three ingredients. These, you will cook for me in a dish—only three. We will meet back at the bus at noon." That leaves us three hours to shop. Plenty of time.

We nod and return the smile, taking his money. The whole thing has a Christmas morning feel to it. As if Santa Claus himself were handing out wads of cash straight from his gift sack.

"Bon, off you go. Find it: *l'inspiration!*" And with that, he waves us off, into the market.

I hang back as the others disperse, eager for even five minutes of one-on-one time. This man has captured the Holy Grail of the French culinary arts. He is part of an elite group of about two hundred chefs in history, out of which only two are women.

To put my chances into perspective, in 2007, Chef Andrée Rosier became the first woman to win the MOF title since its inception in 1923. She was twenty-eight years old. Twenty-eight! Rosier began her first apprenticeship when she was sixteen, meaning I'm already a year late. That's a lot of time to make up for.

"Are you coming?" Pippa calls out behind me. She's standing next to Lucia, who is bent over a glorious display of tarts.

"I'll be right there," I call out. "Grab me a cheese tart."

Pippa gives me a thumbs-up. I turn to face Chef Legrand, who is tipping our driver. My heart is hammering against my chest and my palms are a sweaty mess. I quickly rub my hands against my pants in case Chef Legrand reaches out for a handshake.

"Chef?" I tap him on the arm. When he turns around, I instinctively take a step back. Up close, he's solid and broad chested with thick limbs. He's so tall that if he were to raise his hand into the sky, I'm convinced he could catch a passing cloud. Snake Eyes seems small and scrawny by comparison despite being the tallest in our class.

"How can I help you, mademoiselle?" he asks, his face returning to the all-consuming smile.

My mouth goes dry. I clear my throat and try my best not to gush.

"My name is Isabelle Fields." I pronounce my name with the proper French intonation.

"Oh, l'Américaine, oui?" he asks. I get the dreadful feeling Snake Eyes has been talking about me.

"Well, my mother is French, and although I grew up in Chicago—we have almost twenty thousand restaurants, you know?—she taught me how to cook from a very young age. And we travel to France at least once a year. My grandmother lives a hop, skip, and a jump away, in Nice," I say, all in one breath. Not only am I borderline apologizing for being born in the wrong country, to one wrong parent, suddenly I've become the kind of person that says "hop, skip, and a jump away." Who says that? I must sound like a total idiot.

"I guess, what I am trying to ask is . . ." My mind struggles to find the right words. Now that I'm here, at the source of the world's culinary wisdom, I can't seem to put into words exactly what I want to know—which is everything. I settle for, "What does it take to make it?"

He considers my question for a moment, nodding with what I interpret as amusement. If he thinks I'm some talentless, dim-witted girl, he doesn't show it.

"*Sa vie,*" he finally says.

I lean forward, waiting for the explanation to his "one's life" response, but he appears content with his two-word answer. I don't want to come across as dense, but I need to know *exactly* what he means. So I ask, "What does that mean for you?"

"This is an excellent question," he says, flashing his ultra-white teeth and thousand-kilowatt smile. "I will explain like this. In 2010, divers found 168 bottles of champagne in a ship-wreck off the Finnish Åland archipelago in the Baltic Sea. These bottles were 170 years old." He pauses for effect, as I wonder how it's possible a sunken pirate ship relates to my question.

"The bottles sold at auction. I bought one bottle of Veuve Clicquot—a very rare bottle, you must understand this. Some eighteen thousand euro it cost me. When I received my MOF, I drink this bottle. Now, I am worthy of this champagne." His left eyebrow is slightly raised and his head is cocked to the side. I get the distinct impression he is very pleased with his story, which has left me absolutely dumbfounded.

"But, you know . . . how did you get there from where I am"—I point at myself—"to MOF." I point at him, as if it's not clear who's who. "What did you do?"

He furrows his brow. There's virtually a neon sign on his forehead that reads, *The answer is obvious, little girl—you just don't get it.*

"Your life. *This* has to be your life. When you are awake. When you are asleep. Never stop. Your entire life—this is what it takes to be the best. This is why people make a special journey to eat my food. They fly across continents! You must do whatever it takes. Sacrifice everything. Owe nothing to anyone. You are number one or you are a stove monkey—there is no second or third place. Understand?"

"Yes. Okay." I nod, taking mental notes of everything he's saying, even if it sounds a tiny bit extreme. But, I mean, what do I know? Right? My mental notes stack up until they drown out the faint voice in the back room of my thoughts, arguing this guy is nuts.

"Every day I put on my MOF title. The colors we wear," he says touching the red, white, and blue ribbon around his collar. "We are the only chefs allowed to wear this. You see why I can drink the expensive champagne? This champagne and I are the same. Exceptional."

I thank him, then back away slowly, feeling unworthy of even standing in his shadow.

I find Pippa and Lucia sitting on a bench, digging into a box of tarts.

"One cheese tart for the señorita," Lucia says, handing me a pastry wrapped in parchment paper. We walk down the market path overlooking the east bank of the Saône River.

"So? What did Papa Legrand have to say?" Pippa asks.

We stop to finish our tarts and watch the parade of boats cruising along the river.

"I'm not really sure, to be honest," I say, still pondering his advice. "Something about being worthy of a bottle of champagne recovered from a shipwreck. And giving one's whole life to the craft."

"Well, that's certainly helpful," Pippa says sarcastically.

I shrug, taking another bite of my tart while admiring the backdrop of pastel buildings and Fourvière Hill on the other side of the river. Perched atop the Hill, the Basilique Notre-Dame de Fourvière looms impressively over the city. Its white façade and four main towers glisten on this bright, sunny day.

"How are we supposed to pick only three things?" Lucia asks. "There are over a hundred vendors here."

"We have three hours . . ." I offer.

"Actually, make that two hours and forty-five minutes," Pippa corrects.

"That's practically an eternity. Enough to walk around and see what inspires us," I say, savoring the last bite of my pastry and crumpling the napkin into a ball.

"*L'inspiration!*" Pippa exclaims, opening her arms wide as she mocks Chef Legrand. "Was it me, or is there just something dodgy about that guy?"

"What do you mean?" Lucia asks.

"I don't know. It's like he was trying too hard," Pippa says.

"Maybe it's because we're used to being berated by Chef Troissant. We've got some kind of Stockholm syndrome," I say, and we all chuckle.

"For the record, I feel no sympathy toward our captors," Pippa says, "and I have no sympathy for phony charm."

"I thought he was really nice and approachable for someone with so many titles," I say.

We stroll down the path, scanning vendors' tables as we go. There are booths on both sides of the walkway, selling a plethora of culinary delights: sausage covered in buttery pastry dough, succulent peaches dripping in juice, giant wheels of cheese straight from the dairy farm. I stay away from the Époisses de Bourgogne and any other kind of stinky cheese.

As we walk, I take it all in—the tiny samples I collect from table to table, the cacophony of conversations in French, and the intoxicating smell of the *poulet rôti* carts challenging you not to buy one of their rotisserie chickens. I marvel at the construction of the carts—a masterpiece of street food cookery. A tall rotisserie wall rises into the sky holding row after row of chickens roasting in their own fat. The grease pools in a large pan at the bottom, where potatoes are cooked. Lala would love this. She may have even asked Grampa Roger to build her a roasting cart in their backyard.

We lose Pippa at an oyster stand. "I'll catch up with you later," she says. She's inspecting a box of fresh-caught oysters and haggling over the price.

"Is that an empanada truck?" Lucia asks, moving toward a truck with a sign that reads *Señor Carlos Empanadas*. "It is! I have to get one. You want one?"

"I'm good," I say, setting my sights on a mushroom stand up the path. "I think I found my first ingredient."

Over a dozen varieties of mushrooms are displayed on the table. Handwritten chalk signs provide names like *cêpes*, *morilles*, and *girolles*. I bring a black, trumpet-shaped mushroom to my nose, fully taking in the pronounced aroma of forest, earth, and dampness. This one is called the trompette de la mort. I don't let the name intimidate me. Instead I take it as an omen, that I'm about to kill my competition. These so-called trumpets of death are imbued with a sweet and woodsy aroma. The texture is soft enough to stand alone as a main ingredient in a pasta dish.

I ask the vendor for half a kilo. He weighs the flower-looking mushrooms and places them inside a paper bag.

"Merci," I say as we exchange euros and he passes me the change.

My other two ingredients have to complement these beauties and be distinctive enough to grab Chef Legrand's attention. I'm thinking a fresh pasta—a tagliatelle? I scan the booths, searching for signs of a nonna. It will take the supernatural skills of an Italian grandmother to craft the kind of pasta I need.

A forkful of real Italian pasta has a toothy texture and rich flavor. But what's more, it makes your soul yearn for the carb-induced rapture that follows. Nothing short of this will do for my dish.

I take my time with each pasta vendor, asking questions about their methods and the quality of their ingredients. Most are lacking. Frustrated, I walk to the end of the market, where I come across a small stall with a little girl clutching a cash box. She's adorable in a yellow dress and pigtails.

"Bonjour," I say in greeting. She smiles and starts rambling in Italian, pointing at the pasta displayed on the table, completely oblivious to the fact I don't understand a word she's saying. I'm about to walk away when I recognize the one word guiding my quest: *nonna*.

"Nonna?" I ask.

The girl nods, slides off the stool she's been sitting on, and runs down the row of tents.

"Wait!" I call out, but she's gone.

Crap. How much time do I have left to shop? I check my phone. Thirty minutes—and counting. *Double crap!* Where did all my time go?

I hunt through the stands, desperate to find this kid, who I pray will take me to her nonna. After a few minutes, I see the girl walking back in my direction, mercifully with a grandmother in tow. The culinary gods must me watching over me today.

I follow her and her grandma to the pasta booth, regretting every second I've wasted today.

I ask the nonna for fresh tagliatelle, which she leisurely produces from a basket under the table. This woman is certainly not in a hurry. And it's up to me to keep my neurosis in check and be polite. Problem is, I still don't have a third ingredient, and I'm quickly running out of time.

I offer the nonna a few euros, but she doesn't take them. Instead, she holds both palms up in front of her, signaling me to wait.

"I can't wait," I mutter in English, holding a respectful smile.

Nonna retreats to a table in the back and takes FOREVER

to return. When she does, she's barely holding on to the giant wheel of cheese in her hands. I quickly set down the bag of pasta and cross inside the booth to help her carry the thing. It weights a ton.

We gently place the wheel on the table, next to the display of pastas. When I step back, I catch the inscription on the rind: *Parmigiano-Reggiano*. The king of cheeses.

Thank you, Nonna! I've found my third ingredient.

This wheel has the Consorzio's seal of approval—they're like the federal police of cheeses—and the gold seal, which means it was traditionally produced, aged thirty months, and carefully inspected in and immediately around Parma, Italy. *This* is one of the best cheeses in the world. And the perfect complement to the ingredients I already have.

I don't want to jinx it, but I'm feeling pretty confident about my dish.

I pay the little girl and thank the nonna for her help. I even manage "Grazie!", one of the handful of words I know in Italian.

Not long after, Chef Legrand and Snake Eyes walk up the path and stop at a booth three tables down from where I'm standing. It strikes me that their once-sparkling smiles are now surly scowls.

Chef Legrand shakes hands with the attendant of the sausage booth and they exchange a few pleasantries. The chef asks after the vendor's family, and the *big* smile momentarily makes a comeback. He orders a kilo of sausage with pistachios and pays. Meanwhile, Snake Eyes stands back, uninvolved. He mills around with his hands tucked into his pockets, staring at the pavement. I've never seen him look so sullen.

Chef Legrand thanks the vendor, then walks down the path with Snake Eyes, heading in my direction. I move to the side and step into a flower stall, disappearing from view behind some buckets of lavender.

Chef Legrand and Snake Eyes are engaged in a conversation I can't hear, but from what I can see the argument looks intense.

Chef Legrand gesticulates with his arms and speaks in rapid French. Snake Eyes interjects every so often, his face taking on the shade and texture of an overripe tomato. The muscles of his jaw form hard lines and deep ridges have appeared on his fore-head. He says something to his dad then takes off toward the river bank, in the opposite direction.

It figures. Some people just can't appreciate how good they have it. If my dad were a MOF, I'd be glued to his side, trying to absorb every ounce of knowledge seeping from his pores. But my dad is not a MOF; he is an investment banker turned cherry farmer. Not exactly a source of *"l'inspiration!"*

A truffle vendor calls out to Chef Legrand by name. They're close enough that I can overhear their conversation.

"Just for you," the vendor says, revealing a small basket from behind the table. He uncovers the contents and offers it to Chef Legrand. "White truffles from Alba," he says in a low voice.

Chef Legrand's eyes widen, as do mine. It takes every ounce of self-control I possess not to leap across the path to peer over Chef Legrand's shoulder. I mosey around the lavender, trying to get a glimpse of the crown jewels of the culinary world, but it's useless. Truffles are about the size of a baby potato, and the basket is obstructing my view.

"But we are not in season," Chef Legrand says, bringing the basket to his nose.

"A rare pre-season find," explains the vendor.

"How much?" the chef asks.

The vendor holds up three fingers. "Three thousand. Per half kilo," he adds.

I almost choke on my own spit. I pull out my phone and do a quick currency exchange calculation. It comes out to a little over $3,300 US dollars per approximately one pound of truffles.

I think of all the things I could buy with $3K: a used taco truck off Craigslist; a round-trip ticket to Hokitika, New Zealand, for their Wildfoods Festival; an authentic Italian espresso machine (with its own view of the Mediterranean!).

"I'll take a full one kilo," Chef Legrand says.

The vendor carefully wraps the basket and gives it to Chef Legrand, who cradles it like he's holding a baby.

At this exact moment, I realize I have two options. I can stick to the schedule, since by now I'm supposed to be back on the minibus. But let's face it, we're not leaving the market without Chef Legrand. Or I can put on my big girl panties and ask to see (and smell) the Alba truffles.

"*Quien nada arriesga nada gana,*" I hear Lala say. If I don't risk making an ass of myself, I'll never know the pleasure of holding a truffle from Alba. So I straighten myself to full height, inch my chin upward, and walk over to Chef Legrand.

For a moment, I casually linger next to him, inspecting some of the more inexpensive truffles on the table.

"Oh, hi there," I say, pretending to be surprised.

Chef Legrand glances down at me and smiles politely.

"Looking for truffles?" he asks. "Bernard here can help you."

Bernard shoots me a crooked smile from behind the table. "What can I get for you, madame?"

"No, I . . . I . . ." I stutter, lowering my eyes to the basket in his hands. "I already have my ingredients."

Come on Isa, big girl panties. I suck in a deep breath and go for it.

"I didn't mean to pry, but I overheard you talking about the Alba truffles."

Chef Legrand considers me for what feels like an eternity. His blue eyes pierce mine, narrowing as if he's trying some kind of mind trick. I stay very still and don't look away, my feet planted firmly on the sidewalk under me.

"Curious little thing, aren't you?" he mutters.

"It's just that . . . they are so rare," I explain.

"Yes," Chef Legrand says with a nod. "Yes, they are."

And then something like a little miracle happens; he passes the truffle basket into my hands. I take in a breath and peer at the irregularly shapped, knobby spheres. I bring the basket closer to my face and draw in the fragrant aroma. It's heavenly. Earthy and nutty, slightly garlicky with a deep musk. I am holding one of the most expensive and sought-after foods in the world. I gently slide one finger over their surface, tracing the uneven texture.

"Wow," I whisper, reluctantly passing them back to their owner.

"And the flavor . . ." Bernard muses, bringing his closed hand to his mouth and kissing his puckered fingers. *"Indimenticabile,"* he exclaims in Italian.

I look back at Chef Legrand, hoping for a translation.

"Unforgettable," he says with a hearty laugh.

I laugh too, in disbelief of this turn of events. I'm hanging out in a beautiful French market, on a glorious summer day, buying Alba truffles with a MOF. How did this happen?

Back at the restaurant, we quickly get to work on our dishes. Chef Legrand explains we can use some basic items from the pantry like butter and spices, but nothing that will distract from our three main ingredients.

"The spotlight must shine on the flavor of your ingredients. Simplicity with depth—this you must learn," he says, pacing around the kitchen.

I think of his "your life" advice and wonder if I'll ever be worthy of drinking 170-year-old champagne. What would that even taste like?

"Bon, get to work," he tells the class.

I fill a large pot with water and set it to a rolling boil. Separately, I plunge my trumpets of death into a cold bath to remove the grit before slicing them into delicate strands, then toss them in a hot pan with melted butter. They cook until they are soft and tender.

"Ah, beautiful." Chef Legrand materializes in front of my station. "Excellent choice of ingredients."

I'm thankful the heat coming off my stove masks the redness surging to my face. This is the first time since I arrived in this kitchen that a chef has said a kind word about my food. It's nice to know someone appreciates it. And a MOF, nonetheless. It doesn't get any better.

He watches as I drain the tagliatelle and toss it with a mixture of mushrooms and butter. I sprinkle grated nutmeg and white pepper, then coat the pasta with the Parmigiano-Reggiano until all the ingredients are integrated. My presentation is minimal. I select a plain white pasta bowl and sprinkle extra cheese on top.

Chef Legrand wastes no time grabbing a fork and digging into my dish—before I can even taste it. My heart has stopped beating inside my chest. How I continue to live and breathe defies the laws of human biology.

"Mademoiselle," he says after he's taken two full bites, "this deserves a glass of champagne." He winks at me, then turns to the class and says, "Someone found *l'inspiration!*"

I almost pass out. A few students grunt across the room, but it only adds to the pure joy swelling inside my chest. I glance at Snake Eyes. His full attention is on a filet, which anyone can see is on its way to being overdone.

Chef Legrand passes my dish around the class and makes everyone taste it.

"Quality ingredients. Beautiful combination. Lavish and simple at the same time. I could eat this entire dish," he says, taking another forkful.

My face is glowing so bright it could put out the sun. Newfound confidence explodes inside me. I can do this. I can get this apprenticeship. I'm so going to win.

The half-eaten pasta plate returns to my station, and I'm finally able to taste my own dish. The cheese and butter merged into a silky cream and the mushrooms add a hint of drama to the plate. Their smoky flavor is a perfect pairing with the Parmigiano-Reggiano.

Maybe my dish is not worth a special transcontinental trip, but at least it's worth a special ride on the bus.

After everyone has left, I stay behind to pack up yesterday's coq au vin leftovers and take them to Papi. Chef Troissant has yet to assign points on that dish or give us any clue on how we did.

On the way to the lockers, I pass her office. The door is slightly open, enough to reveal my crêpe cake sitting on her desk, half eaten. I mean, literally an entire half of the twelve-inch cake is gone. The smile I've been carting around since my pasta dish triumph only gets bigger.

My legs prance across the kitchen, toward the locker room so I can store my things before going home—no more sleeping in my apron.

I stop before entering. I can't see them, but I can hear Chef Legrand and Snake Eyes arguing. Chef Legrand keeps his voice above a whisper but I manage to piece together *cuillères, perdant,* and *embarras*—spoons, loser, and embarrassment.

I peer around the corner to catch a glimpse. Snake Eyes is staring at the floor, and his shoulders are so hunched over he looks a foot shorter.

I try to recall yesterday's spoon order, and I'm pretty certain Snake Eyes remains in second place, after Lucia. That girl may be lost in translation but her technique—dead chickens aside—is by far the best in the kitchen.

"Chef Troissant hates me," Snake Eyes tells the chef, sounding like a whiny five-year-old complaining about his teacher. "I'm the best in this kitchen. Everyone knows."

Holy macarons, could this guy be more full of himself?

"If you are the best, you should be number one—not second place. Second best is not worthy of my name," Chef Legrand hisses.

"I'll do whatever it takes," Snake Eyes says.

"Whatever it takes," Chef Legrand repeats like it's the family mantra. "The Spanish prodigy is in your way. But a little bird tells me she has no classical training. How can this be? How can *she* be number one? And keep your eye on that American girl."

Snake Eyes snorts in disgust. "Fields? Please, Father."

"That girl wants to win." Chef Legrand steps in closer. "Americans are nice until you get in their way. Then, they bring out the big guns."

At this point I decide to take my apron home with me. Not only am I annoyed with Snake Eyes's visions of his own grandeur, but this whole "whatever it takes" business is making me queasy. What exactly did Chef Legrand mean by it?

I've already surrendered most of a normal high school experience, time with my family, and romantic relationships. Is this not an indication I'm committed enough? What else is there to give?

Maybe Chef Legrand is right. Maybe I need to focus *more*. Be *more* creative. *More* determined. Take every and any opportunity to get ahead. Not a moment wasted.

Maybe it's time I bring out the big guns.

Chapter 14

The Real Chocolate Cookies

"No cooking today?" Diego asks as I walk onto the patio. It's Saturday morning, not a cloud in the sky, and almost eighty degrees outside. He's working his way through a plateful of poached eggs, toast, beans, tomatoes, cheese, and what looks like an entire slab of bacon.

"Just because I'm not cooking doesn't mean I'm not creating," I answer, twirling my hand next to my head in the manner of a mad scientist. "Something's always cooking up here."

"You got that right," he mumbles into his plate. He's sitting by the patio table with Beluga at his feet. The dog is gnawing on a piece of bacon.

I ignore him, returning to my morning goal. Nothing is going to ruin my good mood. I'm still reveling in the pasta dish success and the encouragement from Chef Legrand. As a reward, I'm allowing myself a little pool time this morning. It may not be the same as drinking a bottle of champagne found in a shipwreck but, for now, it'll have to do.

Chef Troissant is evaluating our progress over the weekend, and on Monday morning I'll know my new spoon standing. The thought of walking into the kitchen on Monday morning makes my stomach turn with anxiety. Week three will be decisive. *Whatever it takes to win.*

I will need something to set me apart—hence the thinking.

Lots of thinking. Even if I'm in the pool, I can still run though flavor combinations in my head.

For an additional burst of *l'inspiration*, tonight I'm meeting Lucia and Pippa for dinner at a traditional *bouchon Lyonnais*—complete with checkered tablecloths and sausages dangling from the ceiling.

"Let us know if we need to move. Wouldn't want to get in the way of your creative process or anything," Diego says sarcastically.

I look at him and make a face. "I'll let you know."

"Oh, I know you will." He snorts and bites into a piece of toast.

I smirk, refusing to allow his snotty mood to ruin my morning.

Looking at him, all I can think is how happy I am I didn't kiss Diego that night by the pool. What was I thinking?

He may be gorgeous, but from what I can surmise, unlike me, this guy has no ambition in life. None.

I unwrap the towel tied around my waist and toss it onto a lounger. Mom bought me a bold blood-orange-colored one-piece that highlights the bronze tones in my skin.

I'm not the bikini type—too many fleshy bits exposed. But this suit, with its low neckline and high-cut leg, is just as sexy.

I'm feeling so unusually confident that I reach for my pony-tail and let my hair down. It falls around my shoulders in waves.

As I walk into the pool, I wonder, is this is the kind of bathing suit—and body—a guy like Diego would find attractive?

I glance at him, and to my surprise he's staring at my midriff. He stops midbite on a slice of bacon before looking away, swallowing hard and clearing his throat.

I bite my bottom lip, suppressing a smile.

Watching him looking at me is a guilty pleasure at odds with the die-hard feminist part of my brain that insists my body is not an object to be sexualized for the amusement of the male gaze.

I put the thought aside for a moment. It's my body, after all. I can do with it whatever I want.

And it's those very thoughts, of what I would like to do with it, that make my cheeks turn hot with embarrassment.

I really need to get my head out of the gutter.

I've never been so glad to be wearing these big cover-half-your-face reflective sunglasses. He can't see me sexualizing *him*.

I take my time wading into the water, then slide forward and swim the length of the pool. It's cool and refreshing.

"Are you getting in?" I ask, folding my arms over the edge. I try to make it sound more like a question than an invitation.

"I'm good," he says.

"That's right—the chlorine thing. I forgot. Is that really a thing?"

"Yes, it's a thing."

"I think you're scared," I say. He slowly shakes his head, but a grin appears on his lips. "I think you don't know how to swim."

"You really got me there," he says dismissively.

"Come on, what is it? I want to know."

He sets down his fork and turns in his chair to fully face me, his gaze shuttered.

"I've been in a pool for more than five hours a day since I was four. I've inhaled enough chlorine to open a new hole in the ozone layer. So yes, I guess you can call it an allergy."

"Five hours?" I ask.

"That's what it takes. I logged eighteen thousand meters a week on average," he adds.

"I have no idea what that means."

"A lot of pointless back and forth. So, to answer your question, I know how to swim. I just choose not to."

He returns to his breakfast, folding a slice of bacon and stuffing it into his mouth.

Beluga walks to the edge of the pool, reaches over with his head, and tries to lick my face.

"I think your dog is thirsty." I move my head back, just in time to avoid his wet tongue. "It's all that bacon you're feeding him. It can't be good for him."

"He likes it," Diego says, pouring water into Beluga's bowl. "*Vente, Beluguita,*" he coos in Spanish.

Beluga follows Diego's hand into the bowl and drinks until there's nothing left. Diego adds more water and gives him another piece of bacon.

"Why did you quit?" I ask. "The swimming, I mean."

"Because I hated the person I was turning into," he says, turning back toward the table. He loads a fork with eggs and beans and takes a bite.

"What kind of person?" I ask, genuinely curious.

"The kind who didn't care about anything but winning. I had no life outside of school or swimming. Not that it mattered much. Friends and competition don't really go together. It's lonely at the top—right?"

"The top?" I eye him skeptically.

"I made Olympic trials last year."

It takes me a moment to realize what he's saying. Was he really that good? Who would give that up?

"And you quit?" I prod. "Just like that?"

He nods. "Just like that." He drops his fork onto the empty plate and pushes it away before taking a small espresso cup between his fingers.

"That's the craziest thing I've ever heard anyone do."

"It was the best day of my life. I'm not even kidding." He chuckles to himself, bringing the cup to his lips.

"Is this why you won't call your dad?"

"Are you always this nosy?" he teases.

"To be fair, it wasn't like you and Margo were whispering. I mean, all of Bessenay probably heard you."

"Uh, yes," he concedes. He sips on his espresso and sets the cup down in front of him. Then turns his upper body toward me and says, "Swimming was his thing, not mine. Now he wants me to go to Cambridge for economics, like he did. Me, a finance guy . . ." He shakes his head and shrugs. "I only applied because I thought I wouldn't get in. I never intended to go. And I certainly never intended to continue swimming once I went to university. I'm so done."

"All that work for nothing?" I tilt my head to the side, as if somehow a different angle will help me make sense of his decision. I have no idea what it takes to get into Cambridge, but at a minimum his grades must be excellent. And I can only guess that not many people make Olympic trials. And based on what he's saying, he's worked practically his whole life to achieve these things. I can't imagine ever making his decision. I've worked too hard, come too far, to let it all go. And what's more, I'm not a quitter.

"I don't get it," I say.

"Not many people do."

Papi saunters onto the patio before I can ask Diego exactly how one gives up on life at eighteen. And what exactly he intends to do next.

"My two favorite people," Papi says as he approaches. He's wearing his preferred cherry farmer outfit—worn jeans, plaid shirt, and a brown felt Stetson hat he bought when we took a family trip to Idaho a few years ago. Mom picked it out.

"Hope you don't have plans for the rest of the day," Papi says.

"You're looking at my plans," I reply, treading water.

"A couple of cherry pickers came down with the flu, and we're short a few hands. Could use your help," he says in his best Mr. Midwest Nice Guy tone.

"I have to prepare for Monday," I say.

"Aren't you off all weekend? You can prepare tomorrow," he argues, impatiently.

Diego gathers his things. "I'll go change," he tells Papi. "Happy to help."

I give him the stink eye as he walks off. Now I'm left looking like a jerk for not wanting to pick cherries for the rest of the day.

"Next week is gonna be brutal," I say.

"Isa, honey, you've been spending every waking hour on this . . ."

"Because that's what it takes," I immediately retort, thinking of Chef Legrand's advice. "I need time to think of new recipes. Thinking is part of the process, you know?"

"I'm just asking for a few hours, Isa. Margo and I need a little help around here. The baby is coming soon, and the room isn't ready yet. We have a lot on our plates right now." He wipes sweat from his brow, even though it's not really that hot out. It's still weird seeing him like this—dirt under his fingernails, hair and beard grown out. This new "rugged style" makes him look old and worn out. Suddenly, I feel sorry for him.

"Fine," I say, stepping out of the pool. "But I'm not wearing overalls."

He hands me my towel and smiles.

"I'll make you a deal," he says. "You can keep all the cherries you want. Maybe you'll have enough for a pie. No flambés, though."

"So funny," I say, wrapping myself in the towel. "Is this deal supposed to benefit me or you?"

He throws his arm over my shoulders and walks me inside.

"Well, you said you had to practice for school, right? I'm just trying to help you out, honey."

"Right . . ." I wriggle from under him and he stops moving.

He stares at me and I can see the confusion and hurt in his eyes.

"I'm not making her pies, Papi. I can't." A knot forms in the back of my throat.

Papi's warm hand lands on my shoulder.

"Isa," he says in a raspy voice. "I miss her too." He blinks a few times, and I pray it's not tears I see glinting in his eyes. Papi never cries. He bears his emotions with an impassive expression that used to drive Mom nuts. "I wish you came with subtitles!" she'd yell at him in a heated argument. But I don't need subtitles to see the toll of grief on his shoulders. It weighs him down, more than he'll ever admit. *This*, he can't walk away from.

"I can't," I repeat, fighting back my own tears. I step back, pulling away from his touch even though I want him to hold me. I want us to cry together for everything we've lost. I want him to cradle me in his arms and tell me this all-consuming sense of loss will eventually go away and we'll be a family again.

I clear my throat and the words "I'll meet you in the orchard" come out instead. I walk away, angry at my inability to find the right thing to say. When confronted with this asteroid-sized ball of guilt, grief, and anger burning a hole inside my chest, words fail me every time.

***

I wait until Diego and Papi leave to come down from my room.

The beauty about baking, I've learned over the years, is that it serves as a great substitute for therapy. Today calls for an emergency session.

I open the fridge and pull out a tub of chocolate chip cookie dough, made with the chocolate discs I bought at Pâtisserie Lulu. They were the perfect size, flavor, and consistency. Jakub is sure to love these. I want him to have the best possible, ultimate chocolate chip cookie.

The French, I've realized, take the chocolate chip cookie for granted. They use some chocolate chip aberrations they call *pépites de chocolat*—tiny, sad, wrinkled chocolate pieces that resemble old raisins—as substitutes for the American counterpart.

Many people think chocolate chip cookies are the bottom rung of the baking ladder, but that's an amateur's assessment. Anyone can make hard cookies with sparse chocolate chips. It takes a master to bake a chewy cookie with the right amount of crisp around the edges and enough chocolate to please even the most discerning chocolate connoisseur.

In this case, the master recipe belongs to MOF pastry chef Jacques Torres, who coincidentally now lives in America. He once taught a day course on just these cookies at the French Pastry School in Chicago. Of course I went.

There, I learned that chocolate discs are preferred to chips. They help spread the chocolate goodness throughout the cookie. And most important, the dough must rest in the fridge for at least thirty-six hours to allow the gluten to loosen and to meld the dry ingredients with the wet.

Every time I pull one of these trays from the oven, I feel like a winner.

I pack the freshly baked cookies in a tin and head to the orchard. I ride my bike there, guided by the sound of a Polish Roma song. The music plays in the background as the cherry pickers glide up and down ladders propped up on trees.

I lean my bike against a tractor, where Diego is loading buckets of cherries onto the bed.

"I thought you weren't cooking today?" he says, eyeing the tin box in my hands.

"It's not cooking, it's baking," I say, searching for Jakub. "There's a difference."

He raises an eyebrow, questioning my statement.

"It's relaxing," I add.

He shakes his head. "I'm curious as to what you actually do for fun."

"What do you mean? Baking *is* fun."

"Exactly," he says sardonically. Then reaches for the lid. "Anything good?"

I move the tin away. "These are meant for someone." I spot Jakub playing with his toy truck under the shade of a tree.

"Trying to lure a farmhand?" Diego teases.

"Jealous much?"

"I'm not gonna lie. I am a little jealous of whoever is getting those." He glances at the tin, but in the process his eyes travel up my body in a way that leaves me gasping. Where the heck did all the air go? We're standing outside for crying out loud!

"I, um . . . I . . . I guess you can have one," I say, reaching inside the tin.

"Gracias," he says, biting into the cookie. "These are amazing."

"Yeah, I know," I say. "I got this special chocolate."

He scoffs and shakes his head.

"What?" I ask.

"You really need to work on your thank-you skills." He puts the last bite into his mouth and goes back to work.

When I finally say thank you, he's too far up the tree to hear. I guess I'm so used to having my food critiqued that it's hard not to instantly explain myself.

The moment Jakub sees me, he drops his truck and runs to meet me. He takes my hands and leads me to his blanket under the shade of a tree.

I sit next to him, give him the tin, and point to the piece of paper that reads *chocolate chip cookies* in Polish.

He smiles and jumps up and down, clapping his little hands and singing the Polish word for cookies, *ciasteczka*. I laugh hard, taking in the pure joy on his face.

When he finally opens the lid, his eyes widen at the mountain of cookies inside. He slowly reaches for one and brings it to his mouth.

The smile on his face is worth all the chocolate chip cookies in the entire universe. His eyes immediately close—a tell-all sign of culinary ecstasy. He devours one cookie in three bites and pulls out two more—one in each hand. I kick myself for not bringing him some milk so he could have the full experience.

"*Les meilleurs ciasteczka*," he tells me in a jumble of French and Polish.

"The *best* cookies? Wow, Jakub. I am honored." I add a *merci*, thinking of Diego. I'm fully capable of saying thank you.

"*Pour plus tard*." He can have the rest later, I tell him, and close the tin before he eats them all in one sitting. These cookies are highly addictive; I know from experience.

Jakub trades me the tin for a kiss and runs off to his parents.

"I'll have you know, I am not opposed to fighting a little boy for that tin." Diego sneaks up behind me.

"He can jump in a pool if he wants to get away from you," I hit back.

"That's a low blow," he says, amused. "That was nice of you."

I force my eyes to meet his. "Thank you."

"See, that wasn't so hard, was it?" His face breaks into a smile.

"Don't push your luck."

He sighs and shakes his head. "Why are you always so difficult?"

I'm stunned. "I'm not difficult," I'm about to say, but then he suddenly takes hold of my hand and I'm left speechless. His touch is so casual and unreserved that it startles me. Why is he holding my hand? And why does it feel like it's the most natural thing in the world?

"Come up this tree with me," he says, pushing me onto a ladder.

I climb first. He meets me at the top on his own ladder. For a while we pick fruit in silence, tossing cherries into the empty buckets attached to the top of the ladders. It's menial work, but something about it brings me an unexpected sense of satisfaction. I get lost in the folk music swelling from the ground below, with the festive jingling and rattling of a tambourine. My body sways from branch to branch as I reach for new clusters of cherries.

Diego climbs down and repositions his ladder across from mine. Now we're facing each other. My eyes keep wandering in his direction, even though I'm trying hard to keep my focus on the tree. There's something captivating about the way the muscles on his arm tense as he reaches farther into the boughs. His brow is furrowed in deep concentration. When he catches me staring at him, he smiles. My breath catches. I hold his gaze and smile back.

"Do you have plans tonight?" he asks. He leans on the side of his ladder, closing the distance between us. I do the same. As a result, we end up hidden inside the canopy, completely covered by leafy branches.

"I'm meeting Lucia and Pippa in Lyon for dinner," I say, debating whether I should ask him to join us. Mostly, I fear he will end up embroiled in one of those rapid Spanish conversations with Lucia that I find impossible to keep up with. I don't want to sit on the sidelines wishing I knew every detail being said—wishing I knew every detail about him. But then I gaze into those deep brown eyes and see an unguarded openness that takes me by surprise. It's as if I could reach out and touch him without moving an inch. All my resolve leaves me.

"Do you want to come?" I ask, going against my own qualms.

"Yeah, that sounds fun."

"I'm leaving at seven. Papi said I can take the car, so just meet me up front."

"I'll be there."

"Great," I say, tamping down any excitement in my voice. This is not a date, after all. We're just agreeing to meet at a certain time and drive together to a discussed location, where we will meet other people. There is nothing datelike about the evening. A date would constitute us being alone, doing date things, like kissing and such. There will be no kissing tonight. None.

By late afternoon, we have picked a gazillion buckets of cherries, enough for a lifetime supply of cherry pies.

"Feels good to do something with my hands," Diego says when we load the last bucket onto the trailer bed. He has patches of sweat and dirt all over his T-shirt and face. But under all the filth, there's a lightness about him that wasn't there before. Even his shoulders seem to hang looser.

Diego and Papi drive the tractor back to the warehouse. I take my bundle of cherries and ride my bike back to the house.

As I pedal through the fields feeling proud of the day's work, I give myself permission to muse *what if*—what if it was a real date? What if there was a kiss?

Chapter 15

Fried Cow Stomach Is Not Sexy

We push open the glass door and enter the bouchon. Inside, we're greeted by a full house. A soundtrack of French conversations, accordion music, and laughter fills what little space is unoccupied.

"Do you see any open tables?" Lucia asks.

I scan the small restaurant. It is everything I expected—checkered tablecloths, a collection of ceramic pigs congregated by the bar, clusters of framed pictures, walls covered with old newspaper clippings and ancient posters.

"We may have to share a table," Pippa says. "They do that here."

"*Bienvenue!*" A blonde woman welcomes us with open arms. "Table for four, oui?" she asks, smiling.

We nod and follow her to a booth in the back of the restaurant. I walk slowly past the other tables, trying to get a sense of the menu. I recognize the braised calf head in vinegar and the blood sausages with apples. There is little to no thought for presentation. The plates are mostly utilitarian, a mere means to gather and serve the food.

Pippa slides into the booth first, while Diego, Lucia, and I awkwardly linger in the aisle. I want to sit next to him without it looking obvious.

Diego slides in first, sitting across from Pippa. But it's Lucia who sweeps in and grabs the seat next to him. There's nothing subtle about the way her arm presses against his, or the lack of space between their bodies. She's not worried about being obvious at all.

A glance passes between Diego and me across the table. He shrugs as if to say, *It's not my fault.* My head shakes slightly to say *It is.*

Lucia makes some joke in Spanish and Diego laughs. *So funny!*

Why did I think this could work? Why did I go against my own instinct? I should've never asked him to come.

"Care to share?" I say, forcing a smile.

"It's not funny in English," Lucia says.

Suddenly, the tension inside the booth feels like cold grease, so dense you could cut through it.

"I love the napkins," Pippa says too enthusiastically. The cloth napkins are hastily folded on our plates. A custom checkered print features a pig suspended over the name of the restaurant, Café des Fédérations.

When the waitress arrives it's a welcome relief. She rattles off a list of what are considered classic bouchon dishes: pike fish dumplings, pork sausage in red wine sauce, fried tripe, and cake of chicken liver.

I read on a travel blog that these dishes date back to the sixteenth century, when bouchons mostly existed as stops to feed the postmen traveling across the country. Later, in the seventeenth century, the sizable food portions nourished the masses of new industrial-era workers. This café is more than a restaurant— it's a taste of history.

"We should try a few things," Pippa says. "Maybe we start with the house appetizer?"

The waitress nods. "Will you be having wine?" she tentatively asks.

We decide to order one bottle of the house wine. I mean, the wine *is* part of the French experience.

"Diego, what have you been up to?" Pippa asks.

"Not much really." He shrugs. "I've been helping James—Isa's dad—do some work on their cherry farm."

"I love cherries. I love farms," Lucia interjects. "My grandfather was an olive farmer."

"Where, exactly?" Diego asks.

"Andalucía. I grew up on his farm. On the days I didn't have school I would help pick olives. He taught me how to make the best olive oil. I even know how to infuse it with citrus and herbs." Lucia has turned toward Diego so that she's basically talking only to him. It's strange to see this side of her. It makes me want to pull her hair out by the roots. I don't care how good she is in the kitchen—she's being a real shrew tonight.

I turn to Pippa and say, "I grew up on a farm too. In Kansas. My grandma had an apple orchard and chickens. She taught me how to make pies."

"I grew up in London," Pippa deadpans. "My Jamaican granma hated cooking . . . and baking. She's more of an eater." She chuckles to herself, then tosses her head to the side and asks, "I thought you grew up in Chicago?"

"I spent the summers in Kansas." I bite my lip, hating this competitive vibe when we're supposed to be enjoying ourselves. "Shouldn't we be looking at the menu?"

"Oh, we lived on the farm year-round." Lucia clearly feels the need to clarify the extent of her farm experience. "My parents have a few acres where they grow all sorts of stuff."

"In Barcelona?" I ask curiously; I'd thought she was a city girl like me and Pippa.

"Isa, we have farms in Barcelona. Well, technically, in the outskirts," she explains as if this should be obvious. "I'm a farm girl at heart." She giggles.

What is she doing?

If she's trying to impress Diego, she'll have to try harder. He's been a farmhand for only a week. It's not like he grew up toiling the fields with a horse-drawn plow.

Our wine and appetizers arrive. The spread of dishes takes over the table.

"All right, ladies, please explain," Diego says, reaching for the bread basket first.

Pippa points at each item. "Black sausage, beet salad, lentils with cerverlas sausage in mayonnaise dressing—it's an acquired taste—board terrine, and Lyonnaise charcuterie. Bon appétit!" She raises her wine glass and we join in by clinking our glasses.

I take one sip of my wine but it's too bitter, so I set it down.

"You have to try this," Diego tells me, dropping a piece of black sausage onto my plate. "Have it with the bread."

"I'll have one also," Lucia says, lifting her plate so Diego can place a piece of sausage on it. "Gracias," she says. "This feels like home." Then she launches into some story in Spanish that I guess is meant only for Diego. I'm having trouble translating some words I've never heard, so I decide to completely ignore whatever is happening on the other side of the table and just focus on my food.

"This is bloody great, no pun intended," Pippa says, biting into the black sausage.

I follow her lead. The meat is light and creamy, almost like a mousse.

"Seriously, this is the best sausage I've ever had," I tell Pippa. "What do they put in this thing?"

"Spinach, I think," she says.

"Really?" I quickly finish my entire portion.

I ask our waitress for water and push aside my glass of wine.

"Are you going to drink that?" Lucia asks. Her own wine glass is already empty.

"Nope, help yourself," I say, giving her the glass and instantly regretting it. Her eyes are taking on a glassy sheen and the space between her and Diego seems to have narrowed to nonexistent. Diego is squeezed between the wall and Lucia, who is all but sitting on his lap.

The scene is beyond annoying. I scan the room, counting

the sausages dangling from the ceiling and reading the vintage posters on the walls.

"Are we sharing?" Pippa asks. "I want to try a few things."

"I'll share with you," I tell her.

"Looks like those two will be sharing," Pippa says with a snort. But I don't think it's funny. In fact, none of this is funny.

Lucia has downed her second glass of wine in what must be record time. The result is her arms have transformed into tentacles.

What. Is. She. Doing?

My eyes cut to Diego, and I can see he looks as uncomfortable as I feel.

"Maybe we should order some food," he tells me. "And no more wine for her."

"I've never seen anyone get pissed so fast," Pippa says.

Now, Lucia is *only* speaking Spanish. She slurs some version of "don't be a party pooper" and reaches for what is left of the wine bottle, which thankfully is empty.

The waitress returns and we place our orders. Lucia can't make up her mind, so we ask the waitress to bring her a soup.

"Stew of pork cheeks?" the waitress asks.

"Perfect," I say, glaring at Lucia, whose own cheek is leaning against Diego's shoulder.

The waitress leaves, and for a while we sit in an uncomfortable silence.

"So . . . Pippa, how do you like the culinary school?" Diego leans forward, trying to extricate himself from Lucia.

"I guess it's harder than I thought it would be," she says.

"Oh, please." Lucia waves her off. "Piece of cake," she says, snapping her fingers in midair.

At least now we know what kind of drunk Lucia is—an obnoxious one.

"Lucia is currently at the top of the class," Pippa explains to Diego. "Her cooking skills far exceed her drinking skills."

"I am the best cook." Lucia drapes her arms over Diego. "Maybe sometime I cook for you, eh?"

"We already have a resident chef, but thanks," he tells her. He glances at me with a half smile.

"I can make you a paella. Or a gazpacho. Or estofat de pop i patata. Whatever you want, I can make it," she says into his ear.

"I think I need to get some air," Diego says. "Excuse me." He gently moves her out of the booth, then steps outside.

"Maybe you should have some coffee," Pippa tells Lucia.

"I'm fine," she says.

"You're being stupid," Pippa says curtly.

Lucia considers us for a second. "You're just jealous," she says.

"Now I really know you're pissed." Pippa laughs to herself.

I wave to our waitress and order the strongest coffee they have.

"This is why I don't have girlfriends. They're always jealous of me," Lucia says to no one. "I thought coming here would be different."

"We're not jealous of you," I respond.

She looks at me intently. "You know what your problem is?"

"I didn't know I had a problem." I awkwardly chuckle, trying to keep things light. But being an expert on conversation train wrecks, I know this one is already off the tracks.

"Your spoon is at the bottom, *that* is a problem," she explains, grabbing a spoon from the table. "And you cook like you're trying too hard to be French. You're not."

"My mom *is* French," I remind her.

"You're as French as me or Pippa here." She points at Pippa with the back of her spoon.

"Leave me out of this," Pippa says, stacking empty plates on the table.

"I have dual citizenship. I could be a MOF someday," I say. "Besides, all the top chefs are classically trained. Everyone knows that."

"Exactly. *This* is your problem." She redirects the spoon toward me. "You want to be like everyone."

I stare at her in disbelief. Is this what she's thought of me all along? Then why even pretend to be my friend?

Troissant was right. This is not a team sport.

I edge forward, open my mouth to say something . . . anything, but then Diego returns.

"What did I miss?" he asks, sliding into the booth across from me.

Our food arrives and the moment for a comeback passes. I lean my head against the leather upholstery in defeat.

"Try this first." Lucia lifts a piece of fried tripe between her fingers. "It's tripa frita." She brings the tripe to Diego's mouth and feeds it to him.

Would it be rude to leave halfway through dinner? Let's face it, I'm not the kind of girl who can make eating a cow's stomach look sexy.

"Oh! I have an idea. We should go dancing," Lucia squeaks, wrapping her arm around Diego and forcing him to sway.

"Let's eat first," he says. "I'm starving and you need something to soak up that wine."

Lucia pouts. "You don't want to go dancing with me?"

"I'm up for whatever you ladies want to do." He unfolds a napkin over his lap and scans the dishes on the table.

"This looks amazing." Pippa reaches for a fork and digs in first.

I load up my plate with the flathead quenelle and drizzle crayfish sauce over the puff pastry. Then add some chitterling sausage on the side.

"Are you okay?" Diego asks. His hand reaches across the table and touches mine. The sides of our palms press lightly against each other until my insides feel as mushy as the quenelle swimming on my plate. Our eyes meet briefly, and my stomach flips—the same as that night by the pool with the ukulele.

"You need to have another one," Lucia interrupts, holding a tripa frita in front of Diego's face again.

"I'm fine," I say, pulling my hand away.

Diego grabs the tripa frita from Lucia's hand before she can put it into his mouth.

"You have that look on your face," he tells me. "I know it well by now."

"I'm fine," I repeat forcefully.

Last-place spoons don't get the apprenticeships or the cute guys. Clearly, both are reserved for the winner. And clearly this is not a date.

We get home shortly after midnight.

"Thanks for the invite," Diego says, putting the car in park. "It was interesting . . ."

After the disaster dinner, we went to Le Lavoir Public, where a guest DJ from Berlin packed the club. Our night of dancing crashed to an epic end when Lucia accidentally spilled her drink on another drunk girl. They almost got into a fight, so security kicked us out.

"Maybe next time you and I can—" Diego stops midsentence when my phone dings with a string of incoming texts.

I pull it out and read the messages off the screen.

"Looks like Lucia crashed at Pippa's apartment," I say, tapping on a photo of Lucia passed out on Pippa's couch. I show the phone screen to Diego, who snickers.

"Let's never do that again," he says.

"No kidding."

"So," he says, rubbing the back of his neck. "What are your plans after the summer? You know, if you don't get the apprenticeship. What are you gonna do?"

"What do you mean?"

"Your dad said you still have to finish high school. Right? Are you going back to America?"

"The apprenticeship will count toward my graduating credits," I explain, knowing full well that's not what he's asking. "It's my senior year. Like a year abroad."

"Yeah, but you know . . ." he says hesitantly. "I know you're working your butt off, but only one person is getting this. And sometimes these things have nothing to do with talent."

My eyes narrow, as if to say, *Get to the point.*

He stammers. "I'm not saying you're gonna loose. All I'm saying is, what else would you like to do?"

"Huh?" Nothing about his question registers an answer. Did I not prepare for this outcome? What's my plan B? Oh right, I don't have one.

I blink a few times, trying hard to think through the mental fog. What does my future look like outside of that kitchen?

A deep, dark abyss stares back at me. There's nothing. I can't see myself doing anything else. This is it. This is all I have.

"If you could do anything else, what would it be?" he presses. "What would make you happy?"

I shrug. I don't have an answer.

Chapter 16

Snail Stew

On Monday, I'm the first one to arrive at Chef Troissant's kitchen. It's the start of week three and the pressure to excel is mounting.

If my spoon is still at the bottom of the rack, I want to be all alone when I see it.

I stand in front of the rankings, drawing deep, long breaths. "Thirteen," I murmur, scanning the bottom of the rack. It's not there. I step forward, searching for those two numbers, one and three written together.

When I finally find it, my first reaction is to raise both fists into the air and repeatedly jump.

I laugh and jump. Jump and laugh. Both fists still raised, I twirl in a big circle and extend my arms in triumph.

Number thirteen has jumped to the middle of the rack. Halfway there.

Yay, me!

This could only mean that she loved Mom's coq au vin and my mille crêpe cake. I would hug Chef Troissant for this, but I'm guessing she's not the huggy-huggy type, so instead I hug myself. And my spoon jump also means I got serious points from Chef Legrand and my "exceptional" pasta dish.

I bask in my own sense of achievement as I don my uniform—which I finally traded out for the right size—and tie on my apron. I pin my hair into a bun and position the toque over my head, not a hair out of place. I gaze at my reflection in the mirror and stand a little taller. Today, I *look* the part of a winner.

The other students slowly fill the kitchen. Everyone's first stop is the spoon rack. The reactions are a jumble of gasps and murmurs in various languages.

I take to my station and methodically work in silence. I sharpen my knives and refill my spices—first the fleur de sel, then the pepper mill. The tiny black peppercorns flow into the container one by one until it is full. I screw the grinder back on tightly and adjust the coarseness mechanism to fine, the way Chef Troissant likes it.

Lucia and Pippa arrive together ten minutes before the start of class. Pippa and I exchange a nod from across the room. She gives me a thumbs-up when she sees my spoon has jumped to sixth place. Her spoon is right under mine. Lucia's remains in first place and Snake Eyes's in second.

"We have to go out again," Lucia says as she approaches her station. "We didn't get to dance." She pulls her apron over her head and smiles. "That was kinda crazy, huh?"

"Um-hum," I say with a nod.

"I promise I'm not usually like that." She half smiles awkwardly.

Like what? An overpossessive, maniac drunk idiot pawing all over Diego? A spiteful wench, giving me backhanded insults? Or a sloppy drunk getting us kicked out of a club?

Lala used to say, "If you don't have anything good to say, *mejor no digas nada.*"

I nod, then turn to my mise en place. "I'm kinda busy here."

"Oh, sorry," she says, turning to her station and suddenly very focused on retying her apron strings.

When Chef Troissant makes her big entrance, I'm ready. In fact, I'm more than ready.

"Alors, today we will commence preparations for the final examinations that will take place in one week," she announces. "The final exam counts for fifty percent of your overall scores."

She waits for the nervous whispers to die down. "Today we will prepare one dish so you understand the process. I will give you instructions, which you must follow precisely."

Her helper hands every student a pencil and a blank sheet of paper.

"This is a very traditional method of examination. The dishes are technically demanding, and you have a set time to prepare your dish," she explains. "Half of the challenge is craft. The other half is mental. Who will break under pressure?" Her eyes bore into the class, but I feel like she's only watching me.

I will not break under pressure. My jaw tightens and I grip the pencil hard between my fingers.

"You will have two hours to prepare a first course. When time is up, your dish must be plated and ready to be judged. Alors," she says, "fricassée d'escargots."

I transcribe her instructions verbatim, feeling like I've been training for this moment for two weeks.

"Plate four escargots on a thirty-centimeter moon plate. Position three oignon perlés blancs in the moon center. Top with one red chanterelle mushroom. Add four pieces of lardon positioned between the escargots—no more, no less. Pour four spoonfuls of fricassée broth over the escargots. Finish with a five-centimeter slice of chargrilled baguette balanced on the red chanterelle." She pauses and scans the room. Half the students' faces are stricken with panic. A silent prayer hangs in the middle of the room: *Please repeat the instructions.*

But all she says is, "Alors, you may begin." Then she turns and walks away, a sadistic smile on her lips.

I read the instructions five times before my scribble and the mishmash of languages starts to make sense.

"Did she say to use beurre blanc?" Lucia whispers. "After the four escargots . . . I didn't catch that."

I stammer. A tiny voice in the back of my mind says, "three white pearl onions," but the words don't form aloud. Instead, I give her a silent nod.

"Weird. She wants white butter sauce on a fricassée?"

I shrug and press my lips tight against each other. My stomach churns with guilt but I ignore it.

"Then I'll make the best beurre blanc she's ever had," Lucia says. I watch her walk toward the pantry with the confidence of champions—a confidence I'm about to strip away.

What are you doing?

I put down my knife and consider telling her I was mistaken. *This is no way to win*, I tell myself.

But the remorse lasts all of half a second. I think of how insignificant she made me feel last night. "You want to be like everyone," she said—the worst insult you can hurl at a chef. And then she practically threw herself at Diego.

My Diego!

Okay, Isa. Dial it back. Where the heck did that come from?

You need to keep your eye on the prize: the apprenticeship. NOT Diego.

I glance at the spoon rack and see the shiny first place position staring back at me—daring me not to make it mine. One year in a three-Michelin-starred kitchen and the consummation of everything I've been killing myself for. It will be absolute proof I have the chops to make it as a chef—even if I wasn't born in France to culinary royalty.

Whatever it takes.

So I ignore the unease and stuff down the guilt. Now is not the time to be a Goody Two-shoes.

Whatever it takes, I repeat to myself as I slice into the chanterelles, feeling like they'll turn my hands red.

The two hours given for the assignment fly by. We all work in silence in a kind of tunnel vision that only adds to the sense of isolation in this kitchen.

When the time is up, we set our dishes next to our numbers on the kitchen island.

Lucia's face drops as she notices the broth on everyone else's plate. She glances at me, and I look away.

If she asks why I didn't correct her, I could just say I misheard the question. It was an innocent mistake—it happens, right? I mean, the kitchen is such a noisy place. She can't expect me to have perfect hearing, for crying out loud!

"What is this?" Chef Troissant picks up Lucia's dish and probes it with a spoon. She dips the tip of her spoon onto the white butter sauce on the plate and brings it to her mouth. *"Beurre blanc?"* she asks to no one. "Whose dish is this?"

At first no one says anything, but after an unbearably long pause, Lucia raises her hand.

"I want everyone to taste this," Chef Troissant instructs the class. "Alors, everyone, bring your spoon. Have a taste."

Lucia's face goes from terrified to pleased. Her cheeks have taken on a rosy glow. My face probably looks green by now—I feel so nauseous.

I hesitantly take the plate and taste the sauce, then pass it on to the next person. The thick butter drops like a bowling ball inside my stomach.

I glance at Lucia. She reminds me of one of those sacrificial virgins about to get tossed into a vat of scalding water. I want to preemptively apologize, but what could I possibly say?

Hey, sorry for sabotaging your dish. But let's face it, you had it coming. Not much of an apology, I guess.

"Everyone had some?" Chef Troissant asks the class. "Bon, please, Mademoiselle García, tell the class when exactly did the broth for le fricassée d'escargots change to beurre blanc?" Chef Troissant pauses long enough for everyone to sense the air around us has stopped moving. "Is this the Spanish version?" she asks disdainfully. "Or did you come up with this all on your own?"

Chef Troissant waits for an answer, but Lucia is stunned into silence. The glow on her face has transformed into a sheen of sweat.

Chef Troissant clicks her tongue as she picks at the plate,

moving pieces of food around. "And where exactly are your three white pearl onions? Did the snails eat them?"

Snake Eyes snorts into his hand.

At this point I wish I could become invisible.

Lucia's eyes cut in my direction, a move that is not lost on Chef Troissant.

"Mademoiselle Fields cannot help you this time," Chef Troissant snaps. She steps closer to Lucia's station and slowly enunciates, "Three *oignons perlés blancs* in the moon center. Was that not clear enough for you?"

"Je suis désolée," Lucia mumbles, her bottom lip quivering.

"If you cannot follow my instructions, you will not succeed in this kitchen. I don't care how well you can cook. Do you understand?" Chef Troissant takes Lucia's plate and tosses the whole thing—plate and all—into the garbage bin. My worst nightmare.

My mouth fills with saliva and I honestly think I'm going to puke. I suck in a deep breath and then another, and another.

"If I ask for fricassée d'escargots with three white pearl onions, I want a fricassée d'escargots with three white pearl onions. In any kitchen, you would be fired. In a three-Michelin kitchen, the chef would put your head through that wall," she spits.

The silence that follows is deafening.

Chef Troissant steps in front of my dish and asks, "Should I even bother with yours?"

My legs wobble under me, and my stomach is so queasy I can barely look at my own plate.

Chef Troissant grabs a snail shell between her fingers and pulls out the escargot with a fork. She brings it to her mouth and chews.

"Good depth of flavor," she says after she swallows.

"I did a quick wine and garlic marinade," I manage to explain. My back is so stiff, it feels like it's made of quick-dry cement.

Chef Troissant pushes aside the chargrilled baguette to uncover the three white pearl onions and the chanterelle mushroom in the center of the plate. If she is pleased by my presentation, she doesn't show it.

She takes a spoon and tastes the broth. "A little more salt next time," is all she says before moving on to Snake Eyes.

When she is done scrutinizing our dishes, it becomes evident only Snake Eyes and I followed the full instructions. Everyone else lost marks on taste or presentation. But it was Lucia who got the worst of it by leaving out an ingredient and forgoing the broth.

At the end of the day, I snatch a glance at Lucia. I can almost feel how hard she is trying to hold it together.

You need to say something.

Before I let myself make that mistake, I rush out of the kitchen, tear off my uniform, and chuck it into my locker. I shut the door and rest my forehead against the cold metal surface. My eyelids shut tight, wincing at a sudden ache in the pit of my stomach.

You need to say something.

Behind me, someone enters the locker room, clapping slowly. I turn around to find Snake Eyes ambling toward me.

"Well done," he says, pressing his shoulder against my locker.

My eyebrows furrow in confusion.

"I underestimated you," he adds.

"What are you talking about?" I zip my backpack closed and get ready to leave.

"Drop the act. You know what you did. I heard the whole thing."

Snake Eyes towers over me, forcing me to look up to meet his eyes.

"First you pretend to be her friend," he says, "and then, when she least expects it, you plunge the knife into her back." He laughs—a dark, harsh laugh coming from somewhere deep inside of him as he mimics the act he's just described. "I can't wait to see what you have in store for me."

"Please, don't flatter yourself," I say, throwing my bag over my shoulder.

"Just know that what goes around, comes around," he says like a curse as he exits the locker room.

I follow him out, where Pippa is standing by the door.

Her face is crumpled into what I can only guess is disappointment. She looks away when she sees me, turns around, and leaves.

It dawns on me then: I've become Barbara.

I am the devil.

I'm going to be sick.

What have I done?

Chapter 17

Baby Food

"Can I help?"

The baby's room is half-covered in drop cloths and plastic sheeting. Papi is painting the walls a shade of yellow called Lemon Delight.

"Brushes are in the bucket," Papi says. He turns down the music playing in the background—some Bruce Springsteen song that was popular three decades ago.

Margo is assembling a hot air balloon mobile that includes a baby giraffe and an elephant floating inside tiny baskets.

"Honey, do you want Isa to make you something for dinner?" Papi asks Margo. "You've barely eaten today."

"I had a salad for lunch. I'm not feeling well," she says, attaching the mobile to the crib.

Papi glances in my direction. His eyebrows tick up. Since I've been here, this conversation has played out in practically every room of the house. Papi tries to get Margo to eat. She responds with some version of "I'm sick." What else is new?

Apparently, these days she only enjoys Chinese takeout.

"I can make you a broth," I offer. "It helps soothe the stomach."

"No, thank you," she says dismissively. "I'm off to bed." She leaves the room and closes the door behind her.

I grab one of the brushes, fill a small container with yellow paint, and start working on one of the walls.

"Sometimes I get the feeling she doesn't like me," I say, after a long silence.

Papi sighs. "You just have different personalities. Give her time to adjust. She's not used to being around kids."

"I'm not exactly a kid, Papi," I say.

"Fine, teenagers. Young adults," he adds with a smirk. "Adolescents."

"She doesn't seem to have a problem with Diego," I say bitterly.

"Just give her time," Papi repeats absentmindedly.

We paint in silence for a while. Papi uses the roller while I follow him around the room, painting the edges he's missed.

This baby will be arriving soon, and I still can't figure out where I will fit in Papi's new life. Sometimes it's hard to believe that in less than a year, our family has changed beyond recognition. Maybe it's time for me to move out and move on. But how do you move on from the people you love?

"Can I ask you something?" I say.

"Anything."

I stop to refill my paint bucket, thinking of what I really want to ask. I want to know why he left us. But it hurts too much to put this actual question into words.

"What is it about her?" I ask instead. "I mean, why her?"

Papi stops moving the roller, eyes still set on the newly painted wall. He lets out a breath that fills the room with sadness.

"I don't know, Isa," he says tentatively. "She makes me feel different."

"Different how?" I ask, unsure I want to hear the answer.

He glances back at me, something like caution in his eyes.

"You can tell me," I assure him.

"I enjoy this life," he says after a pause. "I have you, and Margo, and the new baby. And I'm not tied to a job at a desk."

I nod in understanding, even though the gesture isn't true. I never heard him complain about his job before. I had no idea he didn't like it. Maybe there's a lot I don't know about him.

"And this might be hard to grasp now, but I had to step up and do the right thing," he says, pushing the roller hard up and down the wall as he starts painting again. "I want us to be a family."

Do the right thing?

I let that statement sink in for a moment. Before I left the kitchen, my spoon had jumped to third place as a result of the fricassée d'escargots debacle. Lucia's spoon dropped to second place, right under Snake Eyes, who took first. If he wins the apprenticeship, it will be my fault.

I dip my brush into the paint bucket and slide it across the wall slowly, instantly transforming the surface from white to yellow. My eyes closely follow the change in color, and I'm weirdly thankful for the sense of instant gratification.

"I just don't get it. How is this the right thing?" I ask, completely focused on my brushstroke.

"You'll understand when you grow up," he says.

"I'm grown up now, Papi." I stop moving the brush to clean a drop of paint on the floor. It leaves a smudge under my thumb. "Try me."

Even without seeing his face, I can tell he's frowning. That's what he does when he's lost in his own thoughts.

"I don't know, honey—it's hard to explain. I guess your mom and I got caught up in things. Work, pressure, getting older, just . . . lots and lots of noise. When the noise finally died down, we realized there wasn't much left to hold on to."

The music track changes to an eighties ballad by a band called Journey—one of Papi's favorites. He stops rolling paint to turn up the volume.

"Was that when you met Margo?" I swallow hard at my own question.

Papi moves the roller up and down until the wall is completely altered. The happy shade of yellow is a stark contrast to the joyless mood currently filling the room.

"We met at a party. Things were already falling apart for your mom and me," he says.

"What party?" I ask, wanting to know every sordid detail of how our lives shattered.

He lets out a loud exhale. "I don't think we need to go into all that."

I nod at the wall while holding back a long list of questions. Did he leave Mom because they fell out of love? Or because Margo got pregnant? And if she wasn't pregnant, could he and Mom have worked things out? Could Mom forgive him?

I ponder the what ifs as we continue to paint in silence, not once looking at each other. A few brushstrokes in, I realize I may never get the answers.

Later that night, I bump into Diego in the downstairs hallway on my way to bed.

"Where are you going so late?" I ask.

He's strapping on his helmet and zipping up his leather jacket, ready to head out the door.

"Into town," he says curtly.

"It's almost midnight." I nod toward the clock on the foyer console.

He shrugs dismissively.

I tuck my hands inside the pockets of my robe, sensing a weirdness between us.

"What? You got a date with Cinderella?" I tease, wondering what's gotten into him.

He unbuckles his helmet with one hand and takes it off, then cradles it under one arm.

"Lucia called," he says sharply. "She was crying. Something about some snails. She said you said something. Or didn't say something?" He stares at me with an expression between confused and expectant.

I tighten the straps of my robe around my waist and fold my arms over my chest.

Tell him.

"There may have been a misunderstanding," I say quietly.

"She says you sabotaged her, Isa. Is that true?" His dark

brown eyes bore into mine. The intensity behind them forces me to look away.

"I didn't mean . . . But come on, *trois oignon . . . beurre blanc*? Sabotage? Really? Is that what she said? She wasn't sure about an ingredient. She asked me, but I must have misheard her or something. It's so loud in that kitchen." I stumble through a diatribe of incoherent thoughts, trying to come up with an explanation that doesn't sound like a lie on top of a lie. But listening to myself, it's clear I'm doing a really crappy job.

Diego moves closer—close enough that I can smell the scent coming off his jacket, something like wind and open road. The smell makes me want to lean my head against the soft leather covering his shoulder and wrap my arms around his waist. Do all the things I've never done before.

"Isa," he begins to say, holding my gaze as he speaks. "Did you sabotage Lucia's dish?"

Judging by the tension lines that abruptly take over his forehead and jaw, he already knows the answer.

Suddenly I feel bare naked and exposed. My arms wrap tighter around themselves, as if they could somehow shield me from the cloud of shame hanging over my head.

"You humiliated her in front of the entire class." The accusatory tone in his voice is more than I can bear.

"You can't be in that kitchen and not know French!" I spit defensively. "When did I get appointed to be her translator?"

"She trusted you!" Diego spits back. "She thought you were her friend."

"There are no friends in that kitchen," I scoff, remembering the things she said that night at the restaurant.

You want to be like everyone.

"Listen to you," he says in a cold, harsh voice, shaking his head slightly. I can't tell if it's out of disappointment or aggravation.

"It may not feel like it right now, but that craving to win turns you into a cancer. It kills all the good and transforms you into the worst version of yourself."

I open my mouth to tell him he's wrong, but he raises his free hand, stopping me.

"You may want to ask yourself if this apprenticeship is worth becoming this other person." His hand gestures in a way that makes me look away in self-disgust. I want to run away and hide, but my feet are cemented to the floor. If I leave now, I fear Diego will always see me like this—an awful, backstabbing friend.

God, how did I get here?

His phone dings in his pocket. He takes it out and the light of an incoming text illuminates his face. It also sucks what little air is left in the room.

"I have to go," he says, slipping the phone into the back of his jeans.

We stand in the hallway facing each other, the tension around us heavy, almost solid. I know I should say something, tell him that I'm not this monster he's making me out to be. But I can't find the words or the energy. I'm completely lost in a web of conflicting emotions.

A few more seconds of silence pass between us before Diego finally turns to leave.

When the door closes behind him, all the feelings I've been keeping at arm's length come rushing in with the strength of a sneaker wave. Why didn't I ask him to stay? Why didn't I confide in him?

If I had, maybe he could help me feel something that is not anxiety, or guilt, or regret, or even grief. I could get lost in him.

The thought both comforts me and scares me to no end.

I take the steps up to my room and climb into bed. Our conversation plays out in my head a thousand different ways. Every single time I say all the right things and he stays. He climbs into bed with me, and for once I'm not the girl who always has to be in control. Instead, I let go. I let go of everything.

But then reality sets in. I'm not the kind of girl who makes him stay.

Chapter 18

Fartichokes

The next day, Lucia calls in sick. As a result, the station to my left is empty and I only have Snake Eyes to my right.

"Did you poison her?" Snake Eyes asks with a smirk. "How very seventeenth-century French of you."

"What is wrong with you?" I hurl back. My head is throbbing with the kind of headache that follows a night of no sleep and too much thinking.

"I hear belladonna was used back then." He looks around him and whispers, "I know a place that sells the berries."

"Please stop talking." I stare at him, incredulous. Is he suggesting we poison Lucia? And how did I get sucked into this conversation?

I make a mental note never to take any food from Snake Eyes's hands—especially dark berries.

Chef Troissant enters the kitchen carrying a basket of vegetables under her arm. She doesn't greet anyone as she walks about the room, setting a different vegetable on each student's station.

When she reaches Lucia's station she clicks her tongue. "*Malade*," she says under her breath in a tone that implies disbelief. Her eyes land on me and I feel a cold shiver run down my spine.

"Mademoiselle Fields, I believe you have earned these sunchokes," she says, placing the funny-looking tubers on my station. "I want a soup. Keep the skin. Make it potent."

"Oui, Chef," I respond with a nod. Snake Eyes covers his mouth with his fist to suppress a laugh. When Chef Troissant is out of hearing distance he aims a farting sound in my direction.

"I'm sorry, should I get you a whoopee cushion while you're at it?" I deadpan.

"I don't know this whoopee. But you may need a cushion to sit after eating that soup." He laughs at his own joke, which I don't get.

"What are you talking about?" I ask, quickly losing what little patience I have left.

"You'll see."

I ignore him and get to work on the sunchokes. I melt butter in a pot and use it to sauté chopped onions, leeks, and garlic. I add vegetable broth and drop in the sunchokes, leaving on the skin as Chef Troissant directed, and wait for them to fully cook. Using an immersion blender, I puree the soup until all the lumps have disappeared and it's smooth. Then I stir in cream and seasoning. For my presentation, I garnish with toasted pumpkin seeds and a drizzle of pumpkin seed oil.

Chef Troissant works the kitchen, moving from one station to the next as students announce their dishes are ready. She dips a spoon or fork into their plates and passes judgment in one-word verdicts like "overcooked," "tasteless," and "unoriginal."

I raise my hand to indicate I am ready for a tasting. Chef Troissant looks at me from across the room and narrows her eyes. The ominous feeling from the start of class returns, and this time I know I'm not making it up.

My stomach goes into overdrive. *Does she know about the beurre blanc? But how?* A rope of tight knots forms in my abdomen and climbs all the way to my throat.

Chef Troissant doesn't say a word. She doesn't even look at my soup. She pulls a spoon from the pocket of her chef's coat—like she had planned this all along—and hands it to me with an acerbic, "Eat."

"Pardon?" My mind whirls. She wants me to eat my own soup?

"Eat," she repeats, pushing her spoon into my hand.

Everyone stares in silence.

My hand trembles as I reach for the spoon, knowing something is very wrong with this picture.

She's trying to break me, I tell myself. This is part of the test.

I take the spoon, dip it into the soup, and bring it to my mouth. It has a delicate artichoke flavor with an earthy aftertaste.

I move my hand to set down the spoon but Chef Troissant pushes the plate toward me and says, "All of it."

I pause for a beat, trying to sort out what's going on. Chef Troissant crosses her arms over her chest and shifts her weight from one foot to the other. Her eyebrow arches as if to say, *I don't have all day.*

I load up my spoon and eat the puree. I pause again, thinking maybe she will leave now, but she doesn't. She's just standing there! Like some crazy chef statue.

Meanwhile a rhythmic pounding inside my head has taken my temples hostage. It literally feels like my head is about to explode into an atomic bomb-sized mushroom.

I eat another spoonful. And then another. I keep doing this, like a robot, until the dish is empty and the room is spinning at warp speed.

"Bon," Chef Troissant says when I'm finished. The left side of her lips slightly ticks upward as she says, "My regards to Mademoiselle García."

My stomach grumbles as I watch the back of her pristine white coat walk away from me and disappear into her office.

I glance in Pippa's direction, but she looks away like she's trying to avoid me. So instead of doing the sensible thing and just letting it go, I walk over and flat-out ask her, "What's going on?"

"You tell me," she says, cleaning the sides of her dish. Her vegetable was an eggplant, so she prepared an eggplant Provençal that looks and smells amazing. But my stomach is not having it. It rumbles again, so loud Pippa can hear.

She puts down her towel and sighs.

"I heard you," she says.

"I think the entire kitchen heard me," I say, wrapping my arms around my stomach. That soup did not go down well. At all.

Pippa's face softens. "I'm talking about yesterday. I heard you talking to Snake Eyes in the locker room. And Lucia told me what you did. It's not right. We need to stick together."

My fingers dig through my scalp. At this point, I don't know what hurts more—my head or my stomach.

"I didn't mean to . . ." I say. "It was a mistake."

"Then you should tell Chef Troissant," Pippa says. "It's not fair."

I think of the repercussions of such a confession: no more apprenticeship, no more Michelin-starred kitchen.

I'd rather live the lie.

"Especially as it looks like she already knows," Pippa tells me.

"What do you mean?" I ask, gripping the sides of her station for support.

"She gave you fartichokes. And made you eat them," she calmly explains. "The skin is the worst part."

My face goes blank. What is she talking about?

"They're notorious for their bowel-busting terror," she adds. And somehow *bowel-busting terror* doesn't sound any better when said with a British accent.

As if on cue, my stomach thunders like it's about to burst in terror. I run to the nearest bathroom and barely make it in time.

I tell myself to research poisonous foods when I get home. If I ever get out of this toilet, that is.

I stop by Monsieur Barthélemy's stand on my way home. I'm preparing "*un bouillon de légumes,*" I tell him, grabbing a bunch of carrots from a basket for a broth.

"Where have you been?" He sings the question in his heavy French accent. "My vegetables miss you."

"Very busy," I say, and then explain in French the whole apprenticeship thing.

"Bah, Michelin!" he hisses with a dismissive wave. "The best chefs go crazy for those tiny macarons," referring to the French nickname for the little rosettes in the guide that indicate the number of Michelin stars a restaurant received.

"Just last week . . . What was his name? He killed himself!" The memory of Chef Bernard Martin's death comes back to me. Has it only been a week? It feels like a lifetime ago that Pippa, Lucia, and I were talking about it in Grattard's kitchen.

Monsieur Barthélemy searches for something behind his booth and returns with a worn copy of *Le Figaro* newspaper. He shakes his head in disapproval, holding the pages for me to see. A headline proclaims "TV Personality and World's Best Restaurant Chef Dead of Apparent Suicide." I take the newspaper from his hands and read.

Last month, Le Illusionaire was named the world's best restaurant on the prestigious La Liste released by the French Foreign Ministry. Yesterday, its 44-year-old owner, celebrity chef Bernard Martin, was found dead of an apparent self-inflicted gunshot wound at his home outside Paris.

Martin was a young star in the competitive world of high-end dining, having earned his third Michelin star when he was only 36 years old. His charming personality fueled the success of the beloved food and travel TV series *Places Untraveled*.

His death came the day before the Michelin guide was to announce its ratings for this year. Rumors had circulated that reviewers for Michelin were not as impressed with Martin's new, modern take on classic staples.

"He gave everything to his craft," said Le Illusionaire's sous-chef and Martin's close friend. "A true creative genius and a kind soul. It hurts to think of a world without Bernard in it."

Monsieur Barthélemy's voice takes on a grim tone as he says, "Chasing perfection, they say. If you ask me, there is no such thing."

I stare at Chef Martin's photo on the page. His lips are smiling but there's something like sadness in his eyes. A knot forms in the back of my throat. I can't even begin to imagine what kind of pressure led Martin to take his own life. How scared and desperate he must have felt in that moment. And how incredibly tragic he didn't realize his life was worth so much more than a bad review.

"What does it matter, these macarons, anyway?" Monsieur Barthélemy asks, waving a bunch of dill in his hand. "Here, you will need this for your broth." He drops the herbs into my basket.

"It matters a lot," I say absentmindedly. "Reputation, success, fame; more people want to visit your restaurant, eat your food." It's something I read in *Art Culinaire* magazine, but looking at Chef Martin's photo I'm suddenly questioning everything I thought I knew about the career path I've chosen.

What the *Art Culinaire* article left unsaid was how much exactly these things do matter. Enough for someone to completely forgo a life outside of the kitchen? Enough that they become so identified with a role that nothing else matters? Enough that they don't see a future? Enough that they don't feel how much they're loved?

Is this what I'm doing?

I swallow hard.

"Reputation and success, bah!" Monsieur Barthélemy fusses again. "They are traps, these things. They own you. And they take away your peace in here," he says, pointing at his head, "and here," gesturing at his heart. "I have no reputation, no success, no fame. But I am very happy man." He smiles wide and throws a free head of garlic into my basket. "Best garlic in all of Bessenay," he says with a wink.

I add a few onions and also pick up some leeks and potatoes. I take a ginger root in my hand that looks too similar to a sunchoke. "This is ginger, right?" I ask.

"Of course it's ginger! What else would it be?" he protests, then adds a bulb of fennel to my basket. "Fennel—aromatic," he says, wafting his hand in front of his face.

I pull a twenty euro note from my purse and hand it to him. "Merci."

He takes the money and gives me back some change.

"You come back soon," he says before turning to help another customer.

I linger for a few seconds and finish reading the last part of the newspaper article.

The day after Bernard Martin died, the Michelin guide was released. His restaurant retained the three stars, but Martin wasn't around to see it.

I thought I couldn't possibly feel any worse today, but I was wrong.

Whenever anything in her life went wrong, Lala would say, "*Más perdimos en Cuba, morenita.*" And perhaps she did lose more in Cuba.

Lala left Havana with only two suitcases to her name. Her entire life was neatly folded and packed inside those two bags.

I think of all the things in our Chicago brownstone that would be difficult to leave behind—the framed family photos scattered around the house, a handstitched quilt made by Grampa Roger's mom that Lala passed on to me, and a painting of a Mexican landscape my parents bought on their honeymoon. All of these reminders would be gone, as if the memories they represented never existed.

Six months after she arrived in Miami, Lala married Grampa Roger. They settled in a two-bedroom bungalow in Coconut Grove, the best he could afford on his salary as a Latin American studies professor at the University of Miami. "I never thought I would be that happy," she once told me. She had a new life in

Miami, but she had also managed to scrape together pieces of the old one: her aunt and cousins lived nearby, everyone around her spoke Spanish, and if she needed a taste of home, she just had to drive over to Versailles restaurant for a roast pork sandwich.

Within the year they were expecting my dad. "I wanted him to grow up surrounded by a big family, people who love you and care about you, who have a shared history," she told me. But it wasn't meant to be.

Grampa Roger's mom got sick. "Mary wanted to die at home, so moving her to Miami wasn't an option," Lala told me. "We had to respect her wishes. She was born in this house, and she lived here her whole life. It was the only home she ever knew. I understood what losing one's home does to you. It takes away a piece of your soul, morenita."

That summer, after Grampa Roger finished teaching his spring semester course on the Chilean Revolution, they moved 1,500 miles from their cozy little house in Coconut Grove to a hundred-acre farm outside of Kansas City.

Once again, Lala left her life behind to start over. But this time there was no big Latin family, no aunt, no cousins, no Spanish, and no roasted pork sandwiches from Versailles. Instead, she lived in a big farmhouse where she used her nursing background to help her sick mother-in-law, who she had never met. "I cared for her like she was my own mother," Lala once said proudly.

Lala didn't speak English at that point, and Mary didn't speak Spanish. The only place they could communicate was in the kitchen, where Lala would make Mary her caldo de gallina, or *la sopa levantamuertos*, as she would call it, because it apparently "could revive the dead." And Mary in turn would teach Lala how to make her Blessed Pies.

"Mary taught me to write down all my recipes," Lala said. "Back home we just knew what to do. I learned from Mami and my tías. Only a few things were written down. But Mary had a shelf full of notebooks."

I still remember that shelf. The notebook pages were yellow and dusty, but every pie recipe ever baked in our family kitchen was written there.

"I wanted my own notebook. So I watched how Mary did it and I started writing down my own recipes."

Mary didn't have a daughter. And Lala's mother had already died. Between the food and the love in that kitchen, they became each other's family.

"We didn't need words, mija. On pie days, Mary bounced out of bed and we picked apples in the backyard. I brought her café con leche and we sat out in the sun for a while. On those days, the color returned to her face. We peeled the apples, kneaded the dough, and cooked the syrup. Mary taught me how to lay the apple slices on the baking dish and how to cover them in syrup. Then she would place the pie inside the brown paper bag and close her eyes before putting it in the oven. At first, I didn't know what she was doing. All I knew was that a peace took over that kitchen like a warm blanket. Later, when I asked Roger what it meant, he said she was praying over her pies so whoever ate them had joy in their heart. She didn't need words to teach me how to bless the pies. I just felt it."

Back at Villa des Fleurs, I drop off the basket of vegetables in the kitchen and head to my room. I pull my suitcase out of the closet and slowly unzip the top. There is only one thing I haven't unpacked: Lala's handwritten cookbook. The moment my hands touch the red cover fastened shut with kitchen twine, all the grief returns like milk that came to a boiling point too quickly, rising and spilling around the edges of the pot.

The love and loss both swell inside me until my eyes sting with tears. I move the book to my desk. I can't bring myself to unknot the twine and open it. I find myself wishing I were back in Lala's kitchen so she could pass on the final step of her

signature recipe. It's not written in her book; I know because I've looked so many times that some of the pages have come undone.

I think about making her pie and trying a blessing of my own to see what happens. But it's so hard to believe in blessings when you feel so unworthy.

Chapter 19

Dots, Dots, Dots

On Thursday, the only reason I get out of bed and drag myself to the restaurant is because we were promised a two-day pastry intensive at the end of the third week.

The thing I most love about baking is its precision. Baking is a science. I like having specific directions that leave little room for mistakes. And there's something relaxing, even meditative, about following a recipe from beginning to end.

Today, Lucia is back in the kitchen. We don't look or talk to each other; instead we stand by our workstations, ultra-focused on our mise en place, sharpening our knives or doing whatever busywork will keep us from having to make eye contact.

I can't help but wonder what happened that night she called Diego. How exactly did he console her? I only have myself to blame, but the question has been eating at me for two days.

I realize Chef Troissant has entered the kitchen only when a wave of excited murmurs moves across the room. My knife falls out of my hand the moment I see him: Chef Pascal Grattard stands next to Chef Troissant, a vision in his impeccable white chef's coat. He is tall, handsome, with deeply tanned skin and bright, platinum hair. His eyes are a shade of light green that makes him look almost otherworldly. And when he smiles, the most adorable dimples take over his cheeks. The photos I saw online and in magazines do him no justice. Seeing him in the

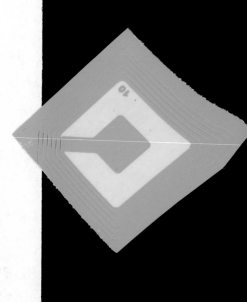

flesh is something else entirely—like a culinary god descended from the heavens and graced us with his presence.

Everyone in the culinary world knows the name Grattard. He is his own brand of genius.

Chef Grattard began working in his uncle's kitchen while he was still a kid. In his teens, he apprenticed at a high-end kitchen in Paris. By his midthirties, he became a MOF and opened La Table de Lyon, which has retained its three Michelin stars for twelve years.

Chef Grattard has written a dozen cookbooks and even has a documentary that bears his name. He is not only a genius, he is a legend. The flavor combinations that routinely come out of his kitchen are unheard of. Like the liver parfait and mandarin jelly appetizer, his brilliant idea to combine chicken livers and foie gras into a kind of meatball that is dipped into a mandarin jelly concoction, then frozen so the jelly has a mottled orange peel effect. The final result resembles a real mandarin and supposedly melts in your mouth like soft butter.

A few years ago, he created this intensive program to pass his culinary lineage on to the next generation of haute cuisine chefs. The man is a visionary.

A hi barely squeaks out of my mouth.

"Welcome to La Table de Lyon," he tells the class. Never mind we've been here for almost three weeks. Where was he hiding? "I hope you have enjoyed yourself. This is a very demanding course—world-class."

We all nod and smile.

"Chef Troissant has kept me abreast of your progress. Today, some of you will begin the pastry course."

I move closer, hoping for more details. What exactly will we be baking?

"But I have come here today because there are three people who have earned a special place. Mademoiselle García, Mademoiselle Fields, Monsieur Legrand," he announces. I freeze. Did my name just come out of his lips?

"You will be coming with me," he says, all dimples and heavenly eyes. He looks straight at me, like he knows who I am.

"You are the top of the class and you have earned a spot in my kitchen. You will be helping us prepare for our very special dinner tomorrow. And for the next two days, you will be working side by side with some of my best cooks. You will get a feel for the job at hand. And we will know if this is the best fit for your talents," he says. "You may come with me."

The mood in the kitchen instantly transforms from excitement to disappointment, maybe even jealousy. Only the three of us get to see what's behind the curtain.

I should be ecstatic right now. Euphoric, even. But Chef Grattard's invitation also means I won't be participating in the pastry course. And I won't be learning Chef Troissant's baking methods. Since I've been here, I've discovered her dessert creations are the kind of masterpieces others copy.

My shoulders slump in resignation. I have to let it go. I'm not about to blow this opportunity of a lifetime over a piece of cake. As if in a trance, I walk behind Chef Grattard and follow him down a long corridor into La Table de Lyon's kitchen.

Lucia moves next to me with wide-eyed anticipation and a big smile on her lips. Even though we're not friends anymore, and it's super awkward between us, I'm happy she'll be in that kitchen with me.

I glance at Snake Eyes behind me. His lips are curled in what I guess is apprehension. What is he so worried about? I thought he was a pro at this.

The clinking of pots and pans gets louder as we approach the real kitchen. I can already hear the sizzle of a sauté and the bubbling of a rolling boil, the whirl of the food processor and the spattering of hot oil. A decadent smell of lobster stock infuses the air even before we reach the door. This is what I've been working my fingers to the bone for: to stick my spoon into every sauce until I memorize every single ingredient, to learn the correct way to sauté a delicate fillet of rouget—to master the craft. Grattard's kitchen is like the summit of culinary creation and we have arrived.

When the swinging door opens, it's like being at the gates of heaven and St. Peter himself holds the door for me. I go in, not knowing I've actually just passed through the gates of hell.

Lucia, Snake Eyes, and I stand uncomfortably close to each other. We are surrounded by crates full of glistening fresh vegetables, all polished to a shine. I've never seen vegetables this clean. Even the leaves on the greens are so bright, they look as if they were injected with nuclear chlorophyll.

We move aside as a shipment of equally polished eggs arrives. The kitchen is uncommonly small for a high-end restaurant, but what strikes me the most is the eerie quiet. A few cooks purposefully move between stations and most stand in one place, working with a speed and rigor that seems impossible to re-create. No one speaks. No one stops what they are doing to look at us. All I see are the tops of their white toques protruding from the pass along the stations.

"Chef Troissant tells me you have come a long way in the program," Chef Grattard says. My chest fills with pride and pure happiness. I guess I had been wrong about Chef Troissant all along. I had nothing to worry about.

"I designed this program to seek out the greatest talent. Only the very best will find success in my kitchen." His voice is gentle, and his facial expressions have a modest quality that stand in sharp contrast to the man I read about. Some say that part of the legend surrounding Chef Grattard is the brutality with which he runs his kitchen.

France is the birthplace of the *Brigade de cuisine*, a kitchen hierarchy system similar to the military. In Grattard's brigade, it's been reported, dissent sends you straight to the guillotine.

But now, having met the chef, the myths seemed exaggerated.

The cooks around us don't seem like the victims of an auto-cratic society. Instead, I see a man assembling a rabbit terrine with layers that almost float one above the other. This dish is a combination of architecture, chemistry, biology, and physics, and he seems to be an expert in all.

"You will work with Hugo," Chef Grattard says, patting a young man with a tattoo of a hog on his arm. Hugo's shoulders stiffen at the touch. "Hugo will show you to your stations. We have a lot of work ahead of Friday evening—it's a seven-course meal. Our guest is a very important man, very important." He winks with a smile. Maybe the French president? It wouldn't surprise me; Grattard has cooked for him in the past.

"Our guest will bring a small group of his close friends, around forty or so. The restaurant will be closed to the public, of course. This is very private event. Everything must be perfect. Perfect. Perfect. Perfect." As Chef Grattard smiles, Hugo winces ever so slightly. It's an almost imperceptible movement, but I notice the distress lines around his eyelids. They are the same lines Papi carried around for years while he was at the height of his finance job.

"Bon," he says. "Hugo is in charge." And just like that, he walks away and disappears into a tiny office off the side of the kitchen.

The moment the chef leaves, Hugo remembers how to breathe.

"Let me be clear, I'm not your babysitter," he says. His lips are so tight they may split open. Even Snake Eyes seems to be taken aback.

"We don't need a babysitter," Snake Eyes tells Hugo.

"Did I say you could speak?" Hugo's voice stays even, though anyone can tell this guy isn't messing around.

"This is not the little play kitchen," Hugo hisses. "Here, you do what you are told, no questions asked. I don't care what you think. I don't care how you feel. I don't even care if your mother dies during the lunch shift. Do. Your. Job. *Comprend*?"

Snake Eyes and Lucia nod. I nod too, because let's be honest, this guy is freaking scary.

"Follow me," he says. We walk behind him down the line, tripping on each other.

"You," he tells Snake Eyes, "peas."

Snake Eyes's eyes widen but he doesn't say a word.

The biggest bowl of peas I've ever seen sits on the counter.

"Remove the peel. Then take out the tiny sprout inside. The pea must remain intact," Hugo says, as if this explanation actually makes any sense.

I know he said no questions, but I am genuinely curious as to why the hell anyone would waste their time peeling a pea. I raise my hand and wait to be acknowledged.

"Is my accent too thick for you?" he spits. "Did you not understand my instructions?"

"I'm just . . ." I stutter at first. "I'm just curious, why do you remove the sprout?"

Hugo's eyes narrow. "Thinking will not get you far around here, girl," he warns, the *girl* sounding like an insult. "Chef Grattard is convinced the sprouts make his dish bitter."

"That's absurd," I mutter, because clearly I have a death wish.

Snake Eyes elbows me in the side. "Shut up," he whispers. I'm about to give him my best *you shut up!* response, but then I see the terror on his face.

Hugo steps forward at the exact same time Lucia and Snake Eyes take a step back. A cold chill runs down my spine as I come face-to-face with Hugo. He smells like cigarette butts and his teeth are stained brown. I'm horrified into silence.

"That is not for you to judge. In fact, thinking is the fastest way to get removed from this kitch—" Hugo stops abruptly. A cook working on the station across from us is cursing at a food processor. He punches the machine and a batch of croutons flies everywhere.

"You idiot!" Hugo yells at the man. He points at the machine, saying, "Lock the top. How many times do I have to tell you? If your croutons explode one more time, you are out on the street." The cook doesn't respond. He grabs a broom, cleans up his mess, and starts all over again.

Hugo then turns his wrath on us. "You are here to execute Chef Grattard's vision. You're not here to think. If Chef Grattard wants you to put a turd on the plate and cover it in the rarest Almas caviar, you don't ask why, you just do it."

So gross. What is wrong with this guy?

He forces the bowl of peas into Snake Eyes's hands and says, "All yours."

Snake Eyes mutters "Oui, Chef" and gets peeling. What happened to the brash son of a MOF who gave Chef Troissant a run for her money? Is it possible he checked his balls at the door?

Lucia and I follow Hugo past the bread station, where a tall deck oven emits about 500 degrees of heat. I feel sorry for whoever has to work that station. It must be like working inside a sauna all day.

Again, I notice the many security cameras in the kitchen. Every room has one. I know theft is a big thing in high-end kitchens, but all the electronic eyeballs feel a bit stifling.

Up ahead, a few cooks mill around the espresso machine, making themselves coffee drinks, but the moment they see Hugo walk the line, they scram.

When we arrive at the salad station, Hugo stops and says, "You two are on dots." He pulls a small notebook from his pocket and scribbles something on the paper. "You have all day to practice. Tomorrow they must be perfect. Perfect. Perfect," he says, mimicking Grattard with a voice full of resentment.

"You will use five different sauces," he explains, motioning to the dishes on the counter. "Cover the plate in alternating sauce dots—the entire plate. Dip the tip of the needle in the sauce and carefully dot the plate. The space between the dots must be the same—exactly ten centimeters."

A knot forms in the pit of my stomach as I take in our impossible task. It's not only impossible, it's completely mad. And to top it off, Hugo drops a tower of oversized platters in front of us. These are not dinner plates; they're practically serving trays.

"What are these?" I ask, unable to keep my mouth shut.

"Dot. Dot. Dot," is his only response.

For the first time all week, Lucia and I look at each other. Our faces bear the stunned visage of war survivors. But this is not war, it's a kitchen, and we have yet to survive.

I open my mouth, intending to bring up the onions-and-snails incident, but can't seem to find the right words. I don't even know where to start. How do you apologize for backstabbing a friend? How do you make it right?

Meanwhile, Lucia is moving things around our work station so we can both have quick access to the sauce dishes. She swiftly engineers a system to maximize the small space and organizes the ingredients in the order we will use them.

"This should work," she says in a taut voice.

"This looks great. Thanks," I say awkwardly.

After what seems like an eternity of painting tiny dots on the plates in the most uncomfortable silence, my wrist is about to fall off my hand and my arm is cramping all the way to my shoulder. My hand is so stiff, my fingers are stuck in the shape of a claw. I don't know how much longer I can do this. Is there such a thing as teenage arthritis? Because if there is, by now I'm sure I have it.

"This is it: number forty," I say, letting the sauce needle fall from my hand. I can barely hold it anymore.

A few seconds later, Chef Grattard suddenly reappears by our station. Which makes me wonder if the cameras also carry sound.

He's standing by our station, arms crossed over his chest, the jovial smile gone.

My eyes are so tired from looking at dots that I can barely keep his face in focus. All I see are dots in five different colors. Maybe he will realize what a crazy task this is and give us something else to do. I'll settle for washing dishes at this point. The dishwashers, with their reggae music and plenty of workspace, seem to be the happiest members of this kitchen. They bounce around from station to station, putting things back on the racks. No one seems to bother them with unreasonable demands.

Lucia and I step aside so he can take a good look at our plates. I'm wondering if he will clue us in on what he plans to plate on these dishes. His famous lobster salad? His crustacean gelée? Instead, all he says is, "These are no good." The earlier gentleness in his voice has been replaced by an intensity on the verge of violence. My left eye starts to twitch. I press my eyelid with a finger to keep it from spasming.

"Five sauces, five colors. Like the prick of a needle on the plate. Same distance apart," he says, as if that is not what we just spent four hours doing.

"Again," he says, then turns to the guy at the station next to us and says, "Babette wants her meal now."

The poor guy looks like he's about to pass out. He has dark circles under his eyes and half his eyebrow is missing. Did he scorch it off?

"Oui, Chef," he responds barely above a whisper.

After Chef Grattard leaves, I watch the guy cut a steak into perfect cubes. He can't be that much older than me, but he looks as if he's been to hell and back.

I want to offer some help, but there's no way a) I'm gonna risk talking or b) I'm gonna leave the dots. So instead I watch him work, terrified that this will be me in a few months.

He cooks the meat to medium and gently drops each cube inside a tall crystal dish. He serves the dish on an elaborate tray and walks it back to Chef Grattard's office. When he returns, he is plucking out his eyebrow with his fingertips like he's about to have a mental breakdown.

I need to get my twitchy eye under control. *Now.*

Shortly after, Chef Grattard returns carrying the same tray and crystal dish, the meat only half eaten.

"You call yourself a cook?" Chef Grattard asks him in an even tone. "You can't even make a meal my dog will enjoy. She ate two cubes and only sniffed the rest. What am I supposed to do with this steak? You have wasted my steak."

Chef Grattard slams the tray on the counter and walks back to his office. The cook just stands there, picking at his half-missing eyebrow, shell-shocked. None of his colleagues offer any consolation.

While a few of us prepare for the next day's dinner, the regular kitchen staff still has to execute today's lunch service. Across the pass, a cook juliennes turnips on a mandoline until they come out translucent. A tray of veal bones goes into the oven and a pan of onions caramelize on the stove. Big hunks of rib eye get transferred from a cart to the worktable. The bloodied cuts of meat land with a loud thump on the counter. Behind us, a blender runs while someone pours olive oil into a garlic mix. The delicious aroma of roasted garlic fills the kitchen but is quickly replaced by the clean-ocean smell of fresh fish. The slightly briny scent lingers after the fillets have been stored in the fridge. In time, the serving staff starts to arrive, their starched white shirts in hand.

Through all of this, the kitchen remains strangely quiet. It occurs to me that this is not an everyone-is-focused kind of quiet. And what I'm hearing is not silence; it's fear.

My stomach clenches. My throat tightens. My shoulder blades pull back so tight, my back might break. I turn to Lucia, desperate to connect with another human being, desperate for someone to acknowledge the insanity of this place, but she's back to the dots. So I do the only thing that will make time pass. I grip the needle hard and drown my fear in dots, until dots are all I can see.

Chapter 20

Geese Fat and Bubbly

Before going home, I slip into the test kitchen to wrap some leftover chicken in wine sauce, a dish I made yesterday. Papi loves this stuff.

I'm surprised to find Pippa is still here this late. She's cleaning the area around her station, where a beautiful croquembouche tower is displayed on a cake stand. Glimmering strands of spun sugar are draped over the profiterole stack.

I hesitate, since we haven't really spoken since the sunchoke soup disaster. I miss hanging out like we used to. I've never had friends like this. And I went and made a mess of things.

"Wow," I say, sounding like I'm trying too hard.

"Yeah, it's nice, huh?" Pippa's eyes are set on the pastry tower. She fumbles with a strand of spun sugar and I can sense the tension between us bothers her as much as it does me.

After a long pause I add, "I didn't plan to do it . . . misleading her, I mean. It just happened." I gesture apologetically with my open palms.

Pippa stares me in the eyes. And as uncomfortable as it makes me feel, I hold her gaze. I want her to know how truly sorry I am.

"How can I trust you won't do the same to me?" she asks. The question stings. I hadn't thought of it that way. "It's hard enough being a woman in the kitchen. We don't need to tear each other down."

Pippa shakes her head. She must see the hurt in my face because she looks away.

"I wouldn't . . ." I stutter. "I got caught in the moment. It was stupid and childish. I feel like crap about it. You guys are my friends."

"Strong women lift each other up," she says in a gentler tone. Her hand reaches for my arm. The touch has a grounding effect. "You need to talk to Lucia. Set things right."

My face goes hot with embarrassment and shame.

"I know," I say in a low voice. I just don't know how, exactly, to make it right.

Pippa nods. Her shoulders relax slightly, and her features soften somewhat.

We both turn to admire her creation in silence.

"Did you make this in one day?" I ask, incredulous.

A satisfied smile appears on her face. "Yes, we did. Chef Troissant is some kind of pastry genius. I mean, she hasn't written any books or won any big titles. But she's crazy good."

"It's perfect," I say, leaning in to sniff the buttery scent of the profiteroles.

"Do you want to try one? I have some leftovers."

"I would love to." She hands me a delicate pastry and I put it into my mouth. It's airy-light and filled with vanilla bean cream. Absolutely delicious. "This is amazing." The last thing I want is to feel jealous, but I do. Pippa got to stay behind and craft this spectacular dessert.

I remind myself I was one of the chosen allowed into Grattard's precious kitchen—one of only three. I should feel extremely proud of myself. But now, staring at this gorgeous tower of cream puffs, I wish had been left behind with Pippa.

"How was your day?" Pippa asks. "Lucia was walking on sunshine when she left. She said it was exhilarating finally being in the real kitchen."

"It was fine," I say while reaching for another profiterole and stuffing my mouth with it. Pastries make a great avoidance tool.

"Fine?" she asks, her tone doubtful.

I point to my full mouth and manage to say, "These are so good," between bites. I ignore the curious look she's giving me.

"Are you sure you're okay?"

"Yeah," I say. "Why?"

"You don't look fine to me. You seem down."

"Long day." I won't admit, even to myself, how miserable I really feel.

"When are you going back to London?" I ask, attempting to steer the conversation away from me. "Maybe we can hang out or something before you leave." It's supposed to be a casual question, but it comes out loaded with all the baggage from our last outing and the drama I've created in our threesome.

"Not for a while," she says tentatively. But then her face breaks into a smile she can't seem to hold back. "I got a job at Pâtisserie Lulu. I'm assistant baker."

"*What?* That's amazing!" I reach out for a hug. Pippa hugs me back, which I take as a sign of progress. Maybe our friendship isn't dead after all—more like in a coma.

"Wow, congratulations. How did that happen?" I ask.

"I went by a few days ago to taste their canelés—oh my god, she has the rum shipped in from Martinique, it's amazing—and Chef Lulu was speaking with a customer. I introduced myself and told her how much I loved her pastries, and that I was part of this program. Then she said she was looking for an assistant baker if I was interested. I said yes, right on the spot."

"That's amazing," I say again.

"I start next week. Right after our final exam on Monday."

I'm trying really hard just to be happy for Pippa and to celebrate this wonderful accomplishment. But I can't help feeling sorry for myself. Her excitement is palpable. She knows exactly what she wants and where she wants to be. I wish I had her clarity.

"I have to go," she says, pulling out her phone and staring at the screen. "I'm taking this little guy home before it gets soggy. My flatmates can't get enough of our assignments."

I help Pippa pack her croquembouche, careful that the spun

sugar stays intact. Then I hold open the back delivery door as she walks into the alley carrying a tall box full of pastries.

"Take care, Isa," she says, disappearing into the busy street.

I close the door and lean my back against it, hands falling limply to my sides. I've painted myself into a corner and there is no escape. While Pippa and the others get to savor the joys of baking, I get to pinprick sauce dots onto a plate for hours on end. Maybe tomorrow will be different.

I'm startled by Chef Troissant, who stumbles out of her office carrying a half-empty champagne bottle under one arm and a glass flute in the opposite hand. At first, she doesn't notice I'm in the kitchen. She pulls a stool from the kitchen island, sits, and refills her glass.

When she lifts her head, she seems genuinely shocked to see me standing by the back door.

"What are you still doing here?" she asks, slurring her words.

"I was about to leave," I say, walking toward her. "Just wanted to get what's left of my chicken." I pull my apron over my head and fold it on the table. "It's for my dad," I say, sounding apologetic.

"Ah, I see," she says. "Might as well get yourself a glass." She pushes the champagne bottle in my direction.

I stare at the bottle, wondering what to do. I've never been to a French school, but I'm pretty sure I'm not supposed to be drinking with my teacher.

"What?" she asks. "Ah, you're American. Not until you are eighteen, oui? I won't tell anyone." She brings her index finger to her lips and makes a shushing sound.

I go get a glass to appease her. The last thing I want is to turn Chef Troissant against me right before the final exam.

I fill my glass only halfway.

"Alors," she says, and I notice her eyes are rimmed red. She raises her glass and gives me an expectant look, so I raise mine to meet hers.

"À *votre santé*," she says, clinking my glass. I take a small sip. This all feels super weird.

"Are you okay?" I ask, trying to sort out what to do. Do I call Pippa to come help me? Or do I just leave?

"You want to be a chef, oui?" she asks. Her eyelids are heavy and she's propping her face up with one arm leaned against the kitchen island.

I nod, afraid to say the wrong thing. After the dots, this is not how I wanted my day to end.

"Let me tell you something," she says, now pointing her index finger at me. "The kitchen is a man's world. You want to succeed? You need to rip your heart out. Drop it in a hot pan and let it sizzle. That's what it will take." She stumbles back to the wine fridge and returns with an uncorked bottle of champagne.

"Perrier-Jouët," she announces. "The best."

The bottle she's holding is worth about $500. I know this because Papi used to get it for Mom on their anniversary. The last bottle he bought is still unopened in our house back in Chicago.

Chef Troissant pops the cork and giggles like a schoolgirl.

"This is a good one," she says, examining the bottle. "You pour," she tells me.

I do as I'm told even though I'm second-guessing every decision right now. I half fill both our flutes, trying to pace myself. I don't want to end up plastered in front of my teacher, even though I doubt she will remember any of this in the morning.

"It was an accident, champagne. Did you know this?"

I shake my head. I did not know.

"The wine was bottled after the initial fermentation. The bottles exploded and the corks popped. *Le vin du diable*, they called it."

The devil's wine. How appropriate.

I sip on my glass and the bubbles burst in my mouth, leaving behind a flowery sweetness.

"That was nice . . ." I say as I set down my glass. "It's getting kinda late, though . . ." I grab my apron and take one step back.

"Five years I give to this man," she says. "All this time,

waiting for a recommendation. Maybe a restaurant in America, New York or D.C. Anywhere!"

She pushes out a stool with her foot and I take it as a suggestion—an order, really—to sit and listen.

"But no, instead I'm fifty feet away. Behind the curtain." She scoffs. "I have talent too. That mandarine foie gras everyone talks about? That was my idea. I came up with that, not him."

She seems to be waiting for an answer, so I say the only thing I can think of. "Yeah, the foie gras is awesome."

"Thanks . . ." Her voice trails off.

"Is there some in the fridge?"

"You're right. We should have some foie gras," she says, suddenly wide-eyed and animated. "To my foie gras!" She clinks my glass and downs hers like it's grape juice.

I finish the rest of my champagne, already feeling its mind-numbing effect. This stuff is like a liquid anesthetic. The anxiety that only moments ago felt like a sharp knife has transformed into a dull blade. My mind is so dazed that I don't even think about the poor, tortured geese whose livers are systematically overstuffed to make the foie gras. Normally I would be too ridden with guilt to enjoy it.

Chef Troissant returns with a spread of crackers and a foie gras terrine that takes half a day to make—surely someone will miss this in the kitchen tomorrow. Then she drops a blue booklet in front of me on the table. "Pâtisserie Clémentine. Opening soon."

I take the book in my hands and flip through the pages written in French. It's a business plan complete with financial projections and architectural drawings of the store. A big sign in gold letters reads *Pâtisserie Clémentine* over a quaint storefront with bright flower baskets hanging on both sides of the front door. The interior drawings show plenty of space for a long pastry display cabinet, a coffee bar, and a few dozen café tables. I flip to the business goal section, where it reads: "To provide artistic products of distinctive quality, made by a devoted team, led by Chef Sabine Troissant."

"You're opening your own place?" I ask, surprised. I read somewhere that in France it is rare to find a woman at the helm of a pastry shop. For both Pâtisserie Clémentine and Pâtisserie Lulu to be female-led and in the same town seems too much exception to fathom.

"This is my dream," she says, digging into the terrine with a cracker. "When I started here I had so many ideas, so many things I wanted to do. But that kitchen can be like a spoiled child. You give and give and give, and never get anything in return." She pauses, staring at the bubbles rising inside her champagne flute. "I feel so far away from where I wanted to be. Did you know two years ago I made the semifinals in the MOF competition?"

My jaw drops to the floor. There is nothing like the MOF tryouts in the world. Seventy to eighty candidates compete in the most grueling two-day competition against perfection. About sixteen normally make it to the finals. I realize Chef Troissant is not just a great pastry chef. She's one of the world's best.

"But the semifinals are just the beginning. For the next year you need to prepare, find a MOF consultant, a coach, and a full-time assistant. It's very hard work." She swishes the champagne around in her glass.

"How was it? The finals. Were they as crazy as everyone says?" I ask.

She shrugs, pursing her lips.

"I wouldn't know," she says. "Grattard said it was a busy time at the restaurant and he could not do without his pastry chef. Then I spoke to Legrand, asked him to mentor me, but he said he would not go against Grattard's wishes. I had to bow out."

"Why didn't you just quit?" I ask, leaning over the island.

"My mother, Clémentine, was sick at the time. I needed the job."

"Wow," I say. "That sucks."

She gulps down what is left of her champagne. When she

reaches for the bottle, she accidentally knocks it over and it spills all over the floor.

We both break out laughing.

"Go get another one," she says.

I do as I'm told and walk over to the wine fridge. I find a bottle of very expensive Veuve Clicquot, the same brand Chef Legrand bought from the shipwreck.

Even if this bottle wasn't found at the bottom of the sea, I decide Chef Troissant also deserves to drink her own bottle of Veuve Clicquot. She may not have the stupid MOF title, but in her own way this woman is exceptional.

I bring her the bottle.

"Excellent choice," she says, pulling out the cork. She pours two glasses.

"To your pâtisserie," I toast, and our glasses clink. "May it be the best in all of France! Hell, the whole freaking world!"

We laugh together, then launch ourselves into the terrine until we are fingering foie gras off the table. Now this is what I call high dining.

"This is so good," I say as I lick my fingers.

"My recipe," she says with both pride and disdain. "But who cares, right?"

She staggers to a standing position and zigzags back into her office. I follow her just to make sure she doesn't trip and fall. I'm not faring much better. The entire kitchen appears out of focus and I'm holding on to the wall for support. Thank goodness I didn't finish that last glass.

I ease her onto a couch, prop a pillow under her head, and cover her with a blanket. Before she passes out she says, "Why was the cake missing a piece? It was excellent in flavor but had a hole in the middle."

It takes me a moment to realize she's talking about the mille crêpe cake.

"Because an infuriating Spaniard who lives with me has no appreciation for the culinary arts," I say.

"Infuriating, huh?" She looks at me and smiles. "You like this Spaniard?"

"He's just so . . . chill all the time! It makes me crazy. And he drives this stupid motorcycle with a stupid sidecar. Who does that?"

"Do yourself a favor and call him to take you home. And clean up before you leave."

She curls up and turns away from me. I guess this is my cue.

I stand by the door, watching my passed-out teacher. What just happened? I don't even know.

What I do know is this: I am too lightheaded to get home on my own. I pull out my phone and call Diego. Dang, I'm that kind of drunk.

Chapter 21

Two Bacon Cheeseburgers
and Fries, Please

"Wow, you look . . . rough," he says.

"Don't turn on the charm just for me." I try to stand and fail miserably. That champagne landed like an alcoholic bomb in my stomach.

"Hold on to me," he says, reaching around my waist and lifting me from the ground.

I've been waiting by the alley behind the restaurant, where the kitchen cooks come out for their cigarette break during dinner service. The smoke around their faces makes them look even more worn-out and downcast than they did at lunch.

I get to my feet but stumble. Diego holds me by the arms and helps me up, but instead of standing I end up leaning on his chest with my face pressed against his collarbone. He doesn't move, so my nose traces the edge of his collar, taking in the smell of wind, earth, and open fields on a sunny day. It reminds me of my grandparents' farm.

"You smell like home," I say, inhaling deeply. My head rests on his shoulder and I close my eyes. I'm drifting, feeling there is nowhere else I want to be but sunk into his chest. Everything starts to fade away.

"Okay, come on. We need to get some food in you," he says. "And coffee. Lots of coffee."

"Can we just stay here?" I mumble.

"It smells like pee," Diego says, completely oblivious to the fact I'm having a moment. "Let's go—I know a place around here."

"Wait," I say, raising a finger to his face. "I need to know something."

He stares down at me expectantly.

"Did something happen between you and Lucia?" I ask. "Are you together? Like together, together." My finger stabs his chest, demanding an answer. I'm sober enough to know that if they're a couple, I need to back off.

"I'm not betraying her again." I take a fistful of his shirt, trying to steady myself. "I don't want to be that person. I don't want to be a cancer." The last words come out teary and remorseful.

Diego sighs under the weight of my body, which is again resting against him for support.

"You're not a cancer. I'm sorry I said that," he says, brushing my hair off my face with one hand. "Lucia and I, we're just friends. Nothing happened. Okay?"

"Okay." I take a gulp of smoky alley air and relax my hand on his shirt.

"Can we go now?" He swings my backpack over his shoulder, then grabs my hand. I decide in that moment I like how our hands fit together. He has what I would call grounding hands— solid, rough, and callous-ridden—the kind of hands that have been helping Papi pick cherries all week, the kind of hands that can prop you up when you are standing or pick you up when you fall.

Neither of us speaks as we walk down Lyon's cobbled streets. All I can do is follow him, and his sole focus seems to be preventing my face from hitting the road.

We turn onto a narrow promenade, busy with locals and tourists coming in and out of restaurants and shops. A chorus of laughter, music, and conversation fills the street, along with the smell of seared meat, stale alcohol, and sweat. I squint at the sudden burst of bright lights illuminating the alley, a combination of streetlamps and neon signs.

Outside one of the restaurants, small café tables covered in white linen are arranged on the sidewalk. Not one seat is empty. As we walk by, I glance at the dishes resting on the cloths. Everything looks so . . . ordinary. Hunks of meat float in a pool of sauce with mountains of mashed potatoes or overcooked vegetables beside them. Nothing like the expertly crafted dishes I watched being prepared in Grattard's kitchen all day.

I'm unbelievably relieved.

"Burger 'n fries," I call out to Diego, but he doesn't hear me over the music flowing out of a bar. He's ahead of me, given there's no space to walk side by side. I tug at his arm and he turns. "Burger 'n fries," I repeat. "That's what I want."

His face lights up as if I've given him the best news he's heard all day. "Burger and fries for Mademoiselle Chef. You want cheese with that?"

"Yes. And bacon."

"I know just the place. It's down this alley."

We walk into a small restaurant called Butcher, a simple establishment with bare wooden tables and condiment caddies that include your own ketchup bottle. The only piece of art is an oversized red pig propped on a ledge over the dining area.

It's so absolutely unsophisticated that it puts a smile on my face. And the burgers . . . oh my god, the burgers are huge, served with hand-cut fries in uneven sizes—no batonnet cuts here. I never thought the day would come when I would crave nothing more than an uneven fried root vegetable.

The place is packed so we find two seats by the bar.

Diego hands me a menu but I already know what I want.

"Bacon cheeseburger and fries," I tell the bartender.

"Two," Diego says. He also orders a beer for himself.

For a while, we watch people milling around us. A young hipster couple is making out at the end of the bar like their plane is about to go down. The bartender just slides the drinks in front of them and walks away. Next to us, a group of friends is toasting someone's birthday with the French version of the "Happy Birthday" song.

"Here, drink this." Diego pushes a glass of carbonated water in my direction. "You'll feel better."

I drink, knowing this is not what I need to feel better.

There were so many times today in Grattard's kitchen when the pressure got so intense, I couldn't even breathe. What I need is to stop the crazy voices telling me that no matter how hard I try, it will not be enough to succeed. I'll never be good enough.

"What happened back there? You sounded upset over the phone," he says.

I tell him about Chef Grattard and the special dinner I'm convinced is for the president. I also tell him about the dots, the meal for Grattard's poodle, and Chef Troissant's binge. I tell him everything.

Diego brings the beer glass to his lips and drinks a big gulp.

"Do you realize how messed up this all sounds?" He laughs in astonishment.

He's right. It's so absurd, it's laughable.

"What happened to all the dots you made?"

"Straight in the dishwasher," I say and then start laughing like a maniac. I laugh until my chest cracks open and the knots in my shoulders loosen.

"Why don't you leave? That place is full-on loco."

"I don't know," I say, unexpectedly questioning my motivation for being in that kitchen in the first place. "Grattard is the best. When people leave his kitchen, they either take a higher position in a five-star restaurant or they open their own place. He's like the Godfather or something. You know, the gangster movie?" It's one of Papi's favorites.

"Revenge is a dish that tastes best when it is cold," Diego says with a thick Italian accent, nodding like Don Corleone.

We both laugh. I laugh mostly because his imitation is terrible in an endearing way.

"It's a privilege to be allowed in that kitchen," I say.

"But what's the point if you're going insane in the process?"

"Just because you gave up doesn't mean the rest of us have to." The moment the words spill out of my mouth I wish I could reel them back. His face falls, and he turns to look straight ahead. *Crap. I really need to get myself a filter.*

"I'm sorry. I didn't mean that," I say, but it's obvious I hit a nerve.

"I made a choice and, given the chance, I wouldn't change a thing. I'm done caring what other people think."

I nod. His words sting a little. Does he care what I think? It hits me then that I care what *he* thinks. Probably way more than I should, given I don't know how to feel about him. What I know is that he's different from every other guy I've ever met. His life is wide open to possibility.

The problem is, I don't know if mine is. And I'm not sure *different* is something I want or need right now.

"Let's talk about something else," he says, clearing his throat. "Have you been to the Presqu'île?"

The Presqu'île was in every travel guide I read before coming to Lyon. It's a peninsula that is home to many of the city's historic sites.

"I haven't done much other than cook since I got here," I say.

Diego's eyebrows arch. He doesn't say anything. He doesn't have to.

"I know, it's pathetic." And just because the champagne hasn't completely worn off and I'm feeling slightly rebellious, I say, "Let's go tonight. After we eat, you're taking me on a tour."

Diego laughs. "Don't you have to be back at that place tomorrow morning?"

"Yes, but so what? Do they have Red Bull in France?" I ask, knowing I'll have to pay for tonight's little adventure come morning. But there is something about Diego, with his worn jeans and his faded T-shirt, and the beaded leather bracelet wrapped around his wrist—something that makes me not want to care. Whatever it is, it inspires me to be reckless. To forget about the dots and the poodle and the possible presidential dinner. It makes me want to reach out for another possibility.

Our food arrives and we eat our burgers with juice dripping from the sides of our mouth. They're perfect. We then both wolf down the thick fries slathered in ketchup.

"That was so good," I say after I've emptied my plate.

Diego is still working on his fries. "Remind me never to share with you," he teases.

I smile and catch my reflection in a mirror behind him. *Good god, I do look rough.*

"I'll be right back," I say, leaving my barstool and turning toward the bathroom.

When I take a good look in the restroom mirror, even with the low light I barely recognize myself. My hair is a mess that hasn't been combed in days and dark circles are starting to appear under my eyes. I unzip my backpack and rummage through its contents, searching for anything I can use to make myself look human again. I find Mamie's emergency makeup kit wedged in the bottom of the bag. I forgot to take it out. Thank goodness. I made fun of it then, but now I'm grateful the woman is a beauty savant.

I pull my hair out of the bun I've kept it in all week and let it fall loose around my shoulders. There's a bottle of dry shampoo in the kit, so I glance at the instructions and read: "Absorbs and removes oil, sweat, and odor." I spray it all over my head—twice. I search on my phone for a hairstyle that can disguise dirty hair and settle on a loose chignon.

There's even a facial wash in the bag, so I clean my face before I put on some makeup—powder, blush, and mascara so my eyes don't look like I came back from the dead. To finish, I daub on the red lipstick Mamie picked out, a color called Flaming Lips. *Just what I need.*

When I walk outside, Diego does a double take.

"Ready?" I ask.

"You look pretty," he says, rubbing the back of his neck with his palm. "I mean, you always look pretty. But this is nice too."

I reach for his hand, embracing the swell of electric energy inside my chest. I step in closer, until our bodies are almost touching. He looks down at my face, down to my lips and up to my eyes, and suddenly it's not just my lips that are flaming; every part of me is on fire. I like this. Feeling affixed to him somehow. Being so close I can sense the warmth of his skin. Catch the musk of his cologne. Experience the solid, steady presence that is him.

He leads me out of Butcher and into the street. We walk down the promenade, heading toward the river. I'm still feeling a little lightheaded, but the food helped soak up the champagne. Enough that I can walk on my own.

We leave the side streets and walk down the Quai Romain Rolland main avenue, following the Saône riverbank. It's a mild summer night and everyone is out and about, it seems.

We stop to watch a dinner cruise motor up the river. The boat's dim lights cast an eye-catching glow onto the water's surface.

"We went on one of those one time, Margo, my dad, and I," he says. "You would hate it." He laughs to himself, nudging my arm.

"Why? It looks nice." I nudge him back.

"The steak was overcooked and the potatoes didn't have salt. It's a bit of a tourist trap."

"Ah, but seriously, what were you expecting?"

He shrugs. "It's more about the experience, I guess."

The boat passes us, moving slowly up the river. The big windows on the side panels are meant to look out, but from our perspective they paint a picture of the scene inside. Dozens of people appear to be enjoying their ordinary meal of overcooked steak and bland potatoes. I watch a man reach across the table and kiss the woman on the other side. The last thing on their minds, I'm sure, is the food.

If that were Diego leaning over to kiss me, I'd probably not care about the overcooked steak either.

"It was a great night, actually," he says. "Margo and Dad even danced after dinner."

"Why did Margo and your father break up?" I ask as we start walking again.

"He works and travels all the time," Diego says with a twinge of resentment. "He was never home. It was always just Margo and me. She felt so bad that neither one of my parents were around that she would come up with these elaborate excursions on the weekends."

"Like what?"

He laughs at whatever memory comes to mind.

"This one time, we had just watched *Casablanca*. You know the movie?"

I nod. I mean, who hasn't seen *Casablanca*?

"We finished watching this movie and she gets a call from dad saying he's not coming home for the weekend. He has to extend his business trip or something. She hangs up the phone and gets this wild look in her eyes. The next thing I know, we're on a plane heading to Morocco."

"Are you serious?"

"I swear. It's only a two-hour flight. So we spent the weekend trekking around Casablanca." He smiles at the memory, a genuine smile. "I even got to skip swim practice. That was the best part."

We cross the river at a pedestrian bridge but stop halfway to take in the view of the cityscape. A dance of multicolored lights bounces off the grand historic buildings reflected in the river. The ripples add to the almost mystical, scenic feel.

There is so much history behind these buildings, it is hard to wrap my head around it.

We cross the bridge to the Presqu'île. The peninsula is a stunning array of medieval buildings, luxury window displays, and crowded restaurants. The streets teem with history and life—an intriguing mix of old and new, modern and classic.

"The place I want to show you is down here," he says.

I nod, still unable to comprehend how I ended up on this beautiful street, on a perfect summer night—walking next to this ridiculously stunning guy who makes me want to do impulsive things.

We follow a few narrow streets until we arrive at Place des Terreaux, where a four-story fountain of a horse-drawn carriage is the centerpiece of the plaza.

"Fontaine Bartholdi," Diego says. "It was sculpted by the same man who created the Statue of Liberty."

"It's beautiful." I step close enough to touch the outer rim of the pool around the fountain.

"Wait here. I'll be right back." As he walks away, he holds up all the fingers on one hand and calls out, "Gimme five minutes!"

"Where are you going?" I ask, but he's already taken off across the plaza. I lose sight of Diego, so I sit on a bench with a full view of the fountain.

Magnificent is the only word to describe this sculpture. A goddess-like woman sits atop a Romanesque chariot. She holds the reins of four wild stallions. The horses rear and plunge forward, held only by bridles and reins made of water weeds.

I am instantly captivated by the woman's calm and relaxed demeanor. Instead of freaking out and letting go of the reins, she leans back lightly with a dispassionate expression on her face. She has this under control, and she knows it.

I want to climb up the fountain and ask her what's the secret. How can she be so serene and steady when she's getting pulled in four different directions?

Diego returns a few minutes later carrying an ice cream dish in each hand.

"Hope you like waffles and ice cream," he says, placing a dish in my palm. "They have like a hundred flavors. You would've been there hours."

I smile because, I mean, we just ate a giant cheeseburger! With fries! Is he ever not hungry?

"Thanks," I say.

"You're welcome." He passes me a spoon and our fingers briefly touch, sending a shiver up my arm. I become keenly aware of his full lips and the shadow over his unshaven jaw.

"See, that wasn't so hard," he says, digging into his ice cream.

I take a spoonful of mine. It's chocolate, super creamy, and not too sweet, with just a hint of sea salt.

We eat enjoying a full view of the fountain. An uninterrupted stream circulates down the carriage, between the horses, and then crashes back into the pool. The mist blows in our direction.

"So, you think I'm a dropout?" He tears off a piece of waffle with his fingers and takes it to his mouth.

The question catches me off guard.

"I . . . no . . ." I stumble.

"Listen," he says, "I know it looks like I'm flailing around, but this is exactly what I set out to do."

Our eyes meet, and for a brief moment I see him, the real Diego. Walls down Diego. No nonsense between us.

"I'm sorry," I say, holding his gaze. "It's not that I think you're a dropout. Well, it's not that exactly. I just don't get it. How can you quit something you've worked so hard to achieve? What made you do it?"

He turns in the direction of the fountain and takes a spoonful of ice cream.

"I met this monk," he says.

"Huh?" I pivot sideways on the bench and cross my legs, leaning toward him. My knee brushes his thigh but neither of us moves away.

"I was browsing at this bookstore I go to from time to time. I like sitting in the aisle and reading through the stacks. But this one day, there was a monk there."

"Like a priest?" I ask.

"No, a real Buddhist monk. With the robes and the shaved

head," he says, turning to meet my gaze. A smile passes between us and I nod, urging him to continue. "He was giving a lecture about living a meaningful life or something like that. So I sat down, and it was like *bang!* Someone turned on this light inside me: my life had no meaning. It was as if I already knew it, but I needed to hear someone say it."

I don't feel a light go on inside me, but I do wonder what kind of meaning he's talking about. Is it the Lala Blessed Pies kind of meaning or the Papi having a midlife crisis and becoming a cherry farmer meaning? It seems that every time someone in my family tries to find so-called meaning, my life gets turned upside down as a result.

"So what happened next?" I ask.

"I stayed after the talk and spoke to the monk for like an hour. I told him I hated everything about my life: the swimming, the practice, the competition, the loneliness . . ." He pauses, scanning the plaza. "I just felt so . . . out of control. I had worked since I was five to achieve something I suddenly realized I didn't want. I couldn't even stand the smell of the pool. It made me sick. Still does. And I was so angry all the time. I hated everything."

I stare down at my ice cream and move the spoon around. It's mostly melted.

"What did he say?" I ask.

"He looked at me and said, 'What would happen if you just stop?'—and it was the most amazing moment of my entire life. I'm not even kidding. That was exactly what I wanted. I wanted to stop. I wanted to get off the hamster wheel and do nothing. So I did. And here I am in Lyon, sitting in a plaza built hundreds of years ago, eating ice cream with a beautiful girl who once tried to kill my dog with a cleaver. It doesn't get any better than this."

We both laugh. I jokingly plunge my ice cream spoon toward his chest. Diego grabs my wrist and looks at me hard.

Before I can overthink it, before I can come up with a million and one reasons why this thing between us is a very bad idea, I lean forward to kiss him.

He pulls back, still holding my wrist against his chest. "Are you sober?" he asks.

I nod.

"Are you sure this is what you want?"

I lean forward into his chin and close my eyes. I take in that scent of home and whisper a "yes, yes I am" before my lips connect with his.

As we kiss, my hands follow the contours of his chest. His wrap around my hips as he pulls me in closer . . . pulls me into pure sensation. Feeling his lips on mine and his hands exploring my body makes me forget about tomorrow, and all the days that came before and will come after. What kind of kiss does that?

This, right now, this is what I want. This is what I need.

Chapter 22

Cheeseball

The cruelest thing about death is how it forces you to keep living in a world where the people you love most no longer exist. They vanish to a place you can't reach and leave you with only their memories.

Exactly one year ago, Papi and I drove up the gravel driveway leading to Lala's farm for the last time.

I distinctly remember the moment her old Victorian farmhouse came into view. My heart swelled with a rush of joy every time. There was something magical about the place, like those countryside manors in old movies. It had three floors full of various rooms that wove in and out of each other. A long wraparound porch with big, white columns greeted us as we approached.

Lala stood by the back door wearing one of her flowery dresses, waving as we pulled in and parked. On the days we visited, she always wore heels and red lipstick. She also had her hair and nails done at the salon.

I slid into her outstretched arms and pressed the side of my face against hers, taking in the scent of Maja soap on her skin. I already missed her smell, even though I had just arrived.

"Mi morenita. Que Dios y la Virgencita me la bendiga," she said, blessing me in Spanish. She kissed me on the cheek, then rubbed off the lipstick smear with her thumb. "Let me look at you." She pressed my shoulders back with both hands so she could get a full view of my face. "Mi niña bonita. Even more

beautiful than last year." She wrapped me in her arms again, kissing my cheek a second time. I hugged her back, not wanting to let go. When we finally released each other, she announced lunch was waiting for us in the kitchen.

Then she turned to Papi, kissing his cheek. "You look tired, mijo. *Que te pasa?*" She inspected his face, frowning as if she had found some terrible, unspoken news in his eyes.

"*Hablamos después,*" Papi muttered. Did he really think I didn't know what that meant? *Later,* he told her, as in *when Isa is not around.*

We stepped inside her kitchen. Every smell in that room had a mouth-watering effect. Warm bread rolls rested in a basket on the farm table that served as an island. Pots of what I guessed were white rice and black beans lay covered on the six-burner stove, releasing the rich smell of cumin and oregano.

Papi and I exchanged a knowing smile. We were in for a treat.

Lala pulled a pan of slow-cooked pork butt out of the oven. My stomach growled the moment the smell hit my nostrils.

"This has to rest for thirty minutes," she said.

Papi and I groaned.

"But I'm hungry now," Papi whined, regressing a whole thirty years.

"Go take your things up to your room. Wash your hands. Everything will be ready when you come down," she said, ushering us out of her kitchen.

We complained some more but eventually did as she said. We had woken up before dawn and headed to the airport, flown to Kansas City, then driven an hour to the farm. We were both tired and hungry, usually a bad combination for either of us.

My bedroom was on the second floor, a large room with big windows and baby-blue wallpaper painted with roses. It was dainty and unapologetically pastoral—completely at odds with my modern, all-white bedroom back in Chicago. But part of me longed for this room the rest of the year. The same part that missed its four-poster bed and the vase full of wildflowers sitting on the night table, next to a small jar of Vicks VapoRub that Lala used as a cure for pretty much everything.

In the city, sleeping with an open window wasn't a choice. Too many ambulance sirens and cars honking. Here, the only sounds creeping through the open window were the chirping of crickets and the gurgling of a nearby stream.

But mostly, I missed waking up without an alarm and flowing through my days without having to follow a set schedule. Even though it always took me a few days to adjust to Lala's slow-moving country lifestyle, when I finally fell into that easy rhythm of things I deeply enjoyed it. Here, we strolled through the fields, picked flowers, and took half a day to make one pie. Here, I had all the time in the world.

After I washed my face and hands, I returned downstairs. Lala had set up the dining room table complete with white linens and her best crystal and china. Papi sat in the head chair, where Grampa Roger used to sit. Lala and I sat next to him, across from each other. She passed the serving dishes brimming with glossy white rice, black beans in a thick sauce, croquetas de bacalao, the roasted pork she'd cooked for thirteen hours at low heat, fresh yeast rolls, and sweet plantains.

"Where did you get these?" Papi asked, taking six plantains all at once.

"I drove to the international food market. They have all sorts of things," she said. "I even found some guavas," she said to me. Her cascos de guayaba with cheese were a rare delight.

Before we ate, Lala thanked La Virgencita for our safe travel and for having us home with her. I was just thankful for the mountain of delicious food I was about to eat.

Every flavor at that table will forever be engraved in my mind. The smokiness of her pork, with its spicy burnt crust and meat so tender it fell apart on the first bite. The combination of garlic and cilantro she used in her beans, in a sauce so thick, it coated every grain of rice.

This was Lala's best, the recipes she carried in her heart from Cuba. Those recipes survived a revolution and a lifetime of living in the rural Midwest. The city girl in me didn't know which was worse.

"How are your cooking classes going?" she asked me, moving a few more plantains to my plate.

I shrugged. "They're fine. I'm learning a lot of technique, I guess. But I already know most of that stuff. I'm ready for something more challenging."

"We'll play around with some recipes while you're here, okay? I'm trying out a new strawberry-rhubarb pie for my friend, Pauline," she said. "She loves my buttery crust."

I later learned Pauline was one of Lala's needle recipients.

"Can you make that Cuban cheese ball stuffed with meat before I leave?" Papi asked between bites.

"That's a Puerto Rican thing, not Cuban," Lala said. "A friend of mine in Miami gave me the recipe."

"It could've come from Mars and I'd still eat a whole one by myself." Papi chuckled, stabbing a piece of pork with his fork and taking it to his mouth.

"What is it?" I asked Lala.

"You hollow out an Edam cheese ball—you know, the one with the red wax around it?"

I nodded, picturing the cheese ball in my head.

"You hollow it and stuff it with minced meat. Then bake it until the cheese melts. Jaime loved it when he was a little boy."

"I love it now! But you haven't made it in years," Papi said. He finished his first serving and moved in for seconds. Papi never ate this much back home. At Lala's he ate like he was storing food for months or had a second stomach to fill.

"Fine, the next time I drive to the international market I'll get the cheese ball," she promised.

"Teach Isa how to make it," Papi said. "No reason why I should only have it once a year."

Lala and I both rolled our eyes at him.

"How is Adeline doing?" Lala asked, passing the bread basket around the table for a second time. "She hasn't called me in a while."

My eyes immediately turned to Papi, searching his face for a reaction. He cleared his throat and told Lala Mom was fine, which I knew was a big fat lie. Mom was far from fine. And I knew exactly why.

She had become quiet and withdrawn. She stopped playing her French music when she cooked—if she actually cooked. The weeks before had been a parade of takeout dinners.

Lala nodded, patting Papi's hand on the table.

After we finished eating, we were so full we could barely move. But even in that state, we always found room for Lala's dessert.

"For Jaime, apple pie," she said, placing a pie dish on the table.

Papi rubbed his palms together, his face contorted into a goofy grin.

"Hope you have another one of these back there, because I'm not sharing," he said, digging in.

Lala playfully smacked him on the shoulder.

"And for my Isabela, cascos de guayaba." In front of me, she set a small dish with four guava shells preserved in syrup and three big slices of white cheese. And even though my pants were about to snap open, I was so full, I ate my entire dessert.

"I just got a new hammock in the back. It's been waiting for you," Lala told Papi.

He moved from the table to his favorite place in the garden, a spot where Grampa Roger had hung a hammock years ago so Lala had a place to read her romance novels outside. She would lie there for hours, rocking back and forth while holding a book titled something like *Deseo Prohibido* or *Corazón Salvaje*—always written in Spanish, always with a shirtless man on the cover.

Lala and I cleared the table and stacked the plates and pots inside her farmhouse sink.

"Lala, sit down," I said. "I'll do the dishes." I knew she had probably been cooking up a storm since the crack of dawn.

"You want a cafecito?" she asked, reaching for her tartan thermos.

I nodded. I could never replicate the creamy texture of her coffee no matter how many times I tried. I was certain it had something to do with the old cloth strainer she used as a filter, or the way she heated the milk on the stove.

She poured the coffee into two porcelain cups.

"Remind me where your mother is again?"

I shrugged, not wanting to get into it. I couldn't bring myself to speak about what I'd seen on the street that day between Dad and Margo.

"What's going on?" she pressed.

"I don't know. I'm trying to stay out of it." I swallowed the knot in my throat. I wanted the image of them kissing deleted out of my brain. And I was so tired of keeping secrets. Most of the time, I felt like a traitor around my own mom.

"Sit with me for a moment, mijita," she said, pulling out a stool for me. I sat next to her and took a sip of her coffee. The familiar flavor warmed my heart in ways I could never explain.

"I want to tell you something, nena. It may not mean much right now, but maybe later . . ." She paused to sip from her coffee cup. There was a stillness in the kitchen that served as a quiet prelude to her story.

"Before Castro came marching into Havana, I had all these things I wanted to do," she recalled. "I had gotten my nursing degree—top of my class. I had my eye on a doctor at the hospital— very handsome man. He had a beard and broad shoulders, very, very handsome." She grinned playfully, and I got a glimpse of the young woman I had seen in black-and-white photographs.

"I wanted to get married, have children, and live in one of those big houses in Miramar—by the beach—where I could wake up listening to the ocean every day. That was going to be my life. If someone had told me how things would actually turn out, I'd told them they were crazy. Me? Living on a farm in Kansas? Married to a gringo?" She laughed to herself. "I hate the cold. I'm still an island girl in here," she said, touching her chest. "But life is like that, mija. You make all these plans, you have all these dreams, and things don't always work out the way you planned." She reached for my hand and held it in hers. Her paper-thin skin was soft and warm and somehow capable of passing on every bit of love she felt for me. "I want you to know this uncertainty is not necessarily a bad thing. Sometimes everything needs to fall apart so we can find the life we are meant to live. ¿Me entiendes?"

"Don't you miss it though? Don't you miss your life in Havana? Don't you wonder sometimes what it could have been?"

"You can't live in the past, Isa. If I had stayed, who knows what would've happened. I would've never met Roger. We would've never married. He would be married to some gringa instead. And Jaime would've never been born. Neither would you. And this moment, right now, would not exist. So I guess we can thank Castro for this." She chuckled, squeezing my hand.

Back then, I couldn't imagine a world without Lala. So yes, I was thankful for whatever confluence of events led to that precise moment in her kitchen.

"You have to open your heart, morenita. Open it big and wide for whatever comes, even the bad stuff. If you do that, I promise you will find your way. And when you look back, you will see it was a beautiful life. I promise."

That was July. By the new year, the world somehow continued to turn without Lala. I tried to open my heart big and wide like she had said. But it was too much to take in, all at once. Instead, I hid in the kitchen where a recipe served as a clear step-by-step plan. In the kitchen, order always ruled over chaos—until it didn't.

Chapter 23

A Googly-Eyed Plate

I'm back in Grattard's kitchen before dawn. After changing into my uniform, I walk straight to the espresso machine and make myself a triple shot, hoping that a steady caffeine drip will get me through the day. I also make a café au lait for Lucia; I know she likes those. Call it a peace offering to get us through the day.

I got exactly two hours of sleep. Back in this sobering, cold, stainless steel environment, I'm questioning some of the choices I made last night.

Nothing could've prepared me for that kiss. When Diego's lips pressed hard against mine, I was certain no one ever had felt as alive as I did in my own skin.

It all happened as if in a dream. His hands clutching the curves of my hips. His fingers creating sensations I didn't even know existed. His breath, warm against mine, was heavy with wanting.

I kissed him back, sinking my fingers into the roots of his hair. Leaning my head back, so his lips could trace the lines of my chin until they found my neck.

A shiver runs down my spine at the memory of his mouth kissing my collarbone.

It was thrilling and sexy and everything I imagined Diego could be and more.

When we got back to the house, we curled up together on one of the lounge chairs by the pool. Diego fetched a blanket big enough to cover both of us. After a while Beluga turned up and plopped himself by our feet. He was asleep and snoring in no time.

"What are you doing this weekend?" he whispered, kissing me on the nose.

I shrugged, unable to remember any plans.

"Come with me to Barcelona," he said, running his fingers down the back of my neck. The room spun in every direction at his touch.

"You'll need to get permission from my dad."

"That can be arranged. I know someone working on the inside."

I smiled and kissed him hard on the lips.

"Okay," I said, pulling back. Okay, as if he was asking me to stroll down to the market and not travel to another country.

Exhausted, I fell asleep in his arms.

Who needs eight hours of sleep? I thought in a haze.

Me. That's who.

The possibility of sex, I now realize, does weird things to your brain. Memory loss, for one.

What are you doing this weekend, Isa? Not going to Barcelona, that's for sure. My final exam, the one that will decide my fate in this kitchen, is scheduled for Monday. What are my plans? Going over every technique, method, and recipe I can get my hands on.

I pour a spoonful of sugar into the hot espresso and stir, allowing the crystals to thoroughly dissolve before drinking.

I'm facing the start of a grueling sixteen-hour day, and I'm already tired and cranky.

I find Lucia at our station, diligently working on her mise en place.

"Good morning," I mumble, setting down the café au lait in front of her.

"Thanks," she mumbles back, taking the coffee. Unlike me, she looks as fresh as a peach in July.

We get to work in silence, diligently prepping our station

for the madness ahead. I move about awkwardly, praying I can get through the day without making any significant mistakes or calling unnecessary attention to myself. I gulp down my coffee, eager for the caffeine to kick in. But instead, it goes straight through me with not so much as a jolt of energy.

"I have to go to the bathroom," I say. "I'll be right back."

"Good luck," she scoffs.

"What do you mean?"

"You'll see."

When I reach the bathroom, I jangle the door a few times but it's locked.

"What the heck?" I say to myself, unaware Snake Eyes is passing behind me.

"You have to get the key," he says, walking away.

"What key?" I ask.

"Can't you read?" he snaps before disappearing behind a tower of baking trays.

Someone's in a mood.

I glance back at the door and see a torn piece of paper I assume is the sign. A message in French reads we need to ask Hugo for the key.

Seriously?

It takes me fifteen minutes to find Hugo, who's in the receiving dock inspecting a shipment of oysters. My bladder is about to burst.

"When and where were these caught?" he says abruptly to the delivery man—a tall, middle-aged man with a crooked smile and rough hands.

"*Je ne sais pas,*" the man answers dismissively.

"If you can't tell me when and where these were caught—I want exact time and location—you can take them back. And tell your boss that Chef Grattard wants the exact time they came out of the water, not the time they made it to shore. Do you understand me?"

The delivery man seems immune to Hugo's condescending attitude—that or he flat-out doesn't care.

"I'll be back," the man says, returning the box of oysters to the back of his truck and slamming the double doors shut.

"*Imbécile*," Hugo mutters as the truck drives away.

I tap Hugo on the shoulder.

"Excuse me, Chef," I say, watching him flinch at my touch.

He turns around, glaring at me like I've just run over his cat.

"I need the bathroom key," I say, pressing my legs together.

Hugo releases an exasperated sigh. He glances at his watch and says, "Didn't you just get here?"

I blink a few times. *Is this guy serious?*

"I really need to go," I say with a mix of fear and impatience. No one told me I would need a diaper.

He strides back inside the restaurant and I follow. We stop at his station, where he produces a red logbook and a pen. The book lands with a thud on the metal counter.

"What do I do with this?" I ask.

"Write down the exact time you go in," Hugo says, fishing a key from his chest pocket.

"To the bathroom?" I ask, incredulous.

"In time and return time here." He points at a new blank page on the log. "Write your name. Chef Grattard wants to see everyone's name."

I oblige because I don't know how much longer I can hold it.

I finally get to pee. My head leans back in absolute relief. Then I wash my hands and face. I splash water on my hair and pull it back into a bun at the nape of my neck so my toque can rest on top of it.

I stare at my reflection in the mirror. My eyes are sunken from lack of sleep.

"Barcelona," I scoff.

In two days, Grattard, Troissant, and Hugo will decide who gets the coveted spot in Grattard's kitchen and opportunity to learn from the master himself. It dawns on me, though, that the master may be more of a madman.

Still, a madman with the power to change your life forever.

I step out of the bathroom. Hugo is outside, waiting.

"The average time is five minutes," he says, frowning at his watch. "Not ten."

I hand him the key, turning an appropriate response in my head. Before I can speak, he walks away.

I write my out time in the log, wondering if every high-end kitchen operates like this. And how does anyone last any longer than a month working under such conditions? I'm no expert but this seems insane.

"You just missed him," Lucia says when I return to our station. Judging by her strained expression, I can't decide if she's talking about Hugo or Grattard.

"Who did I miss?"

"Chef Grattard. He was just here. He wants to see how the dotted plates look on the table . . . in three hours."

"All forty dishes?" I ask, helping her organize the various sauces.

"All forty," she repeats, her voice taut.

"We can do this," I assure her. "We got this."

Who says the kitchen is not a team sport?

We divide the plates, twenty each. It takes about fifteen minutes to craft each one. We have less than three hours to finish. It doesn't take a mathematician to figure the timing doesn't add up.

Dot, dot, dot . . . I have no idea where the times goes. Hours later, my mouth is parched and my hands are shaking. Halfway through the morning, the wall fan behind us broke, unleashing a heat wave over our station. My skin is sweltering, my face drips with sweat, and I have a monster heat-induced headache.

I grab an ice cube from a tray in front of us and slide it against my lips. I'm not drinking water. Water equals pee. And pee equals the pee book. I'm not going though that indignity again.

My vision spins with dots by the time a server approaches our station.

"Are these ready?" he asks, a pleading expression on his face. "Grattard wants to see the dishes now." His dress shirt has big sweat stains under his armpits. "Please tell me you are finished with these."

I dip my needle into a bowl of sauce and create the last dot on my twentieth plate. Lucia is finished too.

"Last one," I say, pushing the plate in his direction.

"Take them away," Lucia says.

We watch him cart away the plates. When he's out of view, our eyes meet and we burst into uncontrollable laugher.

"That was crazy," I say, gasping for air.

Lucia is bent over herself, trying to get a grip.

"By plate ten, I thought I was going to go blind. All I could see were those stupid dots."

We lean into each other through another bout of manic laughter. We're soon both wiping fat tears from the corners of our eyes.

When the hysterics finally subside, I reach for Lucia's arm and say, "Listen, about the other day . . ."

"I would like to think it was a mistake," Lucia interrupts. She slides her hands into the pockets of her coat and squares her shoulders. The power in her posture makes me feel even smaller for what I did.

I'm certain the guilt on my face speaks for itself but none-theless I say a quiet, "Yes, it was a mistake—a stupid mistake."

Lucia sighs, then turns to me and says, "Look around you; we are the only two girls in this kitchen. Instead of wasting our energy backstabbing each other, like they do, why don't we focus on helping each other. That's what I want to do, anyway."

I nod. "That's a good plan."

"Should we go see how the plates look? There's air-conditioning in the dining room," she says.

"Lead the way."

We stand by the server pass, which offers an unobstructed view of the dining room. One long table spans the length of the restaurant, with a lavish array of flowers and candles as the centerpiece.

"I heard the fish guy say Grattard had the tulips flown in from Holland this morning," Lucia says.

"Did this fish guy say who's coming to dinner?" I ask, taking stock of the gold-rimmed chargers and glassware on the table. Every piece has been exquisitely chosen.

"He thinks it's a repeat customer. Some prince from a royal family in Asia," Lucia says. "Whoever it is, they have money to burn."

"No kidding."

Chef Grattard himself oversees every detail. The server tasked with carrying our dotted dishes carefully places each one on the table as if he were handling explosive material. Every plate, we overhear, has to be at exactly the same distance from the edge of the table. How they will re-create this effect when all the guests are seated, I have no clue.

When the last dotted plate is set on the table, and the server steps to the back of the room, the chef's ultimate vision is revealed.

"Wow," I whisper, afraid that even the tiniest sound will disturb the artistry I'm bearing witness.

"Did you see the way the dots catch the light?" Lucia whispers, one hand half covering her mouth.

A couple of years ago, Mom and I went to see an art exhibition in Chicago by a Japanese artist named Yayoi Kusama. Mom got the tickets months in advance, which was necessary as it ended up being a sold-out show. Kusama's "infinity rooms," as she calls them, were strewn with hundreds of thousands of dots. Her dot obsession is only rivaled by Grattard's. The museum tour guide told us Kusama was the kind of artistic genius who could force spectators into the unknown. Mom and I agreed. It was like stepping into someone else's imagination.

Staring at the dotted plates, I realize Grattard is not serving a meal. He's creating a life-altering experience.

"Wow," is all I can say.

"Fish guy said he's serving the lobster claw salad on our plates," Lucia says giddily.

We exchange proud smiles. And for the most ephemeral of seconds, we relish in a shared sense of accomplishment, as together we watch Grattard pace around the table.

"Off the table," Grattard suddenly bellows.

Lucia and I jump in fear.

"What's going on?" she murmurs.

"No dots. I don't want the dots. Get rid of the dots," Grattard barks, snapping his fingers at the server. The poor man stands paralyzed at the back of the room.

"What's wrong with our plates?" I whisper, unable to compute the scene evolving in front of us.

The server can't get to the dotted plates fast enough. Grattard, losing whatever patience he has left, grabs the plates himself and tosses them into a dirty dish bin.

"Dots? Why am I doing dots?" he shrieks. "Do you see this?" he asks the waiter.

There is so much fear on the server's face that his left side has developed a nervous twitch.

"Can you see the curve of the lobster claw? The nest of lettuce? It's all wrong. I want all these plates gone!"

A whole morning of punishing work is tossed into a dish bin on a whim.

Lucia pulls on my sleeve to get me to move. Like the server, I too am paralyzed.

"Let's go," Lucia says, sounding dejected.

We return to the sauce station in silence. All the other cooks have also gone unnaturally quiet. Even the hum of the kitchen equipment seems to have temporarily subsided.

Chef Grattard bursts into the kitchen and slams shut the door to his office. Someone drops a pot in the back, but the way it clinks and clanks, reverberating on every surface of the kitchen, it might as well be a bomb.

"What do we do now?" I ask.

"Wait, I guess."

During the downtime, I submerge my hand in a bucket of ice water. The cold helps ease the stiffness from holding the needle tool way too tight for way too long.

A short time later, Chef Grattard reappears, calling out for Hugo.

Hugo sprints from the back of the kitchen like he's been called to put out a fire. And maybe that's exactly what he'll need to do.

"We are doing something new," Grattard tells Hugo, loud enough so the cooks in the back can hear.

Lucia and I peer through an opening in the sauce station. We have a clear view of Hugo but not Grattard. Hugo rings a towel in his hands with enough force that he could probably rip it apart if he pulled a little harder. He mumbles something I can't hear.

"What did Hugo just say?" I whisper.

"I think he said we don't have time for something new," she whispers back.

"Whose name is on the door?" Grattard bellows. "My name. It's my name. I decide if we have time."

Grattard gives Hugo a sheet of paper. "This is what we are serving. I want to see it in an hour."

I don't have to see what's on the paper to know it will be extremely complicated to execute and will look absurdly elaborate on the plate.

After Grattard locks himself back in his office, Hugo glances at the white piece of paper in his hands. I swear on Lala's grave, his soul seems to eject out of his body the moment his eyes land on the page, like the man just gave up on his life because of whatever is written there.

Not only do I feel sorry for him, in that exact instant I realize I don't want to be him. Not ever. Not by a long shot.

When Hugo finally snaps out of it, the first words out of his mouth are, "Listen up, you good-for-nothing scumbags! I'm not repeating myself! You"—he points at one of the cooks—"find me twelve tins of black osetra caviar."

The cook nervously shifts his weight from one foot to the other. "Chef, where am I supposed to go?"

"The market. The fish vendor. I don't care where you go. But either come back with twelve tins of caviar or don't bother showing up. Ever."

The cook scrambles out of sight. He leaves out the back door with his toque still balanced on his head. If this guy doesn't come back with the caviar, his only culinary future will be in a McDonald's kitchen.

Hugo calls out the other ingredients. "Crabmeat, seafood gelée, cauliflower puree." The staff moves so fast they are tripping over each other. Someone is dispatched to buy crabs since, like the caviar, this is not an ingredient we keep on hand. A cook is asked to make the seafood gelée from the stock we have, and someone else is tasked with the puree. And just as I am wondering what my role will be in this bedlam, Hugo drops a stack of large gold dishes at our station.

"You and you," he barks at Lucia and me. "Memorize this." He tapes Grattard's sketch in front of us. "You will plate."

I glance at the sketch, then at Hugo. My first thought is to tell him he has lost his mind if he thinks we can plate this . . . thing. But then I catch his eyeballs bouncing around inside the sockets. Yes, he has lost his mind.

He leaves, then returns with a handful of squirt bottles and specialty spoons. "You will need these," he says before he leaves for good. I watch him disappear into the walk-in cooler and lock the door behind him.

"That man is about to crack," I say.

"Hugo?"

"He just locked himself inside the walk in. It's thirty-five degrees in there."

Lucia takes the sketch and studies it.

"Amazing," she says. "This is . . . It's a work of art."

She hands me the paper. On it, Grattard has drawn what will surely be his latest masterpiece: a shiny round layer of black caviar sitting atop a delicate mixture of crabmeat, which is floating on a pond of seafood gelée. The pond is dotted with cauliflower puree. He doesn't call them dots, though; he calls them pearls.

"How many pearls is this?" I ask, trying to do a quick count on the page.

"Sixty," Lucia says. "Plus the sixty tiny green spots on top."

"Is that gold?" I ask, pointing to the garnish at the center of the dish.

"Twenty-four karat gold leaf."

"Of course."

Panic starts to set in.

"We have to plate forty of these in an hour?" I ask, my voice tight with stress and fear.

"We just have to go a little faster than last time," Lucia says. I don't know if she's trying to reassure me or herself. "We need a system."

We work fast, organizing our station and debating a plan of action.

"Efficiency is key," I say. "We can use a squeeze bottle for the puree pearls."

"If you do the pearls, pass the plate to me so I can finish the green dots with a needle," she adds.

Cooks from other stations drop off the components of the dish. The green sauce for the tiny dots appears, then the cauliflower puree. The head of the fish station brings the seafood gelée and the crabmeat mix, both of which smell amazing. The only thing missing is the caviar. I pray for the guy who got sent on that mission. He might as well leave the country if he can't find the twelve tins on time.

"Where is he?" Hugo yells, slamming shut the door of the walk-in behind him. I guess the cold air didn't help.

As if on cue, Caviar Man runs into the kitchen carrying a

small cardboard box. It all happens in slow motion after that. He shouts, "I got it." His shoe gets stuck under a floor mat. He trips. The box glides through the air. The lid opens and out fly twelve tins, like tiny projectiles, some hitting Hugo square in the head.

No one dares to move. The last can hits the floor, swiveling in circles and making a metallic brushing tone. When it finally stops, Hugo picks up a can that landed by his feet and quietly drops it off at our station.

Lucia and I work in silence. At this point we can anticipate each other's movements.

We plate the crabmeat and the caviar at the center of the plate using a mold ring. Then, very slowly, pour a pool of seafood gelée around it.

But when it's time to create the cauliflower puree pearls, my hand starts trembling like I have some disease of the nervous system.

These pearls require surgical precision. I have to squeeze exactly the right amount of puree out of the bottle and onto the plate to create a perfectly sized pearl while not disturbing the gelée pond.

"Hold your wrist," Lucia tells me.

I wrap my left hand around my right wrist to keep it from trembling.

"Almost done," she says to someone behind me. I don't have to turn around to know Hugo is breathing down my neck.

I grip the squeeze bottle tighter, moving steadily around the plate. I have to create three rows of pearls before I pass the dish to Lucia. It takes every ounce of concentration in my body and mind not to screw this up. After my sixty pearls are finished, I get out of the way and let Lucia do her thing with the green dots. When she steps back, I pinch the gold flecks with a set of tweezers and drop a small amount at the center of the caviar circle.

Hugo, Lucia, and I step back at the same time.

"It's beautiful," Lucia says.

"Don't you think it's a little creepy?" I ask.

"What do you mean?"

"It looks like a swamp creature with lots of eyes," I say. "Like the dinner is staring back at you."

"Just give me the stupid plate," Hugo says, sounding both hopeless and exhausted.

As I watch him walk into Grattard's office, shoulders hunched as if he's carrying the whole kitchen on his back, I can't help but wonder if Hugo ever had any joy in him. And if he did, where did it all go?

Chapter 24

Lemon Granizados

Someone is knocking on my door. The thought comes to me from the deepest corner of my sleep mind.

I left La Table de Lyon after our forty swamp-creature salad plates were served and our station was spotless. It wasn't the president who came to dinner after all, but some lame oil magnate and his retinue of uber-rich buddies and their wives. They drank enough champagne, spirits, and wine to fill an Olympic-sized swimming pool. Excess seemed to be the official theme for the evening.

The party toasted and clapped hard for Chef Grattard when he entered the dining room. We heard them say the meal was "legendary." Grattard never came by the kitchen to thank the people who actually prepared it. It was disappointing but to be expected, I guess. In that kitchen, we're all cogs in Grattard's great machine.

"Isa, are you up?" Diego's voice travels into my room. I squint my eyes open and see his figure backlit against the doorway.

"I'm sleeping," I mumble, covering my eyes with a pillow. But he walks in anyway and sits on the side of my bed.

"We leave in thirty minutes. Have you packed?" he asks.

Crap. The weekend Barcelona thing.

I groan under the pillow, fully awake now and trying to process Diego sitting on my bed.

"Come on. Get dressed. I made you coffee." He gently pulls

away the pillow and wafts the open travel mug against my face. The smell of coffee, milk, and sugar is irresistible. I'm an addict, what can I say.

"That's not fair," I say, grabbing the mug and pushing myself to a seating position. "Barcelona, huh?"

I know I can't go. There is no way I can go away for the weekend with my final exam two days away.

I pull my legs in and wrap my arms around my knees.

From my point of view, the back of his head is washed in light coming from the hallway, and he looks like he has a halo around him. My eyes land on his lips and every sensation of every kiss comes rushing in. An intense ache settles in my stomach. I tighten my grip around my folded legs and force myself to look away. Why is it so hard to say what I have to say?

"I'm sorry, but I can't go," I whisper. "I have my final on Monday. Maybe some other time?"

Diego throws both hands into the air. "You know everything there is to know in that kitchen," he argues. "What more can you possibly cram in two days?"

I shrug.

"For one, my soufflé is still not up to par."

He rolls his eyes and stands.

"And besides, I can't just go on a whim," I blurt out.

"Why?"

"Why what?"

"Why can't you go on a whim?"

Our gazes meet. I stare into the dark brown of his eyes, fighting the urge to get lost in them. Part of me is scared of where this might lead. Scared of letting go.

"I can't," I say, quietly.

"Here's the deal," he says more firmly, "I already made all these plans because you said you wanted to come. I had to pull some serious strings to make this thing tonight happen. But we have to be in Barcelona by six."

I open my mouth to argue, but he doesn't let me.

"And it will mean a lot if you get your butt out of bed, and for once let someone else take care of you. Who knows, I may surprise you."

He turns to leave but stops by the door.

"I'll be downstairs. I'm leaving in fifteen minutes—with or without you."

He doesn't even close the door when he leaves.

Ugh! This. Guy. I hit the mattress hard.

I stare at the open door, arguing with myself. My head is telling me it's irresponsible to even consider the possibility of doing anything this weekend other than preparing for this exam. But my heart disagrees. My heart is ushering me to get dressed and out the door.

"Arrg," I say aloud. "Why is this so confusing?"

My head and my heart compete for an answer, but I've already made up my mind. I jump out of bed and into the shower. In minutes, I'm dressed and holding a backpack with a change of clothes and a few toiletries.

"Where are you?" I call, rummaging around my room in search of my cell. I find it under my soiled apron, sitting on top of Lala's cookbook.

I haven't opened the book since it arrived at our Chicago house in a box addressed to me. A letter from some estate manager Papi hired said Lala left all her kitchen stuff to me. Everything was wrapped in tissue paper and styrofoam. The only two things I took out were her tartan thermos and the cookbook. There were too many memories inside that box to deal with them all at once.

I reach for my cell but find myself also reaching for the cookbook. I stuff both into my backpack and dash out the door.

In exactly fifteen minutes, I'm stepping onto the gravel, backpack swung over my shoulder and a mug in my hand.

"The dog stays," I say, dropping my bag into the sidecar. "I'm not riding to Barcelona covered in drool."

Diego tosses me a helmet. He doesn't bother hiding the amused grin on his face.

"I can't believe I'm doing this," I say, taking a long sip of coffee.

"I knew you had it in you."

"Thanks for the coffee. It's perfect."

"I've seen the way you make it. I was going to put it in that thermos you like to use. But it would've been hard for you to drink on the road."

I smile, lean in, and kiss his cheek.

"Thanks."

"You're welcome." His arm wraps around my back and he kisses me on the lips. My legs turn to human jelly at the warm feeling of his mouth on mine. I close my eyes and kiss him back. Wherever he's taking me this weekend, this is only the beginning.

We pull away and he takes my hand to help me inside the sidecar and settle onto the small leather seat.

"Where are we going, exactly?" I ask.

"You'll see when we get there."

"Does my dad know you're kidnapping me and taking me to another country?" I fasten the helmet strap under my chin.

"Of course he knows. What kind of man do you think I am?" he says, that sly grin appearing on his face.

Truth be told, I never stood a chance against that grin.

He pulls down the visor on his helmet and turns the ignition key. His boot kicks down the start pedal and the motorbike roars to life under us.

We pull out of the driveway just as the sun is coming over the horizon, bathing the cherry trees in a soft morning light.

This is nuts. What am I doing?

I sit back and watch the scenery speed past us. Cows roam the pastures. A farmer feeds chickens around a coop. A store clerk opens his shop for the day's business. A deliveryman drops off a few boxes of lettuce. A stray dog barks at the motorbike, running behind us like he thinks he can catch up. Diego and I speed past the fields of Bessenay, but to me it doesn't feel like I am moving forward. Instead, I feel like I am leaving something behind.

Papi is poised to start a new family but I am still grasping at the family we used to have. I miss our old family so much that sometimes it feels like someone carved out my insides. There's a big hole where we all used to be: Papi, Mom, Lala, and Grampa Roger.

How do you even begin to let go?

Once we hit the major highway, we leave Lyon behind us. The Rhône River is to our left as we ride for hours, the wind in our faces and the sun climbing high over us. We pass a few gas stations and convenience shops on the side of the road, and eventually stop for a quick baguette lunch at a café near the highway. A truck driver pulls up next to us, honks his horn, and waves. I wave back. I suppose he thinks this is all so very cute: two kids on an impromptu motorcycle road trip in the south of France. Yeah, it's kinda cool, I guess.

We cross the Spanish border at Le Perthus, a town perched on mountains and split down the middle between the two countries. Then we ride along the Mediterranean highway surrounded by fields and mountains in all directions as well as the occasional town. After so many hours on the road, it's a relief to see a blue highway sign welcoming us to Barcelona.

This is Diego's home. I perk up in my seat, eager to take it all in. Maybe I'll finally understand why he ditched his old life.

We exit the highway and enter the city. The streets immediately become a maze of apartment buildings, shops, historic landmarks, public parks, and big open plazas. The one thing I notice, though, is the slow-moving way people saunter along the sidewalks—with a sort of laid-back attitude that seems to come naturally to coastal residents. I watch a group of middle-aged women hanging out at a café, talking and laughing with no sense of urgency. I decide that for today, this will be me. I too will be the slow-moving, sauntering, no-sense-of-urgency kind of girl.

I take off my helmet as we enter the city center and become overwhelmed by the 360-degree view of medieval architecture, broad boulevards lined with shady trees, and charming cobbled streets.

"I love it," I say, loud so Diego can hear me over the sputtering of the motorcycle.

He glances back but the helmet visor conceals his expression. I imagine that all-consuming smile hiding underneath.

We pull into a parking spot by one of the big plazas and he cuts off the engine. A sign reads *Plaça Catalunya*.

"Welcome to Barcelona," Diego says, taking off his helmet.

He dismounts and walks over to the sidecar to help me stand—help I'll need, as my legs are half asleep. I take his hand and step out into him, into his arms.

"I'm so glad you came," he says, kissing me softly on the lips. How can his lips have this crazy earth-rattling effect? Every. Single. Time.

"I want to see everything," I say.

"I'll show you as much as I can in twenty-four hours. We may have to skip the whole sleeping part, though."

"Who needs sleep?" I say, stretching my arms into the sky to get my bearings.

"This is where the tour starts: the city center," he says, throwing his backpack over his shoulder. I also take mine. He stores the helmets in the back of the sidecar.

We walk aimlessly at first so I can take in the historic buildings looming on the periphery and the massive fountains throwing mist into the air. There is a verve to the Plaça due to multiple roads converging into it, like energy streams flowing into one massive hub.

Around us, children run carefree and a flock of pigeons gathers by a food vendor. Rows of evergreen trees dampen the noise of traffic. Public gardens burst with purple and pink flowers. Big statues tower over pedestrians. There are drink vendors, ice cream vendors, food vendors, and souvenir vendors—there is even a man selling balloons in the shape of cartoon characters.

Diego and I exchange a smile. His face beams with some kind of national pride as he explains that this plaza is the meeting point between the old town and the new city.

"It marks the beginning of Las Ramblas," he says, "the central boulevard that cuts right through the middle of the city. Anything you have ever dreamed of, you will find on Las Ramblas."

"Anything, huh? I'll have you know that I have high hopes for this place."

"I wouldn't expect any less from you."

"I like this, my own private tour guide," I tease, bumping my arm against his. "Am I going to have to tip you at the end?"

"I'll think of something," he says with that heart-stopping grin that makes all the heat in my body rush to my face.

We join a large group that has gathered to watch some street performers. A hip-hop tune blares from a boombox and everyone is clapping to the beat of the song.

A kid, probably about our age, contorts himself in gravity-defying ways. His body lifts vertically into the sky while he supports himself with just the palm of his hand. Then he goes horizontal, almost levitating, with his fingers bearing all the weight. His fingers move slightly as the rest of his body circles the plaza. The crowd goes crazy as he further unfolds into a seamless combination of yoga, martial arts, hip-hop, and acrobatics.

I dig into my bag and pull out a few euros to drop inside the collection hat. Diego does the same.

"These guys are amazing," Diego says. "They belong in a circus or something."

"Back home, he would get hired by a dance company in a heartbeat," I say, thinking of people I knew at school who had danced their entire lives and still couldn't do what this guy just did. "It's strange how some people just have a gift."

"What do you mean?" he asks.

"Some people just don't have to try to be good at something. They just are," I say. "It's so frustrating for the rest of us."

We leave the performance and walk toward a drink vendor selling granizados. I learn this is Spain's version of a slushy. Diego orders an orange-flavored one and I ask for the lemon. It tastes sweet and refreshing, just like iced lemonade.

"Why do you think it's not fair?" he asks.

"Because while the gifted are walking around with a lighter in their pocket, the rest of us are rubbing two sticks together. And it doesn't matter how good you are at rubbing sticks, you will never be as effective as the girl with the lighter."

Diego looks at me like I've officially lost it. "Is this about your cooking?" he asks.

I shrug. "Maybe."

In a way, it is about my cooking, but it is also about the difference between someone like Lucia and someone like me. In the lighter versus sticks department, I'm left rubbing twigs. "This was one of the best days ever"—that's what she said before we left the kitchen. I so badly wanted to feel the same way. But all I could genuinely feel was pure exhaustion. I was so sick of rubbing sticks all night that I couldn't even enjoy the fire when we finally got a flame going.

We walk by an empanada truck to the side of the plaza with the logo Señor CheChe Empanadas. I wonder if it is related to the one at Le Marché Saint-Antoine, the one Lucia liked so much.

Diego bumps my arm softly and nods toward the truck. "They make the best apple empanadas."

"You must know, I come from a long line of apple pie enthusiasts," I say, taking a sip of my granizado.

"Oh yeah . . ." He chuckles.

"My grandmother, Lala, was the Wyandotte County Fair pie contest winner ten years in a row," I say. "It was a record."

"I've never tried this pie, so my money's is still on Señor CheChe."

"So wrong."

He leads me by the hand as we walk to the food truck.

"Una de manzana y canela, por favor," he orders in Spanish. The truck vendor hands him a freshly fried pastry wrapped in a napkin.

"Here you go," Diego says, giving it to me. "I think your abuela may have some serious competition."

"Have some respect. She was like county fair royalty." I bite into the empanada. It is indeed delicious, but it will never compare to Lala's pie. For one, the apples are missing that juicy crispness that was the signature of Lala's orchard. It's also missing that extra pinch of nutmeg that gave her syrup a nutty-sweet aroma.

"So?" he asks.

"Not even close." I laugh, sharing the empanada with him.

"Do you get to see her much?" he asks.

"She died about six months ago."

"I'm so sorry," he says.

I stare ahead and take a long sip of my drink. I don't know if it's the beauty of this place, or having Diego by my side, or tasting the sweet apples, but suddenly I feel so moved I could cry.

"Hey," he says, grabbing my hand. The warmth on his skin is enough to make me feel connected to someone. "You want to sit for a second?"

I nod, then follow him to a bench.

"Tell me about her," he says as we sit. I repeatedly stab the ice in my cup with the straw, trying to sort out where to start. My eyes follow a pigeon helping himself to some leftover popcorn.

"She was amazing. She had this laugh . . ." I instinctively touch my chest. "It came straight from her heart." My eyes sting with tears but I keep going. It's been so long since I've shared Lala with anyone that now that I've started, I can't stop myself. "Her kitchen was like this wonderland. She was one of those people with the gift—she had her own fire, you know?"

He nods and reaches for my hand. His touch gives me permission to continue.

"Everything she made was exquisite. Even her butter! Oh my god, she would add honey and thyme from her herb garden. It was the most delicious butter ever. And when she served it—it's crazy—she would put this little dish of her special butter in front of you, and in that moment you felt like the most special person in the entire freaking world. Like someone loved you so much that they had come up with the best butter ever made, just so they could share it with you. And now all that is gone."

I blink and a few tears stream down my face. Diego brings his thumb to my cheek and wipes them away. I lean in a little closer and hold his hand in mine, needing so badly to feel the presence of someone who cares. "I miss her so much that it physically hurts."

Diego squeezes my hand in silence and I squeeze his back. There is only kindness in his eyes. It softens the defined features of his face in a way I haven't seen before.

"I'm sorry, Isa," he says. "But I'm sure she knew how much you loved her."

I shake my head, finally releasing all the self-hatred and blame I've been carrying. And regret. So much regret. It eats at me every time I think of her.

"I never got to tell her any of this," I say. "I hadn't spoken to her for a while when she died. I kinda pulled away in the last months."

"Why?"

"I was being selfish," I say, the truth squeezing my heart.

When Papi told me she got sick from those needles, I was so angry I couldn't even bring myself to call her. I was too afraid of what I might say. How could she leave me when I most needed her?

"Anyway," I say, taking a deep exhale. "Papi keeps wanting me to make him her apple pie, but I can't even open her cookbook."

"Maybe you just need to give it time," he says.

I nod, feeling my heart open a little. It's not the big and wide-open heart Lala would want, but it's enough to let me reach out to someone and deal with what's inside.

We sit in silence for a while and I drink the last of my granizado. There is more to be said, but right now I just want to be in the present. Be with Diego.

"Okay, then. So where do we go from here?" I ask, eager to do something in this city of his.

Diego stands and reaches for my hand.

"This is all part of the journey, Isabela. Enjoy it." He starts walking in the direction of Las Ramblas.

I don't know if it's the way he says my name—with the same singsongy Spanish intonation only Lala used—but I find myself trying to shake a peculiar feeling: that somehow Lala has a hand in this little road trip. I can't even begin to comprehend how that could be possible. But I know it's true. The same way I know when my chocolate chip cookies need to come out of the oven—I just do.

Side by side, we enter the crowded boulevard they call Las Ramblas.

Chapter 25

Tapas, Tapas, Tapas

And of course, he's right. There is everything you could possibly want or need here—an absolute cornucopia for the senses.

We walk by cafés serving sandwiches made with cured ham and Manchego cheese and delicious churros dipped in hot chocolate. On the other side of the street, a woman poses for a portrait painter who is meticulously capturing the refined lines of her nose. Next to them, a street performer dressed like some sort of winged gargoyle dances to the beat of Andean indigenous flute music. All of this is happening at once in some strange, imperfect harmony.

A million different things compete for my attention as we walk—the ripples on the street pavers that resemble water currents, the Barcelona postcards displayed on a souvenir kiosk, the smell of melted chocolate wafting from a nearby candy shop, and the color riot breaking out in a flower stand up ahead.

"Let's stop there," Diego says while nodding toward the flower stand. "I need to get something."

"Are we going somewhere in particular?" I ask, watching him pick up a bouquet of bright orange peonies. They are a shade of orange I have never seen in a flower before, like the petals absorbed all the color from a summer sunset.

Diego pays the vendor and thanks him in Catalan.

"Right down this street," he says, taking a firm hold of my hand. As our skin touches and we fall in step next to each other walking through this amazing place, I come to believe this day could not possibly get any better.

We leave the main promenade and head down a cobbled side street, shaded by a canopy of trees. Apartment buildings rise into the sky, painted in various shades of terra-cotta brown. Each floor has a long balcony with ornate black iron railings. The sound of conversation and laughter falls over us like rain.

"This is it," he says, stepping into an alcove that forms the entrance of a building. He presses a button on an intercom, and after it beeps he speaks into the box. "Es Diego," he says, switching to Spanish. A woman's voice tells him to come up.

"After you," he says as the front door buzzes open.

Inside, we are greeted by a shaft of light pouring from above, washing the old Spanish courtyard in sunlight. A fountain serves as the centerpiece. Potted plants and a few tables and chairs are scattered around the space. My American mind finds it odd the building residents have their doors and windows wide open onto the common space, as if they aren't worried at all about someone looking in or dropping by unannounced.

It occurs to me, this is probably how Lala lived back in Havana—with the windows and doors thrown open into a beautiful courtyard and life happening all around her. Makes me wonder what it would be like to live like this—in a wide-open space where everything and everyone are always welcomed.

We climb four flights of stairs all the way to the top floor. The sound of lively guitar music and laughter gets increasingly louder as we approach. When we arrive, I'm not surprised to see the apartment's front door is open.

"Dieguito!" A woman immediately wraps her arms around Diego for a hug. She kisses him on both cheeks. "I haven't seen you in years! How have you been?"

Her hair is arranged in a bun at the nape of her neck and pretty green earrings dangle from her ears. Her skin is glowing bronze and there is a youthfulness in her smile that doesn't match the wrinkle lines around her eyes.

"Isa, this is Clara," Diego tells me. "She's married to one of my swim coaches, Pablo, aka *El Jefe*. Best youth coach in the league."

The mention of her husband's nickname makes Clara laugh. "The kids still call him that. Can you believe it?" She turns to me, bringing me in for a hug. "So good to meet you." Then kisses me on both cheeks. It's a sweet gesture.

"I'm so glad you could make it tonight," she says.

I smile and nod, even though I have no idea what exactly we are doing here.

"Thanks for making room for us, I know it was a last-minute request," Diego tells her.

"Oh, don't be silly. Pablo was so happy to hear from you after so many years." Then to me she says in a sarcastic tone, "Diego went on to the big leagues and forgot about the little people he left behind."

"I did not," he says, indignant.

She squeezes his arm playfully. "It's okay. We forgive you." Her palms gently land on our backs, ushering us both inside the apartment. "Let's get you seated. The other guests have already arrived. I promise it's going to be a lovely evening."

My curiosity only grows. What other guests? What's going on?

Clara leads us into her living room, where a shelf full of awards draws my eye. Instantly, I recognize the rosette.

"Is that a *Michelin*?" I ask, stepping closer to the shelf. I've seen it in photos, but it shines brighter up close. The words *MICHELIN Guide* are written above the name of a restaurant, San Pascual. In between is one rosette, indicating the number of stars and telling the world Clara's food is "high quality" and "worth a stop."

"Oh yeah, I forgot to mention, Clara is a chef," Diego whispers, a mischievous smile on his lips. A flash of pure satisfaction crosses his eyes.

"*You* have a Michelin?" I ask Clara again.

"Yes, but that was a long time ago," she says dismissively. "In another life." She winks and smiles.

Nothing about her calm demeanor, or her fresh makeup, says she is a chef—at least not like any of the ones I've met. The only cheflike quality about her is the long blue apron hanging from her neck and expertly tied around her waist.

"Diego told me about your classes. How is Grattard treating you?" she asks.

I search for Diego. What else has he told her about me? But he's already making himself at home, taking off his jacket and storing our things in a coat closet.

"It's good," I say politely. "I'm learning a lot."

"I studied in Paris," she says. "It was insane. I have no idea how I survived those years." She chuckles to herself.

"We got these for you." Diego hands her the flowers.

"*Ay, gracias.* You didn't have to," she says, bringing them to her nose. "I love how they smell. Aren't they beautiful?"

I nod, distracted by the sound of laughter coming from her terrace.

"Now, come and join the party. What can I get you to drink? Is sangria okay? I made a lovely white sangria with champagne. Used mint from my garden. It is delicious."

My eyes cut to Diego, as if to say, *No way I'm drinking champagne.* Just the sound of the word makes my stomach churn.

"Maybe later," Diego tells her. "I read on your website that you have a special orxata on the menu?"

"The best! Two orxatas coming right out," Clara says. "Now, go and take your seats. There is some bread and salad at the table, something to get you started."

Clara disappears into the kitchen, leaving us alone with her awards, including the large Michelin star staring back at us from the shelf.

"What's going on?" I whisper-yell the moment she leaves. "Why didn't you ever mention you know a top-level chef?"

"Whoa—easy, tiger. I wasn't hiding her." He titters to himself. "I was on social a few days ago and caught a photo Pablo posted of him and Clara making one those flambés you like.

Except they didn't burn their kitchen. She lets him use the blowtorch. You should talk to her about that."

I roll my eyes.

"Anyway, I remembered Pablo always used to bring her desserts to practice when I was a kid. Loved her flan! So I reached out to him, trying to connect you guys. To be honest, it was a selfish move—I was hoping you could talk her out of her flan recipe so you could make it for me."

I shake my head. "Of course."

"But come to find out, she's some big-time chef. I had no idea. That's when I learned about her dinner club thing. I called Pablo again and managed to get us two reservations."

I stare at him blankly, trying to understand the full scope of what he just explained. *Did he arrange all this for me?*

When I don't say anything, he rambles on. "You have to understand, Clara is booked months and months in advance. I practically had to beg. I think they pulled two extra chairs for us."

"You did all this for me?" I ask quietly.

He reaches for my hands and holds them in his. They are comforting and sturdy. I want them to wrap me tightly and not let go.

He leans in and kisses me on the forehead.

"I want you to enjoy yourself, okay?" he says, pulling me closer. "Tonight should be fun. Let someone else do the cooking."

I lift my face to meet his, stepping onto my toes so I can reach his lips.

"Thank you," I say. I've never meant it more.

"*De nada.*"

"You could've told me we were visiting a Michelin chef—and a woman at that."

"Pablo said she doesn't make a big deal about her awards."

"Are we going to her restaurant?" I pull out my phone to search for San Pascual. I bet it's amazing.

"This is it," he says as we step onto a rooftop garden overlooking the city. A large table runs the length of the terrace, where about two dozen people are already gathered.

"What is it?"

"Her restaurant."

"At her house?"

Diego doesn't answer. He's already five steps ahead of me, blending into the party.

Everyone's attention is set on an older man propped on a high chair, playing a Spanish guitar. His voice is throaty and rough but full of emotion as he sings something that sounds like flamenco pop. The lyrics are about falling in love with someone he once saw walking down the street.

Diego pulls a seat for me at the end of the table. I take my place and notice the place card with *Isabella* written in beautiful cursive.

Everything about the way the table is set screams attention to detail—the delicately knit tablecloth, the bright wildflowers in mismatched vases, the votive candles I know can burn for six hours, the embroidered cloth napkins that read *Buen Provecho*, and the cardboard menu cards presenting a three-course dinner. Clara's presentation is both whimsical and exquisite.

"Do you know these people?" I ask.

"No, these are Clara's customers. Apparently, she's been doing it for years. She calls it *Club de la Cena*, the Dinner Club."

Most of the guests, I realize, must be tourists. I catch the sound of a conversation in German and another in Portuguese. Their laughter sounds the same in any language.

"Last year a travel magazine did a story on her, and she couldn't keep up with the reservations. She only takes twenty-four people at a time. It's very exclusive." He elbows my arm gently.

"These are some serious brownie points you've just earned," I tease.

"What's a brownie point?" he asks.

"You know, when you do something nice for someone else."

"But does it translate into actual brownies?"

I laugh. Of course he'd find a way for this to result in more dessert for him.

"I'll make you the best brownies you've ever had," I tell him in a slow and deliberate voice. His hand lands on my knee, and I feel my own body melt like hot chocolate.

His cheeks go red as he says, "I can't wait."

I'm relieved when a server brings our orxata glasses and leaves a full pitcher on the table. I grip my glass and gulp down about half its contents in an attempt to cool myself.

"This is really good," I say, refilling my glass. Diego explains the milky drink is made from a tuber called chufa. I love it. It's creamy and refreshing—exactly what I need if I'm going to get though dinner with Diego's fingers drawing circles on my knee.

The woman sitting next to me passes a bowl of salad. "Do you speak English?" she asks.

"I do," I respond.

"This is so yummy!" she says with an American accent.

"Where are you from?" I ask.

"Atlanta—I mean, originally from Puerto Rico, but I've lived in Atlanta for twenty years," she explains. "You?"

"Chicago," I tell her, feeling incredibly far away from home. "By way of France."

"Here, have some bread," the Atlanta woman says. She hands me a breadbasket and a plate of butter spread. "Chef Clara bakes it herself, I'm told."

Diego and I take turns serving ourselves from the salad bowl. Pieces of pear and dates are carefully arranged over a bed of arugula. The menu says the dressing has maple syrup, lemon zest, and mustard. My first bite is nothing less than divine. The flavors and texture are spot-on. The bread is equally amazing. It has notes of rosemary and garlic, and with the honey butter spread is simply decadent.

"There's nothing like this back home," the woman says. "I mean, sure, we have great restaurants, but this is an experience. You know what I mean?"

My mouth is full of warm bread, so I can't respond.

"You go to a restaurant, you eat your meal, and then you

leave. Here, you meet new people, you share a meal—something unexpected—you listen to beautiful music. It's pure joy. I will remember this."

The guitar player tells the guests he will now perform a Gipsy Kings cover called "Love and Liberté." His fingers run through a guitar solo full of everything that makes Spanish love songs sound so genuine, all passion and heat.

Diego leans into me halfway through the song and whispers, "Are you happy?"

It is an unexpected question and one that makes me stop. I turn my head to face him and I'm lost in his eyes again. I find only kindness staring back at me. I nod, unable to speak.

"Good," he says. "Very good."

I realize that for the first time in what seems like forever, I feel something other than pressure or anxiety, worry or sadness, or grief. For the first time in a while, my life feels full of color, and flavors, and sounds—which says a lot given I have been in a kitchen for the last three weeks.

The server takes away the empty salad plates and re-sets the table with clean dinner plates and utensils. Her unassuming but efficient serving style could compete with some of the best servers at La Table de Lyon. After she refills the guests' sangria glasses, she brings out the main course: multiple trays of tapas.

Diego leans over. "I told Clara how much you like tapas," he says.

"Please say you did not tell her that story," I say, blushing with embarrassment. That was not my finest hour.

"Of course I did," he says.

"God, you are the worst sometimes." Sadly, I know that to him, it's only a compliment.

The server sets a tray in front of us, then presents each dish. "Wine-braised chorizo, shrimp in garlic sauce, lobster empanadas, rolls stuffed with serrano ham, country cheese and fig preserve, patatas bravas with aioli, traditional ham croquetas, and gazpacho shooters." She fills our water glasses and tells us *buen provecho* before leaving.

"I don't know where to start," I say. "Everything looks incredible."

"Give me your plate," Diego says. When I do, he fills it with a sampling of everything.

When the plate makes its way back to me, I pick up a lobster empanada between my fingers and bite into the crispy brown dough. The lobster has been slowly cooked in a tomato sauce with small pieces of potato, green olives, and red peppers. I've never tasted anything like it.

"Do you think she will share her recipes?" I ask, digging into the ham croquetas. The bread surface is a mouthwatering prelude to the savory meat mixture inside.

"Doubtful, but you can try," he says while placing the last of the empanadas on my plate. "Pablo told me she guards her recipes like one of those mythical three-headed dogs."

"Cerberus," I offer between bites.

"That one," he says, pointing with his fork. "Some guy she worked with tried to steal her flan recipe once. It didn't go down well. In fact, it's probably best you don't ask for her recipe, even for me. I'd hate for you to be forced into hiding."

I think of Lala, Barbara, and our family's pie recipe. And Chef Troissant with her mandarine foie gras, an idea Chef Grattard took full credit for. I guess it's the same no matter where you live.

"Save room for the dessert tray. You won't want to miss out on that flan," Diego says. "It's all over the food blogs."

I stare at him in disbelief. "Since when do you read food blogs?"

"I like to be prepared." He reaches for another empanada and lays it on my plate. "I know you want another one."

I smile. A girl could get used to this.

I make my way through Clara's food, wondering how this perfection can happen outside of a professional kitchen and in awe of the cheerful atmosphere she created as the flawless stage for her sought-after meals.

On the horizon, the sun begins to set, and a string of lights comes on above us, crisscrossing the length of the terrace. As the guests comment on the merits of the food, I hear someone say she stayed an extra day in Barcelona just to come here. "Totally worth it," she tells the others.

By the time we finish dinner there are no leftovers on the tapas trays—I mean nothing. Even the smallest crumbs of patatas bravas have been devoured.

I lean back, trying to remember the last time I enjoyed a meal in such a way. The memory that comes is from my last summer at Lala's farm. Tonight feels like I'm back in Kansas.

"Do you like pie?" I ask Diego.

"I love pie," he says. "And even more if it's made by county fair royalty."

"How about a descendant of county fair royalty?"

"Like a pie princess?"

"Yeah, something like that," I say. Because maybe, just maybe, I'm ready to bake my way back home. And pies are meant to be shared; at least that's what Lala used to say.

Chapter 26

Spanish Flan

How did I manage to exist for seventeen years without knowing how to make the perfect flan?

I'm full, but that's beside the point. I take the last spoonful of Clara's flan to my mouth and enjoy every last bit of it, until the plate in front of me is tragically empty.

"I'm not even going to ask you if you liked it." Diego laughs to himself. He graciously ate the other desserts on the tray and left me the only slice of flan.

"Seriously, you have to get me her recipe. I will do anything. I will wash the dishes. I will be her slave for months. I need to know what kind of magic she puts into this thing." Because there is nothing short of magic in this dessert. It has a creamy consistency that tastes of caramelized sugar and vanilla without being too eggy. The problem with most flans is that the milk-egg ratio is way off.

The guitar player pauses, speaking into the microphone. He tells the guests Chef Clara wishes to thank them personally. Chef Clara saunters out of the kitchen and is met by applause. We give her a standing ovation.

"Gracias," she says, blushing. "Please, sit, enjoy a cordial courtesy of the house."

Our server comes by with a tray of small liqueur glasses and places one in front of each guest.

"Thank you all for being part of the Dinner Club," Chef

Clara says into the mic. "And thank you to Rosa for her impeccable service and Manuel for his beautiful music."

Everyone breaks out in applause again. I've never seen diners applaud a chef like this, with such gusto and authentic enthusiasm.

Chef Clara seems to respond in kind. She raises her hand to her heart and says, "It was my privilege to create this meal for you. I truly hope that you enjoyed yourself, and that you have a wonderful time in Spain and a safe journey back home. Come see us again."

Chef Clara walks about the table, personally thanking everyone. There is a sheen of sweat on her face, but no real signs of exhaustion. She looks genuinely happy to be interacting with her customers. At a big restaurant, this would be almost impossible. People come and go in a mostly anonymous manner.

After the cordials are enjoyed and Manuel has played his last song, everyone leaves, merrily pouring into the street below us. Chef Clara joins us on the terrace as Rosa clears the table.

"There's an extra piece of flan in the fridge with your name on it," Clara tells Diego as she sits down.

"And this is why I'm so happy Pablo married you." Diego squeezes her shoulder. "I remember, we all told him, 'Pablo, if you don't marry this woman, you are the world's biggest idiot.'"

Clara laughs, tapping the table with her hands.

"If it doesn't involve the pool, he is in no hurry," she tells me.

"He was the best coach I had growing up," Diego adds, his voice full of emotion.

"He was heartbroken when he found out you quit," she tells him. "You're lucky he's not here. He still talks about you coming back."

"Where's El Jefe, anyway?" he asks with a smirk. I chuckle at the coach's nickname, The Boss.

"He took our son to visit his abuelita in Manresa. They will be back late tomorrow. You will be gone then, right?"

"We have to leave after breakfast. Isa needs to prepare for an exam," he tells her.

Between the tapas and the flan recipe, I'd all but forgotten about my final.

"I'll be right back. Going to go claim my piece of flan. Isa ate the one you brought to the table. Didn't even offer me a bite." He grins and walks away.

My cheeks blush red with embarrassment.

"He told me I could have it," I explain.

"Swimmers . . . their stomachs are bottomless pits."

"Oh my god! Yes!"

She shakes her head and laughs. I join her.

After we catch our breath, I lean in to ask the one thing that's been on my mind the entire night.

"What made you leave the restaurant business? Seems like you were pretty successful."

She shrugs, undoing the bun at the nape of her neck and letting her long, dark hair fall loose around her bare shoulders.

"I grew up in a small town outside of Barcelona. We didn't have fancy restaurants, but my mother always prepared these four-course meals for us. We made flan, tres leches, all sorts of cakes. It was wonderful. And then I moved to Paris to attend the Cordon Bleu and stayed there to do my *stage*—I think Americans call it the internship, right?"

I nod.

"I was introduced to this world of cooking, and at first it was like the star on top of the Christmas tree. But then you work from one in the afternoon to one in the morning, on your feet the whole time. And the only break is to go to the bathroom—if you have time! You rush to get ready, you rush during service, you rush to clean. Rush, rush, rush . . . it never ends."

"But you got all those awards," I argue.

"Yes, but the more awards you have, the more people expect from you. I remember about five years ago, Pablo and I were talking about having a child. I was so naive, I thought I could juggle becoming a new mom, being a wife, and having a demanding career. And everything was going to work out perfectly because

I was this modern superwoman. After I had Sebastián, things got so crazy that one day, after I returned to work—I was still breastfeeding—I was going through the menu of the day with the staff, you know?"

I know exactly what she means. I watched Hugo do the same thing in Grattard's kitchen.

"And I noticed everyone was staring at me like I had just dropped from space, like an alien. I thought they were just stressed because we were serving a new dish for dinner, but when I went to the restroom I realized my chest was all wet. I had forgotten those milk pads that go inside the bra. And the worst part was I didn't have time to run home to change because I had to get the dinner service ready. It was a total disaster. I wanted to crawl inside the walk-in cooler and never come out." She laughs at herself.

"What did you do?" I ask, horrified. My arms instinctively fold over my own chest. How does that even happen? I don't even want to know.

"I stuffed my bra with paper towels and changed my chef's coat. What else was I supposed to do? Dinner must go on." Clara sips from her wine glass as if this was no big deal. I hope she's not expecting an answer.

"But you could have kept going, right? You didn't have to quit." I press the issue, because I want her to keep going. I need her not to quit.

"I could have, I just didn't want to," she admits. "I was miserable. I was trying to be in a million places at once, trying to please everyone. Meanwhile, I was getting out of bed grumpy every single morning. I was a complete mess."

"So what did you do?"

"I decided it was time for a change. I did some research and built a business model around how I envisioned my life to be. I made all those awards work for me." She pauses to take off the top of her apron. "I knew I wanted to spend more time at home with my family, be there for my son, I wanted to cook, and I wanted to be creative. So my plan was to organize these private meals for small groups—a manageable number. Then I hired Rosa and Manuel to make it more of an experience, with the music and the professional service. People love that. That was five years ago, and I wish I had done it sooner. You have to find what suits you and makes you happy. This makes me happy."

She eases back in her chair with a smile on her lips and takes another sip of wine.

I am thankful Clara is sharing her life with me, but at the same time I feel like her journey only proves you need the classical training and the awards to later do your own thing and truly be successful. If there is another way, as Diego says, is this really it?

Regardless of all the unanswered questions that remain, there is one I absolutely need the answer to:

"How do you make your flan?" I ask, almost pleading. "I need to know. I mean, I drove seven hours in a motorcycle to get here. I'll do anything."

Clara considers me for a moment.

"I don't just give away my recipes, you know."

I nod. "What can I do to earn it?"

Clara gazes at me, her face suddenly somber. "If everything I've heard about Grattard is true . . ."

"You have no idea," I interject. "Whatever you've heard, triple it."

"I think you've already paid for this flan with blood, sweat, and tears."

"So many tears," I acknowledge.

She pauses as if deliberating. I anxiously wait for the verdict.

"Okay, I'll tell you how to make my flan. I think you've earned it."

I clap repeatedly, bouncing with joy on my chair.

"It was my grandmother's recipe. You will need two cans of condensed milk, two cans of whole milk, six eggs, and vanilla. Pour everything into the blender for thirty seconds. Caramelize the baking pan before you pour in the mixture—use lots of sugar. Then bake for eighty minutes in a baño de María. Easy."

"Ah! Two cans of condensed milk," I repeat. This is it; this is the magic.

"Everyone else uses one can. It's not enough," she says.

I smile, feeling like she has just given me a huge gift. And in some weird way, it's all thanks to Grattard.

Diego walks back toward the table, holding the plate of flan at chest level as he takes a bite.

"You just ate a three-course dinner," I remind him.

"Mine had four courses," he says, digging into the flan. "I'm that special."

"You better be careful, Dieguito," Clara tells him, tapping his stomach. "Those abs won't last long outside the pool."

"Don't you worry about my abs," he responds. "Did you give Isa your recipe? I'll volunteer for the trials."

"I'm sure you will," I snicker.

"Listen, señorita, my people invented flan. The taste is seared into my taste buds." He places the empty plate on the table. "You need me," he says, meeting my eyes.

An electric current silently moves between us, across the table. Everything becomes absolutely still, and yet somehow he touches every part of me. Clara's patio fades as I realize I do need him. I don't know when or how it happened, but he's right. I don't want to let go.

Clara clears her throat. Her hand is playing with one of her earrings and she's suppressing a smile.

"Yes," Diego says, startled. "What was that?"

"I asked if you're seeing your father while you're in town." Clara says. "Pablo said you had a bit of a fallout."

Diego shrugs but doesn't answer. The smile on his face withers.

"I'm sure he only wants what is best for you," she says, rubbing his arm.

"We have different ideas of what is best for me," he says,

pushing the empty plate in front of him. "Anyway, can we help you clean up?"

"No, no, you go and explore the city." She pulls a key from a pocket in her apron and hands it to Diego. "You can sleep on the pullout couch. I made the guest room for Isa. When will you be back in Barcelona?"

"Soon," he says.

I glance at him, wondering what that means. How soon? And for how long? It never occurred to me as I ventured into needing him that he may be leaving Bessenay. A knot forms in the back of my throat at the thought of walking onto the patio at Villa des Fleurs and not seeing him stretched out on a lounger with Beluga lying at his feet. I never thought I could even miss that dog.

We leave Clara's apartment and take a taxi to Barceloneta Beach. The weather is clear and a full moon hangs from the sky, perfect for a stroll by the ocean.

The beach is crowded with restaurant-goers and pedestrians, so we walk toward a pier, where a few people are gathered at the end—mostly couples speaking in hushed tones.

Diego sits on the wooden boards, his feet hanging over the water. I take off my sandals and join him, letting my bare feet swing next to his. My body leans into him and I rest my head on his shoulders. The warmth of his touch travels from my side through my chest. Our feet entangle below, pulling the same heat all the way to the tips of my toes.

We don't speak as we watch the lights of a large sailboat cross the bay in the dark.

"We can leave a little later tomorrow, if you want to visit your dad," I say. At this point, an hour or two will not make much difference. The best I can hope for is that I'll be able to finish the test.

"I don't know, Isa," he says, his voice suddenly soft and

vulnerable. "I feel like he doesn't see me sometimes. Like I'm just a trophy son. I'm sick of it."

I take his hand and pull it into mine. Our fingers intertwine as our bodies move in closer. I've never felt like this with a guy—so just *me*.

"If I talk to him, he's only going to bring up Cambridge and the whole swimming thing. He thinks I'm wasting my life. Nothing I say is going to change his mind."

"What if it's not about that?" I say. "Maybe it's just about not being angry with him anymore." I think about Lala and my own dad. It's time I start listening to my own advice. What's the point of holding on to all this resentment? When do I move on and stop reliving all our collective mistakes? When do I let go of my own?

"It doesn't mean he doesn't love you," I add.

Diego lets out a deep sigh. His eyes are set on the water as he says, "There was never a time when my life wasn't scheduled. He never asked me what I wanted to do."

After a long silence he adds, "And I never asked myself," his voice resigned.

"How come?" I ask.

"I don't know." He shrugs. "I was too busy shaving a tenth of a second off my time, stressing over the position of my feet or how my hands were pointed during entry. Did you know that the ideal finger separation for optimal propulsion is point-three-two centimeters?" He shows me the separation between his fingers.

"That's so sad . . ." As the words trail off, I think of all the exact measurements I've had to memorize to succeed in Grattard's kitchen: the brunoise cut, measuring one-eigth of an inch cubed; the julienne sticks, one-eighth of an inch by one-eighth of an inch by one to two inches. And so on and so forth. It *is* sad.

"I just want time to figure out what I want to do. I don't think that's too much to ask. Do you?" He looks at me, expectant.

I press my lips and shake my head no.

"You can tell him that," I say. "And if he doesn't understand, then at least you tried. But you can't hide in Bessenay forever and pretend he doesn't exist. That's not a good way to start your new life."

The waves lap at the columns of the pier as we both stare out into the infinite ocean. A soft breeze carries the sounds of music, laughter, and conversation from the beach, filling the momentary silence between us.

"What about you? Are you staying in that restaurant?"

"I don't know," I say. "I don't know that I can turn down the apprenticeship if I get it. It's a big opportunity. It would be stupid to say no."

"Whatever you do, just make sure it's what you really want. Otherwise, what's the point?"

The point is, if you want to be the best, you have to train under the best. The real question on my mind, however: Is it worth the pain?

We leave the pier to walk on the beach, and I find myself enjoying the cool sensation of the waves breaking at my bare feet. Diego reaches for my hand and holds it gently as we walk. Our bodies lean into each other once more as our feet sink into the wet sand.

It's a perfect night. One I'm not sure I want to end.

Pippa's voice echoes in the back of my mind, egging me to "have a good time."

"We should head back soon," Diego says. "It's getting late."

I nod, my heart thumping inside my chest. We haven't talked about the possibility of sex, but I know it's coming. I can feel it in every cell of my body.

We take a cab back to the apartment. Diego never lets go of my hand. I rest my head against his shoulder and close my eyes. This is so much more than a good time.

The cab drops us off in front of Clara's building. We take the stairs until we're inside. Diego locks the front door behind us, then turns to face me. My open palms come to rest on his chest. His heart is drumming as fast as mine.

He kisses my forehead first, then the tip of my nose, then my lips. Everything about the way his lips search for mine, the way his hands find the small of my back, says he wants this, wants me, as much as I want him.

I kiss him hard, pressing all of me against all of him. His mouth slips down my chin and gently explores the contours of my neck. I lift my head and a soft moan escapes my lips. My hands slip under his shirt, fingers digging into his hot skin. The intensity of our limbs wrapped around each other leaves me gasping for air in the best possible way.

My head is spinning like I've had too much to drink.

For the briefest of moments, my eyelids flutter open and I catch a beam of light shimmering on the metal surface of one of Clara's culinary awards.

I close my eyes and tighten my grip on Diego's torso, trying to recapture the heat of the previous moment, but something has shifted inside me.

The fear of losing myself completely in someone else niggles at the back of my mind. Doubt quickly creeps in.

This thing between us—whatever it is—has only just started and I've already jeopardized everything I've worked so hard for by coming on this trip.

Yet, given the opportunity, I wouldn't take it back.

Diego's lips brush the tender skin above my chest and I shiver as if intoxicated.

What I don't get is, how can I give myself completely and still be wholly me?

I wrestle with my thoughts and all these new emotions for answers, but none come.

My hands slide over his shirt and come to rest on his chest. His skin blazing under my palm.

I turn my head so that my cheek is resting against the soft skin of his neck. My lips start to relax as I try to calm down my own racing heart. As I try to formulate a coherent thought.

After a long silence, I manage to whisper, "I'm not ready."

Diego presses his forehead against mine.

"Not yet," I add, touching his neck with my hands.

"Haven't you heard? I have all the time in the world," he says, kissing my earlobe and sending goose bumps down my back. "Clara has more leftover flan in the fridge. Wanna join me?"

I suppress a laugh, afraid of waking up our host.

"Are you always thinking about food?" I ask, following him to the kitchen. He opens the fridge and pulls out a plate of flan and two spoons.

He gives me a *Do you have to ask?* look that only makes me want to laugh harder.

"See? Even Clara knows," Diego says, pointing to a sticky note attached to the plate that reads, "In case you're hungry when you get home."

"Give me one of those spoons," I say, sitting next to him on the living room couch. It's a big sectional with a chaise large enough for two.

The hours pass as we raid Clara's fridge, eat, and laugh, sharing random stories of life across both sides of the Atlantic.

When we are both so tired we can barely keep our eyes open, Diego leans back and I rest my head on his chest. I fall asleep to the soothing sound of his heartbeat.

Chapter 27

Mallorca Sandwich

"A re you sure you don't want to come in?" Diego asks.

We're standing outside the front door of his father's apartment building—a collection of modern lofts encased in floor-to-ceiling glass windows. It's in what is clearly a trendy part of town with lots of green spaces and luxury stores.

"I'll be at that little bakery on the corner," I say, gently squeezing his arm. "Take your time."

Diego leans in and kisses me, his hand resting between my cheek and my neck. It is a slow and tender kiss, one that implies, *I'll be right back.* I lean into his hand and kiss him back. With every kiss, I discover a new sensation, like walking into one of those ice cream shops that advertises a hundred different flavors—you find a new favorite every time.

He steps back, still holding on to my hand.

"Try their mallorcas," he says. "They're my favorite in the whole city."

I reluctantly let go of his hand and watch him walk inside the building. He briefly turns, so I give him a reassuring wave. Then he crosses the threshold and disappears into a corridor.

I head down the street toward the small bakery I'd seen on our way to the apartment. Inside, the sweet smell of mallorca bread is intoxicating. I stand by the register and order two bags with a dozen rolls each. This way Diego can bring some flavors from home back to Bessenay. For myself, I order a toasted ham and cheese on a mallorca roll, and a coffee.

On my way to a table, I notice a rack of cookbooks for sale next to the storefront window. They're all in Spanish, but I'm drawn to one in particular with a black-and-white photo of a boy sitting on a bakery counter. He reminds me of Jakub. His legs dangle over the side and he's holding two baguettes up in the air like he just won a contest. It's adorable.

I pick up a copy and do my best to translate the words written on the back jacket. The author, a man in his eighties, promises to teach you all the secrets of how to create the perfect loaf of bread. His family fled Nazi-occupied France in the 1940s and carried their recipes in a suitcase all the way to their new home in Barcelona, where they have lived ever since. I learn that his family opened this same bakery shortly after they arrived.

I get so lost in this man's story that I don't hear my name being called behind me. I turn to face a server holding a tray with my food.

"The mallorcas you ordered will be out shortly," he says in Spanish, then leads me to a table by the window.

I set the book on the table, the little boy staring back at me from the cover. In the background, I notice an old lady leans against a doorframe with her arms crossed over her chest. She's smiling at the boy.

I bite into the sweet mallorca, as if through this bread I can somehow connect with the boy in the picture and the old man who wrote this book. They're the same person sharing two different experiences: joy of childhood and wisdom of time.

I open the cover flap and scan the biography page for words I can translate. His family rebuilt their French bakery in Barcelona, and the recipes have passed on to a new generation. In the process, they also added new recipes, such as the mallorca bread, to honor their new life in Spain. He calls it his family's *legado*, which after checking the translation app on my phone I learn means "legacy." "Anything handed down from the past," I read.

I sit there in total stillness, letting the old man's words sink in—deep, deep into my heart. I glance out the window to the sidewalk, where people are walking by. A woman rides her bicycle with a basketful of flowers. A girl about my age talks on her cell phone. There's a lot of coming and going in a million different directions. Meanwhile, I'm sitting here, alone, feeling like I can't go anywhere until I face my own legado. The one I've been avoiding for six months.

It's time, I assure myself. A sudden unwavering resolve drives me to pull Lala's cookbook from my bag and set it on the table in front of me.

I never thought it would be so freaking hard to open a book. All my grief comes to the surface as I touch the tattered red linen cover. Some of the fibers around the edge of the hardcover have further unraveled.

I slowly undo the cooking twine knot Lala tied to keep the pages from falling out and turn the cover. My skin tingles with the rush of happy memories that follow. But my eyes sting at the feelings of loss that always come right after.

I stare at the first page, where Lala wrote her name. Her handwriting is the kind of old-style cursive they don't teach anymore, with letters that flow neatly into each other and flawless loops and tails.

Under her name is a quote written in Spanish from someone named Carme Ruscadella. It reads, "The history of gastronomy is the history of the world."

I search *Carme Ruscadella* on my phone. Turns out she is the world's only seven-Michelin-starred female chef, and she is from Spain. Lala never mentioned her, which only serves as a reminder that there was a lot about Lala I didn't know.

I read Ruscadella's bio and learn she had no classical training. She came from a family of farmers who taught her how to cook as a young girl.

"What are you trying to tell me, Lala?" I murmur into her book.

Very gently, as to not disturb the delicate binding, I flip through the familiar pages.

Her recipe for roasted pork is here, and so is the one for her guisado black beans. On the border of the pages, she's written notes such as "Fiesta de Reyes, 1961" or "This is Jaime's favorite."

I find a recipe for an enchilado de mariscos, a Cuban seafood stew from what I can gather, with the note "Last meal in Havana, 1970." Her entire life can be traced back through these recipes. About halfway in, I find the recipe for her apple pie. At the top of the page reads a quote from my great-grandmother: "The best-tasting love is one slowly baked in the kitchen. —Mary Fields." A few pages later, I find the recipe for Cascos de Guayaba a la Isabela with the note, *"Para mi morenita, nacida con azúcar y miel en las venas."* I may have been born with sugar and honey in my veins, but there are a few grains of salt and hot spices too.

I blink a few times and swallow the giant knot lodged in the back of my throat. I'm trying so hard not to cry but every cell in my body wishes I could go back to her kitchen one last time— that I could, even if it's just for a second, dip my fingers into her pineapple cake batter or watch her roll the dough for her pie crust. I want to take in the scent of her Maja soap and listen to the joy in her heart as she laughs.

But I can't. I will never get to do any of those things again. So instead I flip through the pages until I find an empty section at the end, waiting to be filled with new recipes and new stories.

I pull out a pen and write in my own. I title it "Clara's Flan," and under the title I write one short line, like Lala used to do: "From Barcelona to Kansas, with love."

I write Clara's recipe through an onslaught of tears. I wipe them off with the back of my hand, but more come.

"Are you all right?" Diego appears by my table. "What's wrong?" He sits and puts a bag down on the floor next to him.

I clean my face with both hands, breathing in and out slowly.

"Everything is great, actually," I say, reaching for his hand across the table.

"Are you sure?" His thumb caresses the top of my hand.

"I'm sure." I nod. "How did it go with your dad?"

"Fine, I guess," he says, ripping off a piece of my sandwich and putting it into his mouth. "Are you going to eat the rest of this?"

I push the plate in his direction and he digs into my leftovers.

"Fine?" I ask.

"He told me if I wasn't going to university, I had to get a job." He pauses to chew. "Ah, these are the best. Can you make these?"

"Can you stay on point, please?"

"He wanted me to get some job at the firm where he works."

"And?" My pulse goes from zero to a hundred in half a second. Is he staying in Barcelona?

"I'll be right back. I'm starving." Before I can protest, he stands and walks to the register.

It's moments like this that make me want to strangle him. I watch him talk to the girl at the register. She smiles at him and giggles at something he says. For crying out loud, does he have the same effect on everyone? He returns a few minutes later, carrying a plate. Meanwhile, my heart is about to burst out of my chest. How could he not tell me he was planning to stay in Barcelona all along? And how did I not think this was a possibility?

"If you are staying here, I can just take the train back," I say. My shoulders tighten, and my lips press into a thin line. I close Lala's book and tie back the twine. "It's not a big deal. I'm sure Papi and Margo can ship your things back."

He's staring at me, not saying anything. He's simply chewing on a piece of mallorca like nothing is wrong.

"And I'm sure they can put your dog on a plane or something. I doubt you even have to come back." I stuff Lala's book into my backpack and zip the top closed.

"Where do you get these crazy ideas?" he asks, wiping his hands on a napkin. "I'm working at the cherry farm. I'm not leaving."

His words sink in and I briefly close my eyes in relief. A smile spreads across my face. He's not leaving. He's staying—with me.

"James offered to take me on full-time for the season."

"Was your dad okay with that?"

"He wasn't about to throw me a party, if that's what you're asking." Diego leans back in his chair, crossing his arms over his chest. "He'll just have to get over it. I'm not the person he thinks I am. Can you really see me wearing a suit and tie? Working behind a desk? Please."

I take him in fully—the tight white T-shirt that barely contains his arms, the messy hair that somehow manages to look sexy every single day, and the day-old stubble on his face that tells the world he just doesn't care what it thinks. Diego doesn't belong behind a desk, pushing papers all day; he belongs in the fields and on the open road. Anyone can see that.

"What's in the bag?" I ask.

"My camera," he says, opening the top of the bag to reveal a professional-looking camera and lens. "I want to start taking pictures again."

"Again?" I ask, amused at this new development.

"I took a class in school. My teacher said I was pretty good. I was out in the fields the other day and had this idea for some portraits of the workers. I thought I'd give it a try." He shrugs and zips the bag closed. "I want to try everything."

My phone buzzes and Papi's face lights up the screen. I pick up. "Papi?"

"Where are you guys?" he asks, panting.

"Still in Barcelona. We were about to start the trip back. Is everything okay?"

He swallows hard and goes silent for a few seconds.

"Papi?"

"Margo was bleeding so I took her to the emergency room. We're at the hospital now. She'll need an emergency C-section. Just get here—" The line goes dead.

"Hello? Papi? Are you there?" There's no answer. The call

dropped. My fingers tremble as I dial his number. It goes straight to voice mail.

"What's wrong?" Diego asks.

"Margo is having an emergency C-section. Can I borrow your phone?"

"Sure." He takes his phone out of his pocket and hands it to me. I dial Papi's number but it goes to voice mail again, so I try texting instead. No response.

"He probably forgot to charge it. You know how he is," Diego says in an attempt to bring some levity for my sake. But as much as he is trying to hide his own concern, I can see it play across the tense lines of his forehead.

"He sounded really upset," I tell him.

My thoughts go into overdrive. I search *emergency C-section* on my phone and immediately wish I hadn't. Words like *placental abruption*, *uterine rupture*, and *abnormal fetal heart rate* jump out from the page.

My own heart rate picks up. How can I lose everything again? Just when I was starting to believe in this new life—in our new family. This baby, I now realize, meant a new beginning for all of us—even for me.

What will happen if . . . I can't even go there.

How does one get up in the morning after something like that? Lala dying as an old woman is one thing, but a baby? *My* baby brother or sister.

I don't see how our lives could be the same. Or how I could return to Grattard's kitchen tomorrow morning.

I've learned death is its own natural disaster. It wrecks everything, and everyone, in its path.

"Margo is strong. She and the baby will be fine," Diego says, reaching for my hand and squeezing it tight.

"How can you be so sure?" I pull away, angry at myself for agreeing to come on this trip. "I knew I shouldn't have come here," I snap, standing to pack my things. "How fast can you get us back home? Maybe I should look into a flight instead."

Diego doesn't respond. He just sits there stone-faced, cleaning his greasy fingers on a napkin.

"I'll be outside. Can you please hurry?" I rush out of the restaurant.

The café door closes behind me and I'm standing alone on the sidewalk. I expected the burst of street air to help me find calm, but the busyness around me only adds to the desperation in my heart.

Why is this happening?

I move out of the way to let some customers pass on their way into the café.

After they go in, Diego steps out behind them.

My body edges against a cement wall, searching for support. I shut my eyes and will myself to find some peace in the chaos of my thoughts. But there's no peace to be found.

Death is like the winds of a hurricane; it will obliterate life as you knew it in seconds. It's like an earthquake that ruptures the ground under your feet. And it's like a tsunami that floods your heart with loss and then retreats back into the ocean, dragging away all the happiness within you. I know this. I've lived this already. I can't do it again. Not so soon.

"I know this is hard, but you're not the only one who's ever lost someone," Diego says quietly.

I nod. I know he's right. But sometimes it feels like no one ever in the history of humanity felt this much grief. It's irrational. But death also takes away reason.

"I'm just so . . . scared," I finally say. "And tired of feeling this way."

Diego stands next to me so that our arms touch. Slowly, my head leans onto his shoulder. His body is steady and solid against mine. He brings an arm around me and kisses the top of my head. Under different circumstances, I could stay here forever.

"I know," he whispers, pressing his lips against my forehead. "It's going to be okay."

I hug myself, hoping he's right.

"Excuse me," I hear someone say in Spanish next to us. Our server is standing outside the café with two bags of mallorcas dangling from his hand. "You forgot these."

Diego glances at me, confused.

"I got them for you," I say, making an effort to smile and remembering the cookbook pressed against my chest. "Oh, and I have to pay for this."

"How much is it?"

I turn my copy of *Buen Pan*, searching for a price. "Twenty euro."

Diego hands the server a paper bill and thanks him.

"You didn't have to pay for the book," I say as we turn to walk away.

"Consider it a souvenir." He unzips one of the bags of mallorca and pulls one out. "You don't strike me as the T-shirt type."

"I'm not."

We reach the motorcycle and quickly strap on our helmets.

"How long will it take us to get home?" I ask, suddenly aware of all the love and hope behind that plain, four-letter word.

"We'll be there this evening," he says, helping me inside the sidecar.

I silently pray to La Virgencita for Margo, the baby, and Papi.

"Please," I beg in a murmur over the roar of the bike's engine. And then, I do something I've never done before today: I pray for myself.

Please. Help me.

Chapter 28

Apple Pie

We make it back to Lyon in what I'm sure is record time. The last text we received from Papi said they were going into surgery, but no updates since. I'm worried sick. What if something happened to Margo or the baby? I don't even want to think about all the things that could go wrong.

I send one last nervous text asking if everything is all right, but nothing comes back. I shove my phone into my pocket as we turn onto the hospital's driveway.

There's construction on the building's entrance, which only adds to my sense of anxiety. A big cement truck blocks the main doors and a man with a yellow jacket redirects traffic. The drilling of a jackhammer blends with the blaring of an ambulance siren behind us. Diego moves to the side to let the ambulance pass.

We follow the detour signs to the carpark, drop the bike, and speed walk to the hospital.

The moment the automatic glass doors slide open, we are hit with the smell of alcohol and chlorine. Diego and I hurry down a long corridor with white walls and blinding bright lights, following a string of confusing signs that point in ten different directions. We pass a few people in gurneys being wheeled to who knows where. I scan their faces, hoping none of them are Margo.

I try Papi's phone one more time but it's going straight to voice mail.

"I can't get ahold of him," I tell Diego. My hand is shaking as I redial. Voice mail, again.

Diego and I lock eyes in the hallway, neither wanting to acknowledge the desperation we feel.

"Excuse me." Diego stops a nurse coming down the hallway. He's wearing blue scrubs and carrying a clipboard. Hopefully he knows where Margo is.

After a short conversation in French I don't understand even a quarter of, Diego informs me, "He says the maternity ward is through those double doors," and points at a set of massive gray doors down the hallway.

My heartbeat is drumming so fast I fear an artery might burst. I lean against the wall behind me for support. It's cold as ice.

Diego starts walking in the direction of the doors without realizing I've stayed behind, glued to the frigid wall, unable to move.

On the other side of those doors are two possibilities: An unspeakable tragedy, which I refuse to even consider. Or a new family in which I am already a big sister.

Diego disappears through the doorway, only to return a few seconds later to find me still in the same place.

"What's going on?" he asks, taking hold of my shoulder.

I don't say anything. I can only stand there, paralyzed, until two nurses push a gurney down the hall and I'm forced to move aside.

"Are you going to be sick?"

"What if the baby doesn't like me?" I ask through quivering lips, keenly aware of how crazy I sound. We still don't even know what happened during the C-section.

Diego stares at me. His face is a mix of amusement and disbelief. He finally wraps his arms around me and cradles me into his chest. His bike jacket is open, and I can feel his body heat through the thin layer of his T-shirt. I let my head fall into him and breathe in that familiar, calming scent. I reach inside his jacket and grab two fistfuls of his shirt. I want time to stop.

"That's impossible," he says, kissing the top of my head. "You are going to be the best sister ever. And the baby is going to love those chocolate chip cookies you make."

I laugh into his chest.

I agree. Everyone loves those cookies.

He takes my face in his hands and our eyes meet.

"It's going to be fine, I promise," he says, as if he knows something I don't.

"Okay," I say, desperately wanting to believe him. I step back and release my grip on his shirt. "Let's go in."

He rests one hand on my shoulder and leads me through the doors.

We find Papi in one of the private rooms with Margo resting in the bed next to him. I've never been so relieved to see them. The baby is safely cradled in Papi's arms.

When Papi sees me at the door, his face breaks into a huge smile. He turns so I can see the pink blanket wrapped around my new baby sister.

I smile and laugh and cry, all at once.

"Can I hold her?" I ask, stepping inside the room. The tiny bundle in Papi's arms is all I can see.

Papi places this tiny baby burrito in my arms and kisses the top of my head.

"This is Flora," he says.

She is so tiny I feel she could break if I don't hold her right.

"Hi, Flora," I whisper, bringing her closer to me. Her skin is soft and gives off a kind of pungent sweetness. Her head is covered with dark hair, just like mine and Papi's.

The moment she opens her eyes my heart overflows with so much love that more tears form in my eyes. Suddenly, I understand what Lala meant when she talked about your heart being wide open. Mine feels like it has finally opened wide enough to let in this new family.

I place my pinky finger inside one of her tiny hands. She wraps her little fingers around it like she's trying to hold on. But in reality, it is me who's holding on to her. She feels exactly like my sister. I can already see our future waiting to be filled with lots of shared memories.

Reluctantly, I pass Flora to Diego, who's been patiently waiting behind me. I take a mental picture of the two of them. He is so tall, and his chest is so wide that Flora is dwarfed even further in his arms. Like me, he can't help but smile.

"I've called you like a million times," I tell Papi, pulling out my cell phone. "I was freaking out."

"My phone died," he says. His face looks strained and tired, but there is undeniable joy in his eyes. "The doctor told us the baby was breech. So we went into surgery. She flipped at the last minute. It was a natural delivery." He sighs, letting his shoulders fall.

Papi sits next to Margo and reaches for her hand. All this time she has been watching us silently from the bed with a smile on her lips.

"How do you feel?" I ask.

"A little tired, but I'll be fine," she says. "I'm just so relieved." She squeezes Papi's hand and they exchange a bigger smile.

I glance at an untouched dinner tray next to her bed. The smoked salmon salad and baguette don't look terrible when judged by American hospital food standards.

"Have you eaten?" I ask. "We can go get you some dinner."

"You know what I've been craving this whole time? That chicken in white wine and butter sauce you made once . . . with the mashed potatoes and the vegetables." Her voice is full of longing, as if this chicken will somehow make her feel better.

After all these weeks of not eating my food, I can't believe this is the one thing she wants. It must have been the pregnancy thing all along.

I glance at the clock on the wall; if we leave now, we should be able to get to the house, make the chicken, and be back in a few hours. Which will leave me with zero time to prepare for the final exam.

Lala used to say that love was her secret ingredient. And that when you cook with love, a meal could nourish the soul. This is what I'm meant to do.

So I push away all thoughts of my exam and ask Papi for the car keys.

There is so much love in this room that everything comes into focus. There is so much joy that it's easy to see what I want to do with my talent. And easy to know what I need to do when I return to Grattard's kitchen.

"I'm coming with you," Diego says, after I explain I'm running home to bring them back a proper dinner. "I'm starving."

"You're always starving," I joke.

"It's all your fault, really," he says as we reach the car. "If your food wasn't so amazing, I wouldn't want to eat it."

My cheeks blush at the compliment.

"So, really, you just need to make crappy food. And problem solved," he adds with a grin. "But we both know that's not gonna happen."

I shake my head because he's right. I love cooking too much. And above all, I love that food always brings people together. So I make a mental list of all the ingredients we will need to get at the store—including a few apples. Enough to turn a hospital room meal into a first feast for our new family.

Back at the house, Lala's book is propped up on a stand on the kitchen island. The recipe for our family's apple pie is displayed on the open page.

While the chicken simmers, Diego and I begin to work on the apple filling. The dough for the crust is already resting in the fridge.

"We have to peel and core all these apples," I say.

It took me fifteen minutes to find the right apples at the store. It was a testament to Diego's patience that he didn't hurry me once. Now, in the soft light of our kitchen, they look perfect.

"I'll peel, you core," he says, pulling a knife from the drawer and standing next to me. As is always the case, his body has the effect of making the kitchen feel way too small. But tonight, as we cook side by side, it feels more like a homey coziness, the way Lala's kitchen used to feel.

I find myself wishing she was here with us, helping me get the right amount of nutmeg in the syrup. Instead, I have to rely on the instructions she left me in her book. I turn a new page and an old photo falls onto the counter. I clean my hand on my apron, carefully pick it up, and bring it closer to my face.

"Is that her?" Diego asks, peering over my shoulder.

"That's my Lala," I say, showing him the picture. She's standing next to me, wearing a black dress with bright pink flowers. I must have been Jakub's age. I'm holding her hand and gazing up at her with the most innocent smile.

"She used to call me her morenita," I say. It's weird how one word can make you feel so *you*, honest you.

My eyes fill with tears.

"I know this sounds absolutely insane, but I'm so angry at her for dying," I say. A heaviness lifts off my chest as the words leave my mouth.

Diego puts down the knife in his hand and reaches for my arms.

"Here," he says, pulling out a stool. "Sit down, Isa."

I let him guide my body to the stool, then sit.

"Sometimes I wish I could scream at her for leaving me." I rub the tears away with both hands as the words spill out of me. They feel like a mad rush held back for too long.

"She volunteered with a needle exchange program near her home in Kansas. She used to be a nurse in Havana, so she had some experience with the medical stuff. As part of the job, she'd take used needles from drug addicts and give them new ones. It's supposed to limit the transmission of infectious disease.

"It should've been funny, really—hilarious if you knew my Lala. She was this tiny Cuban abuela, driving around in a van with a box of infectious waste material in the back and half-dozen pies in the front seat. She'd hand out pies along with the needles. It was crazy." I manage to laugh between the tears.

Diego smiles and squeezes my hand. He gives me a kitchen towel so I can clean my face.

"She accidentally pricked herself with an infected needle. It gave her hepatitis and killed her liver."

I stare at the picture in my hands. Behind us, there's a big hydrangea bush in full bloom.

"Why are you angry, though?" Diego asks.

I shrug and swallow hard, rubbing my eyes with the kitchen towel.

"She was like the ground under my feet," I say while staring into Diego's eyes. All the affection in his face completely melts my heart. "I just don't understand—how could she put herself at risk like that? She told me it would be fine, but it wasn't. I know it's not right to think this way, but part of me is angry she picked them over me. I needed her too."

"Them?"

"Bubba, Milly, Mary," I recite, ashamed. "The people she was trying to help."

"I'm sorry," he says, resting his hand on my knee. He reaches for a strand of loose hair around my face and gently moves it behind my ear. "But whether you can see it or not, you're just like her."

"What do you mean?"

"This is how you give yourself, Isa." His eyes are set on mine as he says, "This is how you show others that you care. You go out of your way to make all this delicious food because you know it will make people happy. She was doing the same thing."

A few more tears run down my cheeks at the recognition that Diego is right.

It wasn't only me who lost Lala—all the people she was helping lost her too.

"Come here." Diego pulls me onto his lap, wrapping me in an embrace.

I lean my head on his shoulder.

"I'm glad you're here," I say, reaching around him.

"Me too," he whispers into my ear.

We hold each other like this for what feels like forever. I feel so safe and cared for in this space that I never want this moment to end.

We only pull away when Beluga enters the kitchen. He sits by our feet and whimpers in my direction.

"I think he wants you to pet him," Diego says. "He hasn't been happy with my ear scratching ever since he had you."

I laugh and squat down next to Beluga.

"Come here, you," I say, digging my fingers behind his ears. He leans his wrinkled face toward my hands and makes a low grumbling sound. I sit on the floor next to him and scratch his neck until he climbs onto my lap and rests his whole body against my chest.

"Okay, Beluga. You've had enough. We have a pie to finish," Diego says. He starts to usher Beluga out of the kitchen, but I stop him.

"He can stay, I guess."

Diego smiles. "You hear that?" he tells Beluga, who plops himself down on the floor.

I swear, this dog is something else.

"Now, let's see what kind of sous-chef you make," I say, washing the dog hair off my hands.

We peel, core, and cut the apples. In little time, we have a mountain of apple slices ready to go inside the baking dish.

I reach for a saucepan and gather the ingredients for the most important step, the syrup. Lala's special syrup, passed down from my great-grandmother, was a combination of butter, white and brown sugars, vanilla, nutmeg, and cinnamon. The recipe calls for mixing the apples and the syrup before placing them into the baking dish to ensure every piece of apple is covered.

"Can you pass me the dough?" I ask Diego.

He reaches into fridge, pulls out the ball of dough covered in plastic wrap, and sets it in front of me.

"What if . . ." he muses, removing the plastic wrap from the dough. "What if—this may sound a bit strange, but just listen for a minute—what if she's not totally dead?"

"Okay . . ." I glance at him and chuckle at his nutty idea. "I mean, I saw the casket go into the ground."

"Hear me out. I've been thinking about this . . ." He takes the dough from my hands and sets it on the counter. I turn to face him so that he has my full attention. A deep furrow appears on his brow, and I realize this is what he looks like when he is lost in his own thoughts. I want to memorize this expression.

"You know how some people believe in rebirth?"

"What do you mean?"

"Well, it means that the body and mind are two separate things. So when people die, the physical body dies, but the mind goes somewhere else. Takes a new form."

"This is what you believe happens when we die?"

I stare at him, amused, because this is so not the guy I met in the market three weeks ago. This Diego is so open and unguarded, so easy to fall for. Yeah, so easy. Anyone could fall in love with this guy.

Including me.

"What I'm trying to say is, maybe it's like she's living somewhere else."

"That's deep stuff," I tease.

"You know, there is more to me than an albino dog and an ever-hungry stomach." He brings a kitchen towel to my chin and wipes something away. "You are covered in flour."

I lean into him with a smile. The space between his chest and his arms is my favorite new place outside of the kitchen. He kisses the top of my head, which barely reaches his neck.

"So, you're saying that Lala has been reborn somewhere else?" I ask, my cheek pressed against his T-shirt. I can hear his heart beating faster inside his chest. Mine is too.

"Yes, that's exactly what I'm saying. And because the mind can go wherever it wants, you can somehow connect with her."

"Like telepathy?"

He gently pushes me back so he can see my face.

"I'm being serious," he says while on the verge of laughter.

"Me too!" I try hard to suppress my own giggles.

"Not telepathy. More like what you think and feel affects others. There are studies about this. It's a real thing."

"Okay, so let's pretend for a second that Lala was reborn into some awesome house with an amazing new family. How does that help me now?"

"You can tell her how you feel with your mind. And she'll get the message. It's like a subconscious thing."

"I'm telling you something with my mind—can you tell what it is?"

He rubs the back of his neck, leaving behind a trace of flour on his shirt collar. I wipe it off with a kitchen towel.

"Let me give you a one-word hint: *loco*," I say, laughing.

Diego doesn't budge, though. "She will get the message," he says confidently. He kisses my forehead, steps back, then puts the ball of dough back into my hands. "I'm going to start taking some things to the car. Give you guys some privacy."

He takes off his apron, grabs a bag full of containers, and leaves.

I spread a thin layer of flour over the counter. My hands firmly grip the sides of the rolling pin as I begin to roll the dough. I think of all the times I made this pie with Lala and let myself feel everything again. I don't push the memories away, instead I open my heart wide and let them exist inside me. I allow them to become a part of who I am.

After I finish rolling out the dough, I cut out the lattice strips. Then I pour the syrup-covered apples into the pie dish. Finally, I crisscross the dough strips over them in Lala's special pattern. The end result is perfect and beautiful and exactly the way Lala taught me how to make it.

As I place the dish inside the paper bag, I realize that this pie, with its history of familial love, has the power to heal the splinters in my heart. I put it into the oven and close the door, then lean against the kitchen counter and close my eyes.

"Lala," I start in a whisper. "It's me, your morenita."

For a moment, I give myself permission to believe everything Diego said is true. I tell my Lala all the things I didn't get to say. And I send her all the love I didn't get to give. I want to believe she got my message; that as I honor her legacy, our minds and hearts are connected as one. The moment I reach out into this space of my mind, my skin tingles with a feeling I can only describe as pure joy. Lala's laughter reverberates inside my chest and suddenly I can smell the scent of her Maja soap. I know then, I can let go of my grief, my anger, and my pain. She will always be with me.

Later that night, we return to the hospital with platefuls of delicious chicken, roasted vegetables, and a special dessert fitting the occasion.

Diego and I pass the food around while Papi runs to the vending machine to get us drinks. When we're ready to dig in, Diego takes his spot next to Margo, while Papi and I sit across from each other, sharing an over-the-bed table we borrowed from an empty room.

"Thank you for making all this, sweetheart," Papi says. He's moving the chicken around his plate with a fork like he's not quite ready to eat. "I never told you how sorry . . ." He clears his throat, staring at me from across the table. Our eyes meet and I can see his are turning watery and red. He clears his throat again and looks down at his plate.

"It's okay, Papi," I say, reaching for his hand. Our eyes meet again, and a moment of recognition passes between us.

Even though what he did is not okay, it's okay for him to feel sorry about his mistake and for me to accept this new dynamic between us. For us to live this new life together.

"Te amo," he whispers, squeezing my hand.

"I love you too."

In the confines of that small hospital room, we finish our

dinner and cut into Lala's delicious pie with the gusto of a celebration a hundred times the size. As I watch our extended, complicated family share its first meal together, I realize another thing Lala once told me is true: Food made from the heart will nourish the soul. I can't think of anything better to do with my life.

Chapter 29

Deconstructed

The day of the final exam feels like one of those cooking competition shows, but without the cameras. The lights glare brightly
above us. Tension runs high. The spoons are lined up on the wall,
and for the first time mine occupies the number one spot.

I have finally arrived at the top of the spoon ladder, thanks to
the snails and the dots. Lucia is under me, and Snake Eyes sits
in third place. His fall, I heard, had something to do with Chef
Grattard finding half a sprout inside one of his peas.

"I almost went blind," I heard him tell one of the other guys
in the kitchen. "After the first hour, all I could see was a green
blob. No beginning. No end. A nightmare." He sounded so broken that I couldn't help but feel sorry for him. Grattard finally
got to him. Snake Eyes no longer carries himself with that same
cocky confidence he once had. Something in him changed.

Something has changed in me too. Even though I've finally
gotten to where I've always wanted to be, it doesn't feel the way
I thought it would. That sense of accomplishment followed by
mind-blowing elation is missing. Instead I feel like a cheat, like
I'm taking something away from someone who deserves it more
than me. The guilt has been gnawing at my insides, like a babka
loaf that hasn't had time to cook in the middle—it comes out all
doughy and undone, sticky in all the wrong ways. If you take one
bite, it will make you sick.

Chef Troissant approaches my station. She has been inspecting our work areas since we are not allowed to bring any notes or recipes into the final exam. Every technique must be executed from memory.

"Alors, Mademoiselle Fields," she says, handing me an envelope. "The apprenticeship is yours to lose."

My chest swells both with pride and disappointment. Disappointment at myself for having succumbed to the pressure in order to get ahead. What I did to Lucia was really awful. And what is worse, I never apologized. I need to change that.

I take the white envelope from her hand and stare at my name written in neat cursive. I told myself I would finish the exam, even though I had no time to prepare and even though I'm still not sure this is where I want to be.

"Best of luck, Mademoiselle," Chef Troissant says as she begins to walk away.

"Wait," I call out, almost tumbling over my workstation. Pâtisserie Clémentine has yet to open, but if I've learned anything from Chef Troissant these last three weeks, it's that the business will be a success. She will be the kind of chef who makes others step up their game. And she will also be a great teacher, because regardless of how insane my time here has been, I am better because of her and no one else.

"I was wondering if . . . if Pâtisserie Clémentine will need an apprentice."

Chef Troissant doesn't answer. Instead, she looks at me— into my very soul, it seems—before the side of her lip ticks up ever so slightly. When she finally speaks, a resounding *No* comes out of her mouth.

"Oh, I thought maybe . . ." I mumble, my heart sinking all the way to my feet.

"My pâtisserie will not be a consolation prize."

"No, I . . . that's not . . ." I stumble over my words, trying to explain myself, but she cuts me off before I can verbalize a coherent sentence.

"The test is about to begin, Mademoiselle. Please return to your station."

Of course, the moment I return to my station I know exactly what I wanted to say. That this is not where I belong. Where I belong is in her pâtisserie, learning from the best chef I know.

Grattard's apprenticeship belongs to Lucia, not me.

I turn to my left and watch her fiddle with her knives. She has the kind of manic energy that would succeed in La Table de Lyon's kitchen.

"Hey," I say, touching her shoulder.

She turns toward me, pushing a strand of loose hair into her toque.

"It was great working with you these last few days," I say.

"It was fun, yes." She pulls on the ties of her apron, which are already tight enough.

"I wanted to say I'm sorry for what I did. I mean, with the snails. It was terrible and I feel so guilty about it. I wasn't thinking. I just got caught up in the pressure, you know?"

Lucia nods, burying her hands inside the pockets of her jacket. "I know," she says. "But you didn't need that to win. You have all the talent."

"Thanks," I say, already knowing how I will make it up to her. "Friends?"

"Friends."

We hug it out. And it feels like the beginning of a *true* friendship, one based in admiration, respect, and forgiveness.

On the other side of the room, Pippa has been watching us. I wave at her and mouth *good luck*. She smiles back and waves. Out of everyone in the room, she seems the most at ease. All she has to do is finish the test so she can get a certificate signed by Grattard himself. Tomorrow she will start her new job in Chef Lulu's pâtisserie, which has just been named the best in the city. To celebrate, I'm thinking we should have a bake-off, just the kind of party a few kitchen geeks would love.

"Faites attention!"

All eyes turn to Chef Troissant. She sits alone at the judges' table, next to two empty chairs and a big, bright red digital clock hanging just above her.

Grattard and Hugo have yet to show up. Both will arrive just as the test is winding down, to taste the quality of the dishes. I guess they're too busy or something.

I quickly turn to Lucia and whisper, "Good luck." She nods and says, *"Buena suerte"* in return.

"You will have five hours to complete the three-course meal," Chef Troissant tells the class. "You will be judged on presentation, technique, and the ability to follow Chef Grattard's vision."

I glance over at Snake Eyes. I have to give the guy props for coming back after Chef Grattard's vision turned into his own personal hell. Today, he almost looks humble. Makes me wonder at the power a pea has to break a person.

"You may begin," Chef Troissant says to the sound of envelopes ripping open. They contain a blank sheet of paper so we can write the instructions as Chef Troissant calls them out and a scorecard with our number printed at the top.

I instinctively reach for a pen from my jacket pocket, and when she begins to rattle off the insane dish instructions, I'm ready.

"First course," Chef Troissant says from her place at the table. "Parisian-style gratinated onions injected with onion soup. Four onion balls, very light, very fluffy, filled with warm onion broth. A drizzle of black truffle sauce with a sprinkle of thyme. A crispy Parmesan wafer balanced on top. The second course will consist of a three-centimeter-wide, six-centimeter-high medallion of grilled, soft, rare beef served very rare, very soft. Cover with truffle, mozzarella, and mushrooms, forming a white shell.

"And for the third course, a deconstructed Mont Blanc," she says. I notice a hint of pride in her voice. This is one of the most successful desserts she has crafted for Grattard, where the components of a classic Mont Blanc are separated on the plate to form a whole new invention. I once saw a photograph in a culinary magazine with the caption "Old meets new in this remarkable creation." Grattard took all the credit in the article. But now I know who the real person behind the curtain is—a woman, not a man.

"A caramel drizzle must run the length of the plate," she continues, moving her hand in the air as if there were an imaginary plate in front of her. "Three dollops of chestnut purée positioned in alternating sides of the drizzle line. And at the center of the plate, one dollop of Chantilly cream, which must be topped by a praline bonbon—the most delicious bonbon. Just one, so make it exquisite."

I grip my pen over my paper, waiting for any other instructions. But all that's left is a heavy silence as she presses a button on the judges' table and the digital clock begins to count down five hours.

And so it begins. The test that will determine the rest of my life.

Except the rest of my life doesn't seem to carry the grueling intensity it once did. As I begin to peel the tiny onions for my appetizer, I think of Lala's legacy and the love she put into every meal. And as I prepare the truffles for the entrée, I think of my baby sister and all the meals our new family will share over laughter and conversation. The Mont Blanc makes me think of Diego—the caramel drizzle and the dollops on the plate remind me of the road and the mountains we crossed on the way to Spain.

For five hours I remain in this space—a sort of protective bubble—surrounded by the memories of everyone I love. Not once do I forget an ingredient or hesitate on a technique. The dishes flow out of me almost effortlessly, until there is only about a minute left on the clock and my dishes are completely finished except for one small detail. A praline bonbon that would likely crown me as the winner. It sits on the countertop staring back at me, probably wondering why it's not floating on top of a dollop of Chantilly, the way Chef Troissant instructed.

Next to me, Lucia is piping her cream with the fierceness and focus of a genius. All three of her dishes are impeccable, but then, so are mine. The only difference between us is that if she won, she would give herself fully to Grattard's kitchen, while I would always wonder why I never had the guts to change course. Even if it meant letting go of everyone else's measure of success. And even if it meant I may never get an opportunity like this again.

I reach for the bonbon and hold it gently between my fingers, but I can't bring myself to lift it from the table. The clock is about to run out, and under its red glow sits Chef Troissant.

She's watching me. Across the kitchen, our eyes meet and my lips form a warm smile. One that leaves no doubt of where I want to be.

Chef Troissant's eyes narrow and her head cocks to the side. It's a look of puzzlement, broken only by the sound of a buzzer announcing that time is up. Her eyes shift to the bonbon in my hand, which never made it onto the plate. I watch her face for a reaction—maybe anger or disapproval—but there's nothing there. Only that neutral, emotionless expression that makes you wish her face had subtitles.

A few minutes pass before Chef Grattard enters the test kitchen with Hugo trailing behind. The three judges move to different sides of the kitchen, talking to the students, commenting on the dishes and filling out the scorecards.

My eyes narrow on the small bonbon, knowing that no matter what happens next, I made the right choice. I know this because I only feel immense relief. Like I've been spared from some terrible fate.

Chef Troissant is the first judge to approach my station.

"Perfect technique," she says, marking the scorecard. Her eyes briefly cut to the bonbon and she clicks her tongue. "Too bad that bonbon didn't make it onto the plate."

I stand up straighter, jut my chin, and gather my courage. I have nothing to lose, so I say, "I would like the opportunity to train in your kitchen. I would work hard and learn as much as I can from you. But if that is not an option, I still know that this, here, isn't what I want. I want something more."

"More?" she asks, mildly surprised.

"I want to enjoy doing the one thing I love."

"I don't need an apprentice." Chef Troissant picks up the bonbon from the table and puts it into her mouth.

Inside, I'm crestfallen, but I don't let it show. In addition to all the life-changing culinary lessons, Troissant taught me to keep my emotions in check. If you have to fall apart, do it when no one can see you—over very expensive champagne.

She jots down a few things on her clipboard, and without taking her eyes away from the paper says, "I need a chef's assistant. We begin pastry trials in two weeks. We will open in two months." She looks up to meet my gaze and gives me just the slightest smile. "Chef Fields."

I can't believe what I'm hearing.

A nervous *yes* jumps out of my mouth, but what I really want to do is hug this woman. Chef's assistant! Me!

"I have only one question," I say, my head turning toward Snake Eyes, who is getting a talk-down from Hugo about the consistency of the white foam shell over his beef medallion. "Are you hiring any of these self-declared kitchen gods?"

To my surprise, and that of everyone else in the kitchen, Chef Troissant bursts out laughing with an uninhibited cackle. Her shoulders shake with mirth and her head falls back.

"Not a single one," she says, handing me my scorecard.

The dessert score is so low, given the missing bonbon, that I know I've succeeded at losing the apprenticeship.

I've never felt so happy to fail.

Chapter 30

The Harvest

With the end of summer comes the end of the cherry harvest. As a way to give thanks to the migrant pickers and the local workers, Papi and Margo host a harvest dinner at Villa des Fleurs. Margo asked me to be in charge of the menu, with the condition I make that chicken in wine and butter sauce she loves. These days she can't get enough of my food.

As head of Villa des Fleurs's kitchen for this special occasion, I assembled the best team of cooks I know.

"Consider this my last meal," Legrand (i.e. Snakes Eyes) says as he frets over a broken piece of steamed cabbage. He's assembling a tray of golabkis—Polish stuffed-cabbage rolls—one of the main entrees on our dinner menu.

After Legrand lost the apprenticeship, he shocked us all with the announcement he was done with cooking. He had one too many shots of tequila when most of our class decided to go out to celebrate our final exam results and went full-on confessional, admitting he almost had a mental breakdown over the peas. "I see them everywhere, those green monsters!"

He decided to take a break from the kitchen and head to Paris to pursue a philosophy degree instead.

"I plan to win a Nobel Prize." He actually said this. And without even a hint of sarcasm.

"Maybe you can start a new food philosophy movement," Lucia tells him. She is expertly piping mashed potatoes onto a dish so that they resemble flower petals. "I read there's a group trying to get people to grow their own food." She decorates the center of each potato flower with dots of green sauce. I shiver at the memory of the swamp creature we once created in Grattard's kitchen. This girl just can't get enough.

She won the apprenticeship at La Table de Lyon and, as expected, has been working crazy hours since. But she loves it. While the rest of us hated who we became in that kitchen, Lucia thrived on it. The more Hugo and Grattard throw at her, the sharper she becomes.

"Sorry I'm late," Pippa says, walking into the kitchen. "But look what I brought." She lifts both hands to reveal bags full of fresh bread. "They just came out of the oven."

"Did you make these?" I ask, grabbing a dinner roll from one of the bags.

"I did," she says, passing everyone a roll. "I'm experimenting with flavors a bit. These are sweet potato with rosemary and sea salt. They have a hint of brown sugar too."

I take a bite. It's the taste of heaven, if heaven were made of carbs—which, let's face it, it should be.

"These are incredible," I say. Everyone else nods in agreement, their mouths too full to speak.

"It's only my third batch. I'm still getting the hang of it," Pippa says. "But I love it there. I feel I can be creative and try new things. Do you have a basket for these?"

I find a big basket in the pantry and hand it to her. Pippa covers the bottom with a pretty red cloth and arranges her rolls along with some baguettes and a fougasse, flatbread sculpted to look like an ear of wheat.

"How's Chef Troissant doing with the big opening?" she asks.

"You can ask her yourself," I say. "She's outside." I glance out the window, where I see Troissant talking to Papi, merrily holding a glass of wine in one hand and a canapé in the other. Papi must say something funny or stupid because Troissant laughs, her head falling back in pure delight. She looks like a completely different person than she was in Grattard's kitchen. Younger, even.

"I can't believe she left Grattard to open her own place. I heard he lost it when she told him, even stormed out of the restaurant. What an ass! Why can't he just be happy for her?"

I shrug. "She didn't seem to care much," I say. "We've been super busy preparing for the opening. I think we've both moved on from Grattard."

"He's a selfish prick," Troissant told me soon after she left him. "A creative genius, yes, but a prick nonetheless."

I mean, who wants to give their best working years of their life to a selfish prick? Not me, that's for sure.

"Where do you want these?" Diego walks in with a bowl full of cherries. I make room on the kitchen counter for him to set them down.

"Are you sure you want to do this?" he asks.

"Everyone loves a good flambé," I say, taking a cherry from the bowl and putting it into my mouth. They're perfectly ripe and so sweet. Without a doubt, they will caramelize on the pan when we add the liqueur and set them on fire for the cherries jubilee.

"I have a fire extinguisher ready, just in case." He plants a kiss on my cheek. "And the garden hose. And a water bucket."

"We have a room full of experts. What could possibly go wrong?"

He opens his mouth to respond but I pop a cherry in before he can say anything.

"Not a word," I say, kissing him. He laughs, grabs another cherry, and puts it into my mouth. It's a quick, playful movement, but the soft touch of his fingers on my lips sends a warm electric current running through the length of my entire body. My cheeks flush red. They probably match the color of the fruit.

"All right, you two." Pippa throws a bread roll in Diego's direction. He catches it after it bounces off his chest. "We have work to do—save the smoochfest for later."

A timer dings, and I know it's time to get my pies out. I

open the oven door and the entire kitchen fills with the aromatic smells of melted sugar, cinnamon, and nutmeg. I take out the pies one by one and rest them on the counter. Everyone gathers around as I open the paper bags. I watch their faces soften with a childish grin, the hallmark of a memorable dessert.

"They look amazing," Lucia says, smothering her finger in syrup that spilled over onto the bag. She tastes her finger and closes her eyes with a pleased hum.

The others follow her lead.

"I'll be damned," Pippa says. "You need to give me this recipe."

"A proper tart is more refined," Legrand says, going in for his second taste of the syrup. I had warned him that if he said one bad thing about Lala's pie, I would kick his butt all the way to his philosophy school in Paris.

"But I guess it's good for a rustic dessert," he adds. I shake my head and chuckle to myself. In Legrand's world, that is the highest form of praise.

"These are county fair royalty pies, I'll have you know," Diego tells him.

This time I laugh out loud. Legrand stares at him with a *What the hell is county fair royalty?* expression that is both mildly irritating and highly amusing.

"I think these are ready to go out," I say to Diego. "Can you put them on the dessert table?"

"They may or may not be missing a piece by the time they arrive at the dessert table," he says, moving the pies onto a tray. "I can't make any promises."

"I'm right behind you," I say, picking up the chicken platter. "You really think I'm going to trust you with a tray of pies? It's like having a wolf watch over sheep."

"I have no idea what you're talking about."

We walk onto the patio, where one of the Polish migrant families has improvised a polka band. I catch Jakub dancing next to his dad, who's playing the trumpet. An older man squeezes an accordion, while his two sons play the violin and the clarinet. Someone even built a dance floor made of wooden boards on the lawn.

Long, family-style tables have been arranged on the patio for the occasion. Diego and I strung a few lines of lights from the trees, like we saw Clara had done for the dinner club.

We place our dishes on the table and take a step back to admire our work. Before us, a collection of multicultural dishes is spread in a flawless array of flavors and smells.

"Good job, everyone," I say. "Now let's eat."

We pat each other on the back or arm. Then move to the dinner table, where Papi is seated next to Margo, with Flora on her lap. Troissant is seated across from them, talking to a very handsome farmhand. When she sees me, she raises her wine glass in my direction and smiles. I smile back and nod. Sometimes you don't need words to convey the depths of gratitude between two people.

Food platters are passed from hand to hand. Plates overflow with delicious food. Drink glasses are refilled with lemonade and wine. There is the echo of laughter and multiple conversations in different languages all across the table. But above all, there is friendship, there is joy, and there is love. Lots of love.

Tonight, we not only share a meal, we share our lives.

After the main course, Pippa and Lucia clear the dinner plates off the table. The conversation quickly turns to dessert.

Diego cuts the pies in slices as Legrand scoops ice cream and a dollop of whipped cream onto each plate. I deliver them to the table, enjoying every bit of excitement on our guests' faces.

I don't need a translator to know they're a big crowd pleaser. Not even the crumbs are left.

Diego and I walk our pie plates to a garden wall overlooking the cherry fields. The sun is quickly setting over the horizon, tinting everything in shades of orange and pink.

We eat our pie and ice cream in silence, smiling at the harvest banquet we helped create. It couldn't have gone any better.

"Your Lala would be proud," Diego says, leaning his shoulder against mine.

Our gaze meets, and in his eyes I see the same kindness he showed me the night my sister Flora was born, when we were cooking together in the kitchen. My heart overflows with love for him.

"I wish you could've known her."

"But I do!" he says to my surprise. "She's here."

As I look around the garden and see the joy of people sharing a meal made from the heart, I realize this is Lala's legado—*my legado.*

"To my Lala," I say, raising a spoonful of pie in front of me. When I take it to my mouth, I can only taste love.

Yes, Lala would be very proud of her morenita.

Author's Note

Isabella's story was born from my own teen years, and the role that my abuelos played during my parents' rocky marriage and consequent divorce. My abuelas Cuqui and Josefa's love sustained me during that difficult time. In particular, Abuela Cuqui's house in *el campo*, with its open fields, roaming farm animals, and fruit trees in the backyard served as a much-needed refuge from the storm at home.

My abuelas also taught me the healing power of food made with love. Almost thirty years after my abuela Josefa's death, I can still recall the taste and smell of her guisado beans—unfortunately, she took the recipe to the grave.

Now as an adult, I make a yearly pilgrimage back to my hometown of Sabana Grande in Puerto Rico to visit my Abuela Cuqui and Abuelo Arsenio's rural home. There's always something cooking on Abuela Cuqui's stove, and a sweet treat hiding in her fridge. And even though these days I tower over her, she still wraps me in the kind of hug that makes me feel as if I never left the island.

Dear readers, I hope this book brings you a little joy and maybe some relief from your own family drama. And if you see yourself through Isa's pain, I pray you will eventually transcend your own complicated family dynamics and find your place in the world. And for girls, I hope this story provides a vision of how you can create success on your own terms.

Note on Italicized Text

While editing *Salty, Bitter, Sweet*, my editors Hannah VanVels, Jacque Alberta, and I decided to italicize some non-English words for clarity, since this book contains words and phrases in six different languages. The words that do appear in italics (other than those for stress or other style-based reasons) are only those readers may not be familiar with. In addition, words that are defined and used often in the book are not italicized after the first mention. We also created a culinary guide to help readers follow Isa's journey; turn to the back for those definitions, which might make you a little hungry.

Acknowledgments

After four years of slumming it in the writing trenches, fairy-madrina and agent extraordinaire Saritza Hernandez plucked one of my manuscripts from the cold-query bardo and offered me representation. Thank you for all the positive energy and unconditional support you've poured into me and my work. And above all, thank you for changing my life.

Three years later, another fairy-madrina changed my life by giving me my first book deal, the marvelous editor Hannah VanVels. Thank you for all the love and enthusiasm you invested in transforming my manuscript into a published book.

I am equally grateful to the entire team at Blink/HarperCollins including rock-star publicist Jen Hoff and grammar bruja Jacque Alberta; and the design team at Brand Navigation for creating the most beautiful cover a girl could dream of.

A book is the work of many people, and I had an amazing team of consultants to help me make *Salty, Bitter, Sweet* as authentic as possible. The insanely talented Chef Carla Tomasko of Atlanta's Bacchanalia restaurant shared her knowledge on high-end dining and her story as a Latina working in one of the city's most celebrated kitchens. Fellow Las Musas author Ismée Williams made sure Lala's Cuban experience rang true and held my hand through my first sensitivity report. And French native Virginie Kippelen provided feedback on the French language and setting.

Along the way, I have been lucky to receive the support and encouragement of hundreds of people. And have been humbled by the outpouring of love for my work and this book.

I am especially grateful to my friends in the Atlanta writers community and the members of the Pie Wish Coven. You welcomed me with open arms and inspired me to believe in my publishing dreams in the face of soul-crushing rejection. I have cherished every minute of our writing gatherings, retreats, and the awesome Mingle & Margaritas. Pie wishes are the best wishes.

Which leads me to thank the local bookstores that support our gatherings, especially Little Shop of Stories and Charis Books. Your dedication to helping local authors is unparalleled.

A super loud GRACIAS to the proud Latina women of Las Musas. I am honored to be a part of this trailblazing group of authors. Pa'lante!

During the last six years, I have juggled my job as a CNN producer with my passion as a YA writer. My CNN colleagues have made it easy for me to focus on both and have cheered my dreams along the way. A big thanks—and flan!—to Monte Plot and Jessica Jordan, who read my first (awful) drafts and offered only words of encouragement. And equally big slice of flan to my colleagues at CNN's Special Projects for your daily check-ins and motivation. I couldn't dream of a more amazing group of people to spend my weekdays with.

Outside work, my spiritual community at Kadampa Meditation Center Georgia made sure I didn't lose my mind while juggling so many commitments at once. Their study programs and meditation classes have provided refuge and peace, even on the most stressful days. A huge thanks to administrative director Cindy Parker, education program coordinator Celeste Green, and resident teacher Gen Kelsang Mondrub for their support and dedication.

At home, my wonderful neighbors in the Norcross community have been constant cheerleaders. And the members of our local dinner club have served as testers to many delicious recipes. In particular, I would give a million pies to my lovely friend and next-door neighbor Hazel Ringelstein for championing all my crazy dessert ideas and lending me the occasional egg or stick of butter. I love you, Hazel! And if I'm lucky enough to make it to my eighties, I want to be just like you.

The seeds of this book were sown long ago, when I was growing up in Sabana Grande, Puerto Rico. Most of my family still lives there and have been constant supporters on this extraordinary journey. My heart overflows with gratitude for my amazing mom, Zulma Nazario, whose belief in my dreams helped me believe in myself. Te amo, Mami. Gracias por todo...

And to my sweet stepdad Hector Ramos, my abuelos Cuqui and Arsenio, my tías Noemí Velez and Sonia Colón, and my cousins Lisi and Rosa Ruiz. Even with an ocean between us, you are always in my heart.

The rest of my family lives across the pond, in Florida. A big open-hearted thanks to my dad, Tomás Cuevas, who inspired some of the scenes in this book. Besitos, Papi.

And to my sister, Lourdes Cuevas, for reading some of my first terrible stories and telling me how great they were. Your lies kept me going and I love you so freaking much for it.

Some family you are born with, others you choose. Thank you to my sweet mother-in-law, Diane Perry, for her constant encouragement. And to my amazing step kids, Alex and Caleb Perry, for inspiring Diego, "The Hot Spaniard." You have filled my life with joy and wonder in ways I never expected. I love you guys, more than you'll ever know.

Finally, my writing career would not exist without two extraordinary people:

My kindred spirit, Marie Marquardt, who has been my writing companion since we met at a conference in 2012. Back then I didn't know I was also earning a friend, a sister, and a membership to the FROS club. I love you even though you stubbornly insist *Dirty Dancing: Havana Nights* is better than the original. IT. IS. NOT.

And my husband and best friend, Chris Perry. You have made all my wildest dreams come true and I will forever love you for it. Thank you for giving me all the love a girl could ever want, a home full of happy memories, and most of all, thank you for sharing your life and your boys with me. You guys are everything. I love you.

Isa's Kitchen Notes

Arròs negre: Translates to "black rice." I'm dying to try Lucia's version! Traditional arròs negre is kind of like paella—another classic Spanish dish with seafood and rice—but with a Catalan twist: cuttlefish and squid ink that colors everything black and gives a lightly salty taste.

Bain-marie: Or as Clara calls it, *baño de María*. A technique where you pour a shallow amount of water into a walled pan and then place ramekins or a small baking dish inside—the water keeps the temperature around the dish consistent while it's in the oven. A must for any soufflé . . . or perfect flan.

Black sausage: Sounds weird, but it's actually really good. These are made from blood and the . . . leftover parts of a pig, and flavored with onions and spices.

Bugnes: Delightful, thin little French doughnuts that often look like squared-off *O*'s or even leaves, which are fried in oil and then sprinkled with powdered sugar.

Café con leche: Literally "coffee with milk," but is so much more with Lala's addition of Mexican cinnamon. (Café au lait is also a term for coffee with milk, just French and usually made with really strong coffee.)

Cafecito: Cuban coffee. For Papi and me, it means any coffee that is tasty, sweet, and has some cream. But it is also the special name for coffee made with expresso and topped with crema (a tasty sugar foam whipped with a splash of coffee).

Café créme: French expresso with a touch of heavy cream.

Caldo de gallina: Like Lala called it, this "food to revive the dead" is a chicken soup that is believed to be able to heal sicknesses incredibly fast. And when it tastes anything like my Lala's, I believe it works!

Canelés: Little French pastries that look a little like tall bundt cakes without the hole, but don't be fooled by appearances; they are much more complex. Flavored with vanilla and rum, with a custard center and a dark tan, caramelized outside . . . so good.

Cascos de guayaba: One of my favorites! This popular dish from Cuba is made of guava shells cooked in a syrup with cinnamon (or a similar spice) until they're tender, then topped with whatever you like.

Cassoulet: A stew-like casserole made with white beans, pork in a seasoned tomato sauce (called ragù), and a type of meat (I use the traditional duck) that is cooked in a deep, round pot. It's pretty much the perfect French comfort food.

Cerverlas sausage: Like we had it at the bouchon, these are sometimes served with mayonnaise. It's a mild pork or pork and beef sausage with garlic, mustard, and herbs that when aged becomes a French version of summer sausage.

Champignon: Usually called white or button mushrooms in America. They're probably what you first think of when you think of mushrooms, since they're the most common ones at grocery stores.

Chitterling: A very French sausage, also called andouillette, that is made from pig.

Clafoutis: A French dessert of fruit arranged in a buttered dish, then covered in a thick batter. Once it's out of the oven, you cool it until it's lukewarm and dust it with powdered sugar before serving. I also like to add a little whipped cream on the side.

Compote: Fruit cooked in syrup, and amazing as a dessert topping.

Confit: Meat—usually duck, if you're in France—slowly cooked in its own fat.

Coq au vin: A family favorite. An amazing stew of chicken cooked in red wine, alongside vegetables like pearl onions and mushrooms. Tastes even better the second day!

Crème brûlée: The transformation of cream, sugar, eggs, and vanilla into a velvety custard, with a final sprinkle of sugar on top that is caramelized by that wonder of all kitchen gadgets, the blowtorch.

Crème caramel cup: A custardy dessert with an oozing caramel topping that looks a lot like a French flan.

Croquetas: Also called croquettes in French, these are made from bechamel (a creamy white sauce) mixed with pieces of meat or other ingredients, then rolled in breadcrumbs and lightly fried. Lala's bacalao croquettas had cod and were deliciosas, though Clara's ham version was also to die for.

Estofat de pop i patata: This delicious octopus stew is popular throughout Catalonia. The pop (the Catalan word for octopus) simmers for a long time so it's tender, then stewed with potatoes and onions in a tomato-based sauce.

Fleur de courgette: Literally, it means "zucchini flower," and it's a dish similar to a squash blossom, where the light orange flower is stuffed, coated in a flour and egg batter, and fried. Very tasty.

Fleur de sel: This is a somewhat coarse salt that is sprinkled on food to finish it or used as a garnish.

Fraisier: The ultimate strawberry cake, and a work of art if you ask me. Made of two layers of Genoise sponge (a type of eggy cake) coated with a sugar syrup that is flavored with alcohol, which is then filled with a layer of French pastry cream and topped with almond paste. The best part: thin slices of strawberries decoratively placed around the outside edge of the cream.

Fricassée: A method of cooking meat by cutting it up and braising it slowly in a cooking liquid.

Guisado: The Spanish word for stew; it can be made from almost anything, but the result is almost always a tasty, complex layer of flavors.

Kołaczki: Polish pastry-like cookies that are made from soft, buttery, flaky dough wrapped around a jammy or cream cheese filling. While Jakub wants them year-round, they're usually baked for the holidays.

Lardon: This is a term for small pieces of fatty bacon or salt-cured pork fat, and they're used in a lot of French dishes to add flavor.

Mallorcas: Rolls of sweet, fluffy, egg-based bread that usually have powdered sugar sprinkled on top. Is perfect for breakfast, but the less-sweet version also works great as a sandwich base.

Mise en place: This refers to all the items you need for a dish, laid out and prepped so you can simply throw them in as you need them—like your diced veggies, spices, salt, and so on.

Mille crêpe cake: Very tasty, as my family's "sampling" shows, and also very difficult to make perfectly. The name translates to "one thousand crêpe cake," and while that number of layers is an exaggeration, it is a stack of around twenty identical, thin crêpes with an equally thin layer of light pastry cream between each one, creating a delicate and almost ethereal dessert.

Mont Blanc: The flavors are a lot like the one I made for the final test, just all in one piece. This dessert is pureed sweetened chestnuts that are piped and topped with a little whipped cream. It earned its name because it looks like a snow-capped mountain when it's done.

Napoleon: Rectangular, delicate bar made from several layers of puff pastry with pastry cream or custard, and jam, sandwiched between each one, with a thin layer of vanilla icing and thin ribbons of chocolate on top. *Délicieux!*

Orxata: A cold drink popular in Spain that is made from water, milk, and chufa, which are also called tiger nuts—these are actually the bottom of a weedlike plant and not nuts at all. Because of the added cinnamon and sugar, it tastes a lot like a sweet milkshake.

Paella: Practically the national dish of Spain. Rice is cooked in chicken stock inside a special shallow pan along with shrimp, chicken, chorizo sausage, mussels, peppers, onions, and tomatoes.

Pain au chocolat: A heavenly, flaky bread with a rich chocolate center, and sometimes chocolate drizzles on top as well.

Palmiers: Buttery, flaky, crisp cookies made from puff pastry dough that is usually sprinkled with coarse sugar then folded inward by each side into a roll, cut, and baked to create heart-shaped delights.

Parmigiano-Reggiano: A very special Italian cheese that has earned its place as king. It's a dry, hard, straw-colored cheese made from skimmed cow's milk, with a pale-gold rind and a sharp, slightly salty flavor that hits every tastebud just right. And only cheese wheels that pass a special list of criteria get to be called by this name. This is *nothing* like the parmesan that comes in a shakable can.

Patatas bravas: A Spanish dish of roughly cubed potatoes that are fried and served warm with a drizzled sauce.

Porcini: Nutty, delicious mushrooms that have a big, reddish-brown cap and a thick stem. Perfect gourmet addition, especially in French vegetable dishes.

Profiterole: Otherwise known as a cream puff in America. These are made from a cooked pastry dough called choux (pronounced "shoo") that is piped and baked, then filled with cream, custard, or chocolate.

Provençal: This refers to a dish that is cooked in the style of the city of Provence—which usually means ingredients like tomatoes, garlic, olive oil, onions, mushrooms, and eggplant.

Quenelle: A French technique of forming something into a football-like shape using spoons, then poaching or frying it. You can do it with thick creams, or even a floury mixture with crushed fish—like the flathead quenelle we had at the bouchon.

Ratatouille: A vegetable stew made from a mix of seasonal vegetables (like eggplant and peppers) sautéed in French olive oil, which are then combined into a tomato sauce.

Roosevalt fondant: Not to be confused with cake covering; instead, this is French red-skinned potatoes called Roosevalts that have been cut, fried in butter, and then baked inside the oven in stock so the outside is golden and crispy and the inside is really creamy. The best roasted potatoes you'll ever eat.

Salad Niçoise: A salad with tomatoes, spring onions, tuna or anchovies, olives, and hard-boiled eggs.

Sancocho: Every Latin American country, it seems, has a different way of making this stew, but Lala said all that matters is that is has large pieces of meat, potatoes, and vegetables in a rich broth. Which means it is perfect for experimenting with flavor.

Socca: A type of chickpea crêpe, or pancake, that is usually cooked in a wood oven, then cut into wedges and served hot or warm. (Must-have in Nice—they'll bring from the oven to you by bicycle!)

Sofrito: An amazing sauce my Lala made with chopped onions, peppers, and tomatoes, some olive oil, garlic, and herbs.

Terrine: What is in a terrine varies a lot, but to earn that name the food has to be cooked in a rectangular, straight-sided dish that looks kind of like a loaf pan. Most have layers of meat, and some have vegetables, foie gras, or whatever the chef is inspired to add.

Tres Leches: A sponge cake that is soaked in three kinds of milk—condensed milk, heavy cream, and evaporated milk—and often topped with a layer of whipped cream with grated cinnamon. It tastes soft and sweet and melts on your tongue.

Tripas frita: Tripe is the lining of a cow's stomach; but when properly battered and fried, it's not that bad. Just trust me.

About the Author

Born and raised in Puerto Rico, Mayra Cuevas is a professional journalist and fiction writer who adores love stories with happy endings. Her debut fiction short story was selected by Becky Albertalli as a New Voice in the Foreshadow YA serial anthology in 2019. She is a TV and digital producer for CNN, where she has worked since 2003. She lives in the colorful town of Norcross, Georgia, with her husband, also a CNN journalist, and their cat, Felicia. She is the wicked stepmom to two amazing young men who provide plenty of inspiration for her stories. Follow her on Twitter @MayraECuevas and Instagram @MayraCuevas